With You
and
Without You

With You and Without You

Deborah J. Wolf

KENSINGTON BOOKS
http://www.kensingtonbooks.com

KENSINGTON BOOKS are published by

Kensington Publishing Corp.
850 Third Avenue
New York, NY 10022

All Kensington titles, imprints and distributed lines are available at special quantity discounts for bulk purchases for sales promotion, premiums, fund-raising, educational or institutional use.

Special book excerpts or customized printings can also be created to fit specific needs. For details, write or phone the office of the Kensington Special Sales Manager: Kensington Publishing Corp., 850 Third Avenue, New York, NY 10022. Attn. Special Sales Department. Phone: 1-800-221-2647.

Kensington and the K logo Reg. U.S. Pat. & TM Off.

ISBN 0-7582-1383-2

First Kensington Trade Paperback Printing: July 2006
10 9 8 7 6 5 4 3 2 1

Printed in the United States of America

For the Colonel

Acknowledgments

Everyone has a first step in this process. Mine started with Doug Stumpf, who gave me both the courage and the contacts to go further. I can't thank him enough for his inspiration and for the doors that he opened.

My undying gratitude goes to my dedicated and driven agent, Richard Morris, who never stopped believing that this book belonged somewhere, for searching for the perfect home. Blessings and thanks also to my editor, Audrey LaFehr, who knew from the beginning that we had something and gave me all the right advice to make it work.

For my fan club, and I thank them in no particular order: Kerry and Chris Vogel, Sherri and Dave Parkinson, Cindy and Andy Forssell, Michelle and Andy Peirona, Tami and Chris Mandeville, Amy and Tom Zeifang, Jamie Tilotta and Joe Green, Michelle and Todd Bartell, Patty Zeifang, Heidi Melin, Aimee Priscaro, Gabrielle Tenaglia, Kurt and Lisa Winter, Lili and Kevin Ames, Bill and Jen Pretto, Kristi and Mike Wolf, Julie and Terry Wolf, Terry Wolf, Jr., and Herve Mardirossian for the long road you took with me in making this happen.

For my beautiful mom, and my wonderful father, for whom this book is dedicated, thank you for believing in me long before I ever believed in myself.

For David Hukari, whose life is far more interesting that this novel and who sees everything in moving pictures. You inspire me every day.

Frank Priscaro, there are no words to thank you for the countless versions you pored over, the chapters you read, the sheer push you gave me to do this. Grazie! XO.

Finally, for my lover and the endless hours you gave me. For the nights you put the kids to bed, kept the house quiet, and left me alone to do my thing. I can't possibly thank you enough for putting up with me and for helping me make the dream come true.

And for Jordan and Brodie, who came to me in a dream and were there when I woke up.

1

The silent house is screaming its ridicule at me again.

I turn on the television, turn it off. Turn it back on, turn it off. The glow from the set illuminates the room, the static electricity filling the air; then immediately the room goes dark. Black. Light on. Light off. Light on. Light off.

I pad into the kitchen and take a heavy jelly jar from the maple-paneled cabinet, filling it with filtered water at the refrigerator door, lean back against the granite countertop, and let out a big sigh. My legs are tight. I hadn't stretched properly this morning and I am paying for it.

When I open my eyes, I find myself staring across the moonlit kitchen at my daughter. My oldest daughter. Lydia stands only ten or fifteen feet from me, but she might as well be on a different shore staring off into the horizon, wishing on a star, contemplating a midnight swim. Fourteen, what an ugly age to be. And particularly for her this year.

"What are you doing, Mom?" she asks indignantly, as if my being there is an intrusion on the place where she lives, the peace she needs. Her boot-cut jeans hang low on her narrow hips, an orange and blue Abercrombie T-shirt lifted slightly at the waist to reveal her perfectly flat, almost concave, stomach. She's been begging me to have her navel pierced. I've almost given in just to win a piece of her back, an outing of sorts that might reconnect us in some way. At least for an afternoon, maybe even for the weekend.

She's come down from her room, eyes glazed over from staring at the wall, not from drugs. Definitely not homework; she's yet to get back in the swing. Ninth grade would be a waste for her. Who could blame her? She's lost her father. He's been taken from her in what has been called "an accident." Surely her teachers would grace her with just one more semester to catch up, a few more months to get back on track. But where would she be then? Of course, you couldn't call it much of anything but an accident. A lapse in judgment, a brief fleeting moment when time stood still. People have spent their time asking us how we are doing.

How are the girls?

How are you getting along?

Is there anything we can do for you?

What do you need?

"Just getting some water, Lydia. What's up?" I try this, but she has already turned, her back stiff and straight to me, her shoulders set back in defiance. When she reaches for something to snack on from the pantry, her T-shirt lifts to reveal the small of her waist. She never answers me.

"Honey?" I try again.

She turns, shrugs her shoulders, and with a chocolate chip granola bar in hand, heads back through the hallway and up the stairs to her room. Her haven. The place where nothing is demanded of her, no questions are asked. I know this instinctively from my own teenage years, but then again, this is different. Lydia is hiding. Every night away from the rest of us, deep in a sorrow that has turned from sadness to anger to nothing. Just plain nothing. Perhaps the worst of all grieving emotions.

I have wondered where she goes when she is gone. She can sit for hours in her room now, hours of nothingness. I've wondered how long it can go on, how long it will go on. When I can stand to be honest with myself, I look at my own life. The nights of nothingness, the time spent staring off into the dark night sky, the minutes, the hours just ticking by.

"Lydia?" I call after her. Nothing. "Lyd?"

Finally, "Nothing, Mom. I'm just hangin'."

Her door opens, and then closes again. I hear her push the weight of her back against the door to make sure it has closed, really closed, and then plunk, horizontal, on the bed, Puma backless tennis shoes dropping one, then the other, onto the floor. In my mind I can see her stretched across her quilt, pillow propped under her chin, and her eyes closed to the world.

What to do, what to do, what to do? The witching hour. Too early to go to bed. Too late to start something new. The hour we used to spend together—my husband and I. Oh, nothing in particular, of course. Maybe flip through a travel magazine and plan our next adventure together, television on in the background, pay bills, share a half bottle of wine, an occasional foot rub if I'd ask with that throaty voice that promised it might lead to something better, something more. Something surely he couldn't pass on. Now the hour I hate every night. The hour I wish someone, anyone would call. Too late for a telemarketer, oh, but what I would give for a telemarketer. *Anyone, call. Ring, damn phone, ring.*

I take the steps to the second floor, set the alarm on the keypad at the top of the landing, and watch the small red light click on. Safe, locked in. *Come and get us, world,* I mouth silently in my mind, surveying the living room and front entry below me before taking the last step to the second floor. *I dare you. You've taken everything we had, there's nothing more for you here. Go ahead; take your best shot.*

Straight ahead at the top of the stairs, Becca's room. The girls share a bathroom, something Lydia hates. "She's into all my stuff," she wailed one morning at breakfast, holding up the mashed end of her new lip liner pencil. True, Becca had come to the breakfast table in her sister's brand-new Brown Sugar lipstick, her eleven-year-old mouth stained past the edges of the outline of her lips, clearly applied by a novice. It looked ridiculous, but I didn't tell her that. Instead I only smiled into the eyes that could barely meet mine. Truth is, Brown Sugar isn't Becca's color and it never will be. She won't need lipstick, now or in the years that will age her physically. She is a natural. Beautiful from birth with perfectly manicured eyebrows that looked as if we'd been plucking them from the minute she emerged from the womb. She's been graced with cornflower-blue eyes like her grandmother, the kind of eyes men would lose themselves in. And a natural ability to hold a crowd: Men, women, kids her own age, it really doesn't matter.

Becca is asleep, one muscular leg thrown casually out from under the comforter and across her bed as if someone has drawn it that way on purpose, a book flipped awkwardly at her left wrist, pages turned and open at the spine. She is breathing deeply, a slight hum in the room where she's left reality behind. She falls asleep this way most nights, lost in some story other than the one that has become her life. She's never been a television watcher the way her sister was as a child, before the telephone and the privacy of her own room stole Lydia away. Becca prefers books, will read any chance she can. That or music. With a double dose of soccer thrown in.

Quietly, carefully, I take the book from her and fold the pages back, laying it on the white desk that is covered with the school pictures of Becca's endless circle of friends. Smiles, childhood grins of other sixth graders, untouched by something as horrific as the death of their father. Many of Becca's friends came to Patrick's funeral; I'm sure it was the first for most of them. She barely noticed. Rather, she stood stoically at my side, her clammy left hand clutched in mine, barely a breath on her lips. She did beautifully until it was time to lower the casket and I was so lost in my own thoughts that I nearly missed her sway, then go pale as death on me. She barely made it away from the front of the newly dug grave when she started vomiting violently, a slight murmur going up in the crowd to the left and behind us. I stood next to her, willing strength to my side so that I would not retch myself, and patted her head with a handkerchief monogrammed with Patrick's initials. She took it from me, that handkerchief, and I've yet to see it since.

I lift the covers over Becca and tuck them in at her side, running my hand over her forehead and brushing away the wisps of hair that have fallen across her eyelids. I leave her breathing deeply and knock softly on Lydia's door, opening it before she can answer one way or another.

"Are we running tomorrow?" I ask her. She lies on her stomach, her legs bent at the knees and kicked up behind her, flipping through my latest copy of *People* magazine. She doesn't look at me, doesn't take her eyes from the article on George Clooney.

"Yeah, I guess, whatever."

"Long or short?" I ask her, looking for a commitment, waiting for her to engage in conversation. Patrick would never have stood for this. This flippant attitude, the nonchalant, careless discomfort that hangs between us. He'd have demanded her attention.

"Whatever you want." Flip, next page.

"Long or short?" I ask her again. "You pick. I did long this morning, so I could go either way." I know she's not reading, because she's running her eyes over the pages, checking the captions to see who's pictured from the latest Hollywood party.

"Short, then. I've got to get to school early." She rolls to her back and raises the magazine so it covers her face. I'm not getting anywhere. Get mad or get out? I can't decide. I've had limited energy for Lydia lately. She's been slipping from me. Try as I might to grasp at her, try as I can to bring her back to me, it's as if I'm beginning not to recognize her. I walk over and push down the front of the magazine, studying her face, the wide splash of freckles that spill out across the bridge of her nose.

"What?" she says to me.

"Lydia, what is it lately? Where do you go from me when you're gone? I'm more than a little worried about you, more than concerned that this funk you're in has gone on for far too long. Is there something you need, something I can do for you?"

"Uh, like what?" she answers me with a huff, shifting away and tossing the magazine across the top of her bed. "Can't I just hang out, Mom?"

"Yep. Every right, Lyd. When have I ever denied you that?"

She shrugs her shoulders at me, brushing me off, but I barely budge.

"Hanging out is not what I'm talking about, Lyd. I want to know how I can help you, how we get back some of what we had before, before . . . before Daddy died." I say this softly and my voice catches. No matter how hard I try, my voice catches. She looks away, distant.

"I'm fine. I don't need anything from you. I just want to hang out by myself. Really, I just like it in here. Okay?" She emphasizes the "okay"—a dismissal—and I know this is my cue to leave, but I just can't. I continue to stare at her, looking, perhaps, to fill my own emptiness with something I might do for her, something I might give her. We've been close, always so close. Now we are like two people coexisting under the same roof, our lives revolving around each other, occasionally touching, and brushing by each other. Call it intuition—a woman's or a mother's—but my daughter is changing. My daughter is slipping from me, and like sand, the tighter I hold her in my hands, the more she slips through my fingers.

"Okay, Lyd, I know you want to be alone." I start to back out of her room, still studying her face, looking for recognition of the little girl I swear still lives here with me. I am gently closing the door behind me when, in a voice that has changed, softened only slightly, she says, "Mom, can you drop me at school in the morning?" Suddenly, from somewhere, interest. Something she needs.

"Sure. What time?"

"Eight."

"Okay, better be ready to go by five forty-five for our run, then. Three miles."

"Oh, okay." I start to close the door again when she says to me with a sigh, "I don't know, Mom. I'm just so tired lately. Can you just wake me and we'll see?"

I nod and let her go. Chances are she'll flake on me. She's been less than committable lately.

Down the hallway, and a sharp left to my room. My room. Mine alone now. The place where I sleep by myself. There were times during my marriage when I longed for that. Nights when Patrick returned from a long business trip only to interrupt the routine I'd settled into. My space. My own room. My journal, my corner of the bed, my television program, and my electric blanket set to my temperature. My, how foolish I'd been.

We have a spectacular bathroom. It's easily the best room in the house. Now it's my bathroom. Mine alone. My bathtub. My sink. Two sinks for me—lucky me. Two large framed mirrors to chase my reflection in, the changes in my body, the wilting of my face. A big, beautiful picture window that overlooks the garden. I spend my nights here as I used to, a long hot bath with sea salt or bath oil, the room lit by candlelight, a good book, maybe some music. It's one of the few rituals I can't shake no matter how many memories it forces me to dredge up.

When the girls were very young and Patrick wasn't traveling so often, he would draw my bath while I read them a bedtime story, the three of us tucked under the quilt on Lydia's double bed. After a while, he'd come in and relieve me, sometimes sending me off with a glass of wine, a cup of tea, or an earmarked article he'd want me to read from some magazine he'd picked up at the metro station. I'd go immediately to the bathroom, peeling off my clothes piece by piece and dropping them onto the travertine marble floor. I'd lower myself inch by inch into the bath, letting the water absorb me, pulling my shoulder-length strawberry hair up behind me and into a towel like an Egyptian queen. I'd sit for a few minutes, eyes closed and in complete silence, fanning the water back and forth so that it created a small wave over the top of my breasts. It was always the first time peace had found itself into my day.

It took a while for Patrick to master the temperature, timing it just right with the swarm of good night kisses and begs for juice or water from the girls. I like my baths hot, so much so that sometimes when I'm done I come out a bit sunburned, a pinkish tint to my pale skin. After a while, Patrick would finish with the girls and come to sit by the side of the bath. Sometimes, if I were lucky, he would use a scrub and the loofah on my back. Other nights, he'd just stand at the corner of the door, watching me with a smile and waiting for me to pull my body, long and lean from a constant diet of running and tennis, from the tranquility the water provided. He might stay there for my entire bath, eyes meeting mine, and never tiring of holding that place in my heart that made me ache for him.

These nights I am staying longer in the bath. And often I find myself with the old, small five-inch black-and-white television on, praying not to go deep into some bit of despair, start dropping saline-laden tears into the water, emotionally spent and, before I know it, gulping for air against the sobs that choke me. No one comes for me anymore. No one hands me a warm-from-the-dryer towel, reaching around me to dry my back, to rub the moisture from the small hairs at the base of my neck.

I draw a bath, adding salt and a few drops of the oil that leave the water beading on my skin. I want some time alone to think about Lydia, about where she is, about who she is becoming.

"Everything you do changes you." The conversation I'd had earlier in the day with my neighbor Anna, whose wisdom I savor, floods my mind again.

Lydia has changed; a light has gone out, her inextinguishable energy doused. I am certain the coals still burn; they simply must. I am struggling to find her flame; I simply won't believe the fire has been put out.

I've wondered about the teenager Lydia would have become had her father been alive. I'd never know the path she might have taken, the new friends she might have met, the old ones she might have retained. I'd never know if her first boyfriend, Eric, would have met with her father's approval, or if Patrick would have been so severely disapproving that she would have changed her mind about her choice in men.

I am grateful for Eric; thankful for the smile he puts on her face, his ability to make her laugh. God, it is good to hear her laugh. But, like a sand crab lost in the tide, Lydia has allowed herself to be tossed around, the ebb and flow of first love throwing her sideways, off her feet. With Eric, as with the rest of her life, she clings to nothing and everything all at once, her lackluster shell of a body like a ghost floating through each day.

I don't know how to fix Lydia, but it is my responsibility to do just that; I am her mother, unconditional is part of the contract. I long to heal her wounds, to run a thin stream of crazy glue through the pieces of her that are visibly cracked. I know she won't let me, not easily anyway, but I am determined nonetheless.

2

We wagered that Patrick fell asleep at the wheel of his car before he hit the center median, and without his seat belt to hold him in place, was dead upon impact. A witness to the accident remembered him weaving a bit, slumped in the front seat, fighting to adjust his position and fidgeting in his seat. He'd pulled an all-nighter, preparing for the pitch of his life. That's what he had called it on the phone to me that very morning, while I was barely listening, struggling to get the girls out of the house and to school on time. "Baby," he said, "this is it, it'll make our year."

Miraculously, externally, his body was barely bruised, the damage clearly done to his internal organs, the smart whip that was once his brain left stupefied.

The *incident*, as the police liked to call it, happened on a freeway nearly two hours from our home. After the sales call and running on three cups of strong black coffee, he'd begun the drive home, hoping to make the first meeting for Becca's competitive soccer club, which was due to start training two weeks later. Becca, of course, will never forget this. And it will be a long time before she lets herself believe it wasn't her fault. I cursed him on the hour, every hour for doing this to her. Even though, of course, I knew this wasn't his fault or his intention.

In the first few weeks, we pieced that much of the story together: the sales call that had been the success he'd hoped for, the coffee he'd told me about on his cell phone just after he'd left, promising me that he was fine to drive, that he felt more awake and alive than he had in a long time. But it's the crash, what I imagine to be the sound of crunching metal and the smell of burning rubber, that has become the dream, the nightmare that haunts me most nights.

I wake up in the predawn with the sweats, drenched in this choking dream that has gripped me and started me shaking, cold with anxiety and loneliness. I'm suddenly and acutely aware that one of my daughters is lying next to me, her body curled tightly into a cocoon, her breathing barely a whisper on the pillow next to mine. It's Lydia and I take this opportunity to connect with her, unclenching her locked fist and wrapping my hand inside hers. Her hands give to mine and I'm suddenly flooded with relief. Four thirty. Truly the most haunting of all hours in the morning. There's a reason God intended us to sleep through the dark. I'm awake now and I know it. Doomed to watch the backlit numbers of the old clock radio click away for an hour until I can legitimately pull my body from the bed, throw on my running shoes, and hit the hard pavement. It's there where a rhythm will start, my breathing melodic with the scraping sound of my well-worn running shoes. There where I push and push hard, afraid of nothing other than finding the next breath, and even that doesn't seem to frighten me away.

Until then I roll my body toward Lydia and watch her breathe in through her nose and out through her mouth. She emits a small shushing sigh and I know she's deep in a slumber that won't easily be broken. Her face is soft, childlike, just as I remember from nights when I'd creep into her room and stoop beside her bed to check on her as a toddler, to watch the rise and fall of her chest.

"Oh, Lyd," I say softly, stroking my fingers across her forehead and pushing a wisp of her hair back from her face, "come back to me, baby, come back. Let me love you, let me know where you are on everything, how I can help you." I'm whispering this to her in the shadows of the room, where I can just make out the outline of her face. She does not move, never stirs, but still I wonder if she can hear me. I long for her to wake and sit up with her eyes bright, allowing me to take her into my arms and run my fingernails down her back in long strides.

Our silent war, empty of treaties, is almost more than I can bear.

I turn away from her, then back toward her, before splaying out flat on my back and staring at the ceiling fan I'd had Patrick install. It sits motionless, the stainless tips glittering in the moonlight that floods my room from the sky. Lydia had begun taking refuge in my room the second week after Patrick died. I'd found her first at the door one night, staring me into consciousness, lingering until I couldn't help but wake to find her. When I rolled over, I sat straight up in bed, a sense that something else had gone sour.

"What's wrong? What's happened?" I asked her, immediately awake, pulling the covers to my chin, then throwing them back in a single swift movement that made her jump back in the door frame.

"No, nothing. Mom, nothing's wrong." She hung there against the wall, charcoal-black gym sweats and a tank top, and I knew she needed to come to me. She might as well have been four again, those wide eyes in the night, begging to be somewhere safe and warm. I prepped for a long cry where I could hold her and we could meld our bodies together, instantly longing to heal both of us at once.

"Well, c'mon then, don't just stand there." The covers on her father's side of the bed lay smooth and pulled tight at the corner as they often had when Patrick was away on a business trip. I pulled them back and said nothing further to her when she crept on her tiptoes to the bed, crawling in and pulling the cool comforter back over her small frame. I reached my arms for her, but she turned away and I rolled back over on my side, listening for what might come next. Tears? Talk? Prayers? Nothing, just the deep and contented breathing she'd often fall into as a child on the nights she'd crawl into bed in between Patrick and me, separating us everywhere except at the top of the pillow where we undoubtedly found a way around her to bind our fingers together.

I roll back toward her one more time and stare at the outline of her frame against the dark room, resting my arm across her waist and feeling the immediate heat she radiates. I draw my body close to her, careful not to wake her so that she might find me wanting, no, needing, to be closer to her. I know if she finds me this way, this look of longing stained on my face, I know she'll move away from me, leaving me to stare at her back and clinging to the far side of the bed. That or leave altogether, which she has been known to do on a night when I move too much in bed, finally stirring her awake. If that happened, it would be as if she hadn't really needed me at all, didn't know how she could possibly have ended up in my bed. She might pad off in her bare feet, clinging tightly to the pillow she'd brought with her, attitude following her like the scent of a skunk.

My fourteen-year-old daughter. Patrick had been strict with her, mainly out of exasperation. Lydia had sprouted her hormones early, a ridiculously morose and moody eleven-year-old, then a pouty and know-it-all twelve-year-old, a brooding and solitary thirteen-year-old. Reach, reach, reach, he'd kept reaching for her, and she kept pulling away. He'd reach again, pulling her back to him with a force so strong it would sometimes knock the wind from her, and she'd relent without even knowing she had, ending back in his arms, his little princess who needed him. Then again she'd be off and he'd be left reaching.

"How far will she go from me?" he asked me one night after dinner.

"Farther than you'll ever imagine," I told him. "But she'll be back. Don't worry, she'll come back to you, Patrick. She won't know how to help herself."

Do I believe it myself now? For Patrick she'd be back; I'd always believed that. He was her knight. For years the only man she'd acknowledge in a room. But for me? She could go and

might never return. Might never see the purpose. Lydia is drifting, no doubt about it. For so long I'd believed it was the residue
from her father's death; now I'm not so sure. It's as if she is hiding
something from me, hiding herself from me. As if she doesn't want
me to know her, doesn't want me to see her. She can turn in a
minute, caustic and bitter, as if she wants nothing more than for
me to go far away from her.

It's 5:38. I brush the thick mane of brown hair back from her
face and whisper quietly at her shoulder.

"Lydia?" Stillness. "Lydia." A little louder now, the hint of a
command, often required with Lydia, especially at this hour of
the day.

"Mmm, yeah?" She barely moves from her spot on the pillow.

"Five forty-five. Our run. Let's go, sweetie."

"Ugh," she groans. "No, Mom, not this morning. No, please."
She barely moves, merely rubs her feet across the bottom of the
bed, sending a small ripple across the crimson chenille throw.
Her voice is a whine mixed with a bit of a whimper. "I'm really
not in a place to go. Didn't sleep very well and God, I really don't
feel very well," she tries on me.

I am a pro at reading Lydia's mornings. She half commits to a
run each night, and breaks the promise nearly as often. This
morning her sleep-filled voice doesn't sound very encouraging.
Truth is, I wouldn't mind the run by myself. Or with Becca, who
might be awake, and ready to go. Either way, either option seems
better than pleading with Lydia to get out of bed, then dealing
with her sullen, crabby prance down the streets, her only conversation a complaint about how cold it is.

"Okay, Lyd. You're off the hook. I'll see if Becca wants to go,
and set the alarm on my way out." I don't think she actually hears
any of it, her head still resting in the same position on the
propped pillow, arms tucked just at her waist. I reset the alarm on
the clock radio for her so she'll get out of bed and shower before
I am back.

"Hi, Mom. Short or long?" Becca meets me in the hallway, enthusiasm bubbling from her voice, running her hands over her waist-length blond hair and smoothing it back into a single ponytail. For eleven she is more disciplined than most adults I know. "Is Lydia running?" Becca is dressed in black Adidas, Lycra warm-up pants, and a red sweatshirt.

"Hi, sweetie. Um, no. Lydia's barely made it through her first dream of the night." I push a long strand of hair back away from her bright eyes and tuck it behind her ear. "Short. Your sister needs to be at school early."

We head down the stairs, our steps falling in place, and I take her hand for a minute, pressing it to my cheek. "Did you have a good sleep?"

"Yeah." She smiles at me, freckles spread across her dimpled cheeks.

Becca stops at the wrought-iron front gate to our courtyard to stretch her calves first and then her shins. She pulls one arm across the front of her body, then the other, then swings them both back and forth in front of her body, willing them to life. She is amazingly alert, ready to run, twisting back and forth at the waist and reaching overhead toward the sliver of daylight that is just beginning to break and blanket the sky.

Patrick used to say that Becca was a machine, and it isn't far from the truth. I watch now as she turns on her body, first the legs and then the arms, sucking in the air she needs to kick-start into high gear and take off. She can go in an instant. She is compact, built to muscle her way down a field, across a pool, even the streets of life.

"Go on ahead if you want." I motion with my head for her to take flight while pulling my right leg up behind me, bent at the knee so that my shoe pulls up against the seat of my Lycra running pants. I hate to slow her down, hate to feel as if she were out here just to keep me company because she didn't want me to be alone for one more hour of the day. The streetlights cut through the still dark sky, and when we speak our breath warms the morning air.

"No way, Mom. I'll run with you. It's not so much a big deal to me." I can tell she is itching to get started. She bobs a bit in place now and the blood is starting to pinken her cheeks.

We'd put Becca in ballet at three just as we had done with Lydia. She'd never taken to it, flapped her arms up and down like a wild turkey waiting to take flight and basically stomped her way across the stage during her first recital. By five she was ridiculously bored with the whole thing and begged us to let her try soccer, for which she was a natural, barreling her way across the field and relentless at making sure the ball went between the two posts. Lydia was good about cheering her on, sideline spectator on the Saturdays we'd spend at the field knowing that Patrick reveled in his youngest daughter's ability to play, really play. He'd attended Lydia's recitals, of course, watched her blossom into the near prima ballerina that she was, but this was different and Lydia knew it. This was a bond only Becca would have with their father.

We start together and I am hoping for a good run. My runs are never consistent; I am plagued by bad knees and sometimes have a hard time finding a rhythm, especially if I haven't slept well or the air is particularly icy. Becca challenges me to let go and suck in the air; breathe it in and discard the breath before it stings the bottom of my lungs and makes me contemplate turning around, opting for tea and a half hour of *The Today Show*. She can talk and run and often does both in tandem, loping along the street or path, switching gears on me to keep me on my toes.

I do my part to keep a rhythm with her. Just before Patrick's death she had started to become an almost permanent fixture in my morning run and so together we'd started a ritual that involved mostly us, sometimes Lydia, but mostly us. It is this tempo that has remained most unchanged since my husband's passing. It is this time of morning when things feel the most normal to us. "Can we see the new Frankie Muniz movie this weekend?" she starts. "Meg's mom took her and she said it was so cool."

Barnes & Noble Bookseller
600 Fifth Avenue
New York, NY 10020
212 765-0590
06-29-06 S01003 R005

CUSTOMER RECEIPT COPY

With You and Without You   14.00
9780758213839

SUB TOTAL   14.00
SALES TAX   1.17
TOTAL   15.17
AMOUNT TENDERED
MASTERCARD   15.17
CARD #:   ************5640
AMOUNT   15.17
AUTH CODE   055778

TOTAL PAYMENT   15.17
        Thank you for shopping at
        Barnes & Noble Booksellers
Shop online 24 hours a day www.bn.com
#556360 06-29-06 04:57P Eagan

"Um, yeah, maybe." I'm concentrating on the run, trying to feel the beat of the soles of my feet on the pavement, feeling for the thud, shuffle, thud, shuffle. *Pick your feet up,* Patrick would say to me on the occasions he would feel he needed a tune-up and take to the street with me, usually later on a Saturday morning after he'd slept in, recovering from a nonstop week. *No wonder you're wrecking the hell out of your knees. Roll your feet, heel, then ball. You're running on your toes again, Al.*

"Well, that'd be cool, Mom. I think we should go. Even you might like it."

"Yeah, even me. Your old mom." I sneak her a smile. "It'd be so cool. Who's Frankie Muniz?"

"Oh yeah, right, Mom. Who's Frankie Muniz? Like I need to tell you."

"Yeah, like you need to tell me. He's only plastered on every speck of your wall. Is there a poster of him you don't have?"

"Funny, Mom. You're so funny."

We run for a while in silence, Becca kicking a step or two ahead of me and then dropping back as if to check in on me. At forty-two I'm not slow, but then I've never been a fast runner. I run because it is simply the best exercise for me, the best way to keep my body strong and lithe and toned. Patrick had appreciated that about me when we were younger, but at some point, the exercise simply changed to a habit, something I needed like oxygen to get me through the day.

Down the long bulk of our street and then out onto the cross street that would take us into town if we stayed on it. We turn left and across the field at the junior high where Lydia graduated the spring before. Across the street and around the border of Lytton Park, a wave to a few early morning dog walkers, the heat of our breath leaving in small puffs as we greet each of them. Back across the street and down a few blocks in front of the 7-Eleven, a long right, and then back onto home turf. Just under three miles. Easy for both of us today, a good feeling in the pace and in each other's company.

Becca kicks it into high gear when we hit our street and sprints the rest of the way home. I know by now not to do this or I'm likely to miss the next few days out here. I watch her from behind and she's fearless. Her arms are pumping and her knees lifting her up, heels kicking out from behind her, until she hits the driveway, then stops and bends at the waist and takes in some deep, purposeful breaths, her body heaving up and down from the exertion. She stands up and paces across the front of the driveway, watching me come in.

I pull in behind her and pat her on the butt. "Good run, sweetie. Thanks." My knees are just at the point where they'd have begun aching had we gone on, and I know it'll take a good stretch to work out my age.

"Mom?" She stops me as I start my cooldown. I'm walking back and forth across the front walk, arms above my head, fingers locked and stretching back behind my head. I shake out my left leg to alleviate the dull ache a bit.

"Yeah?"

"Are we gonna move?"

"No," I say instantly without even so much as a breath in between her question and my answer. "Why would you ask such a thing?"

"Just wondering, really." She is quiet, then, "I mean, are we always gonna stay here? This house? This place?"

"Well, Becca, I hadn't really thought about it." This isn't exactly the truth. The truth is, I *have* thought about it. Every day since Patrick has been gone. Why not move? Why stay here with the smells and sights and sounds and memories he left us? His clothes still hanging in the closet, his shoes lined up at attention, a pile of his dry cleaning balled up and shoved in a basket in the back corner of the closet floor. But I play it off the best I can. I want to see where Becca is going with this. "Did you want to move, Bec? Is there a reason you don't want to be here anymore?"

"No, not really. Like I said, 'just wondering,' but sometimes you just seem so sad here."

"I don't know that it's the house, Bec. I'm pretty sure I'd be sad anywhere." I'm still stretching and have taken a seat on the driveway, right next to where the morning paper has been tossed, legs straddled so that I can stretch either side.

"Yeah, I guess so. It's just been such a sad time."

"Yes, Becca. It has been a very sad time."

3

"You're on the road," I said into the receiver, annoyed. "And when you're on the road, you take care of you. That's it, just *you*. I get to take care of the rest, Patrick. All the rest of this shit? All the stuff that goes on while you're gone? That's mine. I get that."

There was silence at the end of the receiver. He knew how I hated the silence. I could make out the faint sounds in the background: Monday night football, his pacing in the hotel room, the sound of the ice I could hear him dropping into a glass. I imagined he'd just moved a tray—room service—out into the hall, and my jealousy raged on. He wouldn't pick up his towels in the morning; he wouldn't make a bed. Someone would leave a paper for him, have his breakfast ready.

It had been a particularly hard day with the girls, constant bickering, a call from Lydia's principal about her third late slip to class, and then the call with his mother.

"It's dinner, Ally, that's all. My mother doesn't ask for much, just our time. That's all she ever wants. I don't see what the big deal is."

"The big deal is that you arrive home Friday, you're playing golf Saturday, and you leave again midday on Sunday. Saturday night was *the* night, the *only* night we had to do anything as a family. You get that, right?"

"We will be doing something as a family, Al. Dinner. It is just a few people at my mom's house. We're in, we're out, and we'll come home and put on a movie if you want. I'll rub your feet and draw you a bath."

"Fabulous."

"Al—"

"What, Patrick, what? It's got to stop, you know. We have such little time together these days. You can't fault me for wanting more."

"I don't. But dinner at my mom's is hardly something to get so sideways about. Besides, Michael will be there, and Sarah. And a bunch of the family we haven't seen in a while. My sister's in town with the girls. A few of the neighbors will be there."

"Hardly in and out, then." I pictured the party, a feast. Barbara rarely did anything in small form.

"Okay, Al, look—"

I didn't let him finish; I knew there was little chance at victory in this argument and I was tired. Too tired to fight; too tired to go through all this on the phone, his voice fading in and out over the miles. "It's okay, Patrick, it's fine. I know the drill here. We'll go. It'll be *fine*," I sighed into the receiver, sinking back against the throw pillows in the oversized chair and clicking off the television. This was Patrick's third week on the road.

"You sound exhausted, babe. What's wrong?"

"I am. And I'm too tired to spend the time I have with you fighting about what little time I'll have with you."

"Tell me about Lyd. Do I need to talk to her? What did Mr. Towner say?"

"Late again. Third time this semester, science. Always science. It's fifth period, right after lunch. She's loafing, that's all I can say about it."

"Put her on," he barked.

"She's long gone, Patrick. I had it out with her over soup and sandwiches tonight and she stomped off to her room, slammed the door, and cranked up the music—"

"And you let her get away with that? Jesus, Ally, what do you think she's going to do?" He cut me off short, refused to let me finish.

I took a deep breath and counted.

"Ally!"

I let the silence fall over the wire; let it settle in good so he knew I was angry. *Six, seven, eight*, another long breath, *nine*, one more long breath in and out, *ten*.

"Al."

"Yeah, Patrick, I let her walk. Right out of the room, right up to her bedroom. I went up there and coddled her later, like a baby. I brought her a fucking bowl of ice cream and told her it was fine, that she could skip out on the detention she'd been awarded, too." I said this to him slowly, with as much sarcasm as I could manage, between clenched teeth. I sat back, started rubbing my forehead with my thumb and forefinger until I finally felt the pressure points give slightly. Patrick knew not to do this with me; we'd been through this before.

Finally, after a minute during which I was certain I could tell he was pacing the floor of his hotel room, he said to me, "Okay, sorry. I get it. I know you didn't let her slide. What'd you say to her?"

"I grounded her, Patrick. Yanked the phone right out of her wall. I think I busted the little plastic thing on the end of the cord, but I really didn't give a shit, you know. I was done. With the attitude, with the mouth, with the posturing, with the whole damn thing. I was just done."

"Good. You had every right to be. Let her stew on it. I'll talk to her tomorrow."

"She'll be in detention till five. Which, as you know, means she'll miss dance."

"Fine."

"Yeah, okay. I got it. I got this one. And the next one, too," I said, just to let him know, again, what I was thinking, really thinking, about his being gone.

"Al?"

"Yeah."

"I'll talk to you tomorrow, okay? Try and get some rest."

"Yeah."

"Night, Ally-cat. Kisses and hugs."

"Okay, Patrick. Night."

It wasn't what I'd hoped for, or even what I'd bargained for. I reasoned it was just what I'd gotten, what we'd lapsed into all these years later. First Lydia, after a long wait and a couple of years spent trying to have a baby. Then Becca a few years later. I'd given up teaching, my passion, exchanged it for what I was convinced would be my other passion: my girls. They were. There wasn't a thing wrong with my life; not one thing I could point to and say, "whoops, big mistake." No do-overs. Few, if any, rocky relationships. Great friends. A wonderful family.

But me? I'd wondered where I'd gone, who I'd become. Dutifully, I was Patrick's wife. Diligently, I was Lydia and Becca's mother. Resentfully, but respectfully, I was Barbara's daughter-in-law. But me? I was having a hard time with the definition. It had happened slowly, like honey pouring from a jar. Patrick on the road so much, and it was hard to feel a sense of wifeliness. Lydia sliding away from us, slipping into rebellion, and it was easy to feel a sense of failure.

And Barbara.

With Barbara, nothing had been easy. Ever. Never good enough. Never strong enough. Never dutiful or diligent or respectful enough for anyone, she claimed. Not Patrick. Not the girls. Certainly not herself.

Barbara. Lady Barb. Queen Bee.

Patrick had long caved to his mother; mama's boy. Long before his father had passed, but worse since. When Barbara wanted something, Barbara got it.

So it was no surprise, none whatsoever, when Patrick called me on Saturday from his cell phone. He'd been golfing, left early that morning with Michael as planned. I'd expected him by one o'clock, two tops. So I was beyond suspicious, and more than pissed, but completely unsurprised, when he called me just before three. He was on his way to Barbara's; she needed help with the tables, help with the caterer, help with the bar. Could I bring him a change of clothes and just meet him there? No need to rush, take your time with the girls.

"Sure, Patrick. Fine. We'll be over as planned. Five."

"Okay, baby. Thanks, thanks so much for understanding." The thing of it was, I didn't.

"Hey, gorgeous," Michael crooned, wrapping me with his arms, unsteady already with a beer bottle in one hand. "Where ya been all my life?"

"Oh God, Michael, you stink. Golf sweat." I unwrapped myself and set down the tray of deviled eggs I was carrying in one hand, the garment bag with Patrick's pressed pants and shirt in the other. "Are we not showering this afternoon?" I licked my lips and came up with the salty taste of Michael's tanned skin.

"Just on my way out."

"You're leaving me? I just got here. You know I can't survive Lady Barb without you," I whispered under my breath, pulling him close for safety. "Take me with you."

"Is that an offer?" he teased, pulling at my wrist. "Come on, let me get you outta here before your husband finds you."

"Too late, Michael. Unhand my woman," Patrick boomed, grabbing me at my waist, his hands settling on the tops of my hips, before he ran one of them over my ass. "You've been trying for years, Michael. Give it up already and find your own woman. Try someone your own age, you might have just a little more luck."

I stepped away from the both of them. "God, the two of you. How can two men get so damn smelly on a golf course? It's not an aerobic sport, you know. What'd you two do, roll around on the grass?" I reached over to kiss Patrick lightly on the lips, brushing them gently, not quite ready to forgive him for ditching me for the afternoon, clearly having polished off his first few drinks with his oldest friend, the both of them at his mother's beck and call. "To the shower, Patrick. You are ripe."

"Okay, okay, I'm going already."

I stood back and watched them as they knocked fists together, the bond of camaraderie deep and at ease between them. "Don't get lost on your way back, man," I heard my husband say to his friend before he headed out of the kitchen and up Barbara's back staircase.

When Patrick was gone I walked with Michael to his car. The late August heat was stifling; it rose up from the cracked driveway and hung at your knees.

"How's her mood, Michael? Give it to me straight, what am I in for?"

He laughed. Michael had refereed fifteen-round heavyweight battles between Barbara and me before. He was the only one who could calm me down when she pushed my buttons.

"You know this, Al," he said to me, using his keyless remote, and I knew what was coming, the constant reminder he was going to give me. "You know this."

We said it together. "She can only get to you if you give her permission to do so."

"I know, I know. But I swear, I'm gonna walk back in there and she's going to tell me I haven't made enough deviled eggs. Or that I made too many. It'll be one or the other, you know. It's never just right. Never."

"It's eggs, Al. E-G-G-S. Eggs."

"*Ally? Ally!* Is that you out there?" Barbara's voice boomed at us from the house. I turned and watched her amble down the side steps, the first two of them, still holding open the screen door to the kitchen. "Ally!"

"Hi, Barb, I'm just on my way in."

"Oh, honey, I didn't know you were here. Don't you go holding Michael up now. Go on you, get," She said to Michael, brushing him off with the wave of her hand. "Get showered so you can help me with this bar. Patrick's not going to be able to handle it himself." She instructed Michael as if she were his mother; she might as well have been all these years he'd been here. He blew her a kiss, bowed slightly to her in mock hilarity that sent me giggling. I knew Michael adored her but he wouldn't put up with her crap, he'd dish it back at her faster than she could scoop ice cream into a bowl. It was one of the things I'd always liked best about him.

We watched her start back up the steps before she stopped and pushed the screen open again, calling for me once more. "Ally? Ally, these eggs."

"Yes, Barb?" I said, just a hint of a smirk hiding in my voice somewhere, waiting, poised for what was coming. I nudged Michael with my elbow as if to get his attention, catch him right up under the rib cage.

"Well, they're just perfect, honey. Just wonderful." My smirk faded, just slightly, just as I thought she'd failed me for the first and only time.

Michael started to chuckle, fiddled with his keys in his hands so they jingled ever so slightly.

"I just don't know how we'll possibly eat *all these eggs*! I just can't imagine why you'd make so many with all this food we have."

I smiled, complacent, satisfied, fed like an overweight cat.

4

Patrick had always hated leftovers. Couldn't stomach them. On the nights he did the dishes, he'd scrape the remains of any meal I'd made, no matter the amount, into the sink. Then he'd push it down into the disposal with a spatula or a wooden spoon for fear I'd serve it the following night.

I was horrified when we first began dating, standing in the kitchen with a serving platter and a few glasses in my hands as I'd cleared the table where we'd eaten. "Wasn't it okay? You didn't like it?" I felt the immediate heat of embarrassment rise to cover my face. I wasn't much of a cook in those days, but I did try. And he had finished what had been on his plate. Was he placating me? An attempt to avoid bruising my ego?

"No, no. It was great, really," he'd said, simultaneously scraping half a pan of my meat loaf into the sink, complimenting me all the while. "But you didn't want it again, did you?" More hot water and a harsh scraping against the metal loaf pan.

"Um, no, I guess not. I mean, I think it would have lasted to lunch tomorrow, but I guess not." I stepped closer to the sink, really looking in to convince myself that it was, in fact, gone.

He crinkled up his nose then and shook his head. "I never got that. Eating the same thing all over again. Why would you want to do that? It's never as good. Kind of gives me the creeps."

"Well, I don't know," I said, suddenly unsure of my eating habits and myself. Casseroles had been a staple in my family; leftovers in the microwave sometimes a way of life for days after my mother had gone on one of her bake and freeze binges. Good God, this man ate no leftovers? "I kinda like meat loaf the next day. White bread, a little ketchup. Just slightly warmed. It's really kind of a waste to throw all that away, Patrick." I speared the last remaining baked potato from the dish and quickly wrapped it in foil before he could toss it in the stainless steel garbage pail.

"No. Don't ask me to eat that, Ally-cat." He stuck his tongue out then and made a little acking sound as if to indicate he would be sick to his stomach, shuddering all over with a twitch. He pushed the faucet all the way to the left so that steam began to rise from the tap, and the scalding water peeled away the remaining baked crust from the side of the pan.

"Fine. I'll eat the leftovers. You eat a nice new sandwich. How about a baguette, a little Brie, and black forest ham? Will that work for you?" I feigned attitude, but I was really mystified. No leftovers. None, whatsoever.

"Yep, that'll do. That sounds just fine." He took me in his arms then and dabbed a bit of the bubbles from the soapy dishwater onto the tip of my nose, then gently rubbed it off, kissing me in the same spot.

"Well, I suppose if you do the dishes, you can have a new meal every night of the week."

The girls and I learned to save the leftovers for Patrick's business trips when I didn't feel like cooking and the girls barely had time for eating. Or on a night when I was left carting them from school to ballet to soccer to cheerleading to a game to home. Sometimes it was near nine when we finally made it home, weary from an afternoon of miles on my four-by-four and painstaking refereeing between conversations.

Because we weren't expecting Patrick home for dinner the afternoon he died, we were scheduled for leftovers. Chicken enchiladas. One of Patrick's favorites the night it was cooked, simply intolerable for him any other time. I was mixing a box of Spanish Rice-a-Roni when the phone rang, and I grabbed the receiver with one hand while stirring in the contents of the seasoning package with a wooden spoon in the other hand.

"Hello?" I simultaneously checked the box to make sure I had properly added the right amount of water.

"Ah, hello, Mrs. Houlihan?" An unfamiliar voice. Great. Telemarketer. Just what I needed.

"Um, yes? Who's calling?" *Let's get right to it. Society for the Deaf and Blind? American Heart Association? SPCA?* I had not checked caller ID, answered it on the first ring.

"My name is Officer Jack Langley, Mrs. Houlihan. I'm sorry to call you with this, but your husband was involved in a very bad car accident."

"Um, what? What happened? Where is he? Patrick Houlihan, right? Are you sure it's my husband?" I checked the time on the clock just above my right shoulder.

"Yes, ma'am. We have his identification. It appears he might have fallen asleep at the wheel. No one else was involved in the accident, Mrs. Houlihan."

"Where are you? Where is my husband?" Oh God, how bad could it possibly be? "I'm sorry," I said to him, "you'll have to hold on." It was just now that I realized the Rice-a-Roni was burning the bottom of the pan; small speckles of rice were baked black onto the bottom. Either I hadn't used the right amount of margarine or I hadn't added the right amount of water. With a single motion, I flung the pan from the stove top and into the sink, threw on the water, and was overcome by smoke and sizzle. "Where are you?" I asked the man again, in a voice I didn't recognize as my own. "Are you sure this is my husband?"

He read me my home address from Patrick's driver's license and told me that he got my home phone number from our health insurance company. I saw Patrick's wallet in my mind. His driver's license stuck in the top insert, his medical card in the second insert, Becca's latest soccer picture and Lydia's latest recital pic stuffed into the billfold. Patrick carried a money clip; his cash would have been folded in his front pocket.

I said, "Patrick's allergic to penicillin" because I could think of nothing else to say and I thought this might be vital information the insurance company left out.

"I'm sorry?" he said.

"Penicillin. He's allergic to—"

"Mrs. Houlihan?" His voice rang clear in my head.

I waited the beat of a minute, the beat of a heartbeat, anticipating his words.

"Yes?" I managed to choke out in a whisper.

"I'm sorry, Mrs. Houlihan, but your husband was killed. The impact of the accident took his life."

He graciously waited a minute and listened for me to collect my breath, for the sobs that started choking me to subside somewhat. "I'm sorry, Mrs. Houlihan," he said to me automatically, in a voice I could tell had been trained for this duty. "Is there someone I can call for you? Are you there alone? We can arrange for the local authorities to check in on you or have you transported here to the location of the *incident*."

This was the first time I heard the police call my husband's death an incident. I imagined the yellow chalked lines on the asphalt, an officer sweeping away broken glass, the traffic that must have snarled on the highway.

"You will need to come here, Mrs. Houlihan, to identify the body. Strictly a formality, of course."

"Of course." My voice drifted off, I drifted off. "Um, yeah, I am alone. But I can call someone. A neighbor. Maybe I should call a neighbor."

I was not at all sure whom to call. I'd always been a sharer of news, hated to keep something to myself. *A regular gossip*, Patrick used to say, throwing me a get-off-the-phone-and-come-sit-with-me look if I'd taken up with one of my girlfriends on the phone after dinner.

Officer Langley provided me with some of the details, and

told me he'd be back with me later in the evening when he had more information.

I said to him again, "You're sure this is my husband? Patrick Alan Houlihan?"

"Yes, ma'am. I'm sorry, but I am sure."

5

I picked three people to call because it seemed like the right number. Three always seems like the right number.

Patrick's assistant, Suzanne, immediately began to sob until I was left calming her down, the portable phone burning against my right ear, my left foot having gone to sleep. She wanted as many details as possible so she could tell people in the office what had happened. "They'll never believe it," she said to me. "Never, never, never. My God, Patrick? My God. Good God. Never." She was crying again, great giant gulps of sobs coming up from her throat. I was watching the clock on the microwave tick away digital numbers backlit in red, aware that I had only a few minutes before it would be time to leave to get the girls. I promised to call her with more news as soon as I had it. She offered to come over and make some calls for me, but I told her I was going to need some time with the girls.

"My God, the girls," she started sobbing again when I clicked off the phone, desperate now to find someone to collect my girls, acutely aware that driving for me at this moment would be like doing so under the influence of some drug I had never taken before.

My neighbor Anna was the only person I knew likely to be able to pull off the grand heist of picking up my daughters without letting on that their lives, without their knowledge, had changed beyond recognition. When I told her what had happened, her voice went strong as an oak over the receiver and she began to anchor me to the ground.

"You'll have half an hour before we're back, unless you need me to stall longer than that. Is someone there with you?" she said to me. When I told her no, she hung up and was walking through my front door in exactly sixty seconds, rosary beads in hand. She was wearing her lavender slippers and I imagined I'd interrupted her watching *Oprah*. She lifted me from the floor, her hands anchored under each of my armpits, and deposited me into a kitchen chair.

"I have to call Michael. He's got to be here when I tell the girls," I said to her. "Half an hour should give him enough time to get here before you're back." She hugged me and didn't let go immediately. When she finally pulled away, tears weighed heavy in the bottom of her eyelids. It was the only time I'd seen her cry.

Michael used his key to enter our house and immediately began banging sharply on the bathroom door when I didn't answer his calling my name.

"Al, you okay? Ally! Open the door." He rattled the doorknob, banging it with the palm of his hand against the grain of the wood. I wasn't sure what he thought I was doing, but the truth was I was washing my face, splashing the water in great handfuls up and into my bangs, down over the ends of my eyelashes. It dripped from every part of my face, onto my chin and then onto the front of my pressed white blouse. Michael pulled the hand towel from the brass ring near the sink and handed it to me. He held himself back, offered no embrace, no hand, but pushed his sunglasses to the top of his head.

"What happened?" His command was altogether frightening and reassuring at the same time, as if it were Patrick himself standing in the hall with me, demanding why there was a small scratch in the base of the car door. Something insignificant that needed to be slightly blown out of proportion. At just over six feet, Michael was wide and his presence in the small powder room was overbearing. His broad shoulders filled the space; even his narrow hips seemed to block the doorway. All at once I was nauseated with his presence, sick with fright. I steadied myself against the wall, deep breaths in and out as if I were ready to hyperventilate at any minute. I brushed past him into the kitchen, searching for a place to draw a boundary around myself.

He was right on my tail, trailing me with accusations. "Ally! Ally, tell me exactly what happened. Pull it together, for Christ's sake."

"I got a call, Michael. Some police officer from Ashland. Patrick had a meeting there today. That big deal he was trying to land, remember? He was just telling you about it the other night. Remember, Michael?" But he didn't nod. Instead he only stared at me, waiting for my explanation. I spoke quickly and in great gulps. The front of my blouse was soaked and clinging to my bra. I peeled the shirt away from my chest and used the cherry-colored towel to blot myself dry, then folded my arms self-consciously across my chest.

Michael was studying me, watching me intently, and making me more uncomfortable than I could bear. I turned my back to him before continuing. "They think maybe he fell asleep, he hit the center median." I repeated this as if saying it over and over would make me understand the impact, fill me with the details and explanations I'd need to start answering everyone's questions. But when I looked at Michael, he was unrelenting, staring at me and waiting for more of the story. "That's all I know," I said finally, waves of both nausea and exhaustion running over me.

He threw his Maui Jim sunglasses across the granite kitchen counter and ran the palm of his left hand across the college-boy-dark curly locks that hadn't changed, hadn't grayed, hadn't receded in the twenty years I'd known him. He'd had his other hand on his hip, holding his solid frame up in exasperation.

My eyes were burning with a stinging feeling and I automatically pulled the palms of my hands up to shield them, trying with strength to rub the reality away.

"Jesus." Pause. "Jesus, Allyson."

I wasn't at all sure he didn't think this was something I'd caused myself as I watched him walk the full floor of the kitchen.

"Where's this guy's number? Did he at least give you a number where you can call him?"

"Right here." I handed him the pink Post-It with the scribbled, shaky handwriting on it, and he picked up the phone, punching the numbers hard into the receiver.

"Michael?" I said to him as he was waiting for someone to come on the line. "Michael?" my voice began again.

He held up his finger sharply to me as he addressed the person who had answered the phone, demanding to speak to the officer who had clearly left me with so little information.

"Michael?" I was pleading now. "What am I going to tell the girls?"

6

Twelve weeks into the season and Becca is playing the best soccer of her life. It's a bridge year for her. She's the youngest on the team of mostly twelve-year-olds, but you'd never know it. She's first on the field, running until she's nearly faint and she requires a hit of oxygen. One might say she's running from something and to something, neither of which she's entirely identified or located. But her new look is fierce, jersey sleeves rolled up to her armpits and waist-length hair pulled tight into a single streaking ponytail behind her.

I'm watching her third game of the Memorial Day tournament with extreme pride and cheering louder than should be allowed at eight-thirty on a Sunday morning when she takes a hit to the gut from a girl who is a good four inches taller than she is. She limps off the field, her left hand holding tight at the side of her rib cage and two of her teammates nearby to check on her. Her face beet red, she refuses tears that spring to the corners of her eyes. More angry than hurt, she won't be out of the game long, and she waves me off when she sees me coming down the sidelines toward her to check, just to make sure she's okay. Michael trots out to speak with the other coach on her behalf, and by the time he's back on the sideline, Becca's begging him to let her back in the game. He holds her out for a few minutes before checking on her

again, bending at the knees to come eye-to-eye with her and patting her gently on the back to make sure she is really ready to go
back in. I know this overprotection that has kicked in for him,
the debt he feels he owes his friend. He watches her intently.
He's watched all of us this year.

When Becca goes in again she scores the only goal of the
game, ensuring her team's place in the finals later this afternoon.
I'm thrilled and fold up my plastic beach chair before picking up
the empty Starbucks mocha cup I'd started my morning with.
We'll be back at the field before we know it.

"Ally-cat?" Michael calls to me from a slow trot as he's heading
across the field, coach's whistle and sunglasses balanced on the
edge of his clipboard.

Michael is the only other person that dares call me by the
nickname Patrick had for me, and even he uses it sparingly, usually when he wants something, so I know I'm in for it.

"Yeah?" I turn toward the sun and am blinded momentarily
until I hold my hand up to shield my eyes. Michael's long-
sleeved white T-shirt is pulled taut across his chest and his long
legs flash brilliant muscles in black shorts. To me, he's no different today than he was at the university, running off with Patrick
in their grass-stained jerseys and muddy cleats for a beer after
one of their own soccer games. But women watch Michael. Jealous
housewives, the mothers of the girls on the team, watch me
when he calls my name. They wonder what Michael could possibly want, taking an extra minute to listen in on our conversation.

"Lunch?" he says.

His tone is both a question and a suggestion, but I know him
well enough to know that it's really his meager attempt to lose
the woman he's been with the night before, who, in bad form,
has decided to tag along with him to the game this morning.
She's at his side now, all of twenty-seven or so, in a sweatshirt and
tight jeans, the heels of her black pumps sinking in the soft,
sloppy field. She's attempting conversation with Michael's sour

daughter, Sarah, who has neither the desire nor the urge to make eye contact with her, let alone aspire to a discussion with some woman she knows she probably won't see again. This poor date. If she didn't look so good in a borrowed sweatshirt and little makeup, you might feel sorry for her. Rather, I'm searching for a way to rescue Michael, do him the favor he needs.

But not that easy. He doesn't deserve my help, so I taunt, "It's only ten, Michael. A little early for lunch, don't you think?" I say to him, teasing.

"Noon," he says, with a look that could melt the still dewy field. "Duke's." He is all teeth, two perfect rows of them, when he grins at me.

Twenty-seven-Year-Old swings her weapon of a purse over a shoulder and skips a few steps to catch up with him, his long loping legs no match for the stilettos. She throws me a weak smile as if to say she'll see me at Duke's as well. I know she will not.

"Yeah, yeah. Fine. See you then." I chase Becca off the field and dig for the car keys in my purse. Patrick would have raised her to his shoulders, half carried her off the field to the car, making a big deal of her in an overbearing and somewhat embarrassing loud boom the whole way. Instead, Becca and I gallop together at a good trot and I do my best to celebrate her victory, knowing that it's especially sweet for her and that she's already itching to go at it again.

Just a few minutes before noon I spot Michael through the long front window at Duke's as I'm pulling the Suburban into the parking lot. He's alone and sucking on a tall beer, one eye on the baseball game on the corner television set that's perched precariously in a corner above the bar. He's showered and the curly jet-black hair is still wet, slicked back at the temple the way he knows women like it. At least on him.

"Where's your friend?" I ask while I take the seat across from him and drop my car keys and wallet on the hardwood table.

He takes another long draw on the beer, motions to Duke for one for me, and laughs under his breath, shaking his head slowly from side to side. "This is what I like about you, Ally," he says and picks up my wallet. "Keys, wallet. Nothing else. Simple." He dangles the keys from his fingers, jingling them alive.

"Really, Michael, they're getting younger," I continue to scold him, for sport. I've seen Michael with all types. Younger, older, married when he was as well, married when he wasn't, psychos. "Pretty soon people are going to think you're dating Sarah's friends."

A regular waitress shows up with my beer and the tall glass of water she knows I'm going to ask for. I smile at her by way of thanks and send her away before she starts a conversation with Michael that could last the duration of our lunch.

"Well," he says, "pretty soon Sarah's friends will be old enough for me to date." He flashes me a wicked grin. "But she's gone. To answer your question." He picks up a menu to avoid further interrogation and pretends to hide behind it, studying it intently.

"Gone? Just like that. Didya get a number at least? Jeez." I pull the menu from his hands. He doesn't need this; he has the damn thing memorized and Duke hasn't changed his menu in all the years we've been coming here. Besides, you don't eat at Duke's for anything other than a burger.

"Yeah, I got a number. She left it on the kitchen table. Little hearts on the note. 'Call me, Michelle.' Good thing she signed her name. I was having a hard time remembering it." He finished his beer and pushed the thick mug to the end of the table. "Jesus, Ally, what the hell am I doing?" A hint of remorse rings in his voice, residue from a late night, followed by the early morning. Michael isn't getting any younger; he can't keep this up forever.

"Same thing you been doing, Michael. Since the day I met you. Thing you do best. Seducing women all your life."

He shakes his head at himself. "Great, great. You'd think I'd have gotten it right by now."

"Oh, cut yourself some slack, Michael. At least if you're going to do it, do it with the best of them. I gotta say, those were some stilettos."

"Not the best soccer shoes."

"No."

He runs his hands through his thick curly hair like he does at least a hundred times a day and looks me square in the eye. "How are you, Al?" Takes a breath and sits back hard against the wood booth. "Really?"

"I'm fine, Michael." I take a long drag on the beer as if it were a cigarette I was inhaling and swallow deeply. It takes me a minute to meet his eyes, but he's a force to be reckoned with and he won't quit looking at me until I finally stop staring at the table, fidgeting with my hands, and stare back at him. He's searching for the truth, determined to dig it out of me, so I stare back at Michael, holding his look for as long as I can bear. He knows me, has known me since the second day at the university when he found me beating the shit out of the soda machine in the dorm lobby, trying unsuccessfully to retrieve the Diet Coke I'd been robbed of. I'm not much at hiding from Michael no matter how hard I try.

"Fine," I say again more softly, followed by a resounding sigh. I look down at the table carved with initials and wonder about the couples they represent. *CV + KW.* A heart around *Sherri loves Dave.* "Really. Not bad." I'm trying to convince him, but doing a poor job convincing even myself, so I know he's got me.

He takes my hands then and holds them in his own, rubbing his thumbs against my knuckles. His touch sends a chill down my spine and back up again. "Man, I miss him." He lets out a long sigh. "Every day I miss him." He turns my hands over, palms up, and rubs them together generously before placing them softly back down on the table and smiling at me slyly. I've never thought of myself as someone Michael might chase; at least I haven't for years. If I had been, he'd have had me in bed years ago before a friendship befell him and Patrick, before he and Leslie had become our closest friends. Still, the sensation of a man touching me, the human contact, has become foreign and I'm haunted by the tingle left behind.

"Yep," I say, taking in a deep breath. "Every day."

The baseball game serves as a good diversion from talking about Patrick. It has become like this for us, lunch or dinner occasionally, and I wonder if I haven't, in some familiar way, taken Patrick's place in Michael's life, if that is what he thinks of me now, a substitute for what he's lost.

"How's Lydia?" he asks me, paying the bill and leaving the waitress a nice tip. "She hasn't made one game. I hardly see her when I stop by. Is she avoiding me?"

I think about it for a minute, weighing my answer carefully. As distant as Lydia has become, it isn't in my nature to sell her out. "She's okay." I dodge, picking at the cuticle on my right-hand ring finger.

Still, this is Michael. He's practically served as the girls' surrogate father the last year. When I finally look up and meet his eyes, he calls me out without saying a word. A minute later I'm confessing in long, breathless, revealing admissions, "No, Michael, she hasn't, not one game. Don't take it personally, she's hiding from everyone. And with me, she's gone radio silent. I'm at a loss. To be honest with you, I just don't know where to go from here. I'm thinking about forcing her to do some time on the black couch, but to be honest with you"—I smile at him quietly, shrugging my shoulders before I admit—"I'm just not sure I'm up for it. Hell, I've been in that damn therapist's office for the last eight months dealing with my own shit. Now I'm going to drag my fourteen-year-old daughter in there to start exploring that screwed-up side of both of our lives? Just what I need."

Michael waits for me to go on; he can sense that I'm not done unloading.

"I'm watching her closely, Michael, really I am. But her mood swings are doing me in. It's as if she drops down, down, down to the bottom, and then she's higher and higher the minute the phone rings, the minute there's a knock at the door and I call her down from her room, the minute Eric walks into the room." I hesitate for a minute while I let my mind wander. "I don't know, maybe she's fine. She's fourteen, you know. Maybe this is what I'm in for," I say to him again.

Michael sits for a minute, absorbing my words, before he answers me. "About this guy, what's he like? Is he all right, Ally? I mean really okay? 'Cause fourteen is one thing for a girl, but it's an entirely separate thing for a guy."

I know what he is getting at and I have to admit I've turned a blind eye to it. So happy to see Lydia smile, if only occasionally, I've welcomed Eric into our home, into our lives.

"He's a good kid, Michael. But she's so damn delicate right now. I really don't know that she knows who she is, where she's going. She leans into Eric as if he can fix her, as if he can support her. She doesn't do that with me like she used to. She's pulled away from me. She's got the most sorrowful, damn hollow eyes that look right through me, beyond me."

"Rein her in, Al. You don't have a choice on this one. She's fourteen. Rein her in."

"From what, Michael?" I naively defend my daughter. "From what?"

"From everything, Ally. From the loneliness she's feeling, from the isolation and the endless searching she's doing. From the desperation you know she's running from, hiding from. Rein her in from this guy before she leans so far into him she can't find her way back. Hell, rein her in from herself."

"Jesus, Michael, I don't know that I have the strength."

"Yes, you do." He swallows the last of his beer and places the tall pint glass hard on the table so that the hollow sound emphasizes his point. "Yes, you do." He stares me long in the eye, daring me to defy him. "And besides, Allyson, you don't have a choice."

I'd never have had this conversation with Patrick. Patrick

would have lectured Lydia nonstop until he'd talked himself out, and Lydia had finally acquiesced under the pressure of pleasing her father. Patrick would have been all over Eric; he would have sat him down in the formal wingback chair in the living room and interrogated the hell out of him, laying down the house rules, the rules of engagement. Patrick would have met his mother by now, would have shaken his father's hand, been by their house to drop Eric off after he'd walked over on a school night just so he knew where the boy lived. Patrick would have wedged himself in where I hadn't gone.

Michael won't let me off the hook so easily.

"You don't have a choice on this. You know that, don't you?" he says again, his voice finally breaking the silence that has settled over our table. He isn't about to solve this for me, but he isn't going to let me walk away from it either. It doesn't mean he doesn't care; he does. So much so, in fact, that he is insistent, refusing to let this go.

"You know that, Ally, right?" he says to me again, reaching over to lift my chin with his cupped hand. "Patrick's not here to do this. You don't have a choice."

"Yeah, okay, I know, I know. I'm just not sure how to fix it yet."

"Don't let Lydia go further than she has. She's in a bad place with all this. Patrick's death hit her hard, maybe harder than any of you. Maybe harder than any of us. But, Al, anesthetic comes in all shapes and sizes. Lydia's still searching for something to dull the pain. I'm not sure how you fix this either, but you tell me if you need me, okay?"

"I will. But this is something I gotta do, Michael. I know she's not the same. I can see it. You're right, I need to come clean with this, with how distant she's grown from me. I've known that for a while now." I laugh then, thinking about the past, before I say to Michael, "When Patrick was struggling with her, he used to ask me, 'How far will she go from me, Ally? How do I get her back?'"

"And what did you tell him?" Michael asks me.

"I used to tell him that she'd go as far as he'd let her." I smile, thinking back on the memory. "But I always told him that she'd be back. As long as he didn't let her go, she'd be back."

"She will, Al. Don't let her go. Pull her back if you have to."

7

Michael sees Becca go down before I do. Much later he tells me that she was dribbling up the right side of the field with good coverage, but from out of nowhere a beast of a girl came at her and took her out. Beastly Soccer Girl kicks the ball out of bounds just near the corner to avoid Becca scoring and, in the process, slides her body under both of Becca's legs, which become entangled and she goes down hard on her left side. Initially he thinks it's her knee that takes the force of it.

I'm chatting with Leslie, who has shown for the second game of the day and who is pissed about Michael's late child support check. I know the check is clipped to the front of his clipboard because I've seen it there at lunch, so I'm just letting her vent for a while, nodding in her general direction and trying to keep an eye on the game.

But I miss Becca go down.

I do, however, hear a sound like none other that I've ever heard. It's a piercing cry that rips through the clear afternoon sky and sends a shudder through the crowd. When I look up, Michael is tearing across the grass to the other side of the field. I know it's Becca that has gone down because I don't see her jersey anywhere on the field and I know that Michael would run across the grass for no other player, except his own daughter.

I'm up and out of my lawn chair and nearly catch him by the

time he reaches her. Her left arm has taken a position so awkward I still struggle to describe it, and she's gone the color of sickly gray. And she's panting. Not crying, but panting, as if she might throw up at any minute. Together we roll her, careful to immobilize her from the waist up, crowded by the gaggle of girls who encircle us, concern washing over their young faces. Michael screams at them to take their position, to fall to a knee, pushing them away from us in wide giant gaps. They go, but I read panic on their faces.

"Mom, what happened? Mom, what happened? Mom . . ." she says to me over and over again. I'm cradling her head and lifting her body at the same time, carrying her with Michael across the field. We are both instinctive, though wordless, about this. It's obvious her arm is fractured, a small chip of a bone broken through the skin just below the back of her left elbow. I pull her head toward my chest to shield her from this, but she's impulsive about the pain and pulls away to see where it's coming from.

Then she goes out on us. Head back, from gray to the palest of white in an instant. Almost breathless.

"Michael, she's out." I'm doing my best to blink back tears.

"Can you drive?" Michael says sharply to me, pulling Becca's good arm, which is limp, around his shoulder and hurling all ninety pounds of her up in a cradle carry as if she were an infant. His white jersey is matted with smears of Becca's mahogany-colored blood. Her limp body rocks against him until he grips her tighter and holds her still.

He says to me again, even more sharply now, "Al, can you drive? Are you okay to drive?" He is full of concern, worry flooding his face while he is searching my eyes for confirmation.

"Yeah, yeah. I can drive. Urgent Care? Should I take her to the clinic?" Leslie's brought my bag and I'm fumbling for the key chain, ripping out my sunglasses and hurling the bottled water that has fallen to the bottom of my bag across the asphalt parking lot.

"No, Al. I don't think so. Take her to Memorial. It's broken. She's going to need it set, no doubt about it. Are you sure you can drive?" He looks at me again, his eyes darting back and forth across my face for something that might convince him it's safe to put me behind the wheel of the car. Michael uses his free hand to open the door just as Becca starts to come to and is screaming.

"Mom! Mom?" she wails.

"I'm right here, honey. I'm here." I'm struggling to get my own door open and throw my bag in. "We're gonna go get that arm looked at, sweetie. Just hang on and hold it tight to your chest," I'm saying to her over and over again.

"Mom, Mom, Mom," she's crying now, a force taking over her body, and she's started kicking against Michael, pushing away from him with her good arm, heaving and arching her body back. "Mom! Mom, where's Daddy? I want Daddy. Mama, Mama, Mama, where is my daddy?"

My God, how do I answer this child?

"Honey, he's not here. Daddy's not here, love bug, but I'm here," I say to her. "Mama's here." From the front seat I'm smoothing back the hair that has come loose from the ponytail, pushing it back from her face and wiping the dirt-stained tears that are smeared against her cheeks. "I'm right here, sweets, right here for you."

Michael has laid her on the seat and she's hysterical. "Mama, Mama, my arm, my arm, it hurts so bad. Mama, bring me Daddy. Mama, please. I need Daddy."

"Michael's here, sweetie. Mommy and Michael are here and we're going to go to the hospital now. I'm going to take you, baby. Mommy's going to take you. I'm right here. I promise I won't leave you." I look at Michael's face for reassurance, but he's as stunned as I am.

"No!" she screams at me. "No, I don't want Michael. I want Daddy." She's pushing him away as he struggles to get the seat belt buckled across some part of her body where it won't interfere with her arm. She's holding the left arm in her right, across her body at her chest, pulling her legs up into a cradle on the seat where she is sprawled.

"Leave your car right at the front, Ally, they won't tow it," he barks. "We're behind you by about ten minutes." He slams Becca's door, then puts both of his hands on my face, his palms cupping my chin. "You can do this, Al. Just keep your wits about you."

I roll down my window as I'm backing out. "Michael," I say to him while he's standing there, both palms running the curls back from the top of his head, breathing hard now. "Michael? Call Lydia. She should be home. Pick her up for me on the way."

"Just go," he says from the curb, waving his hand away at me.

I pull to the end of the parking lot and turn right, slamming the radio off with my free hand and readjusting the rearview mirror so I can see Becca crouched on the bench seat behind me. I used to drive this way when she was an infant, one eye on the road, one eye on the child. "Becca? Becca, honey. It's okay. I promise we're gonna get it fixed right up. Bec? Becca? You'll be fine, sweetie. Really. Mommy's right here for you. I'll stay with you."

She's still crying, giant gulping sobs from the leather seat, and pressing the sweatshirt Michael has given her around the broken arm. There are grass stains on her shoulder, above where she has broken the bone, and a clump of dirt that hasn't freed itself from her jersey. But she won't talk to me now. I keep talking anyway, hoping that she's hearing me, aware that she's miles away, in such pain and so scared. She'd asked for Patrick. I'd wondered when it would happen. When it would come that she'd momentarily forget that he was gone. I'm certain at that very moment she'd have traded anything in the world for him at her side. And I know now as I watch her through the rearview mirror, watch her maneuver her body around and pull herself up with her good arm so that she's level with the window and can stare out at the street, the strip malls slipping by, that she realizes she'd asked for him out of nowhere. It was as if she had woken from a bad dream and called out from her bed in the night for him, certain in an instant that he'd be at her side. Even after all this time, he was the first person she'd wanted, the only person she couldn't have.

Now she is silent, lost in her own dreams of him. Tears rolling, draining down her face, soaking themselves into her clothes.

The nurse at registration takes one look at Becca's arm, the way it is twisted and the angle at which she struggles to hold it, and they take her right away, leading us into a small curtained room where Becca lies on the gurney staring at the ceiling. I stay with her as they rip away at her jersey with a pair of large kitchen scissors and wrap her carefully in a hospital gown. I remove her cleats and am tugging at her shin guards when she tells me to stop, that she wants to keep them on. I take the closest thing to a chair, a round rolling stool in the corner, for solace.

It is twenty minutes or so before a large uniformed guardlike nurse comes for her and starts to roll her away from me, his mus-cled arms expertly steering the bulky rolling bed.

"Do you want me to come with you?" I look at the nurse for the answer and ask again, "Should I go with her?"

"No," Becca reprimands me sternly. Then they're off, Becca looking smaller and smaller on the gurney, like Alice falling down the hole after chasing the white rabbit. Off she goes, away, away from me now.

I sigh and stretch my arms up and over my head. My God, Patrick would have gone crazy here. Pacing back and forth, ha-rassing the nurses, demanding information from the intern who is quizzing the husband of the woman in the next curtained area. He'd have raged about the girl, the beast of a twelve-year-old who'd taken his daughter out, ended her season. He'd be reason-ing the play, retaping and replaying it in his mind, providing the audio version for anyone in the hall who'd take a minute to hear it. He'd have seen it all, committed it to memory, and burned it into the corners of his eyes and mind.

I sit and stare at the clock, listen for the click-tick that signifies another minute has passed, watch the shuffle of those who go back and forth with their clipboards, rolling medical tables, stetho-scopes looped around their necks. Nurses, doctors, interns, nurses, doctors, back and forth, back and forth.

The nurse wheels Becca back into our curtained area and I can see she's dealing better with the pain. An IV pole rolls alongside the gurney. The chart they've started is at her feet and I ask the X-ray tech what they've found.

"We're waiting for the doctor to read the films, ma'am. Shouldn't be too much longer now. She did fine, huh, Becca?"

"Yeah, no big deal." They've shared a joke, these two. And for that, I am instantly grateful to this man.

"You okay, Mom?"

"Yeah, Bec. You?"

"Yeah. Whatever." She's fiddling with the IV cord, flipping it back and forth and watching the slow drip that's making its way through the needle on the top of her hand. "Did you see it? I'd have scored if she hadn't taken me out."

"I have no doubt that you would have, Bec. No doubt at all."

The X-ray shows a broken elbow, fractured in two places and turned at a ninety-degree angle from where it is supposed to bend normally. She will need surgery and two pins to set it straight, which, given that it is Memorial Day Sunday, is an apparent impossibility until the following Tuesday.

"Tuesday? My God, she can't wait in this kind of pain until Tuesday," I say to the attending orthopedist, a doctor who looks young enough to be Lydia's date to the prom next year.

"When can I play soccer again?" asks Becca.

"We'll give her something for the pain, Mrs. Houlihan, and she can wear the temporary cast we've set it in so she doesn't have a lot of movement. You'll need to keep her pretty well settled for the next forty-eight hours. And we'll need her to check back into the hospital tomorrow night so we can monitor her for surgery Tuesday. Let me check the rotation schedule and see when we can get her in. I'll have the nurse follow up with you on the time."

"But when can I play again?" Becca says again, bravely and with slightly more edge creeping into her voice.

"I'm afraid it's a season ender," he says, making some notes on his clipboard, barely acknowledging Becca's eyes, the eyes that are pleading with him. "We'll have to set it for six to eight weeks. And you'll need some rehab after that. Should be fine by the time school starts again." He smiles at her then, pats her knee, and I think she might come off the end of the rolling gurney at him, sink her teeth right into the side of his arm the way she once had done in preschool. But she doesn't. Goes back, instead, to the place she'd been in the car, lost and sullen, blinded by a pain stronger than the one she is enduring physically. Crushed, she slumps against the wall.

"Thank you, Doctor," I say as he leaves, drawing the curtain behind him so I can figure out a way to get Becca dressed in what remains of her jersey. We opt instead for Michael's sweatshirt, cutting the left sleeve out of it and manipulating it over the temporary blowup cast they have used to stabilize her arm. Her hair is matted, her face streaked a combination of tears and dried dirt, her eyes red from sobbing.

"I carry you all the way to the car and you thank me by restyling my favorite sweatshirt into some sort of new fashionable minidress?" Michael's playful boom greets us in the sterile hall, but Becca brushes past him, holding tightly to the sling. She is angry and he is all she has to be angry with.

"Hi," I say to him with a sigh, as he reaches to kiss me on the cheek. I nod her way. "Broken elbow. She's got to be in so much pain, Michael. Don't take it personally."

"I won't, champ. What gives? How long in the cast?"

"We're scheduled for surgery on Tuesday. God, Michael, the bone is twisted to the other side of her elbow, completely opposite from where it should be." I push up my sleeve and show him what I mean on my own arm. "She's out for the season and I think that's what's got her so twisted up about everything."

"Um, yeah, that and the rest of her life the last year. Jesus, Ally, why now, why after all this?" He's watching her at the other end of the emergency room hallway while she is talking with Lydia and shuffling her feet back and forth across the tile.

"That's what I keep asking, Michael. Why now? Why this? Why take this away from her?" I pull out the comb I'd fastened in the back of my hair and let it cascade around my shoulders before gathering it up again and securing it in a loose twist that fans out at the top of my head. "Thanks for picking up Lydia," I say to him.

"No problem," he says, bowing his head, avoiding my eyes. "Is everything okay?"

"Yeah. Yeah, fine. We can talk about it later, Al. But that conversation we had earlier, the one about Lyd? You're dead on with all that."

I look at him over an arched eyebrow, questioning his comment, but am interrupted before I can ask him about it. "Mrs. Houlihan?" The administrative nurse in a pair of surgical green scrub pants and a much too cheery pink and purple top is holding a clipboard and tapping her pencil against it. She's young; the badge hanging around her neck indicates that her first name is Kate.

I'm still staring at Michael, waiting on his words, waiting for him to come clean with me about Lydia. "Michael? Did something happen?"

"Later, Al. It's fine, really." He places a protective hand on my shoulder and nods in the direction of the nurse, who is standing next to us now, aware, but unconcerned, that she has interrupted something.

I turn my attention toward her. "Yes? I'm sorry, what is it that you need?" Michael begins to slide away, but I reach for his arm and keep him at my side. I'm not yet sure I want him trying to make peace with Becca, given her foul mood. Even more, I'm not ready to have him leave me.

"Well, we can't seem to get approval from your insurance company for your daughter's treatment. Do you have some sort of secondary insurance?"

"Um, no. What's the problem with ours?"

"Um, well, um." She's stumbling and looking at the clipboard again, checking her notes and flipping through the pages as if she'll find the answer to my question there. "Um, Mrs. Houlihan, the insurance company seems to be telling me that the insured is, well, deceased."

"Oh, Jesus. Yes, well, originally the insured was my husband. But he died just over a year ago, last February. We were covered under his policy through work. But surely there's some mistake.

We're still insured, the girls and me. I've paid the policy this year. I've had it transferred into my name, you can see that on the insurance card you copied. They've screwed this up somehow."

Suddenly, Kate is very official. "Well, Mrs. Houlihan, perhaps you need to talk to someone at the insurance company. I'm afraid we've done all we can today. There's really no one there who can seem to clear it up for me, if it is a misunderstanding, that is."

"I'm telling you that *it is* a misunderstanding. The policy is paid through September and we have full medical coverage. I think I've got a two hundred fifty dollar deductible or something." I take a minute to rummage through my oversized bag again, handing Michael my cell phone, organizer, compact, and a brush as I search to find my wallet and the insurance card she gave back to me earlier. When I find it, I pull out the card and hand it back to her. "See, right here, there's a date on it right there and it's in my name." I struggle against raising my voice, losing my temper.

"This is the effective date, Mrs. Houlihan, the date the policy began." She says this slowly to me as if I'm an idiot and I can't understand what it is that she is trying to explain to me. "There is no expiration date on the card. That's why we call for verification. And when we did call for verification, for verification of this policy, under this number right here"—with a manicured nail painted bright pink she points out the numbers on the card for me—"they informed me that the policy was under a Mr. Patrick Houlihan and that he is deceased, rendering the policy invalid." She looks sternly at me, disapproving.

"Well, they've screwed up the verification then," Michael says to her. "What is it exactly"—he pauses and looks at the name tag hanging by the bright blue lanyard from her neck—"Kate, that you need? 'Cause we need to get this girl out of here and home."

Kate is visibly taken aback and fumbles for her name tag, aware that he has zeroed in on her. She looks as if she needs to check her own credentials just to make sure this is, in fact, her name. "Kate," I see her mouth under her breath, as if to convince herself.

"Well, actually, we need a check for payment for today's services. Everything but the X-rays. We don't have a total on how much that will be today, but you will be billed separately from that department. Our X-ray technicians work separately from the emergency room, you see."

"Fine." I let the word fall from my mouth purposefully. My voice echoes in the wide hall, bouncing off the sterile walls. "What's the total?" We're still standing midway in the hall of the emergency room, so I make my way to the administrative desk, a roundish island cluttered with charts and medical paraphernalia in the middle of the floor.

She checks her clipboard again and, without looking up at me, says, "Seven hundred and twenty-five dollars."

I stare at her for a minute until she manages to look up at me, and once she does I shoot her a death look that sends her back to the clipboard again. I write out the check, rip it out of the register, and practically throw it at her across the desk.

"Um, Mrs. Houlihan? Just so you know, the hospital will require a minimum deposit of fifteen hundred dollars before they will perform Rebecca's surgery on Tuesday. Unless, of course, you can clear up this misunderstanding with your insurance company."

I'm already loping back up the hall and wave a hand at her from behind. "Uh-huh," I say, "no problem."

8

Becca comes out of surgery in a daze, her eyes not quite focusing and her mouth thick and crusted in the corners. Her left arm is bent at a forty-five-degree angle and has been set in a hard cast, and she wills the strength to knock it against the stainless steel bed rail to see if the cast is solid. Michael's standing next to me and she focuses long enough for him to tell her the cast will make an excellent weapon for the championship games in late August. It's his attempt at giving her hope to play again at the season end, but she's not having any of it. She takes the moist towel I offer her and presses it against her forehead before she asks me in a voice I barely recognize as her own when we can go home.

Lydia and I have promised to check in with each other when she's finished school for the day, but it's nearly four thirty before the hospital releases Becca and I can turn my cell phone on again. "Hey, Mom, it's me. I'm just checking in. Um, how's Bec? I hope everything went okay. Um, I'm skipping ballet this afternoon. Got a ton of homework and I've got to write this paper for English. I'll be at the library. Can you swing by and pick me up there? Page me and let me know, okay?"

I delete Lydia's message, swing my SUV out onto the expressway, and head toward the library.

"We've got to pick Lyd up, sweets. Can you stand it for a few more minutes?" I check the rearview mirror and find Becca slumped down against the bench seat, her cast arm slung across her body and resting in her lap.

"Yeah, Mom, whatever. It's fine." She says this with her eyes closed and doesn't open them to meet mine. Her hair is thrown back in the same simple ponytail, a few strands coming loose at the temple so that they fall across her face, making her look even younger than her eleven years.

"How's it feel? Does it hurt a lot?"

"Nope."

"Never had my arm in a cast," I say to her. "Does it feel like you can't move it?"

She opens her eyes and meets mine in the mirror. "Ah, yeah, Mom. I can't move it. So I guess that's how it feels."

"Oh, sweetie, I don't know what to tell you. I'm sorry this had to happen to you, you know. It really sucks, doesn't it?" We're stopped at a light just two blocks shy of the library, and the late May sun still hangs high in the sky. I imagine Becca's melting in the sweatshirt she's worn from the hospital, sweltering even more under the weight of the plaster. From the front seat I watch her fiddle with the fluorescent-pink gauze they've wrapped around the outside of the cast. Her face is pale, her eyes dull.

"Do you think people can sign this thing? Even over the pink stuff?"

"Yeah, Bec. They can sign it. Take a Sharpie marker with you to school tomorrow." And with that I get the first smile back from her. It's quick and had I not been watching her staring out the window, I might have missed it altogether. But it's there. Something. I'll take anything.

Lydia's holed up in the back of the library, curled on a couch with her head in Eric's lap. She never sees me coming, until I'm nearly standing over the both of them, my hands on my hips, a thin pressed line across my lips.

"Why didn't you just page me? I would have met you out front," she says caustically, brassy. "Where's Bec?"

"She's in the car. And she's sore as all get out, so let's go."

I've got her by the elbow and am ushering her out the front door, Eric tagging behind us in slow dragging steps that swish across the floor. "What's with the paper that's due, Lyd? Certainly didn't look like that was what you were focused on. And why wasn't it done this weekend? I'm assuming this assignment didn't come up today in school with a due date of tomorrow, right?" I'm peeved and she knows it. She's skipped ballet twice last week and we're batting 0 for 1 this week. Her mood is sullen.

She doesn't answer me right away, pauses until I start in on her again. And I do with a vengeance, not ready to let her off the hook so easily.

"Lydia?" I say harshly, the tone in my voice indicating I'm expecting an answer.

Eric circles the car and brushes a kiss on her cheek. He's quiet; he knows they've been caught and he's more than a little uncomfortable with it. Something in my gut tells me it was Lydia's idea. In one move, he throws his skateboard on the broken asphalt and hitches his backpack up on his shoulders. When he's gone, she opens the door and climbs in.

"Hey," she says to Becca, ignoring me again.

"Hey."

"Lydia?" I say one more time. "I need to know what's going on here. You're flaking out on the things that used to be the most important to you and slacking off on your schoolwork."

"Yeah, okay, Mom, so I didn't do it over the weekend. It's done now. Are you happy? It's due tomorrow and now it's done, so you have nothing to worry about. Okay?" She looks out the window at the expansive front lawn of the library and plays with the hem of the skirt she's worn to school.

"And ballet? That's three times you've been out in the last two weeks, Lyd. Marina's going to have a cow and you know I'm going to get the call and hear about it tonight. And you're going to hear about it tomorrow. You've got two weeks to recital. That's it. Two weeks. Is it that much to ask that you prioritize your stuff so you can finish up the school term and not completely disregard the commitments you've made to dance?"

She doesn't say anything in her defense, so I take the opportunity to go on. "It's going to be here before you know it, you know. Are you ready?"

Nothing.

"Lyd? I said, 'Are you ready?' Two weeks is nothing."

She looks pensive, a worried look passing over her face, and as I watch her, she bites down on her bottom lip, hesitating before she says to me, "Don't worry, Mom. I'll be ready. I'll be fine. It's always fine." She rummages through her bag and starts to put the headphones to her CD player on when I throw her a look that says we're not done talking; and she thinks the better of it, opting instead to reach over and switch on the radio station.

I mean to catch another glance at Becca in the backseat, but it's my own reflection I find when I adjust the rearview mirror. My strawberry curls are brushed into two large clips, a limp attempt at securing them off my face, and my eyes are tired. I'm without makeup, and even the little foundation and powder I applied early this morning are long gone by now. My God, I feel old.

I pull the Suburban into the driveway and park it a bit askew. I'm careless now about the amount of room I leave on either side of my car. The BMW is long gone; we're a one-car family. We go everywhere in this car, the girls and I, not unlike the way we always had done, but there's no second car for me to envy, no vehicle for us to make sure we're careful not to ding or scratch when we get in the SUV, book bags, cleats, ballet bags, and such overloaded in our arms. We pile out and swing the doors wide, leaving an empty Diet Coke can in the drink holder at the dashboard.

Lydia heads for her room.

Becca heads for the couch. I remind her that she's got eight days of school left and the homework two of her teachers have sent home to be finished. As if she were dribbling a soccer ball, she uses her left foot to hook and lift the backpack lying next to the couch up and onto the cushion and lands it in the exact spot she wants it. She clicks on the television but turns the volume low and I'm convinced she must be studying something, her notebook flat and open across her lap.

I'm in the kitchen trying to figure out what to fix for dinner when the phone rings. It's Michael, and the sound of his voice rescues me instantly. He offers pizza. And Sarah, who will make an excellent diversion for Becca.

"You feel like pizza?" I ask Becca, putting frozen lasagna back in the freezer, anticipating her answer. I swing the freezer door shut with my left foot and cross the kitchen toward the family room where Becca has pushed aside her books, fully engaged in channel-surfing.

"Who is that?" she asks me from the couch, never taking her eyes off the television set, all the while skipping through the channels at warp speed so that she can't possibly see what's on each station. She stops on ESPN, the only eleven-year-old girl I know who watches Sportscenter highlights.

"It's Michael," I say to her. "He's bringing Sarah."

"Yeah, okay, whatever."

"Well, Michael, apparently it's your lucky day. I got a 'yeah, whatever' from Couch Potato With Broken Arm and I'm stopping there. Not even going to ask Queen of the Bedroom Beyond, but there's a possibility she'll grant us fifteen minutes of her presence when the scent of pepperoni goes wafting up to her room. No olives, please." I'm rummaging through the mail as I talk to him and setting aside the bills.

"Ally, how long have I known you?"

"All my life. Maybe longer," I tease him, sweetly.

"And how long have we been eating pizza during this so-called life of yours?"

"All of it."

"And do I bring you pizza with olives? Ever?"

"No."

"You got any beer?" he asks.

"Of course."

"See you in an hour."

9

Michael and I are stretched each on our respective lounge chairs in the backyard. We've lit a fire in the outdoor stone stove that Patrick and I had added to the landscape a few summers before, more for the sweet smell of the cedar burning than for warmth, and a whisper of the smoke melts into the sky. Michael's smoking, dragging long on a cigarette and holding the poison deep in his lungs. And I'm yearning for one with him and fighting off the desire by convincing myself that the minute I take the first drag, my girls will inevitably walk into the backyard.

He says to me, "You ready for summer, Al? I mean really ready for it?"

"I stopped being ready for things, Michael. Not really much point as far as I can tell."

He stops, turns his head and looks at me hard, then flicks the cigarette into the empty Corona bottle he's using as his ashtray. "Why?"

"'Cause you can't plan for it anyway, Michael. What's the point?" I start rubbing lavender hand lotion into the cuticles of my nails, working the cream into the palm of my hand and then onto each of my too rough elbows. Had it been Patrick sitting next to me he'd have moved to the end of my lounge chair and started in on my feet, rubbing the balls first and then working his way up my ankles. I'd have loved that, the feel of his strong hands easing the tension out of the arches, manipulating the tendons, cracking my toes.

"You can still plan for stuff, Al. Things you want to do, places you want to go. Where do you want to go this summer? As long as I've known you, you've had a new destination in mind. Always wanting to slip off to somewhere other than the place you are. You and Patrick had some great trips together. Paris. Up to Canada where you locked that man away for a week without his cell phone or his computer." He cracks a quick smirk at me and I can feel it, hear it in his voice. "What about the shore?"

"What about the shore?" I say to him, a hint of sarcasm seeping into my voice. I get up to retrieve the last two icy beers from the silver pail, a makeshift ice bucket of sorts, which we've brought outside with us. My hands are oily from the lotion, so I hand one to Michael and he opens it, and hands it back to me when I hand him the other. We both reach for a slice of lime in the small blue dish set on the table between our chairs, and our hands brush against each other quickly, a smile lighting up between us.

"You going? Lady Barb says she wants you and the girls to come down."

"Imagine that. Two weeks at the shore with Patrick's family. No Patrick. No, thanks." I close my eyes to the image. Two weeks with Patrick's family. I can barely stand dinner with all of them now, a never-ending serving of miscellaneous memories and newsy updates of their latest goings-on, things I've grown to resent out of pure jealousy.

"You've got your hands full with that one, I'd say. Expect the phone call any day."

"You know, Michael, she probably is planning for us to go to the shore. Pack up our things, haul our asses down there, and sit with her for two weeks." I take a long swallow on the beer, reach for what's left of the cigarette in Michael's hand, and drag on it hard. "Jesus, you're right, that call's coming, isn't it?"

"Yep. You should go, Ally. It'd do you good. Get away. Go for some walks. Spend some time with the girls. You guys have been going down there for what, fifteen years or something? At least think about it."

"You have got to be kidding, Michael." I say this slowly, still trying to let the weight of his suggestion penetrate through my skin. "A week at the shore with her? Isn't there anything I get to leave behind besides Patrick? Do I really need to put myself, put all of us, through that?"

"She's never as bad as you think, Al. She means well. She just wants time with the girls, you know."

"Great. I'll send the girls. As a matter of fact, that's a great idea. The girls can go to the shore with their grandmother. We'll see how Barbara does with Miss Moody, who'll be sulking around missing her boyfriend, and Miss Cranky, who will be brooding because she can't go swimming and her cast is itching her in the ninety-degree heat. I'll go to the spa for a couple of weeks. That's perfect. I'd never have gotten away with that if Patrick were here. Never. So, see, problem solved." I sit smugly, leaning against the chair back.

He laughs at me then, throwing his head back against the wooden chair and letting a good howl go. "Yeah, I'd say that's just about perfect, Al. Let's see you pull it off."

"I am not going to the shore, Michael." I say this plainly, clearly, confidently. I'm using this conversation as a practice session for Barbara, and he knows it. And he knows I'll need the practice. Lady Barbara can be very convincing.

"Okay, Al." He dismisses me, still grinning.

"No, Michael, I'm not going to the shore. I just can't do it. You don't understand what it's like being with them. All those memories? Never-ending conversations about Patrick. Stories upon stories upon stories."

"Um, yeah, Ally, actually I do. I really get that." He leans his head back against the lounge and takes the last swallow from his beer. He looks at me hard then, and I falter, knowing that he's walked in these shoes every damn day he's walked into my house, every day since Patrick was killed.

"Michael," I say to him, a second too early, just a second before the uneasy feeling might have passed over us. "You know that you can't be a replacement for Patrick. You realize that, don't you?" The words leave my mouth before my heart can pull them back in. And instantly I'm aware that I've cut him, swift and sharp, but even I don't know how deeply.

"I know that," he says to me plainly, and he won't allow his voice to catch, does everything he can to keep straight-ahead focused on the embers burning in the stone stove. "I know that," he says more quietly, contemplatively.

I find it necessary to draw a boundary around myself, the girls and me, in a place I want so badly to control, a place where I've been so out of control for so very long. So I continue, "You don't have to worry about us, either, Michael. I can handle Barbara. And the girls. You know I've got this thing with Lydia under control," I choke out in a sob, trying to convince myself. "And whatever else life throws at us. There's not much more left, you know. It's day-to-day for me. Day-to-day for the girls. But we're doing it. Every day we do it." Without my realizing it, my voice is rising, a high-pitched passionate plea for my own sanity. And with that I have left Michael on the other side. For the first time.

It's not that I wanted to hurt him. God, I didn't. But as reassuring as Michael is to me, as familiar and comfortable as he can make me feel, he isn't Patrick.

"Yes, Ally, I know that, too." He takes a minute to run his hands through his thick hair, stub out the third cigarette he's just started. "I'm sorry," he says, "if that's what you thought I was doing, trying to replace him. I think it's best if I go now. We can talk about this some other time if you want. Or not at all, not ever again." He walks over to me then as I pull myself up from the chair, leaving my arms crossed stiffly across my chest, still protecting myself. But he pulls my head toward him anyway, kisses my forehead, and looks me straight in the eyes.

"I love you, you know that. You and the girls. You're like my family. I can't just let you go, let you drift off. But I understand that you might need something else. Something I can't do for you, can't give you." He's not afraid to look at me, and he does so with such intensity that I'm forced to look away, focus on something other than the pointed, deep center of his pupils, which are piercing right through me.

I listen to the screen on the French door open and slam shut hard before he rouses Sarah from the movie she's watching with Becca, and with loud protests all the way, leads her out the front door. I hear him start the pickup—the truck he likes to drive when he's not schlepping clients around—and back it out of the driveway, honk two short beeps at Lydia and Eric, and drive off.

"Bec, I'm going for a run. Did you finish your homework?" I brush my hands together, start peeling the belt from the shorts I've got on, and move to make my way up the stairs to change. I catch a quick glance of Becca working from her *Adventures in Time and Place* social sciences book. The family room is void of the television for the first time in days, and I imagine she'll be lucky to last twenty minutes before she passes out from exhaustion of the day.

Eight minutes later and I'm in nylon running shorts and a black tank top, stretching for the first time in days on the front porch. I've taken Lydia and Eric by surprise; he's moved to sit cross-legged and a little less close to her, and besides the terse words after our trip home from the library, it's the first conversation I've had with Lydia all day.

"Going for a run, huh, Mrs. H.?" Eric asks me, quietly, when I start stretching. I've got one leg pulled up behind me and am balancing with the other arm against the stucco of the house. My hamstrings tighten, and then give, with the stretch. "Yep. Haven't been in a few days. Lydia?" I chance it. "Why don't you come with me?" *Maybe, maybe, c'mon,* I think to myself. *Come with me, Lyd, come back to me. I know you are drifting from me. Come running back. I'm right here waiting.*

She rolls her eyes and leans back against Eric's chest. "Oh yeah, Mom, right. How can you even run right now? I'm like so full of pizza, there's no way. I'd barf up pepperoni before we got to the end of the block. No way, no, thanks."

"Lovely, Lyd. Okay, fine then. Fifteen more minutes and you've got homework to finish, okay?" I'm watching her absently play with the shoelace on Eric's shoe, drifting, drifting. "Or," I add cynically, not ready to let the earlier argument go, "did you manage to finish it all this afternoon at the library?"

She glances up at me, but doesn't answer right away until I prod again. "Lyd?" I ask, testing her.

"Yeah, I heard you. Okay, fine. I've got a couple things to finish." She runs her hand up and down Eric's leg and then hooks her thumb on the inside of his high-top tennis shoe, daring me to confront her, to banish her here in our front yard. He wraps an arm around her and draws her to his side, leaving me both self-conscious and ill at ease in the presence of their affection. I pray silently that this boy, this first love, neither breaks her heart nor loves her too quickly.

"Bye, Mrs. H.," Eric says, a full wave and a small salute. "Have a good run."

I rarely run in the evenings, almost never at night. But at this hour, nearly eight o'clock and well into sunset, I'm bordering both. Still, you'd never know it. Nearly eighty degrees and muggy, and the sharp high pitch of birds too eager for the dark shadows to cool their nests still rings in the sky.

I'm out fifteen minutes or so and I'm completely thrown off my pace. I'm near sprinting, racing, which leaves me shifting from side to side to avoid the shrill, razor-sharp jab cutting through my right side until I'm forced to slow, walk, stop altogether, breathe, circle a few times, shake out each of my legs, then my arms, stretch both of my calves, then my shins, push on my right rib cage, and finally regain my general composure.

I walk home at a fair pace; let the heat of the run rush to my face and pour over my legs and arms until I'm crimson red. The sky's gone the last bit of ginger, then moments later to gray, then to charcoal and black just as I stop short in the driveway, the streetlights flickering on in unison down the block.

*   *   *

It's four days before Michael calls me, and this is a record of sorts. I'm long over my anger, way past hurt, and rehearsing my apology line by line on Saturday morning when the phone rings and sends me running to check caller ID. My stomach seizes and the palms of my hands perspire when I reach to answer the call.

"Hey," he says, strong and short. And then again, with emotion sweeping into the phone, "Hey, hello. How are you, Al?"

"I'm okay, Michael. And I'm sorry. You just have to know that straight up. I'm so sorry. I just unleashed on you. I don't know why, don't know where it came from." The apology comes pouring out of me faster than I realize, relief rushing over me.

"Done." That's it, just done. And in Michael's book it is. No need for further discussion. It isn't a dismissal, it is just behind him, and he is willing to move on. "I'm actually calling for Becca. I wanted to know if she's coming to the game. Is she?"

"God, I have no idea. We haven't even talked about it, but it's a great idea. It's a perfect idea. She should go, you're right. How do you think of these things?" His voice warms me, soothes me, and I sink into the couch, comforted by it.

"How could I not think of these things?" he says, not the least bit tenuous. "It wouldn't be the same without her."

"Okay, what time's the game? Eleven, right? What time is it now?" I glance at the clock on the kitchen wall and say to him," "Oh God, okay, almost ten. Yeah, she's up doing something in her room. I can guarantee it isn't much of anything. It'll be good to get her out of the house. I'll bring her myself. It'll be good to get me out of the house."

"Are you sure? 'Cause I can swing by and pick her up if you've got stuff to do."

"No, no, it's okay. There's nothing I've got to get done. I'm supposed to be sitting my ass down at the soccer field just like I do every Saturday between now and the middle of July, August if we make finals. We should both come. We're there."

"Okay, Al. Oh, and, Ally?"

"Yeah?"

"It'll be good to see you. Lunch at Duke's?"

Apprehension grips me. I want so badly to let Michael off the hook, but I'm guarded, still guarded. There's a place for Michael in my life, in our lives, but I'm fighting the tides to figure out where it is. "Sure," I say to him finally, quiet in my resolve.

Becca's not at all sure she wants to go to the soccer field. In fact, she's downright resistant, but in the end concedes and throws on a pair of soccer shorts, a Nike Cool Max shirt she can get over the cast, and her blue and white Adidas sport sandals. I pull her hair back into a ponytail for her and she asks me to braid it, which I do with remarkable speed as she sits at my feet.

"I don't need a chair, Mom," Becca says when she sees me start to load two low folding beach chairs into the back of the SUV.

"You sure?"

"Yeah, I'll be fine."

Five minutes into the game and she's pacing the field, checking Michael's clipboard, in the huddle with her team, galloping the distance of the field on the sideline when Sarah scores, cheering louder than most of the adults. Michael was right; it is just what Becca needs.

That and a pizza at Duke's, which she shares at a table with three of the girls from her team, a pitcher of icy root beer between them.

10

I'm literally dragging Lydia to dance class and evening rehearsals the last two days before the spring recital. I tell her I'll meet her in the usual spot, the semicircle driveway in front of the high school, at two-thirty, but when I arrive she's nowhere to be seen. It's hot, nearly ninety, and even the full blast of the air conditioner, sending my car idling, isn't working to keep my prickly legs from sticking to the leather seats. I pull into the only open space in the driveway, an oversized handicapped stall, and take my keys from the ignition, galloping past the main office and into the quad. The smell of jasmine bordering the buildings and the sound of cheerleaders practicing their chants makes me feel young, like I could be here myself, starting over, looking for love in a far corner of the grass.

Which is where I find Lydia, a contented smile creeping over her face.

"Hey, Mom," she says to me when I slow to a walk, approach her and Eric, and tap on my watch to let her know that we're running late. I am conflicted between wanting to yank her by the arm and leaving her there. She's captivated; I can read it on her face, the way she tilts her head toward him, the way the sun registers joy across her features.

"Let's go, Lyd. We're going to be late. I thought I said the driveway at two-thirty."

"Hey, Mrs. H. Sorry," Eric apologizes to me, polite and hesitant at the same time. He knows they're busted. Lydia's hanging on him, waiting to see how I'll react, if I'm going to blame him for her tardiness or let it fly by.

"Hi, Eric, do you need a ride? I can drop you home after I take Lydia to the studio." I'd like him alone for ten minutes, given the opportunity.

"Um, well, yeah, that would be great, actually. It's too hot to board home." He's up on his feet before Lydia, khaki cargo shorts and white T-shirt hanging off his fifteen-year-old lanky, underdeveloped frame. The kid's tall, awkward, and all feet, a size 11 at least, and I'm sure he's still growing. He pulls her up and she meets him just under his chin, wraps her arms around his waist quickly, and pulls at him to come along with us. Eric hoists his skateboard up under his arm and throws his backpack over his left shoulder. His strides are long, but Lydia keeps pace with him. I lope along behind both of them.

We high-step it across the quad before someone from campus patrol can ticket my car. Lydia throws her overloaded book bag in the back of the SUV and grabs the black duffel she uses to tote her ballet gear. Eric folds himself into the middle of the bench seat behind us, his knees coming up to meet his chest, his skateboard and bag crowding him on the seat. I study him in the rearview mirror. He is better looking than most of Lydia's male friends, better built with a square jaw and warm green eyes.

Lydia's a born dancer; she looks the part. She's tall for fourteen, just shy of fifteen now, already five feet seven inches, and I don't suppose she's done growing either. Her limbs are long, and everything about her, from the way she walks across the quad to the way she sprawls across the couch when she's watching television, is graceful. Dancing came naturally to her, still does, though lately she's fighting it. No dedication, no work, no passion for it. I'm certain she'd have quit months ago, opted out for afternoons of giggling and snuggling, letting loose and playing, had I allowed her to do so. I had not.

It was imperative to me that she finish this, at least this year.

She could walk away at the end, but not in the middle. I knew that would be important to her later, someday when she was really forced to look at this year of her life, this awful period of time, and realize that her dad's life had ended in the middle of everything, not at the end when he was finished doing what he was supposed to do, what he wanted to do. I knew someday she'd look back at this and have more pride in herself for it.

"Last week of school, you guys, how does it feel?" I say to them as we're driving.

"Fine. God, I'll be glad when it's over." Lydia's tugging off Eric's sweatshirt, throwing it in the back of the car in a heap. In this heat, I'm amazed she's worn it. He catches it, flips it inside out, and ties it to the strap of his bag.

I glance sideways at Lydia and ask her, "Do you want me to bring you back something to eat between class and rehearsal?" She has four hours of dance ahead of her, class from three to five and then rehearsal on the stage at the college from six until eight. She'll be exhausted by the time she gets home, worn enough to go right to her room, peeling off the bandages she'd have wrapped around her torn toes, rubbing pure alcohol into the worn calluses at the sides of her feet.

"Yeah, some yogurt and a banana maybe, some trail mix if we have some. Definitely some trail mix."

"I've got to go to the store. I'll drop Eric off and pick you up some stuff and drop it back by the studio before I take the groceries home, okay? Susan is taking you and April from the studio over to the college, right?"

"Hmm? Uh, yeah. Yeah, I guess so." Lydia's barely there now. Her body turned and facing backward in her seat, she's just barely hanging on to this conversation with me. I snap my fingers at her. "Lydia," I say, for the second time, "is there anything else you need from the store?" She and Eric are holding hands now, their fingers intertwined, and she's giggling at something he's whispered in her ear.

"No. Nothing else, Mom. Um, thanks."

We pull into the studio parking lot and she grabs the duffel, glancing over her shoulder at Eric. She hops out of the car and waves back at both of us after she closes the door. I watch her shuffle into the studio, headphones looped around her neck, and I know she's not into this; she's left her heart in the car.

"Well," I say to Eric, breaking the silence of the cab of the SUV, "you might as well move up to the front seat. No sense in sitting back there like I'm chauffeuring you around." He scrambles out of the backseat, backpack and skateboard awkwardly banging against the side of the car, and opens the front door.

"Just throw that stuff on the floor, Eric." He does, obediently, and reaches to buckle his seat belt.

I know the way to Eric's home; Lyd and I have been by there to pick him up or drop her off before. But never alone; the two of us have never been alone in the car together. A quiet nervous energy settles over the cab as if we were on a first date.

"So, are you looking forward to summer?" I say to him again, regretting my question as soon as it leaves my lips. I'm not really interested in small talk with him.

"Um, yeah. Yeah, I am. It'll be good to just screw off and hang around with my friends." He averts my curious stare at him, my watchful eye. "Oh, and to hang out with Lydia, of course."

"Anything special you're doing this summer? You and your family going anywhere?"

"Not sure yet. You know, my brother leaves for college in the fall, so we'll probably do some long weekend trips before then. Maybe some camping. My family loves to camp. You like to camp, Mrs. H.?"

"Sometimes. I guess it depends on the conditions. Not too much for roughing it."

"Oh, we really like to camp. We're a family of campers, my mom and dad and brother and me. We go all the time." His enthusiasm drips from the sentences, the description. "Maybe sometime Lydia could come camping with us. I'd really like to show her some of the places we go."

I take that as my cue.

"I suppose." My voice soft, I pause for effect. "Well, I suppose we'd have to talk about that some, Eric. I'm not sure how I feel about Lyd off for a weekend, just the two of you."

"Oh no, Mrs. H., not alone."

I am pleased to see he's blushing, a fine pinkish tint taking hold at the base of his T-shirt and working its way up his neck and under his chin.

"My folks wouldn't let us go alone. We'd have to go with them."

"Eric?" I say, catching him off guard.

"Uh-huh?"

"How do you think Lydia is doing? I mean since, you know, since the death of her father. How does she seem to you? Does she seem different at all?"

"Uh, well, I don't know. I mean, I never knew him . . . your, um, your husband." He says these words gently, delicately, as if he's handling glass. "Remember? I never really knew Lydia before he, um, well, before he died. Even though we were in the same class and all, I just never really hung out with her is all."

We're stopped at a stop sign and I take much too long to pause and look both ways, taking the opportunity instead to take in his face. He is kind, kinder than I have realized. And sweet. For fifteen, he's a find. "Right. Of course. The last year has been such a blur. I don't remember who came in when and where," I say to him, letting him off the hook. His shoulders relax a bit and he sits a little less rigid in the leather seat.

"She's an awesome girl, though, Mrs. H. I really, really think she's just so amazing. Everything that she does, how dedicated she is to everything, the way she really cares about people."

I wonder, for a minute, whom he is describing. His face is animated, his description narrative.

"Yes, well, she's always sort of just been that way, Eric. An amazing zest for life."

"She can do anything she sets her mind to, Mrs. H. I just know she can. I tell her that all the time. That she can just go for things and be who she wants to be and do what she wants to do. I just know that about her. She's so amazing. I just really, really dig her.

You know, I can see us being together for a really long time, like really, really together."

We've pulled into his driveway and as I put the car in park, I listen as he bubbles over, gushing.

"You know," I begin, patiently tempering my pace and my tone, "I'm glad that Lydia has you, Eric. I really am. There's nothing like your *first* boyfriend. I mean your first over-the-top, head-over-heels boyfriend." I watch as his face lights up. "Everyone remembers their first boyfriend, you know, much later on in life when they've met someone they fall in love with. Really, no matter where you end up, there's just nothing like your first boyfriend." I watch as his face falls, his look quizzical. But I don't stop; I continue. I want him to know exactly where I am coming from; I want control over the situation again. I crave control in my daughter's life as if it were a drug I can't get enough of. So I say to him, "I want to make sure that Lydia has some room here, too. I want to make sure that there are some boundaries set between the two of you, okay?"

"Um, yeah, sure." He swallows hard, the nugget of an Adam's apple rising and falling against his thin, long neck.

"What I mean is that the Lydia you see, the one that's all full of passion and energy and life? All those things are usually exact descriptors of Lyd, anyone will tell you that. But I can tell you right here, right now, that we're not seeing that and that we're all more than a little worried about her. For the rest of us, she's moody, sullen, withdrawn. If you hadn't noticed, I'm dragging her to dance class. Her marks are at an all-time low, and it takes all I have to get her to come down and have dinner with her sister and me. I'm more than a little concerned with how exclusive your relationship has gotten, more than a little bothered by the fact that you seem to be the only reason she smiles anymore."

The silence in the car is piercing. The pinkish tint that had started at Eric's neck and worked north has turned crimson and is covering his arms, legs, and face in splotchy patches. He sits silently next to me, unmoving, except for his fingers, which are gripping the door handle, white at the knuckles. One word to free him and I have no doubt he'll swing open the door and run flailing from the car.

Instead I say to him, "I'm not saying you can't see her, Eric. Far from it. Just draw some boundaries, okay? Lie low on things a little this summer. Give her some time to spend with us, some time with her friends. Do you understand?" I reach over and place my hand on his arm, just near his elbow, and the sensation of my doing this makes him jump. He turns to stare at me, the black pupils just dots in his eyes.

I expect that he'll give easily, that I've rattled him enough that we might not see him all summer. He stares out the front windshield, concentrating on something and gathering his thoughts. "Um, yeah, Mrs. H., I think I get it." He takes a deep breath, and with some satisfaction that I've made my point, I take one myself and lean back into the leather bucket seat. "It's just that Lydia's so amazing, you know. She's just really great. I mean, I really think we're just meant to be together, you know. I can really see us together. I'd do just about anything for her. I mean, I guess what I'm trying to tell you is that I really do love her. I'd do anything for her. Just anything at all. No matter what happens between Lyd and me, you gotta know that I'd be there for her. If she needed anything at all, I'd be there for her."

His goofy, lopsided smile means business. He's serious; what he's confessed to me isn't for show, but he has no idea about the impact of his words, no idea of his vulnerability. I sigh, before I say to him, "Yep, she is. Lydia's a wonderful girl." He smiles at me again before he cracks open the door a small amount, certainly not enough to scoot through, and looks back at me to see if I'm granting him asylum.

I'm not ready to dismiss him.

"I'm not sure you completely understood what I was saying, Eric," I start, calmly, resting my hands in my lap. "I'm not saying that you can't see her, Eric. At least not right now. And I'd really hate for it to come to that. I know I can count on you to work through this with us. All I'm saying is give her some space. Give us all some space."

"Oh, I understand what you're saying, Mrs. H., but maybe you didn't hear what I was saying to you." He pauses for a minute, waiting for me to swallow this time. "I'm telling you that I'm in love with Lydia. I won't let anything happen to her, don't worry. No matter what, I'm there for her."

He closes the door hard, throws his skateboard down on the driveway pavement, and pushes his way up toward the house.

I sit for a minute hugging the steering wheel close to my chest and watching him as he picks up his board and opens the front door. He waves at me and still I stare. I lift a hand to acknowledge him going before I bang my head against the steering wheel in desperation. "Damn, damn, damn."

Ten minutes later I'm standing in the middle of the frozen food aisle trying to recreate the shopping list I've left sitting on the kitchen counter. Chicken, milk, OJ, bagels, granola bars, apples, grapefruit, mayo, paper towel, tampons. Tampons. We're out of tampons. I know because I've gone in search of one in Lydia's bathroom this morning when I found myself down to a light-day mini. I make my way three aisles to the left and stand in the wide row staring at the boxes of tampons. Slender, regular, super, super plus. I find the multipack box, and on tiptoes, pull one down from the top shelf. Then another box for Lydia.

I'm holding both boxes in my hand, balancing the rest of my groceries on my hip. For the life of me, I cannot remember the last time Lydia asked me to buy her tampons.

Which means she hasn't needed them.

No.

Impossible.

I shrug it off, make my way toward the bulk foods aisle, but it follows me.

I shake it off, physically, shuddering.

No way. Uh-uh.

Not my daughter. It's not even feasible.

It follows me anyway, that feeling. It grips me the same way I knew I was pregnant with her, before I even took the test, before

I had even peed into the cup. I hoist the blue wire carry basket I'm hauling up on my hip.

My God, what do I do? Put one of the boxes back? Leave it on the shelf, go home, put my own box in the cabinet under my sink, and say nothing to her? Take them both and leave one at the foot of the stairs for her to carry up to her own bathroom? Confront her, sit her down, and ask her straight up? I have no idea. I'm left scooping out the trail mix into a large plastic bag, until it's full, fuller, more than three-quarters filled with peanuts and M&Ms, raisins and yogurt chips, much more than Lydia could eat, and enough for her to look at me like I'm half crazy when I hand her the five-pound bag. I stand, motionless, unmoving, twirling the overflowing bag back and forth in my hand until the blue plastic twist tie is secured tight.

I load the groceries into the car, then sit listening to the full throttle of the air-conditioning blowing at me. I take out my calendar and count back, trying to remember the last time I bought any of us tampons at the store. Tampons. Damn tampons. Shit. The weeks fall backward into months.

Don't worry, Mrs. H., I love her. No matter what she needs, I'll be there for her. Eric's words come haunting back, ridiculing me.

"Hey, Mom," Lydia says to me from the floor when I walk into the studio. She's got the headphones on and is stretching, legs 180 degrees from each other, and she's pancaked to the floor. I've overreacted, this couldn't be. Not Lydia. She's nimble, firm, not a muscle out of place, not a hint that anything in her body has changed.

I pull her closer; I cling to her tightly until she pulls away, pulls back from my grip, raising her eyebrows at me. "Thanks," she says and squints at me when I hand her the bag of food. "You okay, Mom? What's wrong?"

"Nothing, Lyd, nothing." I start to back away, before I think better of it. "Lyd, can we talk? When you get home tonight, can we talk? Just the two of us?"

"Sure, um, yeah, okay, Mom," she says to me, simply. "When I get home."

I go then because I don't know what else to do.

* * *

I'm nowhere near ready when Lydia walks into the house three hours later.

"Hi, baby," I say to her from the couch. I'm on my second glass of wine, careful not to have more than this. "How was rehearsal?"

She flips on the kitchen light and opens the refrigerator, pops a Coke, and comes to sit by me, laying her head down next to mine. "Fine. But promise me this is it for a while. I'm burned out on dancing, Mom. I'm exhausted. I can't take it. I think I just need a break for a while."

She starts to peel the tape away from her bandaged feet, balling together the sterile tape, creased black from the inside of her shoes. I stretch my hand out flat to take it from her, layer by layer.

"Take the summer off, Lyd. Relax. Do whatever you want to do." I hold her hand then and she lets me, just for a minute. "I had a nice talk with Eric on the way home today."

"Yeah? He's really great, Mom. Really, really great to me, you know."

"You know, honey, I imagine he's the perfect first boyfriend. Just the kind of someone you'll remember later on in life when you fall in love and get married. Someday . . ." I let my voice drift. "Someday." I take another long sip of wine, letting it burn the back of my throat, watching her as her image warps through the thick wineglass.

"Mmmm, maybe, Mom, maybe."

"Lyd? I've asked you before, I'm going to ask you again. Is there anything you need? You know, you and Eric. Is there anything the two of you need? Anything at all? I mean, you know I'm willing to talk to you about this? About anything, well, anything the two of you might be thinking about . . ." I let my voice trail off then, hoping she'll fill in my inaccuracies, substitute my stammering for a definitive definition of their relationship.

She's cautious, cagey, watching me carefully with eyes that

match my own, eyebrows that arch the same way as if to ask a question without so many words. "Why? What did Eric tell you?" She asks this slowly, pronouncing each word with caution, as if she is tiptoeing across a briar patch and she's not quite sure where to step next.

I hold the wineglass close to my nostrils and breathe deeply, hoping the rich aroma of the tannins will punctuate my senses.

"Actually, he told me how much he cares for you, how much he really, really cares for you and wants to be there for you. It was sweet, Lyd, very sweet. I didn't realize he had such intense feelings for you, that he cares so much about you. I guess, well, when it comes right down to it, Lydia, I guess I didn't realize just how serious the two of you had gotten."

She swallows hard. I watch her fidget and feel horrible for it, but I watch her nonetheless.

"Yeah, I guess we are."

"So, Lyd, I want to know something."

"Yeah?" she says, tentatively.

I swallow the last of my wine. "When I went to the market today, to get you dinner, you know, when you were at the studio . . ."

"Yeah."

"I bought tampons."

"Yeah?"

The room is quiet, quieter than I have noticed. "Tampons. I needed some. I bought them today."

"Oh."

"Did you need some?" I glance sideways at her, taking in her face, her young, beautiful face, full of promise, full of light.

"Um, yeah, I guess. If I was out. I'm not really sure."

"Well, when was the last time you needed one?"

"Oh, I don't know, Mom, what's with the fifty questions about tampons?" she snaps at me. "I don't remember." She finishes unwrapping her left foot, cracks her toes, and stretches the ball of her foot back and forth, back and forth.

Before I have the chance to prod any further, she races to answer the phone, its incessant ring cutting through the stillness in the room.

"Oh, hi, Grandma," I hear her say from the kitchen, her voice increasing in volume as she comes toward me with the portable phone. I motion to her that I'm not home, at the same time I hear Lydia say, "Um, yeah, she's right here." Then she pauses a minute. "Um, yeah, I guess that would be kinda fun. Well, hang on, let me put Mom on."

Now it's Lydia's turn to beg for the favor. She covers the mouthpiece with her hand and whispers harshly to me, "She wants us to go to the beach, Mom. Please, Mom, no. Please, you've got to tell her no. I want to stay here this summer, I really don't want to go down there." Her eyes plead with me.

Ah, the call.

I slip Lydia a sly smile. *I told you to tell her I wasn't home.* I set my wineglass on the side table before hoisting myself up a little taller in the armchair, a smidge of self-confidence and assurance for this phone call. And then I take the phone from Lyd.

"Hello, Barbara. How are you?"

"I'm fine, sweetie. So good to talk to you. It has been a few days, hasn't it?" Oh, she's worked herself up for this one.

"Yes, well, it has been a bit busy around here. Becca getting used to her cast, the girls finishing up with school for the year, Lydia's recital a few days away."

"Oh yes, I can imagine. I know how you girls stay busy."

Cut the crap, Lady Barb. I dive in, cut her off at the pass. "What's this about the shore?" I say to her. Lydia's still standing in front of me, hands in midprayer. "Please, Mom, oh, please, just this one thing. No beach this summer. Please." I watch her bouncing up and down, her body tense with anticipation.

"Well, of course, you're coming, sweets. All of you. You just must. It's tradition, you know. And this year, well, it's just going to be the best year for all of us. I mean I just really think it'll be good for all of us to get away. You know, we really missed the shore last year after, well, after Patrick . . . of course, I just couldn't see straight to go then. But now, well, Michelle's coming with the kids for a week and of course Ben will be down on the weekend. And Kathleen and the girls will be there, too. So, you know, it'll be just like the good old times."

Is the woman nuts?

"Oh, well, yes, Barb, we always have loved the beach. But you know, we've just got such a busy summer planned, the girls and me. Tennis lessons, a lot of time lounging at the pool, and you know, I've just overcommitted the girls all year long, so I just think it would be good for them to have some time on their—" Lydia is silently cheering, jumping up and down and raising her hands in victory.

Barbara interrupts me, plowing ahead with prowess. "Well, of course, dear, that's what the beach is all about. Some time for them to just do nothing. Just sit with their cousins and soak in the sun. The girls will love it. I've rented an extra house this year, nothing much, just something up the street from our usual place for Michelle's family, so it'll really just be you, me, and your girls and Kathleen and her girls. A regular, what is it they say, babe-fest?"

Um, yeah. Great.

"Well, I just don't see how—"

"I've already gone ahead and booked your flights. I figured you'd rather fly this year. It's got to be better than driving that awful truck of yours for six hours. It will be much better this way. We can all go together. I've got us going out on the thirtieth of June and returning on the thirteenth of July. I'm sure that'll work for you, won't it?"

I sigh deeply enough to let her know that I'm not ready to give in. "Barbara, that's very nice, but . . ." Lydia notes the change in my voice and stops with a mid-herky jump. Her face changes but she urges me on.

"Mom, no, please. No, no, no, no, no, please, please." I shoo her away with the back of my hand because I've missed half of what Barb has rattled off, which sounded suspiciously like seating assignments on the flights she's booked.

"Well, no I, um . . ." I hoist myself up, leaving an indent in the sofa behind me, and make my way across the kitchen to the calendar. Lydia follows me, still begging, until I shoo her off again. She sulks away, perching on the end of the sofa, still listening, silently mouthing more praying.

"Um, no, we're pretty open those weeks. You're right, it is our usual weeks at the shore. Patrick always loved the Fourth of July there." I pause, holding the pen in midair. "No, you're right. He really did love going with the girls, with the whole family."

Damn. Trapped.

"Yes, okay. Fine. Well, okay. Yes, then it's settled." From the corner of my eye I see Lydia collapse onto the ottoman just as Becca walks into the room.

I hang up the phone just as Becca asks, "What's going on?" harrumphing all of herself and her pink grafittied cast onto the couch.

Lydia starts in immediately, "Mom, you can't be serious? The beach? Two weeks? There is no way. Uh-uh. You guys go, but I don't want to. I can't spend two whole weeks at the beach with Grandma."

Becca stares openly at me, gaping, speechless.

I hold my left hand up to both of them and rub my eyes with the forefinger and thumb of my right hand, stopping to pinch the bridge of my nose.

Plainly, and very slowly, I say to my daughters, "Okay, here's the deal. Grandma's got the beach house. She wants us to go. It's two weeks starting at the end of the month. Same two weeks we always used to go. We'll go, we'll have fun, and we'll come home. You'll have the rest of the summer to do your own stuff. Whatever you want. It won't be *that* bad. I promise." I look at the girls, identical on the sofa, arms crossed across their chests and slumped so low they look as if they might actually slide off the end.

"But Dad won't be there," Becca says.

"Duh, Bec." Lydia throws her an angry look that's meant for me. "Jesus, you can be so stupid sometimes."

"I don't want to go," Becca says, and pulls herself into a ball at one end of the couch. Her cast hangs heavy off the sofa and she lets the weight of it drop and slump, her fingers brushing the area rug. "There won't be anything to do there. And"—at the risk of sounding stupid, she dares again—"Dad won't be there."

"I'm sorry, guys. I know it'll be hard without your father. I don't particularly want to go either. But Gram wants some time with you, with all of us. And we love it there. We always love it there. We'll go for walks and eat ice cream and sit out and watch the waves. Your cousins will be there. It'll be fine. Trust me on this." I do my best to sound upbeat, even excited.

"I don't want to go, Mom," Becca says again.

Lydia heaves herself up from the couch and picks up the black ballet duffel from where she'd dropped it when she got home. And with that, she's off, up the stairs and across the landing to her room, until I hear her door close with a full shove and her stereo click on.

11

"We'll come, Mom, I told you we would be there. But someone's got to watch the girls for the weekend. I want the weekend with Ally. It's her birthday."

I listened at the doorway, watching Patrick pace the floor like an antsy cat, back and forth, back and forth. He cupped the receiver in his hand, his voice in loud whispers, yet harsh.

"I don't care if that's the weekend you booked the lobster feed with the Johnsons and the Trents, it's Ally's birthday. I'm taking her away. Kathleen can watch the girls."

I waited for the echo I knew would come back as Barbara's boom.

"I said, 'I don't care, Mom. You aren't hearing me. This isn't up for discussion, or debate, though you seem set on both. Here's your choice. We'll be there for two weeks minus two days or we won't be there at all. It's her fortieth birthday, Mom. We're lucky she hasn't decided to run off to Europe by herself for the week." I heard him open the refrigerator before he said, nearly inaudibly and definitely under his breath, "And who would blame her if she did?"

I stood statue still with my back creased into the door frame, my arms crossed over my chest; a smug, satisfied smile crept across my lips. I heard him snap off the receiver, place the phone firmly on the countertop. When I peeked around the corner, he was leaning against the granite—his arms spread wide and his head hung down in between his shoulder blades. He took a deep breath in and then let it go in a giant burst of relief.

I imagined it wasn't an easy call.

She'd planned the trip without consulting us; she'd been doing so since long before we were married. Quite honestly, she'd been doing it since long before Patrick and I became a couple. There'd been other women—girls, really—who had endured all, or part, of their week at the shore. But the last three years she'd planned it over my birthday. I'd grinned through the onslaught of happy birthdays from countless family acquaintances I barely recognized and could hardly remember but who managed to show up for the dinner planned on the day of my birth. My day had lost its uniqueness; the candles on my cake long blown out before I ever had a chance.

This year would different.

I padded into the kitchen in stocking feet. I stopped behind him and curled myself into him. My stomach melted into his butt, my kneecaps touched the backs of his. I laid my head down on his left shoulder blade and closed my eyes. "Thank you."

"There's nothing to thank me for. It was asinine of her to think that's how we'd spend your fortieth birthday, Al. Crass and rude and selfish."

"Still."

"Still nothing. There's nothing to discuss."

"Where are we going?"

"Not there." He unwrapped my arms from his waist so they fell limply to my side and moved away from me, busying himself with the mail first, then a mysterious and unsuccessful search for something in the refrigerator. He did not make eye contact; he did not talk to me.

I should have felt as if I'd won; I didn't. Not even close. I watched him struggle in silence and felt little satisfaction in forcing him to have chosen between us. I felt anger toward his mother; she dished guilt upon him like ice cream on top of hot pie. It melted and puddled at his feet.

I tried again. "So, if not there, where?"

"Don't know yet, Al. Just not there."

12

Michael's words are ringing in my ears. *You've got your hands full with that one. Expect the phone call any day.*

Damn.

I had been so ready, prepared. I'd rehearsed it no less than a dozen times. There would be no beach trip for us this year. There would be the spectacular silence of the summer, a renewal of sorts, and a baptism in what it was like to just be us. Together. The new version of our family doing things our family did for the first time together. No running around, no hustle of carpools, just us together.

Damn.

I pick up the phone and dial Lady Barbara's number.

She doesn't answer, not on the first ring, not on the second ring, and not until I'm halfway into my message. Then finally, she picks up the phone.

"Oh, hello, Allyson. Was there something you needed?"

"Yes." I pause, gathering courage. "Yes, actually, there is something. About the trip . . ." I'm strong. I'm still. My voice is my own.

"Uh-huh, yes, dear, the trip."

Maybe it's the two, no, three, glasses of wine buzzing happily in the back of my head. Maybe it's Michael's words still swirling in my ears, daring me to defy. But it's something. Something just goes off in me.

"Well, you know, you've planned it over my birthday again," I say to her, with all the patience and tolerance I can manage. "And I just really think this year, this year of all years, that, well, I just think I might want to spend my birthday on my own."

"Oh, is *that* your birthday?"

"Barbara, I need you to hear me out on this. The girls can stay. Actually, I think it'd be great if the girls *did* stay. But I need to be on my own this year. Just me. So I'm going to come home on the sixth. I'll change the flight and leave late in the day after I've had some time with the girls, and they can come home with you the following week."

She's icy, but melts just enough for me to seize triumph. After all, I'm leaving the girls. They're the prizes she's tried to claim before. This feels good. I feel like a woman full of confidence, ability, assurance. A woman in possession of herself. I turn on the jets and let the water swarm and gurgle around me.

I'll pay the price with the girls; I know this. Becca's likely to shun me for a few days, pouting. But she'll warm to the idea; have fun with her cousins. Movies, a weeklong sleepover, and even with her arm in the cast, some soccer to keep her entertained, a Frisbee they can throw around. Lydia will be more difficult. She's likely to sulk and mope for the two weeks leading up to the trip, and for the two weeks there. Whether I stay or not.

This is about me, a celebration of sorts. This is about me making the first decision about me. About being in control of me. Again.

There's no sound in the girls' rooms; they've long checked out for the night. I push Lydia's door open gently. To my surprise, she rolls over and meets my gaze, lifting her arm over her head and burying her face against her shoulder.

"Mom?" she whispers, hoarsely. "What are you doing?"

I'm startled to find her lying awake. "Are you okay, sweetie?" I say, because I can think of nothing else.

"Yeah, fine. I just can't sleep. What's wrong?"

"Nothing. I, um, I just wanted to check on you."

"What time is it?"

"Just after midnight," I say to her, standing very still, studying her silhouette.

"Mom?" I hear her say again, a little louder this time, but her voice still a hoarse whisper.

"Yeah, honey, what is it?"

"Are you sure you're okay?"

"Yes, I, um, I just wanted to check on you. We can talk more in the morning. I know you are probably tired."

"You can come in for a while. If you want, that is." She begins to scoot her body over, making room for me in her bed.

"Um, well, okay."

In one swift move I push the pile of strewn stuffed animals to the floor, where they fall and scatter in various directions, pulling back the covers and folding myself into Lydia's bed, doubling one of her pillows up under my chin and turning my body toward her so that we lie parallel with each other, our faces only eighteen inches apart. I'm reminded of sleepovers, of giggling girls who have spent hours in this bed together, talking and laughing long into the night, long past the point of Patrick silencing them in harsh whispers that grew into threatening intolerance.

I reach out to Lydia and smooth her hair back behind her ear. In the dark her features look different to me, distorted. I can make out her eyes, the shape of her nose, her lips, but these features—along with her high cheekbones, her normally protruding chin—are all fuzzy, not quite one.

"I can barely see you," I say to her.

She yawns so that her mouth forms a large O shape and she sighs, her voice sleepy. "I'm right here." Then again, as if she is full of concern, "Are you sure you're okay, Mom?"

"Yeah, I'm fine, Lydia. Can, can I ask you something? Something I was trying to ask you earlier tonight?" I say to her, my voice barely audible.

She yawns again and I know that she's fading quickly. She is comforted by my presence in the room; I can sense this. Whatever it was that had kept her up has vanished with my company. "Sure, Mom, what is it?"

"About you and Eric." I say this quietly, and I wonder if she senses fear in my voice. "He really cares for you, Lyd. I had no idea how much until he and I were talking in the car today."

In the dark I see her bite her bottom lip. "What did he say, Mom?" She whispers this, pausing between the words. I know she's doing the best she can to choose her words carefully. "I really like him a lot, too, you know. I like being with him."

"Yes, Lyd. There's nothing like it, actually, that feeling of being loved."

"Is that what he told you, Mom?" she asks, barely audible. It makes me wonder, actually, if he's told her himself.

My eyes pour through the darkness for her, straining to see the face that matches her quaking voice. "Yes, he did. He actually did. I gotta tell you, I had to sit a few minutes with it before I could even breathe again. You're only fourteen, you know. Fourteen. It's pretty young for such a big emotion."

"I know, Mom, but I believe him, I really do."

We lie silent for a few minutes, waiting. "So, Lydia, I gotta know something. I need to understand something and I want you to be straight with me, straightaway, okay?"

I can hear her swallow hard, a gulp of sorts in the back of her throat.

"Yeah?"

"Are you and Eric sleeping together? Have you had sex yet?"

She waits long enough for me to know the answer. I hear her chewing on her thumbnail, unsure of what to say to me. I don't particularly want to make it any easier on her, but I do.

"It's okay to tell me that you are, Lyd. It's fine. I just need to know."

"Okay."

"Okay, what, honey?"

"Okay, we are. We have, I mean. Yeah, Mom, we've done it a couple of times."

I take a deep breath and kick the covers back from my side of the bed, exposing my bare legs in short pajamas. I'm sticky and shivering all at the same time. Next to me, Lydia is very still, waiting for me to say something. When I don't, when the silence has hung in the air, stale and stagnant, she finally whispers to me.

"Mom, how would you know if you were pregnant?" She chokes out the words, stopping to catch her breath.

My stomach churns, rolls over, stands back up, and flops down on itself, my mouth filled with the taste of salt. She waits on my answer, never moves. I think it's my hands alone that are shaking, but then I realize my entire body is trembling, my teeth chattering against themselves.

"Well . . ." I search for my voice, and what comes back at me is a deep throaty cough of sorts. "I suppose the first sign would be that your period would stop." I flip on her bedside lamp so I can see her more clearly, and she winces at the bright light.

"Anything else?" she asks, squinting.

I dodge her question, anger seeping into my voice for the first time. "Which is why I was asking you about tampons earlier, Lyd. I sort of was wondering why you hadn't needed them in, oh, I don't know, three or four months."

"Oh."

I say to her, "There are other signs, too, of course. You might feel unwell. Kind of like you were getting the flu. Especially in the morning, that's why people get what's called 'morning sickness.' Maybe your breasts would be tender, especially to the touch. Moody. Emotional. Tired. Exhausted, in fact. Queasy. Unsure of things around you. An overwhelming sense of joy, for most people, that is." This all comes tumbling out of my mouth without my even thinking about it, in a rush of words that must seem to her like a young physician listing off a patient's symptoms on his first morning of rounds.

She takes this all in but doesn't say anything, still lying prone on the bed and waiting, perhaps to see if there's anything I want to add to the list.

"Lydia? Why all the questions about being pregnant?"

She squeaks, "I think I might be."

I move to her, and she sits up so that her legs hang off the end of the bed, long and lithe, tanned by the early summer sun. She holds her hands in her lap, begins to pick at her well-worn leather watchband, and keeps her head down.

The room closes in on me, the overzealous mix of pink and purple on her walls, the myriad of posters overpowering me, making me dizzy. "Lyd, you gotta tell me, how long have you thought this? And what, oh God . . ." I'm lost for words, no more than a whisper in the silence of her room. "Lydia?"

"I'm not really sure, Mom, but I haven't had my period. You're right, I haven't needed any tampons. God, I don't really remember when the last time was that I did need them. You know, I'm not always regular anyway." She attempts to dismiss me.

"How many periods have you missed, Lyd?" I say to her very plainly, very slowly.

"I don't know. Two, maybe." Pause. Silence.

I don't move. I know she's got more coming, I can feel the words on the edge of her breath, not unlike the way she is poised on the edge of the bed, just ready to tumble off at any minute. Finally, "Three, maybe. No more than that, though. I know it's no more than that."

I watch her face as her mind turns, counting the days, the weeks.

"Oh God, Lydia. What were you thinking?" I start to stand, to pace the floor of her room though it is littered with strewn clothes, some CDs, a couple of schoolbooks. I lean on the wide bedpost at the foot of the bed. "*What were you thinking?*" I scream at her, taking her off guard, and she jumps, then cowers against the headboard, hugging a pillow to her midsection.

"My God, Lydia, do you have any idea what you are saying?" I pace again, back and forth, my arms crossed over my chest, my back rigid, a pounding starting at the base of my spine and running up into the base of my neck.

She doesn't answer me right away. But then, from nowhere, "Well, can we find out? I mean, can we do a test or something, just so we know? I'm tired of thinking about it. I'm really tired of wondering about it." She shrugs her shoulders at me, which only pisses me off further.

"Uh, yeah, you bet your ass we can do a test. Right now we can do a test. Go get your tennis shoes. We're going to the store." I hoist myself up, sounding very much like Patrick would have. "No," I scream at her again, taking her by surprise and grasping her by the elbow to steady her toward me, "never mind. You stay here. Becca's asleep, stay with her. I'll go to the store. Shit, Lydia. Stay right here." I close her door firmly, leaving her sitting on the end of the bed, stunned. I go rummaging around for my oldest pair of running shoes, the ones I use now for gardening, running errands, tooling the girls around from sport to activity to home to school.

I'm in and out of the Star Market in less than ten minutes, running through the parking lot, oblivious of the puddles, clutching a small plastic bag with the $24.99 home pregnancy test.

I drive for a mile or so, the rain beating down on my car, sleeting sideways like a winter thunderstorm. The weather is so disorienting that when I stop at the light, I am forced to crack my window and turn on the defroster. I realize I've handled this poorly. I've not taken Lydia into my arms, never asked her a question she could answer, never rubbed her back or even touched her at all, letting the tears pour down her face, letting her release the burden she's been carrying with her.

The light turns green, the car behind me honking incessantly until he finally pulls around me, then stops next to me. He rolls down his window and honks a quick, short beep at me again. I push the automatic window release so that my window goes down halfway and I'm pelted with a swirl of rain blowing all around me, picking up the pieces of my hair that have fallen loose from the twist I had sloppily thrown into a large tortoise-shell comb. I squint at the driver, a man I don't recognize.

"Hey, lady, you okay?" he says to me.

I shake my head at him in bewilderment. "Yeah, yeah, I'm fine."

"You lost or something? Need directions?"

"No. No, I'm fine really. Sorry about that." I begin to roll up my window again, but he stops me, yells across the car at me.

"Lady, turn your lights on. You're a sitting duck there in the middle of the road. No one can see you in this rain."

"Let's go," I say to Lydia as I prop open her bedroom door and stand shivering in the door frame. I'm soaked and sticky, my clothes hugging me tightly. She is waiting in her room for me, curled in the fetal position on top of the quilted comforter we bought her last summer and listening to something that sounds an awful lot like my David Gray album. She doesn't dispute me, but pulls herself up off the bed and follows me to my bathroom.

"Lyd, before you do this," I say, as I'm unwrapping the cellophane on the box, "I just want you to know that we've got a lot to talk about and that whatever happens here, this changes everything. Either way. You know what I mean?"

She nods her head at me and swallows hard.

It's less than a minute before the second line on the test strip turns dark blue. It's no surprise. For either of us. She sits back on the toilet seat and pulls her legs up to her chin, hugs them tight to her chest, and puts her head down on her knees. I'm eye-level with her, down on my knees, and rubbing her shins back and forth, then down around her ankles and over the tops of her slippers. I can't tell if she's crying, but her body heaves just slightly every few minutes as if she's remembering to breathe.

"Okay. Okay, now we know," I say to her, my own tears streaming down my face. I'm actually relieved, the truth floating within the walls of the tiny, cramped room that holds only the toilet and the two of us. She doesn't say anything, so I fill the space with my words. "We'll figure this out. Really. We can, Lydia. It's, it's . . . well, it's something, isn't it?" She keeps her head down, forehead pressed up against her knees.

"Let's get out of here." I stand and put my hands on my hips, waiting for her to make a move. When she doesn't, I pull at her arms, lift her off the seat, and take both of her hands in mine, walking backward. We move over to the bed and I pull back the covers, run my hand over the sheet, and pat at it for her to come sit beside me, on Patrick's side of the bed. I crisscross my legs and pull a square flowered throw pillow into my lap. My jeans are soaked at the bottoms, nearly up to midcalf, and my white shirt is untucked and wrinkled at the waist.

"Daddy would have been so mad," she finally says.

No sugarcoating that.

"Yep," I say to her, nodding my head in agreement. "Yep, he would have been furious. Wouldn't have understood at all, and to tell you the truth, Lydia, neither do I. Neither do I." I pause then, letting her absorb my words. I shake my head back and forth to let her know how badly she has disappointed me, disappointed her father, disappointed herself.

"But I can tell you this. Daddy still would have loved you. And so do I." I pull her close to me and she drops her head into my lap, lets me comb through her coffee-colored hair with my fingers. She's curled up in a ball the same way she used to when she was a child just before she'd fall off to sleep.

"I'm sorry, Mom. I'm so sorry. What do we do now?"

"You know, Lydia, I'm not sure yet. I'm not sure at all."

13

Lydia sucks at recital.

This is what she says to me. "Mom, God, that sucked. I was horrible."

I've slinked backstage at intermission and I find her in the back corner of the large makeshift dressing room, sitting on the floor, back against the mirror, knees pulled up under her chin, headphones on. There are nearly a hundred dancers of all ages in the room. The pitch is deafening.

I look down at her. "Yep, that sucked." Her timing was off, her steps a moment too slow, and she'd missed a lift.

"Are you angry?" she says, her eyes pleading with me not to be, her own shame more than enough for her to bear. I offer my hand and she takes it, allowing me to pull her to her feet. She's changed into her next costume, a perfectly translucent, shimmering silver-blue leotard with nylon sashes that wrap around her arms. Her hair has been pulled back tight into a dancer's bun, low and tight at the nape of her neck, and a ring of ivory silk flowers has been bobby-pinned around the bun. She's due to dance pointe, a solo, after intermission, and the silks on her toe shoes have been wrapped tight at her ankles. Her eyes look tired, weary, as if she's spent the night fighting nightmares, dreams that have haunted her.

I take her in my arms and hug her first, long and tight, and her body goes a bit limp against me like a child ready for an afternoon nap. She slumps against my chest and heaves a sigh. "No, honey, I'm not angry with you. There's nothing to be angry about. And by the look on your face, I'd say you've got disappointed down." I hold her back from me then and take her chin in my hand. "But file it away. You've got plenty to worry about later. Right now, just dance. Just go and dance."

"Thanks, Mom." She pulls the headphones back over her ears and I hear the crackle of noise, barely recognizable as music, come streaming back through the padded earpieces.

Outside, I breathe in the stale afternoon air and hold it until it pierces my lungs sharply. Not a hint of anything different in Lydia; I'd watched her onstage. Every move, every inch of the way her body turned. No widening of the hips, no bulge at her middle. Not yet anyway.

Eric's brought Lydia a bouquet I imagine he had to beg an extra twenty bucks off his father for. It's brimming with red and white roses, vibrant delphinium, stargazer lilies, alstromeria, and more baby's breath than is necessary, and is tied with a large red satin bow. He'd arrived at the theater in pressed khakis and a starched oxford, twenty minutes early, holding the oversized floral display, absentmindedly crinkling the cellophane. Michael's been to the flower market and holds twelve perfect yellow tulips, Lydia's favorite. They sit next to each other in the row we've taken over; Eric is taking notes.

I stumble in just as the lights go down, the room working up generous applause for the start of the second act.

"How's she doing?" Michael whispers to me.

"She's pissed at herself, but she'll live."

"And you?"

"You have no idea, Michael."

I feel the concern that washes over Michael's face; see it without even moving my head to look sideways at him. He's sly, sexy, in a new pair of denims and a black T-shirt.

"Shhh," I whisper without ever moving to make eye contact and put a finger to my lips, hushing him just as Lydia makes her way out from behind one curtain and the full distance of the stage, completely without pause on toe. Seventy-two of the tee-niest, tiniest steps. I know because I count her making them and I don't breathe again until she has crossed the stage. Her head is elevated, arms at her sides, until slowly, so slow you're unsure that they've moved or raised at all, but before you know it, they're there at her head, the sashes fluttering, and then down again.

I don't realize I'm crying until Michael reaches over to lift an errant tear that has streaked down the side of my cheek. The way he does this, the brush of his finger on my cheek, fools me for a moment and I'm left thinking, no, believing that it's Patrick sit-ting next to me. Not unlike Becca, in an instant I've fallen into a world where Patrick still exists. Lydia finishes her dance and, even as she's greeted by the whoops we sail at her from the third row, never breaks a smile, though you know from the look in her eyes that she's more than satisfied; she's glowing, actually lumi-nous. We don't see her again until the finale, when she is assigned to walk with two of the tiniest ballerinas, two four-year-olds in their pink tutus. She guides them by the hand out from the cur-tain, walks them to the front of the stage, twirls each of them twice, and together the three take their final bow. Low and deli-cate, they balance on one knee. I have a mirror image of Lydia's first performance, her in her own pink tutu laced with silver se-quins, her brown eyes wide as can be, searching us out in the crowd; Patrick's voice cheering bravo over the tape.

I watch my daughter, every inch of her that moves and shakes, shimmies and whirls. There's no hint of anything amiss. I have no doubt she's fooled this audience the same way she's fooled me the last three months.

14

With a week to go to Lydia's fifteenth birthday I want to cancel the party I've promised her. She doesn't fight me on this; she actually agrees. But we're both caught off guard by Becca, who corners us at the breakfast table and calls my decision unjust and unfair, all the while staring at Lydia, asking, "What are you, nuts? You've been looking forward to this party all year. Why, Mom? Why do we have to cancel it? All of Lydia's friends are already planning to come. Why?"

"Oh, sweetie," I try. "It's just so close to our leaving for the beach and all, Lydia and I were just thinking of kind of playing it low-key this year."

"Yeah, Bec, it's fine. I'm not really in the mood after all."

Becca stares at us with an open gape, until finally she says, "Okay, guys, what's up? What's going on? I know something's not right. What gives?"

Lydia and I stare at each other, our lips hard, thin lines of silence. She looks to me for guidance, the best way to handle this. Becca ain't budging and Lydia's desperate for me to figure a way out of this hole we've dug ourselves into.

Finally, to avoid controversy, I say to the both of them, "You know, you're right. Lydia should have her party after all."

"I should?" Lydia asks me with raised eyebrows.

"That's better. Jeez, you guys, you were really scaring me. I thought something was really wrong. Who cancels their fifteenth birthday party? Come on!"

We both smile at Becca and nod our heads in agreement, acknowledging our momentary lack in judgment.

When it comes to the party, here's what I had already agreed to:

Lydia and her friends, who may be numberless, get the backyard and the pool. I get to invite a few friends and we are to stay in the house at all times. Except Michael, who is permitted to barbecue as long as he isn't outside too long and doesn't tell any bad jokes.

I had agreed to this in mid-May, nodding my head vigorously, convinced that it would do us all some good. Now it seems a dismal decision, a cruel twist of fate to the secret that Lydia and I share. Neither one of us is in a mood to party.

We'd had our first conversation, a twenty-minute talk that had erupted into tears, when I suggested to Lydia that I'd like her and Eric to take some time apart from each other. I don't know why I'd suggested it, actually. As if the time apart now were going to do any of us any good.

Rather, Lydia and I hadn't even started the conversation about what came next; I'd only told her to hold all thoughts until we'd had a chance to see Peggy Nelson, an appointment I'd been lucky to schedule before we left for the beach. I wanted confirmation of her pregnancy despite the fact that I already knew it to be true. I wanted a doctor to look me in the eye and tell me what my options were, what Lydia's options were.

On Saturday with Lydia's party in full gear, I'm making a second pitcher of sangria for Anna and me.

"Mom!" Lydia's banging on the family room window, dripping wet and wrapped in a beach towel at her waist.

I pull the cord to lift the blinds and crank open the window, trading the air-conditioning for the heat that penetrates from the scorching yard. "Yeah, sweetie, what do you need?" I've kept my promise to her and stayed put in the house but mostly stationary from a spot in the kitchen where I have been watching her and her friends jump in and out of the pool, pull themselves up on the side, and bask in the sun, an occasional chicken fight ensuing.

"Do we have more sodas? Diet Coke. We need more Diet Coke. And some Mountain Dews, too. Oh, and, Mom, is Michael going to start barbecuing soon? 'Cause everyone's pretty starving." I question how this is possible when we're down two large jars of nuts, a tray of nachos, and three bags of chips. I eye the dishes of onion dip that I'd set out earlier. Wiped clean.

"Okay, okay. I'll send him out. Hamburgers and hot dogs, right? Do you want chicken, too?"

"No, Mom, I told you, no chicken. Just what we planned. And the sodas. Can you bring them out right away?"

"Me? M-E? Am I permitted in the backyard to bring out the sodas? Your own mother?" I mock excitement, clasping my hands together and gasping.

"Funny, Mom. Michael can do it if you want, just bring them out, okay? The guys are dying for something to drink."

I close the window and the pandemonium of the eighteen teenagers and the music blowing through the outdoor speakers in my backyard quiets only slightly. I pull out two six-packs of Mountain Dew and Diet Coke before making my way out the side door of the garage and around to the back of the house to dump it in the iced coolers nearest to the pool.

"Thanks, Mrs. H.," Eric yells at me from the pool just before he spikes the volleyball back over the net that's been set across the middle of the pool. I stop to survey the party scene. Lydia's sitting poolside with the towel wrapped around her waist and a T-shirt covering her purple string bikini. She kicks the water up at him as if to say, "Don't invite her out here," and she throws a wave at me, dismissing me quickly with a "Thanks, Mom, I'll let you know if we need anything else."

I start back toward the French doors, stepping around the beach towels, the casually mislaid sunglasses and baseball hats, the discarded shorts and T-shirts that lie across the grass and the flagstone, and meet Michael at the barbecue.

"You're looking nostalgic there, Mum. Gonna go all soft on me?" Michael jabs me with the tongs he's using to turn the chicken, dinner for the adults.

"Fifteen, Michael," I say to him, audibly surrendering my thoughts. "What an age to be!"

"What's wrong? Don't you want to start over?" Michael whistles a reflective sigh and looks positively jealous of the kids thrashing around in the pool.

"No way. God, fifteen, what an age to be. All those hormones. All that prancing around before the boys. More trouble than it's worth, you know. More trouble than they have a right to be getting into . . ." I let my voice trail off.

Michael starts to jump in, but I interrupt him. "And Becca? Becca's right behind her. She's busy taking notes, volumes and volumes of notes. What happened to my sweet Becca?" I scan the yard and find Becca and four of her friends, in the far corner of the grass, lying on their stomachs listening to their CD players and laughing. They've taken refuge there, afraid to join the party, but thrilled to have been included, so much so that they're taking no risks, staying just far enough out of the way to be unnoticed, but close enough to be a part of it all. Becca shifts uncomfortably in the sun, scratches at her shoulder just above her cast. I'm just about to head over with more sunscreen before I stop myself short, realizing this would only aggravate Becca's own sidelined frustration.

"Women," Michael says to me, shaking his head back and forth.

"Oh, c'mon, Michael, these are hardly women."

"Oh yeah?" He winks at me and puts his hands on my shoulders, turning me slightly to the left so I'm square with the pool. "Take another look, sweetie."

They're scattered across my yard, in lounge chairs, hanging at the edge of the pool. Preening, done-up girls. Combs and brushes and pocket mirrors and clips abandoned on the towels, just in case. Boys with bodies they haven't yet grown into; not quite sure what to do with all the moving parts. Too tall to make it all work quite right together. Not enough width to match the length. Bathing trunks hanging low across near nonexistent waists.

And the noise. Avril Lavigne on the CD player. The high-pitched over-the-top cackle of girls begging to be noticed, unsure of where they fit. The hilarity of boys outdoing each other, each one looking, searching for the next joke, the opportunity to pull the next prank at the expense of the person next to him.

The afternoon sun is beating down on the side of the house, so I offer to bring Michael another beer, which he readily accepts. I'm up the first two steps back into the house to get him a bottle and refill my sangria when he stops me quick and says, "Hey, Al?"

"Yeah?"

"What's with Lydia's T-shirt?" He's busy at the grill, flipping and unwrapping, but he stops then and takes the last swig from the bottle of beer he's holding with his free hand. Then he looks up at me for an answer, waiting cautiously.

I feel a lump gather in my throat, a dry sensation in my mouth. "Um, whadda ya mean? I don't know," I say to him, shrugging my shoulders before I throw my attention back over at my daughter, head back and laughing at something one of the guys has said to her before Eric sneaks up on her, towel, T-shirt and all, and pulls her back into the pool. "Sudden case of modesty?" My voice catches, just slightly, and I clear my throat.

He looks at me over an arched eyebrow before returning his attention to the grill. I look at Lydia one more time, struggling to swim away from Eric, weighted down and slowed by the shirt, a cat-and-mouse game starting between the two of them. And then I take the last two steps into the house and head for the kitchen for the beer and sangria.

"Why do you ask, Michael? What do *you* think is with the T-shirt?" I say when I return, curious to know what he's driving at. Michael doesn't ask unnecessary questions. He opens the bottle I hand him and takes a sip before answering me.

"I don't know. Just curious, really." He's scooping the burgers off the grill, stacking them next to each other in a row behind the hot dogs.

My back's prickly in the afternoon heat, my stomach clenched tight in a knot, but I keep at him. "Michael? It's kind of a funny thing for you to notice, don't you think?" I'm wondering if he's sensed something, or if, God forbid, he sees something. I've studied Lydia up one side and down the other. When she emerged from the house at noon, she did so in a T-shirt that ran just to the top of her bikini line. Now it is soaked, drenched, pasted to her body. Still she looks every bit like she has to me this year, developing certainly, but nothing unusual, nothing out of the ordinary.

He eyes me curiously, testing me. "She's been swimming what, twelve years, Al? And I've never seen her wear a T-shirt in the pool. Ever. That's all. And what's more, I've never known Lydia to be modest." He carries the tray of food into the house with one hand, his beer and the used grilling tools in the other. I don't answer him, but I watch Lydia as she comes out of the shallow end, her eyes dancing, her heart pounding away. I think she's happier than she has a right to be at that very moment, and in that instance, I want to take that happiness from her. I'm angry she's not more sullen, that she doesn't spend the day sulking at one end of the pool, ridden with the same guilt I'm feeling. Michael's questions start my mind reeling, the judgment she'll face, and the criticism that will surround her. She peels the water-logged shirt away from her skin and I expect, hope, for her to pull it over her head and fling it in a wet heap on the cement, and reveal the pan-flat stomach I'm used to seeing. But she doesn't. Instead she finds a new towel, a dry one, and wraps this around her body, her long legs and hot-pink-painted toes sticking out like the legs of a flamingo.

"Al, you got more ketchup?" Michael says to me from somewhere far off, his voice coming at me in monotone waves. When I don't answer right off, he says it to me again. "Ally? More ketchup?" I turn to see him standing in front of me, a near empty bottle in his hand.

I clear my throat, and whisper at him, "Pantry. There should be another bottle in the pantry."

"You all right?"

"Fine. Mmm-hmm. Yep. I'm fine." Sweat beads on my upper lip and I clear my throat again.

"Al?" Michael says again. "What's going on? Is everything okay?" I must be shaking; his hands work to steady me.

I dissolve. Just lay my head down and go to tears on his shoulder.

He doesn't say anything while he holds me there. Doesn't hush me or soothe me but merely runs his hand through the back of my hair over and over again in a melodic rhythm. When I pull away from him, I wipe tears and mascara from my eyes and cheeks and rub my hands on my shorts. I take a deep breath, wordless but better, before I turn on the faucet and splash some cold water onto my face.

Michael never asks me about this. Not that moment, not that day, and not later into the night when we sit finishing off the last of the sangria with Anna and her husband, having moved to the Adirondack chairs on the patio farthest from the pool, where some eight or nine of Lydia's friends remain, still laughing but mostly sharing their conversation in hushed tones and whispers.

But he does look at me long into the evening, where the fireflies and the tiki torches flicker in the cooling night sky. I'm well aware of the stolen gazes he lets fall and rest on my shoulders, their care and concern weighted across the table and thrown around me like a chemise wrap placed there to keep me safe and warm.

15

I've forgotten to close the shutters, so I wake Sunday morning to the blazing sun pouring through the white slats and flooding my bed. I've woken with a headache that is ringing at my temples; dehydrated. I reach for the bottled water on my nightstand and pour it down my throat, inspecting the damage in the backyard: littered red plastic cups, endless trails of now stale, crushed chips dumped from leftover bags, a few beach towels, one errant flip-flop lying on the grass, chairs facing in all sorts of directions.

My mascara is smeared and my eyes are bloodshot, but I've looked worse. I run my toothbrush under the cold water and suck on the bristles for a minute.

The house is soundless, silent.

I pull on the same shorts I've worn the night before, but a new bra and tank top, and pad barefoot down the hardwood stairs and past the family room, where Becca and Sarah are asleep, each sprawled on a couch in sleeping bags. I flip on the air-conditioning. It's one of those days you can tell is going to be stifling from every angle.

Father's Day.

I go to the calendar on the corkboard in the kitchen, take the big black Sharpie marker, and make a large and prominent X through the day as if it's already passed us by. It's nearly ten, so I figure it's justified.

There's nothing to do other than start the process of putting my house back in order. I close up the bag of bread left open on the table, then change my mind and toss the few stale pieces into the garbage pail. I put the top back on the jar of peanut butter and return the jelly to the refrigerator. Then I brush away the crumbs left on the distressed kitchen table into the white plastic garbage bag I'm carrying with me.

Lydia stands stretching in the door frame. She's slept in a pair of gray cotton gym shorts and a much too big white V-neck undershirt of Patrick's that hangs down midthigh. She half yawns and stretches while she says, "Hi, Mom."

I put a finger to my lips and point at her sister and Sarah, who both roll over, turn their backs to us, and settle back down into the soft leather. Becca opens her eyes only momentarily, dreamily, squints, furrows her brow, and pulls the pillow up over her head.

I tell Lydia that I've got to get something in my stomach and ask her if she wants something to eat, but she's already in the pantry pulling out a box of mini powdered donuts. I watch her for a few minutes, set on cooking myself some eggs and opening a bottle of iced Starbucks mocha Frappucino, before I reach over and take two at a time. We sit side by side on the granite countertop and demolish half the box, licking the white powder from our fingertips.

I tell her, "I feel like I'm in college again. That's the real breakfast of champions."

I ask her if she suddenly feels older this morning.

"Nah. I feel the same." She pauses and finishes off the last of the glass of milk she's drinking. "Hey, Mom, I know you didn't want to have this party. I didn't really want to, either. But it was fun. I just wanted to say thanks for doing that, for letting me go ahead with it."

I stare at her for a minute before I say to her, "You're right, Lyd, I didn't want to do it. I really didn't want you to be as happy as you were yesterday. I know that sounds horrible, but that's exactly how I felt, watching you with your friends."

She gapes openly at me, unsure of what to make of my cruel, honest confession. "I, uh, well, um, gosh, Mom, I guess I'm sorry."

"It's not about being sorry, Lyd. Not anymore. What's done is done, you know." I shrug my shoulders, laden with disappointment, before I say it again, more softly this time. "What's done is done."

She picks at a fraying thread on the T-shirt, her head hung low and full of thought.

"We've got a lot to talk about, a lot to cover on this. You know what I mean, Lydia? There's no taking a break from what you've gotten yourself into. You don't step out of it for a couple of hours to go celebrate with your friends, drink some Cokes, have a couple of burgers, gossip. And then come back to it. That's not how it works."

"I know," she says, sniveling.

"No, I'm not at all sure that you do, Lydia. I don't want to be cruel, but parenthood isn't like that. Parenthood is all-consuming, all the time, all your life, twenty-four-seven." I'm lecturing, signs of Patrick's voice seeping into my tone.

"I know," she says again, even softer this time, just barely a whisper.

"Look, tomorrow we go see Peggy. I want to know all our facts, all our choices, before we make a single decision about this, before we figure this thing out." I roll the Frappuccinno bottle between my hands, back and forth, back and forth. "We'll see how far along you are, what our options are, what we can do about this, this . . ."

"Baby," Lydia says quietly, still unsure of herself. "It's a baby. And I'm sorry. I don't know how many times I'm going to have to say that to you or for how long I'm going to have to say it. But I am, okay? I'm really, really sorry. You just have to know that. At least know that."

Finally, I say to her, "What do you want to do, Lydia? Have you even begun to think about it? Has it begun to register with you that you are going to have a baby? What, in God's name, do you think we're going to do about this?"

She swings her legs back and forth and nervously gnaws on her thumbnail until I swat her hand away from her mouth and she stares at me. "You have some choices in this, Lyd. You know that, don't you? You understand that, right? You don't have to have a baby, Lydia. There's a good chance you can terminate this pregnancy, if you're not too far along." She squints and blinks at me in the sunlight as if looking at me for the first time all morning, hanging on each of my words.

"I know," she whispers and clears her throat, the words catching as she carefully constructs her sentence. "I know I can do that. But I don't know what to do, Mom. I still don't know." She turns her back and I watch her shoulders slump forward.

"I don't know what you want me to tell you about it, Lyd. I can barely summon the courage to talk about it. It's not something I could have done. It makes me . . ." I stop, brush the hair back from my face, and turn my head to watch Becca turn over in her sleeping bag again. "Well, it makes me sick to think about it, if you have to know. Just sick."

She starts to say something, but I interrupt her. "And by the way, have you talked to Eric about this?"

She shakes her head no.

"You *will* need to talk to Eric, Lydia. You know that, don't you? He has some responsibility in this too, you know. You'll need to find out what he thinks about all this, how he feels about it and what he wants to do."

"Eric won't know what to think. He's not going to know what to do either, Mom. He'll want to know what you think and I won't know what to tell him. 'Cause I don't, Mom, I really don't." She stars to cry now, letting the tears stream down one right after the other on her face. Finally she looks up at me for an answer.

"I feel everything about this, Lyd. Mad, unhappy, sad, angry, frustrated, worried, oh God, how I am worried. Sorry. I'm so sorry that you have to go through this, that I wasn't there for you. Guilty, responsible, even though I'm not, of course, but willing to accept some of the blame. Burdened. I feel burdened with a secret that we shouldn't have to share. Heartbroken. If you must know, I'm heartbroken that this is the way we are dealing with a child, Lydia. A child that you are carrying. Never in a million years did I think this is what we'd deal with this year. Any of this. But heartbroken that this is your first experience with pregnancy, that I can't be thrilled for you, that we're not off registering you at the baby superstore for a stroller and the latest car seat." I stop now because I realize that she's openly sobbing.

"God, Mom, I am so, so sorry. I'll never get you back. It'll never be the same. You're right. It changes everything."

I signal for her to follow me outside to the backyard. The morning sun is already heating the tile patio, the stones warm to the touch. Lydia crumbles into one of the long lounge chairs.

"You have not lost me, Lydia. I am not far from you. I will never be gone. I'm hugely disappointed, yes. And yes, it changes everything. But not the way I feel about you."

In the yard two houses over, I hear a screen door bang open and someone clip-clop across the yard to start the sprinkler.

"Mom? What if I don't, um, terminate the pregnancy?" She says this "ter-min-ate" as if getting used to the word, practicing it for the first time, rolling it around in her mouth. "If I go through with it, what am I going to do with a baby? I'm fifteen, Mom."

"Yep. Fifteen. I don't know, sweetie. I can't really imagine us with a baby. Never thought about it. And to tell you the truth, I haven't had a chance to play that through in my mind yet. So I don't know what that particular movie looks like."

I close my eyes and try to picture it, a newborn toddling through the double doors and out into the backyard, Lydia close behind, watching, babysitting this child, unsure of what to do. And instead I see myself, me and a small child, my own first child, Lydia. Lydia at sixteen months, finally taking her first steps in a powder-blue gingham sunsuit, Patrick urging her on through the microphone on the camcorder. I try again but it's no use. I'm left with my own image, my own profile, me in the dream that sends me reeling backward to happier days when this was all I wanted, craved with every inch of my being. I see myself, thinner, fewer laugh lines, hair still long and stripped back into a single braid down the middle of my back, kneeling down and begging her to come to me, take those first steps.

Lydia starts to apologize again, and I hold up a hand to her. "It's a lot, Lyd. Being a mom is more than you could ever imagine."

She doesn't understand this, of course, but my words silence her. "What do you think about adoption?" she says, finally, as if she's been storing up an idea I can't believe she's even begun to think about.

I let the silence wedge itself into the small space between the two of us. I've underestimated my daughter; while I've spent my days figuring out how to rescue her, she's busily begun trying to construct a solution to the problem. Before I get the chance to answer her, she says again, "Really, Mom, I want to know what you think about adoption. You know, giving the baby to someone else to raise." She looks at me through her brown eyes, unrelenting, searching for approval in the suggestion she is making.

"I don't know, Lyd. I've never really thought about it. What made *you* think about it?" It was a true statement. I'd been caught in a back-and-forth tennis match between killing off this baby and raising it myself; I hadn't even considered what seemed like a perfectly natural choice to Lydia.

"I'm not sure, Mom. I just sort of did. You know, it doesn't seem fair that I have to make any decision about it."

I stop her then, angry at once. My hands clutch her at the elbows; my nails digging into her already tanned arms and with more force than I mean to exert, I shake her. "Actually, Lydia, it is fair. It's more than fair. You made the decision to be fifteen and pregnant. So a decision is exactly what you have to make now. That's what it's about. About deciding what to do."

I've startled her. Her eyes go wide and her face is frightened as if she were a child and I'd caught her doing something I'd forbidden her to do. But she stands her ground.

Her eyes plead with me. "Yes, okay, I have to make a decision about this, I get that. But I don't want it to be a bad decision for me. And I don't want it to be a bad decision for this baby, either."

For the first time I see her put her hand on her stomach, her still flat, still fifteen-year-old stomach. I shiver even though the sun is perched in a cloudless sky, warm on my back.

"This is going to be the hardest thing in my life, Mom. I don't know what this is going to be like. But I want to do something right out of it. Out of this whole year. This whole screwed-up, stupid year where everything has gone wrong and everything just keeps going wrong. Can't I do one thing to make it right? To fix it? Somehow?"

I know she's talking about more than this pregnancy, this baby. I know that she's looking for a way to resolve Patrick's death, to bring us all closer together again, to put this family back together. And I know that she won't find it, not in this baby, not in whatever decision she makes about it. I know that the decision she makes about this, whatever that conclusion is, will be one more thing to grieve about, one more thing to fight through.

"Lydia, my God," I say softly, my voice barely a whisper in the quiet backyard. I sit in silence for a few minutes, letting her question register with me. How would she know? How would she even begin to contemplate the magnitude of the question she asked me? How could she possibly begin to think about carrying a baby for nine months only to hand him or her over to someone else?

Her face studies mine, waiting.

"You're not going to fix this year, Lydia. You understand that, don't you? Get that right, honey. Get that right, right now. 'Cause all this shit that's happened, all this stuff that's come before this? None of it has anything to do with you, okay? You've got one thing to think about, one decision to make. That's it."

"I know that." She sniffs and wipes her nose on her T-shirt.

I'm struck by just how young she looks, T-shirt hanging down past her shorts, hair pushed back, void of any makeup that might make her look even the slightest bit older.

"But, Mom, how could you say that adoption wouldn't be a good idea? I mean, think about it . . . there are tons of people out there who want to have a baby, tons of people who could do a lot more good for this child than I can. Can't you just think about it? Even for a minute?"

"Lydia," I say slowly, exhaling two tons of emotion that come flooding from me with the whisper of her name. "Oh, gosh, Lyd. I think it's a decision you couldn't possibly have any understanding about. I can't imagine what it would be like, going through everything you'd go through with this pregnancy, and then handing a little baby over to someone else. God, Lyd, I don't know. I really have no idea." I rub my eyes deeply, kneading at the folds, the bags, under my eyeballs. "It's like, your whole life he or she would be out there, wondering about you. And you about him, you know? What he might look like, what he might be like, who her friends are, what she likes to do, what he thinks about you and the fact that you gave him away. God, honey. Don't get me wrong, I think it's an honorable choice, more brave than I could ever imagine anyone to be. More brave, certainly, than I could ever have been."

"So you don't think you could have done it, Mom?"

"No," I whisper, barely audible, but with enough force that the word hangs in the air between us. "No, honey, certainly I couldn't have done it. But it never crossed my mind. It was the happiest time of my life, Lyd. The day I found out I was pregnant with you, it was the happiest day of my life. Your father and I wanted you so badly, so very badly."

She's quiet then, staring at her lap. I think she's simply lost in thought until I see the tears falling slowly into her cupped hands. Finally, she lifts her hands to her face, covering them completely, trying, I imagine, to block out the world. She rests herself back on the chair, her knees pulled up to her chest, and sobs.

16

The air-conditioning in the obstetrician's office comes blasting through a small vent in the waiting room ceiling with so much force that it causes the metal cover to rattle noisily. I've moved twice, to two separate rigid chairs, hoping to find a spot where the temperature is slightly more regulated. Lydia, frozen by fear, sits in the first chair just outside the exam room door, one leg bouncing up and down nervously.

I've scheduled the first appointment of the day, and we're early at 8:50. No matter, Peggy Nelson is nowhere near the office, stuck two buildings over on the third floor of the hospital: Labor and Delivery in an emergency C-section. We wait twenty minutes before Lydia says to me, "Shouldn't she be here by now? I mean, we *have* an appointment."

I laugh at her from behind the most recent copy of *Child* magazine, the cover a shot of smiling toothless twin boys in matching navy blue overalls, their towheads shaved to crew cuts. "If it were you having the caesarian, you'd want her there, too." This seems to placate her some and she gets up, switches chairs, scans the pile of magazines for something to read, and then quickly, when another patient comes into the waiting room, sits herself down next to me quietly and burrows into an article.

The new patient looks as if she's ready to give birth now, her swollen feet stretched in cheap drugstore flip-flops. She checks in, then maneuvers herself into a chair and rests her hands upon her large belly. I smile at her and casually ask her how far along she is.

"Thirty-nine weeks. Ugh. We can only hope Dr. Nelson takes pity on me and induces this week."

"Oh, I remember that," I say. "Nothing worse than the home stretch. Is this your first baby?"

She nods her head yes at us. "Is that your daughter?" she asks me.

"My first, yes. I have another at home who is eleven."

"Oh gosh, and you're starting all over again? That's fairly brave," she says to me, a look of disbelief on her face.

I blush red, scarlet, I'm sure, the curse of my pale skin and strawberry hair. "Um, no, not me. Not this time," I tell her, just as a nurse I haven't met before calls Lydia's name. The woman smiles politely at me, but her eye contact is limited.

I follow Lydia into the small exam room and watch the nurse pull out the stirrups as Lydia's face goes pale. I point to the side chair and motion to Lydia to sit down. I take the chair closest to the door and the nurse starts in with her litany of questions.

"First date of your last period?"

"Around March tenth, I think."

"Age?"

"Fourt . . . I mean fifteen."

The nurse eyes me over the top of her chart. "Has she had a blood test yet?"

"No," Lydia and I answer in unison as our eyes meet. "I asked Peggy about that. She wanted me to bring her in anyway. We've done a home pregnancy test. Two, actually," I say to the nurse.

The nurse pulls a white paper dressing gown out of the top drawer and leaves it on the exam table. She tells Lydia to undress from the waist down and flip the switch on the wall when she is ready for the doctor to come in. Just as she is leaving the room, we hear Peggy Nelson in the hall; she comes bursting forth into the room and in a giant sweep takes both of us, Lydia and me, into her arms at the same time.

"Oh, ladies, I am so happy to see you both," she says to us, bringing with her a level of energy she's savored from the delivery she's just made.

Lydia drops out of our embrace, and lets Peggy and me stand there in each other's arms for a few minutes. She holds me and as I feel her energy support me, I fade a little in her arms. We've been friends for years, nearly thirty, since preteens and braces and junior high made us inseparable. Only the university, then med school, marriage, then kids nearly a decade apart, mine older, hers younger, left us drifting, but never far from each other. Peggy delivered Lydia on a ridiculously hot day in June just weeks after she'd started her private practice. She'd delivered Becca on the harvest moon in September just after the clock went to midnight and I had been in labor for thirty-two hours.

When she loosens her embrace, she holds me at arm's length and says, "It's going to be fine, sweetie. Let's see what we've got here, okay?" Then she turns to Lydia, her patient, and starts.

"Hey, kiddo," she says, rubbing Lydia's back. "You need to get changed. I'll give you a minute to do that and then I'll be back. Okay if your mom comes to get a cup of coffee with me, just down the hall here? I've been up since three in the morning with this last one. We'll give you a minute and be back, okay?"

Peggy puts her arm around my waist and guides me down the hall to her private office. Inside, pictures of her three children sit on the credenza behind her desk. Patient charts are stacked in piles on the desk and overflow into a pile on the floor. An overnight makeup bag sits on the chair, a brush and compact resting on top as if they've just been used for the first time a few minutes before. I slump down onto the couch against the window and Peggy closes the door.

"Okay, give me the skinny. How far along do you think she is?"

"Three months give or take, far as I can tell." I rest my elbows on my knees, my head in my hands, and lean forward. "I just cannot believe we are here, Peg. In a million years I did not think this would happen."

Peggy leans against the oversized walnut desk and crosses her arms over her chest. She's wearing a pink sweater and navy blue slacks, a long white coat with her name and credentials embroidered over the top of the breast pocket.

"How long have we been friends?" she asks me.

"Forever. Maybe longer. I think I'm too old to remember how long," I say, looking up at her.

"You didn't do this, Al, you know that, right? You didn't have anything to do with this. At all. All she needs from you now is your support. That and lots and lots of love, but that's a no-brainer for you. What does she want to do? Have you even begun to talk about her options?"

"She says she wants to give the baby up for adoption."

"Really?" She peers at me over an arched eyebrow. "Admirable, don't you think?"

"I couldn't do it, I know that much." I rest my chin in my cupped hands and rub my eyes some more.

"Did you tell her that?" Peggy paces the distance between her desk and the corner window that overlooks the square between the medical buildings and the hospital, watching me carefully.

I nod.

She takes a deep breath and lets it out purposefully. I've known her long enough to feel the weight of her disappointment. "Okay. Then what do you think she should do? What do you want her to do?"

"Oh God, Peg, I have no idea. There aren't many options here, you know. She's fifteen, totally incapable of doing anything about this. Shit, she can't even drive. Can't hold a job. She can barely get herself up and dressed for school in the morning, never mind getting a kid up, dressed, fed before she what, goes off to high school and I raise the baby?"

"It's been done. But only if you want that. And, more importantly, only if that's what Lydia wants. And, quite frankly, it doesn't sound like that's the best option for either of you. Why not adoption, Ally? Why not let her make that choice? It's not a bad decision. There's a lot to be said about how you can do it. How involved

Lydia wants to be. How involved the father wants to be." She stifles a yawn, residue from the night catching up with her. "Who is the father, by the way? Do I know him?" she asks, shuffling through a few of the charts in a pile on her desk.

"Eric. High school boyfriend. Sixteen."

"And his parents? Where are they on this?"

"Good God, I have no idea. I haven't talked to them. I haven't even talked to him about it. Good kid, I think, despite all this."

"All this? All this doesn't make him a bad kid. It doesn't make Lydia a bad kid for that matter, either. It just makes them kids. When it comes right down to it, that's all they are. They're just kids. They have no idea." She moves over toward the couch and slumps down next to me. We lean into each other; she rests her head on my shoulder softly so that I can feel her pulse beating. She laces her fingers in mine and we sit like that for a few minutes before she says to me again, "So, tell me. Why not adoption?"

I take in a breath—all of it—and let it go slowly. "I know she'll regret it someday, Peg. I can't stand the thought of her living her life always wondering, always thinking about a child out there who looks like her, who probably talks like her, who grows up wondering about his mother and what kind of person she was to give him up, just toss him aside like he wasn't wanted. What kind of person does that? Who carries a baby around inside them for nine months and then hands it over to someone else? Who can do that?"

"Al." She stops me, my pleas getting stronger and more emotional. "Al. There are plenty of people who do it. And plenty of happy endings. And there are about a million varying degrees on how it can be done. If you don't want this child to wonder about his biological mother all his life, then let Lydia play a role in his or her life. She can know the adoptive parents, she can be a part of this child's life. In large doses or small increments. Really, it can be done. It's a good choice."

"Uh-uh. I can't get my head around it. Biological mother. What kind of a mother is a biological mother? You're a mother or you're not, plain and simple. You have this baby. You are, for the rest of your life, connected to this child with every thread of your being."

"But you said it yourself, if she keeps this baby, raises him or her for her own, she'll barely know which end is up. You know you'll end up the primary caregiver in the end. It'll just be in you to do it. What kind of life is that for the baby? For Lydia?"

"It's no-win, Peg. I didn't say it wasn't, it is. There ain't nothing good about it. If I had my way, she'd terminate the pregnancy and be done with it. I know you can't wash your hands of all this, but I'd sure like to do away with the evidence."

Peggy winces, then shakes her head at my suggestion. She's performed plenty of abortions, but I know where she stands on them. *A necessary evil, the worst part of my job,* she once told me.

"The scars from that run deep, Al. You have no idea."

"I don't even know if she'll discuss it, Peg. I really don't."

She stands then and offers me her hand, pulls me up to my feet and into another of her warm, full bear hugs, which I accept readily. "Let's go see where we're at, figure out how far along she is and what we can do at this point. There is a best in this, you know. I promise you, it might not be what you want, but there is a best decision."

Lydia looks smaller than usual sitting on the long examining table. Her long, lanky legs stick out from under the white gown and hang over the side of the table, crossed at the ankles. I say to her, "Do you want me to stay, Lydia?"

She nods her head yes and reaches for me to stand next to her, to hold her hand. Peggy motions for me to take my place on the other side of the table and starts in with a series of questions that blur by me one right after the other. I'm aware of Peggy's voice, though I'm not watching her. Rather I'm staring at the ultrasound equipment that has hummed to life, watching the empty screen as Peggy types in *Houlihan, L.* into the patient name field.

"First day of your last menstrual cycle?"

"Sometime around the middle of March, I think."

"Had you been regularly sexually active?"

"A little," Lydia whispers softly.

"How much is a little? Once a week? Twice a week? More often?"

"Um, once a week, maybe. Twice, sometimes."

"For how long? Before you realized you were pregnant?"

"A couple of months, maybe. Since Christmastime."

I hadn't thought to ask Lydia these questions, hadn't bothered. I didn't see the need given the circumstances. What difference did it make the number of times she'd skated through, the times she'd prayed nothing had happened? But Peggy probes with tenderness, puts Lydia at ease, and by the time she guides her to lean back on the table and put her feet in the stirrups, Lydia's talking more freely, answering her questions.

Peggy is clinical. I'm emotional, awed by the moving life that comes alive on the monitor, the small but vital pulse of a being that squirms one way, then the next. Lydia is removed; she barely looks at the screen but stares without blinking at the ceiling, then at the artwork on the far wall.

When she's dressed, Peggy says to Lydia, "Your mom tells me you're thinking about placing the baby for adoption." Peggy's making notations in Lydia's chart, but she clicks the pen in a slow rhythm and waits for Lydia to answer her.

"Uh-huh. That's what I want to do," Lydia answers her, glad for someone to hear her out. I stand with my arms crossed over my chest, stiff, when she dares to sneak a glance sideways at me.

"Have you talked to the baby's father about that decision?"

Lydia stares at the cuff on the jeans she has worn. My oldest and most comfortable jeans. I'd given them up to her this morning after she showed up in my closet, in tears and with her robe cinched tightly around her waist. "No," she says to Peggy. "Do I need to do that?"

"Well, that's probably the best place to start, don't you think? He should probably be a part of the decision. He really does have the right to help you make that decision and he needs to know what you're thinking about."

"I guess so. I just, I just really don't see any other way. It's what's best for everyone, really. Especially for"—her words catch and she clears her throat—"especially for the baby. At least that's what I think." Lydia looks at me again and I turn to stare out the window.

"I think it can be an admirable decision, Lydia, I do," Peggy says to her. "And yes, it's your decision. Yours and the baby's father. There are a lot of ways you can do it. You're going to want to talk to some people about this and I'm going to have the nurse pull you some resource sheets, adoption agencies, lawyers you can talk to. They'll give you a better idea of what you'll go through and what you need to do. As for us." Peggy closes the chart and comes to the edge of the table where Lydia is still sitting. "We're done for today. But I'd like to see you next month. I want you on prenatal vitamins, taking care of yourself, taking care of that baby. I'm giving your mom some stuff for you guys to read, books that will help you explain what's going on, where you are in the pregnancy." She drapes an arm around Lydia and pulls her close into her chest so that Lydia's head is resting on her shoulder. With her free arm, Peggy reaches out to me and I take her hand. Peggy's staring at me, long and hard, when she says to Lydia, "Of course, your mom's been through all this. Ask her questions, she'll answer them for you, help you understand what's going on. And call me, any time you need to. Both of you." And with that Peggy squeezes my hand tightly and holds it in her own.

Finally, just before leaving the both of us, Peggy says, "Oh, do you want to know your due date?"

"Yes," we both say, standing together and eager at once.

"December fifteenth, there or about. A Christmas baby, without a doubt."

17

"They're inappropriate, that's all I'm saying. Simply inappropriate for company," I heard Barbara whisper harshly, reprimanding.

"What are?"

"The kisses, Patrick. There is simply no reason you need to stand in the middle of a party and slobber all over your husband. It's just plain uncalled for."

"Who are you upset with, Mother, me or Ally?"

"What difference does it make?"

"All the difference in the world. Ally didn't slobber all over me. I slobbered all over her. And if you're not careful, I'll do it again, right here, right now."

I walked into the kitchen in bare feet, on the balls of my feet—nearly my tiptoes—and huddled nearest Patrick, who enveloped me into a bear hug, long and warm, under the cradle of his arm. "Hey, baby" he said, "how'd you sleep?" And then, true to his word, bent to kiss me full on the mouth.

"Mmmm, good. Wonderful, actually."

Patrick handed me a mug and nudged me toward the coffeepot. I ran a hand through my hair, standing in crumpled waves every which way, and padded my way past Barbara to the coffeepot.

"Now. What was it you were saying, Mother? Because I don't

want to let this go. I really don't. Let's get this resolved right now."

"All I'm saying . . ." Barbara's tone had improved dramatically, sickly sweet. "All I'm saying is that I think kissing could be kept for a more private place. A little quieter. In my day you just didn't do those kinds of things. Your father and I didn't go around kissing each other, pawing after each other. Certainly you can understand that, Ally?" She turned her attention to me then and caught me midsip, steam rising up from the mug around me. I raised an eyebrow at her, and then looked to Patrick.

"I mean, after all. This was an elegant party hosted by the Murphys. There was really no need for you to stop the evening and toast at all, Patrick. Really no need."

"It was her birthday, Mother. Ally's birthday. You wouldn't think it would so much as spoil the caviar for people to wish her a happy birthday, would you?"

"Well, I suppose—"

"I mean, did you?"

"But of course. Of course, dear. Ally knows we all just adore her. She knows we all wish her a wonderful birthday."

"That's not what I asked you," Patrick deadpanned her, the silence building in the room. He turned to me then, rage mixed with sarcasm. "Did she, Al? Did she wish you a happy birthday?"

"Patrick. It's all right, really."

"Don't sugarcoat it, Ally, did she?" he asked again, his voice rising.

A crimson scarf felt as if it was building at the base of my neck. I felt the heat run down my vertebrae, prickly and hot.

"Mother?"

"Well, of course I did. Don't be silly." She turned to me then. "Of course you know we all wished you a happy birthday, Ally." Her eyes were daggers, her makeup perfect even at such an early hour. I cupped my coffee in my hands, blew into the rising steam. I didn't wish to anger her; I wanted Patrick to stop.

It was our first year here as a married couple; I wanted everything to be perfect. I wanted long walks on the beach, endless games of Scrabble, maybe to finish a book or two. I just wanted Patrick to throw his arms around me and tell me he loved me; I didn't need anything beyond that. The long, wet, slobbering kiss, as Barbara had affectionately referred to it, had been more than enough.

I felt caught between the two of them, each of them hanging on my words, waiting.

"Well?" Patrick said again. "Did she?"

"Oh, Patrick, I'm sure she did, she must have." I nodded my head eagerly and went to his side. I rubbed my face against his arm, the warm familiar smell of his T-shirt. "Surely she did. Yes, of course, at breakfast yesterday morning, first thing."

He didn't believe me, but he didn't push me any further. He knew; he got it. Instead, he planted another long, wet kiss on my lips, lingering there, holding my face in his hands adoringly. Then, as if to pour salt on open wounds, in a voice I recognized as the one I so often hungered for—a voice reserved only for me—he suggested we return to bed.

We left Barbara, sponge in hand, angry eyes following us. I knew it wasn't the last time I'd fib, as a matter of fact, outright lie to her. And still walk away happy.

18

The morning is a mad dash to make it to the airport on time, which we do, but just barely. I keep constant tabs on Lydia. Check her, check her again, look hard at her, follow her with my eyes to the bathroom, trail her to the magazine stand. She shrugs me off, rolls her eyes at anything I ask of her.

Finally Becca says to me, "Mom, is everything okay with you and Lydia? Can't you guys just be excited to go to the beach?"

"Thought you didn't want to go, Becca," I say, much too caustically.

She looks at me quizzically over the top of the book I thought she was reading. I should know better. Becca's always got one eye on everything around her. "Well, if we're going we might as well make the best of it," she answers me.

"Yeah, Becca." I slow my speech purposefully and try to gain control of the words. "Everything's fine." And just to prove it to her, I turn back to the *Mademoiselle* magazine I'm flipping through. I feel Becca stare at me for a few minutes more until finally she returns to her book.

By our third day at the beach, we're crawling all over each other. It has rained since our arrival, the storm clouds building and shifting as we drove in the rented van from the airport to the coast. We've seen two movies, played seventeen rounds of hearts, and ordered takeout twice. Short of walking the mall for the third afternoon in a row, I'm on the verge of a complete breakdown. I've read each of my magazines, some twice; finished one novel and started another; and have filled out all the girls' required school paperwork that I can now file away until August.

I'm standing in the great room facing the beach, which is dark, cloudy, and littered with pieces of broken, scattered driftwood. An angry sea. It matches my mood.

Lady Barbara is finishing her tea, flipping through the paper and crinkling each section as she goes, punctuating every page with a "hmm" or a "tsk-tsk." She's careful to fold the pages back in the same order for me to read later and she stacks the whole thing neatly in a pile at the end of the table before moving to the stainless sink to rinse her cup, place her saucer in the dishwasher. Even Barbara's sensed the mood. But we've given her nothing.

Becca's resolved to stay as quiet and self-contained as possible, lost in a world that involves anything she can do on her own, quietly. I catch her absentmindedly picking at the now frayed and grubby gauze on her cast while she flips the pages of a book or surfs the Net on Patrick's old laptop that I brought with me.

Lydia has dissolved. She's curled up on the end of the couch, keeps a blanket or sweatshirt nearby at all times, even more careful now to hide the secret she's finally come clean with. When she's not staring at the television, her eyes follow me from room to room, begging, pleading with me to allow her to repair the damage. I've taken to avoiding her, mull at her questions and stall at a discussion when she pulls me aside to have one. Regardless, she leans herself toward me rather than pulling away. Bends her body into mine, leans her head on my shoulder, holds my hand, reaches to the most mothering part of me to protect her.

I am silently counting the days to my departure. Aware of every hour, every minute I have left before I leave. I find the only question I can answer for Lydia is, "Yes, I am still leaving on Sunday. You'll be fine. We'll deal with this when you get home."

Becca is the first up on Sunday. I hear her rattling around the kitchen, in and out of drawers, and I smile at the familiar sounds that have woken me on each of my birthdays as far back as I can remember. I lie in bed, let the sun warm the room, and pull open the shutters nearest the headboard. The sky is brilliant blue, the sun painted into the background and glistening off the water in sparkles. *Finally.* The large black suitcase I'd packed the night before sits open at the foot of the bed, just to the left of the armoire that I have emptied. On top of my neatly folded clothes, secured by the two elastic black straps, lie my tickets and a paperback, my straw hat and a plastic baggie full of shells that Lydia handed me late yesterday afternoon.

"Take these home, put them up on the bay window in the kitchen, and think about us," she said, head tilted and hand holding the baseball cap she'd pulled low and tight across her brow. She had on her sunglasses, but through the UV lenses, I could see her eyes peering at me, staring intently at my reaction to her every word, still looking for the continuous approval that she is so desperate for. She spoke slowly and it was the first time I could remember her speaking directly to me in months, her eyes pleading with me.

"I will. Don't worry, Lydia, you'll be fine. Have some fun if you can stand it. It won't kill you to do so." I stole a glance at Lady Barbara then.

The truth was I was glad to be leaving. I wanted to run from this house, the secrets we were keeping, the reality we'd have to face. I wanted a week of nothing to do with any of it. I wanted my freedom back, my life back. I wanted to start over.

It's another twenty minutes or so before the girls come in singing happy birthday to me, loud as they can, off-key and boisterous. Becca bounds over to the bed and throws her weight over the top of the covers as Lydia comes in carrying the white wicker tray on which sits my breakfast. Two poached eggs carefully slit around the edges of the ramekins they've been cooked in, two slices of dry wheat toast, a wedge of perfectly ripened cantaloupe, and a coffee from the pastry shop a block away that I have no doubt Lydia left to retrieve while Becca was in the kitchen. Little white wildflowers sticking out of a honey jar that doubles as a vase.

I tease the girls as I turn the eggs over onto the toast, and take my first sip of coffee. "Gee, I thought I'd beat you two out of bed this morning. I'm surprised you're speaking to me, seeing that I'm leaving you here for another week, heading off on my own birthday adventure," I drone on, watching my girls, each of them, roll their eyes. They've long given up by now; they're staying.

"Well, Allyson, what a treat." We all look up to see Barbara pulling the violet terry robe around her girth, cinching it tight at the waist as she stands in the doorway yawning. "You girls could wake the dead with all that singing." She turns to take the stairs down to the kitchen when Becca calls her back.

"Grandma? Isn't there anything you want to say to Mom?" Becca begs after Barbara in the slyest of voices, itching for her grandmother to lay a big "happy birthday" on me.

"What time's your flight, Allyson?" Barbara murmurs, yawning again, desperate for coffee.

"Three," I say, stifling a giggle, and then, "Don't worry about me, Barbara, I've called for a car to pick me up."

She waves in the doorway and shuffles off down the stairs to the kitchen. I take a big bite of egg and toast all in one, let a bit of the yolk run down onto the plate, and smile at the girls. We dissolve into laughter, the three of us on the bed, both of them perched in their familiar spot, the one they always picked. Only this year they're a little closer to me, a little more within my reach. And there's a little more room in the bed for all of us.

After breakfast I do a little fine-tuning to my forty-three-year-old face while the shower water runs behind me, fogging up the full-length mirror on the back of the bathroom door. I'm nude, naked, and laughing, standing here in my birthday suit, while I pluck a few eyebrows, rub my finger across the top of my eyelids. My breasts are small; they sag only slightly in the mirror and I step back to take them in, run my hands full across my hips and down over my thighs as I turn and take a side view. I've run every day here at the beach, even on the coldest, rainiest days; a survival of sorts. So even the full meals, the nonstop snacking, the movie popcorn hasn't caught up with me this week and my stomach is flat, flatter than I remember it being in earlier days. The marks from the two children I'd carried still visible but only slightly and certainly only to someone who was searching close-up, but otherwise, not a day over forty-two, I think, nowhere near forty-three.

Forty-three? Where did I think I would be? Certainly not here, plotting my escape from this house, abandoning my children, determined to have a piece of my own birthday cake. And still so uncertain about what the next seven days would hold for me. The first seven days I've had to myself, the first vacation I've had to myself, in all the years of marriage. I have no plans; have remained specifically elusive about what I'll do, with whom I'll do it, when I'll be done. The truth is I have no idea.

Later, after my plane has landed and I turn on my cell phone, I listen to my voice mail. It's Michael. Even without a plan, without even the simplest idea about how to spend this birthday night, I should have known that Michael would rescue me. His voice is like a familiar radio station the first time you're back in your car after a long trip away.

His message goes like this: "Hey, birthday girl. Don't *even* tell me you are planning a quiet night at home soaking your forty-three-year-old sweet ass away in some hot bath. Dinner. And I mean the real kind, where they have linen tablecloths and good silverware. You pick the spot. I have reservations at three places. Biba, Luca, or 29 Newbury. Eight o'clock. Which, by my calculations, means you have time for a bath after all. And to pull something fabulously slinky out of your closet. Call me when you land."

I haven't heard Michael's voice in over a week, had vowed not to call from the shore and piss away an hour on the phone bitching about Barbara and the lousy time I was having. I'm very aware of the half-crooked smile that has crept over my face and left me flushed while I make my way through Logan Airport, my black roll-away toting behind me and my large black leather backpack slung low over my shoulder. I feel free, freer than I have in a long, long time. I feel like a woman traveled, returning to her own life, ready to suck everything she can back into herself and come out whole again. I feel single, unattached, unburdened. I've not been to dinner in Boston in well over a year, since the last time Patrick and I went for an all-day marathon-shopping trip.

I weigh the idea of it in my mind and come up happier than I feel I should have a right to. Won't I miss Patrick? The haunts? The regular route we'd taken together, the streets we automatically navigated wordlessly, the stores we approached out of habit and those we skipped by without even a nod? Patrick and I knew Boston; we'd lived there together in younger days, before kids, before mortgage payments and bills, before ballet and the orthodontist. In the days when we'd stumbled home from a bar on a January night and dived under the goose-down comforter together to keep warm. Boston was very much our city.

I stop short in front of the Cinnabon stand, stop so that the people trailing me, watching me with a longing, wispy desire to be me, are forced to move around me. I dial Michael's number. He picks up on the first ring. "Birthday escort service, what's your pleasure?"

"Hi, Michael," I say flatly, stifling the smile that wants to creep back into my voice, across my face.

"Hi, gorgeous. Happy birthday. Happy your day. It's all about you today, you know that?" His voice floats, singsongy and mesmerizing, through the phone line.

"Yeah, well, it feels all about being forty-three," I fib.

"Not a day over forty-two. So, which will it be?"

"Which what?"

"Restaurant? You got my message, didn't you?"

"Yeah, I did. But, Michael, I don't know. I'm thinking maybe I should just stay in after all. Just sit and think back over this year on my own, you know. I've got a lot of shit to deal with, you have no idea—" I start to protest, but he's having none of it.

"Nope. Uh-uh. You're not getting out of this. Dinner. That's the least you owe me."

"I owe you? It's my birthday. How could I possibly owe you dinner?"

"Your company. You owe me that. And I will not let you sit at home and mope around about this, Ally. Dinner. You want to come home after that? Fine. But dinner it is. I'll be there at seven fifteen. Be ready." He hangs up just as I start to stammer into the phone again.

I tug at the black case, which seems heavier than it was a few minutes ago, and make my way through the terminal, up the escalator, and out into the parking garage. The late afternoon sun still hangs heavy in the sky, and the grimy humidity penetrates from the low cement ceiling of the parking structure. I reach for my phone and dial Michael's number again, but he doesn't answer. I hang up without leaving him a message, dial his cell phone without even looking at the keypad, hang up, and then dial home again. The numbers ring into an endless sea of voice mail until I finally give up. He's waiting me out, passing the time until I just cave.

I try his home number one last time, twenty minutes later, just as I'm making my way off the exit and onto the expressway that will take me home. He answers, "You again?"

"Okay, okay, you win. Biba."

I hear him laugh lightly into the phone before he says, "I figured. I canceled the other two ten minutes ago."

19

I choose a dark beige camisole, gold silk beaded wrap, and a short black sheer skirt that most women my age wouldn't dare to wear. The pedicure I've had at the beach still looks great and my Corvette-red toes peek out from under strappy gold three-inch slides. I'm pulling the last tendrils out of a large comb that I've secured in the back of my head when Michael rings the doorbell, then walks in without waiting for me to answer.

"Oh, diva," he says with a whistle when I make my way down the stairs, working the while to adjust the diamond stud in my left ear. I feel a race of blood to my cheeks and allow myself the good grace of his adoring gaze that scans me up and down as I tiptoe carefully down the stairs.

"Yeah, yeah. Okay, so we'll go to dinner. It's just a birthday, Michael." I'm warmed by the smile so quick to jump to his lips. "Just another day. Start of another year." The sun I've collected at the beach complements my outfit and I'm aware of his long stare, the way his eyes follow me as I cross the room.

"Okay, birthday girl, have it your way. Grouchy." He holds open the door and I reach for the black clutch I've laid on the entry table. When I turn to lock the door, he's already doing with his own key, gently guiding me with his hand low on m back, as we walk to his car and he opens the door.

The most comfortable silence falls over the car. We ma

well be headed to Duke's for a burger, fries, and a beer. I kick off the slides, open Michael's CD wallet, and pull out a Sting album, something I know we've listened to a million times before and I know we will listen to a million times from now.

"Can I call the girls?" I reach for Michael's cell phone and begin to dial as he navigates the steering wheel with his left hand, his weight on his right elbow resting on the armrest quite near mine. Becca answers on the first ring and asks me right off what I'm doing. I tell her Michael has kidnapped me for birthday dinner and that I'm not sure when I will return, but hopefully I'll be back when they fly in next week.

Becca laughs. "Sure, Mom, Duke's is like ten minutes from the house. I'm pretty sure you guys can make it back by Saturday."

"Yeah, Bec. Duke's it is. How lucky am I? Big fat burger and fries tonight." I run a polished nail over the skirt and meet Michael's piercing eyes, still holding the miniature phone to my ear. He's silent, letting me take in the girls and all I need to cover with them. "Let me talk to your sister, okay?"

Lydia comes on, exhaling deeply into the phone. "Hey, Mom, what's going on?"

"Hi, Lydia, everything okay?" I ask casually, trying for normal. I picture Lydia in her sweats already, something quiet and thoughtful of mine playing through her CD headphones. She'd been listening to an old Cranberries CD, *Everybody Else is Doing It, So Why Can't We?* Over and over and over.

"Yeah, Mom, everything's fine. It's about ninety degrees here and all muggy now. Like the summer finally really started." And then a bit more quietly, "Grandma's a little nutty. I think the heat's getting to her. We ordered in tonight."

"Well, you're not missing much. It's hot as blazes here, too."

"Okay, well, I hope you're having a good birthday, Mom." She ends with a whimper and my heart goes through the phone to

talk to you in the morning."

I think she's going to hang up then, but she pauses and says more quietly, "I miss you, Mom."

"Yep, me too."

"Okay, Red, don't go getting all soft on me. This is your night. It's about you, remember?" Michael takes my hand for only a minute, something I can tell he's been longing to do, and holds it tightly, running his thumb across all my fingers and then finally releasing it and letting it fall back into place. I tense, and shift in my seat slightly.

"Where's Sarah tonight?"

"Sleepover. With Leslie. They're working on their mother/ daughter bonding skills. Which need more work than a single night. But hey, it's a start."

"Mmm. Not going well, huh?"

"You know, it's their gig. Sarah's gotta remember Les is not me. She doesn't think like me. She doesn't act like me. Most days she doesn't even like me, can't remember why the hell she married me to begin with." I laugh at this before Michael continues. "It's true, you know? I mean it's just different hanging with your dad. I don't care where Sarah lives, I just want her to be happy. I want her to enjoy life, live a little, have some fun. But Les, well, she's still seething over Sarah's decision to live with me. It's just not what's supposed to happen, you know? I mean, who picks living with their dad over living with their mom?"

"I would. Shit, Michael, I'd pick you in a hot minute over Leslie. No contest. You're much more fun. And you gotta be easier to live with."

"I don't know about that. Leslie's neater, that's for sure. And she's got her shit together. You can't argue that either."

"Oh yeah, let's see. Leslie's stricter, which is definitely a downer for a twelve-year-old. Leslie's less easy to talk to, consumed by her career, available on a part-time basis between the hours of eight and nine p.m., completely taken with another man. Yeah, you're right, Michael, Sarah'd be a lot better off there. It'd be a regular picnic."

"Yeah, okay. But it doesn't mean she shouldn't have a relationship with her mother, you know. She should. It's important. Look at your girls. They're not missing out on all that female bonding stuff."

"No." I hesitate only for a moment, then, "But they are gonna miss out on all that male bonding stuff. I'm just not going to cut it there. No way I'm a substitute for their dad. No one could be."

He takes a look at me then, takes his eyes off the turnpike and meets me eye-to-eye, then runs his gaze down the length of my body and back up again. "No, Al, you're not going to cut it on the male bonding stuff." The car goes silent for a minute before he finishes what he wants to say, what I know he's been meaning to say since the minute I walked down the stairs tonight. "You look, you look so beautiful. Just stunning. Like I've never seen you look before."

"Thank you, Michael," I manage. The crimson color rushes to my face, hot on my neck. I fade into the music; let Sting carry me on this ride.

We arrive in Boston and navigate Back Bay, steering down toward the water and taking the long way in before valet-parking Michael's car at Biba. He totes a bottle of red wine, as well as a card with the letter A written on the front of it in the familiar scrawl I know as his. I adjust the shawl, pull it close to me, and practically skip into the restaurant, anticipating our dinner, the food, and the conversation. I feel like a sixteen-year-old schoolgirl out for a prom.

We're seated at the ideal table, just left and to the side of the wood-burning brick hearth in which, when we take our seats, is visible a perfectly roasted suckling pig. I'm enchanted, enthralled, and I know from the look on Michael's face that he has ordered this spot for me, knows how much fun I have watching the kitchen come alive, the chefs dance around each other. He makes too much of a fuss with the wait staff, declaring this all-important day for me until each of them, independently, stops to pay me birthday wishes. Finally after two glasses of the Pinot he's brought along, he relents. But not until he takes my hands, each in his own, while the candle in my white chocolate cake is sputtering, and one last time wishes me a grand year ahead. He says it just like this, "Allyson, I wish you nothing but a grand year ahead. The best. Everything you could possibly desire, and even more, everything you deserve. Always."

"Thank you, Michael. Thank you. Thank you so much for this. For all of this." I wave my hands over the table as he slides the birthday card he's brought toward me and I reach to open it, slip my thumb right up under the wax seal he's placed against the middle of the flap. The cover of the card is a black-and-white shot of a little girl in a big white party dress, her curls cascading out from under a party hat and down in front of her face as she bends forward to blow out the single candle on a birthday cake nearly larger than she is. I smile and open it up, not near anticipating the words that spill out from the inside of the card.

> *My sweet, sweet friend. You radiate this birthday; simply glow in your skin, in your new shoes. May the year ahead embrace and lift your soul, send you forward into places you never thought you'd go, adventures you never thought you'd have. Happy Birthday.*
> *Always, Michael.*

I hold this card in my hands, stare at the words as they blur and dance in front of my eyes, and let the rush of his admiration wash over me until I'm warmed on the inside. When I raise my eyes to meet Michael's, he's staring hard at me. I wait to see what he'll do, but he does nothing, doesn't move, doesn't change his expression, doesn't dare to breathe.

I reach for my water glass, let the ice swirl and crash together before taking a small sip, and slyly, secretively say to him, teasing him just slightly, "Michael? Are we on a date?"

He laughs, a good belly-hearted roar of a laugh that breaks the tension in two. "Oh, shit. I don't know. I don't know what we're on. Drugs? No. That would be far less enjoyable than this."

"You haven't answered my question."

"No, Al, I haven't. I don't have an answer for you. Really, I'm just not that astute at this. And shit, you're much wittier than my normal dates."

"You'll notice I didn't get carded like your normal dates, either. This has got to be a whole new experience for you."

He laughs again, smiles at me while placing his American Express card on top of the portfolio. "Smoke with me?" He nods his way over my shoulder and I turn to find the bar busy and inviting, luring us both away from our table.

"A cigar? Really? You sure you want to do that? We'll be horribly smelly."

"Ah yes, darling, but horribly smelly together. You can take it. Just one. We'll share if you'd like."

We make our way to the bar, to the cigar corner where a large glass humidor houses the best the place has to offer, and Michael lights a Double Grande Zino, puffs on it a few times to warm it up, and then hands it to me appreciatively while I sink low into a deep purple velvet couch. Michael had taught me to smoke, long ago and on much cheaper and smaller cigars. He taught me how to hold one: less like a cigarette and more like a thick marker pen. When he brings me a Glenfiddich on the rocks I know I'm in trouble, but I eagerly accept it and we sit like this for a while, balancing the smoke and our respective drinks, taking each other in and trading stories.

I get louder when I drink, boisterous and animated, and so before I know it we've retreated to a story that I'd like to forget, a college escapade involving Patrick and me, Leslie and Michael, and a three-day road trip during which we were, for the most part, stoned and unaware of the three midterms that had passed us by while we pissed away our college funds in a four-person tent on the beach.

We go back, Michael and I.

Finally he drains his scotch, pulls me out of the chair, and wraps his arms tight and low at my waist. I tense for only a minute before my body seems to uncurl itself at his touch, melting away in the bow of his arm.

"C'mon, lady, let's pour you into the car," he whispers into my ear.

20

I've spent the last forty-five minutes studying this man, sneaking peeks across the automobile's sexy interior space that separates us. At this range, he's nothing I'm used to. He's broader than Patrick, less compact, takes up more space, commands more room. His fingers are longer, the nail beds wider. His bone structure more defined. Eyes more offset. Earlobes more prominent. His jawline is stronger, his chest outlined against the seat and pronounced. The distance at his waist longer, he's taller, his legs less muscular, but lanky. His shoes seem enormous.

Features I've never noticed, not in all the years I've known Michael, the decades of time we've spent laughing together, startle me and stop me cold. You can't call his hair curly at all, but wavy at the nape, then twisted in coils all over the place. And matted at the center from the unconscious wrestling with it, the constant hand-to-head transfer of energy that leaves you wanting to tousle it and make the curls come back and stand at attention. His eyelashes are longer than an infant's would be. There's a small dark freckle, a bit of a mole perhaps, though it's hard to tell without reaching out to touch him, just to the left and behind his right ear, as if it's a hidden treasure planted there to be discovered, licked.

I know not what to do with this. I know not where to go with this. I am completely and unabashedly clueless about how to handle the next five minutes, the five minutes during which Michael will pull his Jag into my driveway, cut the ignition, and come around to open my door. My body has responded in full; the butterflies twirl and dance in my stomach, my armpits are clammy and damp. Suddenly I feel very much like a child, very uneasy, very on-my-first-date-like. And for the life of me I can't place all the years that have grown between us. As comfortable as I am with Michael, I feel, at this very moment, as if I don't know him, as if I have something to fear from him.

So I tell him this.

I tell him I'm incapable of deciding what should happen next; that I can't even quite locate where we are, who we are, at this very moment. I tell him he can open the car door, use his key to unlock my house, come inside, kick his shoes off, and hang with me for one more drink, even lull me off to sleep if he wants to. Or he can simply walk me to the door and turn and drive away. I tell him that I have no objections to either. The Glenfiddich hums in my ears and I'm somewhat aware of my slurred speech, my inability to form complete sentences, the slow meticulous drawl with which I am speaking. Simply put, the alcohol is not helping. Or maybe it is.

He kills the engine and we sit at a slight incline in the driveway like two teenagers, not sure what to do with the passing of time. My hands stiffen in my lap; I rub my thumbs together like a cricket with too much energy.

"Let me put you to bed, Allyson," he finally says to me softly, in almost a whisper, after I've watched the digital numbers on the dash change from 12:32 to 12:33, then 12:34. He pulls the keys from the ignition and pockets them in a single move as he opens his door, closes it firmly, tightly, and moves to come around the backside of the car. I take in the stillness, suck in the recycled air from the car, and commit to memory the scent he's left on the leather seats.

"What are we doing, Al?" he says to me when I drop my purse on the pine table.

"I don't know. It's very out of control, isn't it?" I pause, then turn away from him and head down the hall toward the kitchen. I hand a bottled water to Michael, which he takes from me, cracks open, and hands back to me when I hand him another. "I don't know that I can stand to be this out of control, Michael. So much of my life just sort of flying around me. Not really understanding what comes next. It has been a long time of not understanding what is supposed to come next, you know. Just that out-of-control, undeniably unrestrained feeling of never knowing what's going to hit you next." I pull myself up onto the kitchen counter and let my feet dangle below me; study my perfectly pedicured toes, while I suck on the bottle.

He gulps down his water, reaches in his pocket, and pulls out his keys, the cell phone, and his sunglasses and sets these down on the granite countertop.

"You're doing fine, Al. Damn near as I can tell you've got it pulled pretty close together, right here." He takes my hand and opens it so that it's palm up and he taps with his index finger into the center of my hand. Then he folds my hand back up, lays it down again in my lap, and leaves it there. I shiver at his touch.

"Michael, you have no idea. You have no way of understanding what's going on . . ." He's close to me so I use my legs, reach to steer him toward me at his waist. When he's standing directly in front of me, we're eye-level. Part of me wants so badly to kiss this man, to reach out and enclose his head in my hands and hold it there while I trace the line of his lips with my tongue, brush his nose and eyelashes with butterfly kisses.

Part of me wants nothing more than to run.

"Ally," he whispers and closes his eyes. "Really, you're fine." His voice is low and gravelly, residue from the cigar. He places each of his hands on either side of my hips, runs his fingers just under my legs, and leaves them there as if he could, at any moment and without much effort, lift me and carry me upstairs. With his thumbs he starts, ever so slightly, to massage the sides of my thighs.

When we finally kiss, it's not an explosion. Not for either of us, I'm sure of this. It's just a slightly different, slightly bolder version of the way I'd kiss him if Barbara or one of the girls were standing in the room with us and he and I were saying good night. But our lips part just enough for something to happen, for each of us to be startled, slightly surprised. Just enough for both of us to know that we want to try it again, a little more. Michael does not move away from me, so I'm anticipating that it's coming. He's so close I feel his warm breath on my cheeks, sense the rhythm of his own breathing.

He traces my face with his fingertips, brushes back a long piece of hair that has fallen from the place I'd originally set it, runs his thumb under my chin and along my jawbone in the slowest movement. I'm mannequin still, the retinas in my eyes burning to blink.

"Why is it so out of control, Ally? What's going on? Besides this, I mean. Is there something else? Something you need to talk through? You know you can talk to me . . . tell me what it is."

It's a deep concern, laced with an insatiable need to work his way to the inner me.

I take his hands in mine and hold them, bow my head, and study our fingers intertwined. "You have no idea. I've fucked this all up so badly, Michael. I don't have a clue as to what I'm doing. I go day-to-day with this. Am I allowed to be happy? Supposed to move on? It's only been a little over a year, Michael. Good God, you have no idea." I shake my head. "You won't believe it even if I tell you, and I've sworn to Lydia that I wouldn't. Not yet, not like this, but God." I watch the look on Michael's face change from interest and concern to distress. Figuring I'm too far down the path to turn back, I say to him, "Lydia's pregnant, Michael. She's fucking pregnant. Three months give or take. God, how could I have let it happen? How could she have been this damn careless, this irresponsible?" I wipe my wet nose with a crumpled piece of paper towel. "How could I have been this irresponsible, this stupid to let it happen right here, right under my nose. Damn! Damn it all to hell. God, Michael, a baby, a fucking pregnant teenager. Now I've got to deal with a fucking pregnant fifteen-year-old?" I'm crying openly now, the tears streaming down my face in long streaks that leave mascara running down my cheeks.

I wait for his reaction, wait for him to begin to try to fix things, to try to right them. It's what I expect from him; I know him well enough to know he'll want to control things. Rather, he shifts his weight but doesn't say anything. A minute passes, then another. He's waiting for me to continue, so I do.

"So, God knows what we're going to do with that, God only knows. I haven't even begun to figure that mess out. Of all things to give us now, on top of all this. On top of losing Patrick." At the mention of Patrick's name, he lets my hands go. I feel his body go rigid, and he moves away from me, rests on his elbow against the countertop next to where I am seated.

"And this, this thing between you and me. *What is this?* What am I supposed to do with *this?* What part of *this* do I think is going to help everything else? What?" I scream at the ceiling, throwing my head back and covering my eyes with both my hands. "What are you throwing at me now?" He knows I'm not screaming at him, that I'm left to scream at no one in particular. I rest my head on his shoulder, not in an unfamiliar way, just wait there and take some deep, soothing breaths in and out, listen for the beat of my own heart, which is racing faster than I can keep up with. "There's nothing more comfortable in my life right now than you. Nothing. Nothing more familiar, nothing more recognizable, nothing more normal or second nature. And yet everything about this is unknowing. Everything about it is odd and unnatural and unfamiliar and God, Michael, I couldn't stand it if this, too, all blew up and I was left without you, without any part of us, without knowing what life was like with you at my side. You, who are supposed to be exactly who you are in a different story, in a different movie. You, who knows me better than anyone, maybe even better than myself. You are all I have. You know that, don't you? And God, Michael, God, why this between us, why go to this place?"

He holds me then, wordless, rubbing the tips of his fingers

over my back, up and across the top of where the two sides of my beige satin bra come together.

I pull back from him and with a much stronger, more assured voice, say, "Did you hear what I said, Michael? Never mind about us, never mind about all this. Didn't you hear what I've told you? Lydia, my baby, my little girl, she's pregnant. She's barely fifteen and she's pregnant. Becca's off on some distant shore. Barbara's watching me like a hawk, checking in on me and assuming I'm fucking up both my kids, which, apparently, I am." I look at him square in the face again. "Me? I'm sitting here in the middle of my kitchen with my dead husband's best friend hoping he'll kiss me, or worse. What the fuck happened? How did we get here? How, Michael? What part of normal is this? How much more out of control can it get, Michael? How much more?"

"Are you done, Ally?" he whispers.

"Patrick would hate me for this. All of this. Jesus, Michael, all we are is what's left over." I laugh then, wiping my mascara-smeared eyes with the back of my hand. "Patrick hated leftovers. He used to say there was nothing good you could do with leftovers, no recipe that would make them taste like anything other than leftovers."

He kisses me square on the forehead like a brother would. He holds me back from him then and brushes the hair back from my face. "Ally, my God, you are not a bunch of leftovers. I won't let you subscribe to that. You are a stunning woman, more put together than anyone I know. You pull yourself up every day and move on from this, little baby steps at a time. Some days I swear I don't see you move a bit, but when I turn around again, there you are, two, maybe three steps forward from where you were before. And you do it with more grace and beauty than most women possess. This? All this? This nightmare with Lydia? Even the stuff with us? This is what happens next. This is the stuff you'll walk through, head up with the grace of a woman, the real woman we've all just begun to see."

The second hand on the oversized clock on the wall is the only sound in the room, swinging back and forth just softly enough to create a rhythm in the room to lull me, dull my senses. Michael rocks me silently in his arms until finally I go soft on him and he asks me if I'm ready to go to bed.

He says to me, discerning one moment from the next, "Allyson, I think you should go to bed, get some rest."

I don't attempt to argue with him. Not tonight. Rather, I let him lift me from the countertop, lead me to the base of the stairs. He loops his arm around my waist, the small of my back, and places the palm of his hand full against the low part of my spine before pulling me toward him and kissing me full on the mouth. His tongue stops to explore the tiniest parts of my mouth. I take it in; savor it like the best part of a dream I don't wish to awaken from.

"Good night, Allyson. Happy birthday, birthday queen. Go slumber. I'll see you tomorrow. We'll move forward from there."

I wait on the stairs, watch him turn his back to me and walk across the hardwood floor to the door, close my eyes to him leaving my house, listen for him to use his key to lock me in safely. And then I take the steps slowly. One after the other.

21

My body, on automatic pilot, wakes in the morning at 5:50, begging for a run. The sky is gray, bland; the sun will have to work hard to make her presence known. I take a few minutes, lying as still as I can under the crisp sheet and blanket, and listen to the house. I'm parched and my head is splitting, but it's the first time, in a long, long time, I remember waking to the light and being glad to be alive to see it.

Outside in the dreary morning I stretch long and hard, my mind teasing me into a long run. I start slow, wait at the corner for the green Dodge pickup dropping a stack of newspapers in front of the last house on our block. Then I pick a tempo, my feet stepping in beat to skip the gutters and driveway peaks.

I'm three miles out, then five, six, and finally seven by the time I'm heading back, my legs stretching to carry me against the soft morning wind that circles the bushes, gently rocks the hedges back and forth. It's seven forty-five when I round the corner on our block and spot Anna in her robe and slippers, bending to pick up the paper.

When I approach her driveway, breathless, she peers over her glasses and says to me, "Well . . . welcome home, birthday girl. I stopped by to see you last night and to wish you a happy birthday, but you weren't home. What gives?"

"Out," I say, kneeling to catch my breath and start the reverse stretching process before my limbs start to tighten. "Michael and I had dinner in the city. He was just bound and determined to get me out on my birthday." From an inverted V-position, bent at the waist, I look up and smile.

"The city, huh? Good for you. Somewhere wonderful, I hope." She smells of the bacon she's been frying for John.

"Biba. It was excellent. Just an unbelievable meal."

"Doesn't look like you'll be paying the price. What time did you start, Ally? It's barely morning." She tucks the newspaper up under her arm, adjusts her glasses, and pulls her robe closer to her body, hugging her arms across her chest.

"Six. Just about anyway. Couldn't sleep much more than that. I just needed to go today, you know what I mean?" I squint up at her from a deep squat, working to stretch out my left hamstring.

"I'm off to Miss Linnea's today, you want to go? I can call for a reading for you. Two o'clock?" Then she starts back up the drive-way, leaving me standing on the sidewalk between our houses that round the end of the court and nearly touch each other at one end. She looks back at me before saying again, "If you want, that is? Might be a good idea, you know?"

I laugh. Anna knows I'm more than a little skeptical of Linnea. But with nothing, other than unpacking my suitcase and doing a few loads of laundry, planned in my day ahead, I acquiesce. "Yeah, sure, okay. Fine. Miss Linnea. I haven't had a reading in what, a year? It's got to be a year, at least." I shake my head. "She'll have a ball with me."

"I'd say it is time, Al. I'm sure she'll find the time to fit you in. Drinks afterward? You know, a little birthday celebration of our own, okay? I'll have John pick Nicole up from camp and we can head over to the cantina. "

"There's nothing I'd like better, Anna. Nothing at all. And by the time Linnea's done with me, there's probably nothing I'll need more than a very tall, very cold, very blended margarita."

I let the first image of Michael slip into my mind while I'm in the shower, the hot water pounding at my sore muscles. My mind flies through the night and my knees go weak, tingly, as I replay every piece of it over and over in my mind. I allow myself this little temptation as I shave my legs, wash and deep-condition my hair. The steam rises up around me and fills the oversized shower with a warm fog. I run the palms of my hands over the small of my back, down to the base of my butt, just where Michael's hands had lingered when he'd held me close to say good night.

Miss Linnea. It's not that I loathe the woman; I don't. But she senses my doubt, smells my skepticism. The last time she read my cards she spread them across the table, studied them for a good five minutes, then picked them all up and reshuffled. When she laid them out again on the table she looked down at them once, then at my distrustful face and said, "Why bother? You won't believe the cards anyway." In an instant she gathered up all the cards again, left my forty bucks on the table, and walked out of the room in a huff. I stared at Anna and then fell into a fit of laughter before picking up and pocketing the two crisp twenty-dollar bills. Anna stood stunned in the corner. She had never seen this happen before and, as she admitted to me on the drive home, selfishly hoped it wouldn't damage her relationship with the woman. This made me laugh harder, small fits of hysterics bubbling up as the tears ran out of the corners of my eyes.

Miss Linnea lives in a pink house, coral, actually. There are two front doors, each with its own screen and welcome mat. The door at the right is tacked with a NO SOLICITING sign. The engraved plaque on the door to the left lists the psychic's office hours: every day from ten to three and weekday evenings from six-thirty to nine. Underneath these hours, in small print, reads CLOSED ON THE FULL MOON. Under that, VISA, MASTERCARD, DISCOVER, AND DINERS CLUB ACCEPTED.

Anna pulls back the screen door and knocks on the door to the left. Miss Linnea opens the door and ushers us in. It takes a minute for my eyes to adjust to the darkened room, but I don't Linnea sizing me up all over again, rolling her eyes up and down.

Miss Linnea's table is set on the sunporch, a room painted bright yellow with high-gloss white baseboards and trim that overstimulates the nerve endings. Anna and I follow Miss Linnea and stand next to each other as she takes her seat, a large oversized white wicker throne on the far side of a square glass table. She adjusts her breezy topaz blouse and automatically her hand goes to the triple string of jade beads she has wrapped at her throat. Only when she's set at her place does she look up at Anna and me, still standing side by side, guilty of taking up too much space in the small room. She motions for Anna to sit across from her and assumes I'll find my way to the small stool in the far corner of the room. I look quizzically at Anna and she reads my mind, shrugs her shoulders as if to say, *sure, yes, you can stay.* So I do.

Anna's readings are like a therapy session for her. She comes as often as she feels the need, sometimes once a week, sometimes not for a whole month. Her decision to have a reading varies with her state of mind. When she needs reassurance, she makes the drive to the little coral house, sets out her forty dollars, and lets Miss Linnea do her thing. When she's in need of a boost, a redirection of sorts, same thing. Once, she's told me, she searched for two days for a pair of reading glasses she'd misplaced until finally, late into the evening, she threw on her sweatpants, a T-shirt, and her sandals, and drove immediately to Linnea's for the answer. True to her word, Anna found them, lying on the second shelf of the medicine cabinet in the downstairs bathroom. Who'd have guessed?

I watch Miss Linnea pocket the two fives, a ten, and a twenty-dollar bill Anna has laid on the table and think to myself that with all the constant visiting, Anna deserves some sort of a discount, a frequent reader card. I'm just about to suggest this when Linnea shuffles her cards and lays them out on the table in a slow, methodical movement, the tips of her acrylic-painted nails scraping against the glass. Anna's feet are crossed at the ankles and her right foot shakes back and forth in a swift rhythmic motion. She leans in and rests her hands on the table.

They talk like old friends, like a patient and her shrink.

After a minute where she carefully studies the cards, Linnea says to her, "How's Nicole doing with the new discipline routine?"

"Better. Seems so anyway. She's quicker to respond, more focused on the reward than us taking something away from her."

"Good, good." Linnea fingers the queen of pentacles card. "She needs you to follow through on things. Keep at what you're doing, it's working. Even if you feel like some days all you do is take three steps backward. It's vital you keep the consistency. It's the only way it's going to work. You mustn't doubt this."

Anna shifts in her chair, moves even closer to the table, and hugs herself a bit. She points to a card I can't see, one that is slightly hidden by her frame. I hear her say, "King of wands again."

"Yes, I see that. Still no resolution on John's job, huh?"

"He's overworked," she says to the reader, sighing. "I see the same thing happening to him all over again, sucked into another job he's not completely passionate about. It's taking everything I have to remain compassionate and patient as you suggested, give him time."

I concentrate on Linnea's giant, overweight tabby that has lumbered into the room with us and is busy rolling around on the stone floor pawing at some imaginary bird.

I want to know about my dead husband.

I want to know about my dead husband's best friend.

I want to know about my children.

I want to know about my children's children.

I want to know my own heart and soul's desire that I can't seem to locate, find, touch, or do anything with.

I want to know what I should cook for dinner tonight.

The questions roll around in my head. It's not until I hear Anna push her chair back from the table that I realize she's been saying my name, addressing me over and over again. "Ally?" I finally acknowledge her; hear the urgency in her voice that brings me back from the endless run-on questions floating through my mind.

"Oh, sorry. I must have wandered off."

"A million miles, I'd say, maybe more. Are you ready?"

"Huh?"

"Are you ready? I'm done. Linnea's ready for you. Let's switch seats." Anna appears agitated. She's waiting, I can tell, to see if I'll pass this time.

Anna looks no worse for her experience; softness has crept into her brow, the lines at her mouth have relaxed a little. We switch seats and I position myself at the edge of mine, unsure of what to do, how to start. Linnea eyes me as she places the deck of cards, the one she's just finished using on Anna, on her side table. She reaches both her hands across the table at me, pushes back the sleeves on the silk blouse. Instinctively, I place my hands on the table, in hers, and look up to meet her. Her hands are warm and soft; I can feel the creases that line them. Her nails are manicured, long and polished, the cuticles cut clean. I let her knead my hands, run her fingers across my palms and down toward the wrists.

Finally she says to me, "The wrists. Such a source of energy."

She drops my hands and picks up a new deck of tarot cards, the goddess tarot cards I had noticed earlier spread across the side table. The images are powerful, but gentle, their beauty illuminated by ornate details and colors. I'm drawn to them, have been since I entered the room.

Linnea shuffles the cards and lays three of them out for me, picks them up, and shuffles them again. Lays them out one more time.

"What happened?" I ask her. "Was something wrong the first time?"

"No."

"What, then?"

"Sometimes the cards call you to reshuffle. That's all."

"Should I ask you something? You know, something I want to know about?" She doesn't answer me right away, so I press on. "For the reading, I mean?"

"It doesn't really work that way," she says. "Besides, you don't need to ask me anything. I'll read what the cards tell us. I'll tell you what they say." She eyes me then. "You are ready, aren't you?" she asks, a hint of suspicion creeping into her voice.

Quietly, sheepishly, like a child struggling to overcome the embarrassment of a punishment I'd earned, I shrink back in the white wicker chair. Miss Linnea studies the cards for a while in silence. Then, without meeting my eyes, she says to me, "I am sorry for your loss."

I clear my throat. "The cards tell you *that*? But how could they possibly—"

"No," she interrupts, saving me from further embarrassment. She lifts her heavily made up eyes from the cards to meet my own. "Anna told me. And I read the papers, too. I was very sorry for your loss. It must not have been easy."

I swallow hard the lump that rises in my throat. I feel Anna's eyes resting on my back.

"No," I say. "It was not easy."

There are three cards lying on the table between us when she starts the reading. I say to her, "Is there a reason you've only chosen three cards? Not run a bunch out like you did for Anna?" I shift in my chair and sneak a glance at my friend, who is also studying my cards, sitting high in her chair to read them over my left shoulder. I scoot my chair just slightly to the right, invite Anna closer to the table.

"This reading is called the Three Fates. It helps you gain insight into past, present, and future." Linnea points a dagger of a nail at each of the three cards in the order in which they are meant to represent my life, and I study the pictures, the artwork, on each of these cards as she goes by them.

"I'm not so sure I need to relive the past," I say, smirking. Then am instantly sorry I have done so when I see her frown disapprovingly.

She ignores me and starts anyway. "The card on the left is the ace of swords. This card most often represents the mind. Brilliant thoughts or nightmares. Some people say that those who draw the ace of swords don't know the strength of their own mind, aren't aware of its power, what they are capable of. Others say they're just afraid to recognize it."

I run my hand over the card and reach to touch it, pick it up, glancing at Miss Linnea all the while, watching what it is she is saying to me, absorbed by the power of her reading.

She continues. "The middle card, the queen of coins." She stops to adjust her glasses, take a drink from the large plastic tumbler that sits on a flowered coaster on the table next to her chair. She crosses her hands in her lap, clips her nails against one another in a swift motion that sends a shiver down my spine. "The queen of coins represents a steadfast person, a domestic, someone who is able to provide shelter and comfort to those who would seek it. This could be you. Of course, it could be someone around you, someone you need right now. My sense is that they will offer you qualities of sensibility, maturity, things you may need in your life right now. Some stability, perhaps."

She sees I'm confused, can read it perhaps on my gaping face. She says to me, "I'd recommend you not try to figure it out or piece it together. It doesn't often work that way. Sometimes it won't be clear to you until much later. Much later from now."

Then she carries on. "The right card, the hanged man." She pauses a moment too long, leaves me a space to fill.

"This one scares me a bit." I study the card, the simple but frightening details of the hanged man, tied by one foot, hanging by a cross, his hands bound at his middle. Certainly it can't be good news.

"Yes, the hanged man frightens many, I'd say. Nothing to him, actually. He's peaceful, not suffering. And remember, this card represents elements of your future."

"I think that's what scares me."

"It shouldn't. The hanged man gave up what he knew about this world, climbed up in the tree on his own, proclaimed his own fate. Some think he's neither here nor there, this world or that, but can see, for the first time, clearly into both, as if he's hanging between the mundane world and the spiritual world. Connections he's never understood before, mysteries he's never solved, are finally made for him."

Linnea stops again to take another drink from the bottomless tumbler. Her voice is creaky, authentic, rattled by too many cigarettes and late-night readings. Her eyes are tired and there are more lines in her face than there will be candles on her next birthday cake. She wants me to believe, so she takes my hand, the one resting at the edge of the table, and cradles it in both of her own, holding it closer to her side of the table and forcing me to move in to her. "The hanged man spends much time hanging, nine days, actually. It's not the time he spends hanging that's important. It's what he does with this when he retreats from the cross, comes down with the realization of where he has been."

My hand falls asleep and runs cold.

"Things float, time stands still for the hanged man. He is suspended, and in doing so has sacrificed his position for knowledge, illumination. Sometimes it is vital to make these sacrifices in order to find solutions, in order to bring about change. One thing is certain, Ally, once you've made these, once you've been the hanged man, you never see things quite the same."

When she is done speaking I realize my head is nodding in agreement, bobbing up and down in rhythm with her voice. She studies my eyes deeply, looking for a sense that she has won me over. I do not disappoint her but she lets go of my hand finally, pats the palm slightly, and I pull it back to the safety of my own lap.

She picks up the oversized, well-worn cards, shuffles them back into the deck before laying them flat in a tall pile on the table, then lights a cigarette, blowing the blue smoke away from Anna and me. I lean against the back of my chair, my lips tight together, Anna by my side.

"You wanted to ask me something. Before, when I was getting ready to do your reading. Is there something specific you need to know?"

I long to ask her about Michael, but don't. I'm not interested in steering the fate of the relationship one way or another, nor do I want to surrender to a barrage of questions from Anna over margaritas. I'm motionless in the chair, searching for a way to ask her about Lydia without divulging her pregnancy, the news I've already shared with Michael, have yet to share with Anna.

"My daughter, my oldest daughter, Lydia. She's going through some pretty significant changes in her life. Can you tell me how these will resolve themselves? And how they'll affect Lydia in the long run? Will she be okay with everything?"

Linnea takes a long drag on her cigarette and holds the poison in her lungs before blowing the smoke above her head in a long, whispery exhale. She shuffles the cards one more time, holds them in the single pile in the palm of her left hand before spreading them face down across the table. The cards are so large they stretch from the tip of her middle finger to the base of the palm of her hand, the matching intricate red detail of the backs of each card lying one on top of the other. "Draw one card and place it on the table face up."

I draw the empress.

Linnea takes a final drag on her cigarette and blows the smoke toward the floor of the sunroom before stubbing out what's left, leaving it slightly smoldering in the ashtray on her side table. "The empress," she says as if I've failed to notice. She eyes me mystically.

"I don't suppose you want to tell me what's going on with Lydia?"

"No. Not really." I'm aloof, but not rude. And Linnea senses that I'm protecting my daughter.

"She's going through quite a change. The empress, the mothering card. It will take quite a while to nurture what lies within her, the changes she's undertaking. But fear not, she understands what's happened, is aware of its significance, even at her young age. And she's not as unprepared as you might think. With time, and the decisions she makes, the decisions you must *allow* her to make, she'll be fine with it."

Linnea continues to look deep into my eyes. I'm transfixed on her voice, so much so that I don't notice the tears running down my cheeks until she reaches for the Kleenex box on the side table and offers me one. I take it and blot at my cheeks.

"The strange thing, Allyson, is that I'm not convinced this card was drawn on your daughter's behalf as much as it may have been drawn on your own behalf. You see, sometimes we have a tendency to smother the problem, to want to solve it ourselves, to turn it over and work it until we find the exact right solution. There's no solution to Lydia's predicament. Only choices. She'll have to make them. You can't make them for her. You understand that, don't you? It's imperative that you do."

The empress's gown is decorated with pomegranates, her crown circled with stars. I nod my head. "But, but she needs me so much right now. She's barely turned fifteen. Certainly I have to be the adult in this situation. She can't possibly make the decisions she needs to make on her own."

"You must understand that plants can die from overwatering. Does this make sense to you?"

I study her eyes boring into my own. "But I just know she's going to need my help on this. There's just no other—"

"There are plenty of ways, Allyson. Plenty of decisions to be made. Make sure you know which ones are yours and which ones are your daughter's. That's what I'm telling you." She says this sternly, fiercely, gathering up her cards and lighting another cigarette before she rises from the chair and swoops, in a haze of blue smoke, from the room.

22

I'm still reeling from my reading when Anna and I start off for the cantina in her Volvo and my cell phone rings.

"Tell me you can do dinner," Michael starts, a sense of weariness teamed with excitement running through his voice.

"I can do dessert. But not until later." I'm staring out the window, wrestling with the contents of my bag and searching for a mint to break the pasty, dry taste in my mouth.

"That'll work. Where are you?" he asks.

"Just leaving the psychic."

Michael groans on the other end of the phone, then laughs. "God, Al, that quack is not the answer to your problems."

"They're not problems, Michael. Challenges. Opportunities, maybe. But problems, no. Just ask Miss Linnea. For forty bucks she'll unearth your deepest, darkest secrets, too. And I'd like to be in the room for that. Hell, I'd even pay her to do the reading." And then, when I suddenly remember, I say to Anna, "Oh, Jesus, Anna, turn around. I forgot to pay her."

Anna waves me off. "I paid her. You think she'd let us out of there without your forty bucks? You can buy drinks." She smiles a crooked smile out of the corner of her mouth.

"Deal." I smile back at her and sink farther down into the soft leather. "Can I call you when we get home? We're off to toast our fortunes, and continue my birthday celebration, over a margarita at the cantina. Come to think of it, it may be two or three margaritas."

"Yeah, no problem. Have a good time. Call me later and let me know what you're in the mood for."

"Why don't you just meet me at the house around nine? Bring something wickedly chocolate. I'm in the mood to be bad."

"Um, okay, that sounds tempting," he says to me. "How wicked?"

"You'll know."

I hang up and divert Anna with a question about her reading before she can ask me about my own, or about the wickedly chocolate thing I might share with Michael later.

"What's with John's job? Is everything okay?"

"Fine, fine. You know, Linnea just balances me, reminds me of what's important, that I'm not the one doing the job, that it's his stress, his day, his road. It's either her or a therapist. She's far more interesting, and much cheaper. Forty bucks is nothing. Besides, Ally, c'mon, don't you think she's the least bit fun? It's always an adventure with that woman. I go just for the social aspects."

"Okay, okay, I'll give you that. She's nearly as good as an episode of *Oprah* with some hot guest like Sting or Springsteen. Almost. Not quite."

The cantina is busier than we'd have expected for four thirty on a Monday afternoon. Men in gray pin-striped business suits, ties askew, line the bar drinking icy Modelos and cheering on a Red Sox game. We move to the other side of the bar, find an empty round table, and flag down a waitress. Anna orders margaritas for the both of us, hers blended; mine on the rocks, no salt and with a twist of lime. Our waitress, a college girl on summer break, her toenails painted a fire-red orange and adorned with small daisy appliqués, teeters off in platform Dr. Scholl's. We watch the overaged baseball fans watch her cross the room, lean over the bar, and put in our order with the bartender.

Anna starts in right away. "Okay, give me the lowdown on the beach. Did Lady Barbara behave herself?" She picks a chip from the basket, breaks it in two, and dips one half in the blue-painted bowl of salsa in front of us.

"Oh yeah, a regular saint. I still don't think the girls had forgiven me for making them go. And they were bound and determined to make sure I knew it. Becca read, day in and day out. Couldn't get her nose out of a book, couldn't engage her in any sort of conversation. Uh-uh, forget it. Lydia sulked. But it's what Lydia does best, so at least she was good at it. And shit, it rained. Man, did it rain, as if the gods were shedding their tears on us in pity. "

"Lovely time. Sorry I missed it," Anna says just as Flame-painted-toenail Girl arrives with our drinks, frosty in heavy mugs made for slurping, rather than sipping at, your margarita. The waitress leaves a receipt in front of us, and Anna's annoyed. "Um, miss, you can take this back," she says without looking up, as she hands the waitress the paper receipt and her gold American Express card. "And open a tab."

"Hey, I thought I was getting drinks," I protest.

She waves me off. "Birthday girl, you just sit back and enjoy that margarita. Here's to being home," she says. "To your freedom and independence for a week." With that she raises her mug and we knock them together heartily. "Happy birthday, Ally. You look fabulous, you know. No worse for wear. Even, dare I say, relaxed a little? Somehow I think it has less to do with the week you spent at the beach and more to do with the dinner you had in Boston last night."

I take a long swallow of my margarita; feel the splash of Grand Marnier laced along the top of the glass warm me. It's turned to a gorgeous day, clear skies and just a hint of breeze that helps circulate the fans that are spinning gently down from the ceiling of the bar. There's a light hum of activity in the bar interrupted on occasion by a great spill of cheer and clapping, we suppose, when the Red Sox do something that agrees with the crowd.

She starts in again before I can answer her. "Okay. Spill it," she says. "Dinner at Biba. Dessert tonight. Just what does your week of freedom and independence have in store for you?" Anna eyes me under an arched eyebrow. "What's the story with Michael? Besides, of course, that he's been in your life forever, and is probably more comfortable than that pair of ratty old purple pajamas you have."

"Hey, leave my purple pajamas out of this. They're sacred. Oh God, I don't know, Anna. I have no idea. None whatsoever. You're right. So familiar but so not familiar. Not like this, not in this territory, or whatever it is someone might call it. But Jesus. I mean, c'mon, Anna, he was Patrick's best friend. What am I thinking? What possible good thing could come out of this? I don't know what to do with him. I really, really don't. He's tempting, he's so damn tempting. And God, it feels so good to have someone look at me. Even Michael. Even Michael, who we know would rather be at a bar with a twenty-two-year-old than sitting at home with me eating dessert in front of the television. God, what could he possibly find attractive in me, Anna? Really, what in God's name could he possibly find interesting?"

"Um, hello, Ally? Excuse me, but hot property sitting here. Beautiful babe of a woman sitting right here in front of me. Don't you dare sell yourself short. And okay, enough with the best friend thing. Yeah, okay, so he was Patrick's best friend. He's probably your best friend, too. Present company excluded, of course." She flips her shoulder-length jet-black hair over her left shoulder and helps herself to another chip, dips this one in the guacamole, and takes a bite. She points a finger at me before she goes on. "Don't even think you don't deserve this, whatever this is. Just a little bit of fun with someone you have known all your life? Come on, whatever it is, whatever it might become, you, my friend, deserve to smile even now. Especially now. If he makes you smile, what's so bad?"

"Yeah, yeah, okay. My friend, too, and you're right, he makes me smile." I balance cautiously on the stool, swing my feet back and forth, and stare at the floor like an uncomfortable teen with a schoolgirl crush. "But, Anna, let me remind you once again who we're talking about. It's Michael. I mean, *Michael*. You know, Friday night date with whoever he can find at the bar. Living the good life. Checking his dates' ID to make sure they can actually get into the bar. *Michael*."

"What's so bad? You said it yourself, you've known him forever. You know who we're talking about, the good and the bad. I'm certainly not here to judge you. Like I said, I like seeing you smile for the first time in months, maybe even longer. Lights your face up in a nice way. Makes you kinda giddy. You deserve that, Al."

I'm fingering my margarita glass, running my middle finger up and down the frost that has accumulated on the side of the mug, and blushing. Blushing a furious glow that I can tell has settled across my neck and inched its way up into my cheeks. I try, unsuccessfully, to stifle just the smile Anna is talking about and giggle under my breath.

"Still, I don't know. I don't know what to do with him. It's ridiculous, really. Where do you go with something like this? It goes anywhere bad and I'm out my best friend and the person who changes my lightbulbs. I can't stand to think of my life without him, Anna. What if one of us does something that puts us in a place we can't get out of? What then?"

"It goes anywhere good and you're ten steps ahead of the rest of us. You *know* him," she says. "What's so bad about that?"

"It hasn't *gone* anywhere yet. Let's not get ahead of our skis. I don't think either of us has a clue about what's next. No flipping idea. I'm telling you, we are in uncharted waters and either one of us could bail out at any minute." My stomach is turning flips even as I sit here. I grip the thick mug and lock my hands around it to keep them from shaking.

"Sounds like it will require another trip to Miss Linnea. I'm sure she'd love to have you back. You grew on her this time. Got her locked up tight. Psychics like regulars, you know. I read once that they like to follow your life."

I munch on a chip and run my hands over my skirt to smooth out the wrinkles. "That gives me the creeps, Anna. I don't want

Miss Linnea with her two doors and ten decks of tarot cards studying up on me, reading my cards every night and figuring out what's wrong with me before I even know it. God, I don't know how you stand the woman. She's bizarre."

"She's not. Not really. She's just been doing it a long time. She's good at it, don't you think?"

"Um, I'm not convinced she knows a nut from a nut. And you know, she never answered anything, never let me ask her a damn question. Just laid those cards out there and spouted off some stuff. Sends shivers up your spine, but c'mon, you think she has a clue about what she's pulling out of her ass?"

"Look, Ally, what I can tell you is this. Linnea tells me things I don't realize until much later. I think I'm watching out for them, expecting them, even waiting for them. But even her readings leave me unprepared. No one knows what's coming. It's just coming, straight down the path to us. You can't duck, you can't step off the path. You think you might take another path, follow some different road you're meant to take, but it won't matter. It's just gonna be there. She just keeps me straight, that's all." Then she pauses, laughs at herself and her supposed seriousness. "Besides," she finishes, "what better way to screw off for the afternoon and drop forty bucks?"

Another margarita and a few appetizers later and we've killed the early part of the evening. We're punchy from giggling when Anna calls it quits and we drive the few miles, windows down and wind whipping our hair around, back to the house. I hug her warmly in the driveway and plant a kiss on her cheek, thanking her for such a wonderful afternoon. I've time enough for a bath. I take three magazines and the portable phone with me, and once the scalding water has filled the tub, bubbles spilling over, I make a call to the girls.

Lady Barbara answers, first ring. "We were wondering if you'd call tonight," she says in an accusatory tone even though, when I crane my neck to read the time on the clock in my room, it's only 7:52.

"Of course." I steer her away from throwing me off, rein the conversation my way before she can ask me too many questions, or keep me talking long enough to figure out that I've had three margaritas. "Girls around? How are they today?"

"I'm worried about Becca," Barbara says. "The girl reads more than I can stand. Read, read, read. Isn't there anything else in her life, dear? She should really get out, don't you think? There is more to life than burying her nose in another book. She's missing so much."

I stifle a laugh, thinking about Barbara's unfounded worry about Becca's voracious appetite for reading. "Well, I'd have expected Bec to spend a good time reading, broken arm and all. I suppose we should cut her a bit of slack, don't you think? I mean she could be out on the street corner, you know."

"Allyson, I hardly think that would be appropriate, she is *only* eleven, you know."

I sigh into the phone, just loud enough so that she hears my voice catch. "Yes, Barbara, I know. May I speak to one of the girls? Please?" I hear her set down the receiver, her gardening clogs clip-clopping on the ceramic tile kitchen floor, until I hear her call each of the girls' names.

Lydia comes on the phone first. "Hi, Mom, how was your day? What'dya do? Aren't you bored without us? Maybe we should come home early?" Lydia launches the questions into the phone one after the other, leaving only a breath in between, not nearly enough for an answer.

When she finally pauses, I say, "Very funny, Lyd. I'm fine. Surviving without you. I know, I know, it's a miracle, huh? I'm just back from dinner with Anna. She says hello."

"Have you, um, by chance, seen Eric?" I hear her whisper into the phone.

"No." I've enjoyed the evening where Lydia's problems weren't the first topic of discussion, and I'm in no mood to discuss them now. All I want is to check in so I can enjoy the bath, dissolve myself into the bubbles.

"Okay, well, just in case you see him, you know around the block or something, can you let him know I want to talk to him?"

She pauses and I wait patiently for her to finish. "He won't talk to me is all, when I call him," she says, with a gulping sob under her breath she barely gets out.

"Lyd? Did you tell him about the baby?" My voice is soft; I'm hoping Barbara is out of earshot.

I hear her well up, sniff, and sigh on the other end of the phone. "I tried. I just had to know what he would think."

"God, Lyd, not on the phone. Oh, honey, not the brightest decision," I say to her, wondering what state she's left him in. "Okay, what's done is done," I say, committing to memory the phrase I seem to be most overusing lately. "You're home in a few days. We'll deal with it then."

I hear Becca's voice trail in. Lydia must have handed her the phone because Becca comes on and says to me, "God, Mom, Lydia is so moody. She's driving me crazy. She doesn't want to do anything but sit around and listen to music. All she does is lie around on the couch all day."

I settle myself back in the bathtub, brace my body with my toes at the end of the tub, and take a sip of the Pelegrino I've brought with me.

"Bec," I say, "cut your sister some slack this week, okay? Just let her be and spend some time doing your own thing. How's Grandma? Everything okay? You doing anything fun?"

"Yeah, Mom, it's great, just great." Her voiced is laced with sarcasm, but I let it go.

"How's the arm, Bec? Any problems?"

"I think I have about a pound of sand in this stupid cast, that's all. And I'm going to have the worst tan line ever, Mom. I mean ever."

"Yeah, but when all that sand comes out and the tan line shows itself, guess what that means?"

"The cast will be off!" we say in unison.

23

Michael brings one gigantic chocolate éclair wrapped in a white box with a purple satin bow. He's been to Sweet Obsession, a coffeehouse and dessert bar on the west side of town frequented late summer nights by college and high school kids who start drinking coffee and smoking cigarettes too early in their lives. In his charcoal business suit and tie I imagine he was quite a standout. He's holding the bakery box in one hand, a duffel bag slung over the opposite shoulder, when I answer the front door in black shorts and a T-shirt, my hair piled up into a baseball hat.

"Jesus, Michael, what will the neighbors say?" I chide him when I swing open the door, take the white box from his hand, laughing to let him know that I'm only half serious.

He looks guiltily at the bag. "It's my gym clothes, Al. It's all I had in the car. I never went home from the office. I thought I could change here. If that's okay?" He asks this as a question and I realize I've embarrassed him before he even sets foot in the door. There is an awkward bit of silence between us as he stands, feet firmly planted, on the front mat.

"Michael, I'm kidding. Of course you can change here. Put on whatever the hell you want." I step aside to let him into the entryway and he steps forward cautiously, examining the house as if it were a place he'd never been.

I shut the door and make my way down the hall, leaving him to set his bag down on the hardwood floor and follow me. I feel his eyes on my backside run the distance, the length of my body, my bare legs. Without turning, I say to him, "I won't do this with you, Michael. The awkward thing. Pull it together, for crying out loud."

I hear him laugh, his well-worn wing tips scraping against the soft cedar of the floor. "Fine, fine," he says. "Can we eat that thing? You're going to need a knife and fork. Two forks, if you please. I skipped dinner. I'm starving."

I retrieve the silverware and offer Michael a beer. "Are you crazy?" he says to me. "Got any milk?"

"Of course."

"Tall glass. Don't skimp on that." He pulls back the box top to reveal an enormous, perfect éclair, stiffly whipped Bavarian cream still standing at attention under the weight of the drizzled chocolate-topped pastry. From the family room drifts the sounds of Mark Knopfler's "Golden Heart." We sit on the countertop like two kids, each with a large tumbler of milk and the dessert in between us, eating right from the box. I imagine Lydia doing this, the tips of her fingers scooping up the remaining chocolate. I'm giddy and giggly as pastry flakes and melts into the roof of my mouth.

"Can I fix you something?" I ask him. "Something besides this monstrosity for dinner? You must be hungry, no?"

We've nearly finished the éclair; Michael is scraping the last of the pastry off the parchment paper that lines the bottom of the box. "Uh-uh. But I'll take a glass of wine, if you've got one. White, preferably. It's too damn hot for red tonight."

"Okay. Go change. Put some shorts on or something and we'll sit outside, if you can stand the bugs. There are some citronella candles on the top shelf of the first cabinet in the garage. Let's light those and the fire pit." I hop down from the countertop, toss the empty box into the garbage and the forks into the sink, and reach in the glass cabinets for two wineglasses.

Michael's halfway down the hall when I hear him ask me, "Is the hot tub on?"

"Mmm-hmm, yep."

After Patrick's death, I learned how to light the fire pit. It's something I rarely did when he was alive, a duty he'd automatically assumed. It was not unlike other things I'd picked up. How to pull out the screens on the windows for washing. Skim the pool for bugs. Unclog the trash compactor after Becca put too much spaghetti down it. Change the lightbulb in the garage door opener. It's not that I was incapable of any of this before; these were merely rituals Patrick had assumed on both our behalf.

Michael emerges from the house, barefoot and in blue nylon basketball shorts and a tank top. I'm sprawled on my favorite lounge chair in front of the lit fire, wineglass in my hand, one waiting for him on the table next to me. He takes the glass, tips it to me silently in the soft summer air, and settles himself a few feet away from me into a straight-back chair at the table, just next to the fire. He looks uncomfortable to me, and I beckon him to come closer, pat the lounger next to me to invite him over.

He accepts my invitation but sits upright when he moves next to me.

"Michael, what's going on? C'mon, you've been here what, a million times. What's wrong with you tonight?" I sip at my wine, and wait for him to come to grips with whatever it is that's got him so goosed.

He sits with his elbows resting on his knees, his legs well tanned from weekends and practices on the soccer field. He meets my eyes with a hard stare, like he could go right through me if I'd let him. "I'm sorry," he says. And then he gets up again, and while I draw my legs up to my chest and hug them close to me for warmth even in the balmy night, he paces back and forth in front of me. When he stops and sits on the end of my chair, balancing himself on the cushion, he finally says to me, "I just so badly would like to kiss you. I just am wondering what you are going to do if I kiss you."

I don't say anything for a minute. Neither of us moves. We don't talk, don't reach for each other, don't exhale, no long swallows from the wineglasses. And then finally, I say to him, "Then why don't you find out?"

"I'm working on it, Ally. I'm working on it." He swirls the wine in his glass and moves away from me again, turning his back to me and staring up at the open sky.

"How long do you expect it will take before you have that worked out?" I ask him.

He laughs and sets his glass down on the stone, before he makes his way to the end of my chair and begins to rub the tops of my feet, right across my high arch and up underneath the balls of my feet. "Can I turn the music on out here?"

"Yes, of course."

I hear him fiddling with the stereo equipment and a moment later music softly fills the backyard, drips from the in-ground speakers planted throughout the landscaping. "Will you dance with me?" he says when he comes back, taking the steps two at a time.

I look at him like he's lost his mind, and laugh. "To this?" He's left the radio on a station playing seventies music and Evelyn Champagne King is blasting "Shame" from the speakers. "*You* want to boogie to *this*?" I lift myself up from the chair, ready to take him on.

"Yeah, whatever, just come dance with me."

Michael spins and twirls me across the flagstone, my hair shaking loose from underneath the baseball cap and falling into my face. We're both laughing and smiling, grinning wider than we know what to do with. We dance to this, then The Bee Gees' "Jive Talking," Hot Chocolate's "You Sexy Thing," and finally a marathon number to Don McLean's "American Pie" that leaves us both breathless before the DJ finally breaks in. I'm wide-eyed and shimmery in the night when Michael finally pulls me into an embrace, wraps his arms around the low part of my back, and begins to kiss me long and slow. I'm certain he must be holding the both of us up.

He slides his tongue along the top inside of my teeth as if he's licking his own lips, taking in something very sweet. He pulls my baseball cap off, tosses it onto the chair, and I follow it with my eyes, watch it land on the cushion. He brushes the hair back from my face. I'm without makeup, have not reapplied anything but moisturizer and a layer of clear lip-gloss. Regardless, when he is satisfied with how he has pushed my hair back from my face, he kisses me quick on the lips, more comfortable now in his own skin and with me still laced within his arms.

When he stops, I don't say anything. I just sort of stand there, not sure what to do next, what to think next.

He says to me, "Are you all right? Ally, are you okay?"

I choke down the butterflies swarming in my stomach and stand there staring at him, dumbfounded. "Hmm? Um, yeah. Yes, yes, I'm fine."

"Are you sure?"

"Yes. Fine. Michael, what are we doing?" Neither one of us has an answer.

"I'd like to go hot-tubbing with you. That's what I think we should do."

"Do you have your suit?" I ask him, not entirely certain I won't go in with him if he doesn't.

He releases me from his grip, steps back, and throws his arms open wide. "You're looking at it."

I size him up, the broad shoulders and small waist, the long legs and bony knees sticking out from under his long nylon shorts, his bare feet and long toes. "That'll do, I suppose. Let me change."

"I'm not waiting on you, Allyson." He picks up his wineglass and begins to pull off the light blue and navy blue North Carolina tank top he's wearing. I watch him do this as I have a thousand times, know the exact markings of his chest, the faint scar at his right kidney where part of it was removed when he was very young, the dark chest hair that runs the length of his sternum and disappears in a line into the front of his shorts.

* * *

Patrick's scent has long dissipated, though his clothes still hang in the closet, his shoes still line the built-in shelves. I'm in and out of the closet quickly, purposefully taking no notice of them, and reach in my second dresser drawer to retrieve a one-piece black terry bathing suit that's cut in all the right places. I stop at the vanity to pull my hair back into a ponytail, then wrap it quickly into a twist and secure it with a large black comb.

Michael watches me as I cross the grass with two oversized white beach towels under my arm. I throw these on the deck close to the spa and let myself gently down into the water, clouds of steam rising up around me and hazing my view of him. We sit in silence for a few minutes, each of us with our heads back against the rim of the spa, jets beating on tired muscles.

"Al?"

"Hmm?" I open my eyes and splash some water up onto my face, wipe away the small beads of perspiration that have started there. As much as I love a hot bath, I'm not long for hot tubs; I'll be in the pool in minutes. Either that or sitting up on the side, legs dangling in the water below, steam rising off my body in the night air.

"Can I ask you about Lydia?" He opens his eyes then and watches me from across the water.

It wasn't where I thought he was going and I'm not entirely entertained by the idea of a conversation about Lydia, but I agree anyway. "Of course. I was wondering, actually, if you were going to." I pause and wait for him to ask me a question. When he doesn't right away, I start again. "Michael, you know that I promised Lydia I wouldn't tell anyone about all this just yet. I asked her not to say anything to Barbara, of course. Good God, could you imagine? Anyway, you're not to know. I don't want you to say anything to her, okay?"

"Of course. I understand. But, Al, I imagine Barbara's going to find out sooner or later, don't you think?"

"I guess that depends."

"On what?"

"On what Lydia decides to do. I'm not entirely sure she's

going to have this baby. We still haven't decided if it's a go or not. In which case, Barbara won't know." I look at him square in the eyes and repeat very clearly what I've just said for his benefit. "In which case, Michael, Barbara won't know. You have to promise me that."

"Of course. God, Ally, of course. I wouldn't do that to you, or to Lyd. You should know that."

"I do, Michael. I know."

The sound of the jets cuts through the silent yard. "So is that what you think she should do, Al? End all this?"

I float my way over to sit closer to him on the bench. The water is hot, just over a hundred degrees. "Oh God, Michael, that's a really, really hard question."

"Why?"

"Oh, just that everything about it is wrong. If I say yes, that I want this problem to go away, what kind of mother does that make me, what kind of woman? If I say no, same question." He's patient, doesn't push. Finally, I say to him, "Yes, Michael, I'd like this whole damn thing to be behind us. We don't need this. I want it to go away. Selfishly, I want it to just *go away*."

"How's she doing? I mean, really? Does she have any clue about what this is, what it means? Any whatsoever?"

"How much can you know, how much can you understand, when you are fifteen?"

"So what then, I mean if she won't end the pregnancy, what do you do then? Are you up for raising another baby? I mean it's not like Lydia's going to be able to do it, really."

"No, she's not. She's nowhere near prepared."

"So, would you? Could you? Raise another child?"

From somewhere a scoff escapes me. "Michael, I have turned that question around in my head every which way from here to the end of time. I've imagined being in this house with the girls and their friends, boyfriends, everything just nuts and a small toddler running around. It's not pretty, Michael."

"It has been done, Al. You could do it."

I reflect on what he's said. "I could, yes, I probably could. I'm just not sure about what that leaves us, about what kind of family we become. Don't get me wrong, Michael, I haven't completely knocked the idea out of the ballpark, and if Lydia wants to keep this baby, I guess it's what I've got."

He's quiet for a few minutes, then dips himself full under the water and comes up, shaking the water from the tips of his curly hair. He pulls himself out of the spa and dives into the pool, swimming the length and back before coming up for air.

"How's the water?"

"Excellent. Come in, swim with me." He's hanging on the side, his broad shoulders spread across three wide tiles.

"Michael?" I ask him as I approach the water, bend down to sit next to him, and drop myself into the side of the pool. "What are you thinking about all this? What do you think I should do? I'm dying to have someone talk me through it. Is there any logic in any of it? Anything at all?"

He turns and looks at me. We're very close, maybe a foot, foot and a half from each other. I have one hand up on the side, the other under the water against the wall, balancing my body out from me, horizontal to the bottom of the pool. I'm practicing my kicks, underwater frog legs moving up, in and out in a constant smooth motion.

"I don't know what to say to you about it. I'm not sure what I think about it. Or even if I get to think something about it."

"You're entitled to an opinion at least. And I want to know what that is, certainly. Of course I want to know what that is, Michael."

"What's she want to do, Al? Has she thought about it? 'Cause I think you should let Lyd make her decision about this, Ally. Even if it's not what you want. Even if it's counterintuitive to what you think she should do."

"Why? She's fifteen, she can barely decide what to have for breakfast. Isn't it still my job to make choices for her?"

"Not this one. Not this time."

"She wants to put the baby up for adoption, Michael. That's her choice. That's her great fix in this." I look at him sideways before turning away, filling my lungs, and swimming the distance of the pool underwater, away from him. Suddenly, I want to get away from him. When I come up for air, I don't open my eyes right away. In the deep end, I cling to the side of the pool, letting the water drip off my face, the back of my hair.

He swims to me. "Ally?" I hear him whisper, his face near mine. "Al? Please. Please don't be angry with me. I don't want you to be angry with me. That's why I asked you if you wanted my opinion, if you would care what I thought."

I fill my lungs again, and open my eyes, staring ahead at the ceramic tiles that line the side of the pool. He is very near me, his breath on my ear, my neck. I turn to look at him, and his eyes are pleading with me, hurt settling in like I've never seen before.

"I'm not angry with you. I'm not. I'm just so confused about all this. I just don't think Lydia can begin to comprehend all this, Michael. I don't think she has any idea about making a decision this monumental. I just really feel like that's still my job."

"Maybe it is," he acquiesces. "Maybe it is, babe. But adoption could be the exact right thing to do. Why not? You know most moms would go for an adoption if it were their daughter in this position. Most moms would be so grateful for the rational decision their daughter wanted to make, to do something mature and adult about the whole thing. God, isn't it supposed to be the fifteen-year-old who thinks she can raise this baby on her own? At least Lydia knows, she recognizes she can't do this, Al. You gotta give her that."

"God, Michael, she doesn't know shit." Anger floods my voice, choking in the deep part of my throat. "Yeah, okay, maybe she wants to try to be mature about this whole damn thing, but she never should have gotten here in the first place. Damn it, how did I miss this? How, how, how?"

"It doesn't matter, Al. It really doesn't. You can't change it now, you just gotta find the best thing for everyone involved. You know that."

"That's what I'm trying to do, Michael. It is. Honest to God, I don't want to be vicious about this. I don't want to force Lydia into something, make her take this responsibility on for the rest of her life, but damn it, she did that part. I'm trying to fix it. I'm really, really trying. Can't you see that?"

"Yes." He says this very quietly, his head turned away from me and staring skyward as if taking in all the stars in the night sky. "Yes, Ally, I know that's what you want to do."

We stay like this for a few minutes, both of us clinging to the side of the pool and silent. Finally he says to me, "Just think about it, okay? Think about her making a decision around this and how important that is for her."

"I just can't have her knowing all her life, wondering all the years ahead, about some child out there. I just can't. I'd rather do this myself, help her through this, so she never has to wonder about what-if. All those what-ifs add up to a long road, a really long road of guilt all your life."

"I don't know, Al. All those days of staring a child in the face, a baby you created but can't take care of, might be a fate worse than guilt. And what happens to Lydia then? How does she go on with her life?"

"I don't know, Michael. I just don't know." I swim the length of the pool again, a modified sidestroke, and jump back in the hot tub. When I'm settled against one of the jets, I say, "This baby is our family, you know. This baby belongs to us, don't you see that? Really, Michael . . ." I take a deep breath and hold it in my lungs until it burns. "Really, when it comes right down to it, I just don't know if I can say good-bye to more of our family this year. I just don't know if I can do it."

He doesn't say anything, not for a long while, so we sit together and let the silence settle over us.

Finally, I say to him, "Michael, can I ask you something?"

"Shoot."

"Did you know? I mean, did you have some sort of inkling about this?"

He takes the steps out of the pool, his shorts clinging to him and dripping in puddles around his feet, and comes to sit by the side of the hot tub, dropping his legs into the steaming water. "Yeah, I had an idea about it."

"When? I mean I thought maybe you were trying to tell me something the day of Lydia's birthday. When you asked about her T-shirt and the sudden case of modesty. Was that it?"

"Before then, actually."

"When? When, Michael? And why didn't you say something to me?"

"The day Bec broke her elbow, actually. When you had me come pick Lyd up here, remember? Before I came to the hospital after the game."

"But, but I don't get it. . . ."

"I caught them, Al. Her and Eric. I caught them upstairs. In her room. It wasn't on purpose, of course. She just didn't answer the door when I knocked and I was so frantic to find her and get to the hospital that I just used my key to come in. She was coming out of her room, sort of adjusting the top and skirt she had on. He followed her out."

"Michael?" I whispered. "Why didn't you say anything to me? How could you keep that from me?"

"Lydia asked for my confidence," he said. "She just asked me straight up and I was so taken aback by the whole thing that I agreed to it. I never should have, I know that. I never should have kept that from you."

I sit stunned into silence for a minute. He's shaken, that's obvious. Finally, I say to him, "You're right, you shouldn't have kept that from me. But the damage was already done by then. It wouldn't have mattered anyway."

"No."

He takes my hand then and holds it in both of his, rubbing the palm with his thumb and intertwining his fingers with mine, back and forth, as if he can't sit still. "How can I help you with this, Al? 'Cause you know what? This is going to rock your world. Maybe even worse than Lydia."

The look of concern, emotion that runs deep within him, floods to the surface.

I say, "You sound like Miss Linnea."

"How so?"

"I mean about the effect of this on me. Miss Linnea's convinced I'll play a vital role in it. That I'll need to remember where my place in this ends and Lydia's begins."

"Hmmm, maybe not such a quack after all."

"I don't know how you help with this, Michael, I really don't. You can't fix it," I say, gently, remembering the argument we'd had. "But if you can do anything, anything at all, it would be to stand right here next to me until I figure out what's next. Hold me up when I stumble. Fuck, walk me through it. Walk right here next to me through it."

"Okay. That I can do. Just promise me you'll think about Lydia, okay? And what she wants in this, what she feels called to do. Don't disregard her opinion about it, Al. She has to have some control over this, too. You know that, right?"

"I know. I know she's trying to make the best decision for everyone. I know that the baby should be put up for adoption. I know all this. I'm just, I'm just having . . ." I stammer, trying to find the right words to help him understand. "I'm just having such a hard time trying to figure out how I'll support her when she'll be doing something I couldn't do myself." I can feel the tears burning behind my eyes, mixed with the chlorine and chemicals, my eyes ready to explode at any moment.

"Sweets?" he whispers.

The warm tears are running down my face now, dropping like raindrops into the water. I don't cry gracefully and Michael knows this, has ribbed me about it for years. But not tonight. Tonight he sits next to me, keeps whispering over and over again into my ear that things will be fine, hushing me in great giant soothing tones, working me over and bringing me back with the tiniest, sweetest little kisses on my cheek.

24

I ask Michael to stay. Just like that, it rolls right out of my mouth without any premeditated thought.

"Just stay with me tonight. Please," I say to him when a silence falls between us.

We've moved inside. Michael's wrapped in a towel at his waist; I'm clutching mine tight in both hands, wrapped around my body, like a child clinging to her favorite blanket.

Michael's back is to me when I say this; I can't see the expression on his face. He's reaching into the refrigerator for bottled water and when he turns and hands me mine, all he says is, "Are you sure?"

"Yeah. Sarah's gone, right?"

"Yep."

"Then, yes. Please. I don't care where you sleep, you can have your pick of rooms. I'm just not ready for you to go home and I don't want to be here alone."

"I've got to go to work in the morning. I've got a breakfast meeting at eight."

"Okay."

We're staring each other down, each of us daring the other to take an out. Neither of us makes a move.

"You running in the morning?" he asks me, twisting off the cap on his bottle and taking a long swig.

"Probably." I'm still standing on the large square kitchen tile floor, towel wrapped tight around me, and shivering now.

"Okay. I've got to be out of here by six so I can make it home, shower, change. You promise me you'll get up and run, I'll stay."

"Fine." I start down the hall toward the stairs. "I'm showering. Do you need anything?" He's watching me from behind. I can feel his eyes on my back, and when I turn to see if he does, he's braced against the countertop, arms crossed against his chest and smiling.

"Nope. I'll shower down here." He pauses then before saying, "In the *guest room*."

I laugh, my voice trailing after me as I take the stairs.

When I reappear, my hair combed back and wet against the back of my sweatshirt, Michael's watching CNN, stretched lengthwise on the soft leather sofa. He's so long his feet touch the armrest on the far side of the couch. I stand under the arched doorway separating the family room from the hallway, watch him set intently on the television, until my stare and the shuffle from my slippered feet make him turn and look at me.

"Hey."

"Hi."

"Do you want to watch something with me?" He starts to sit up and change his position on the sofa.

"Don't," I say, holding up a hand to him. "Don't move. You look so comfortable. Can I come lie with you?" I shut the overhead light off, leaving a reading lamp on so that it's not completely dark when I stumble over to him.

He moves over to make his body as slim as it can be on the couch, leaves a spot for me, and I walk over and fold myself into the space he's left. We fit together nicely, comfortably. He flips through the channels before turning the television off altogether.

"You don't mind, do you?"

"Uh-uh."

I kick off my slippers and run my feet, soft from lotion I've worked into them after my shower, in between his shins, where they settle.

When I wake it's near two. The house is still, my neck tight and cramped from lying in the nest of Michael's elbow, his arm supporting my head. I'm cold; the far family room windows are still craned open and a much cooler breeze has kicked up some-time during the night. I pull myself up vertically and shake Michael at the shoulder, whisper his name a few times to bring him back from the dream he's having.

He wakes with a start, opens both his eyes, and sucks the air in fiercely.

"I'm sorry," I murmur. "I can't sleep here anymore. I'm going up to bed. Do you want to stay here, or come up with me?" I stretch, open my arms, and yawn widely.

"Mmmm." He straightens his legs, pushes his arms high above his head, then down at his sides, in a long stretch that makes his whole body shudder. I offer him my hand, help him up from the couch.

"I feel like a teenager who fell asleep on a date." I'm shuffling toward my room, slipping my feet back into my well-worn slip-pers and trying not to trip as I do so.

"Al?" he says from behind me. "Where do you want me?"

"Michael, I'm so exhausted, I swear I don't care. Sleep wherever you want, but . . ." I stop to take him in and I see he's standing firm on both his feet, stuck in place and waiting on my every word. I stop and reconsider what I'll say to him. "Forget it, Michael. Come on. Just come up with me. It's fine. You'll sleep better in my bed than Becca's. And Lydia's left her room a mess. I've vowed not to clean it up. You don't want to either. And I don't know if there are sheets on the bed down here. Come on, really, it's fine." He's farther away from me now, but I reach my hand out to him any-way. He steps toward me, takes my hand, and holds it in his.

He lets me lead him to my bedroom and watches when I pull back the comforter and throw the small square pillows onto the reading chair on my side of the room. I pull the sweatshirt over my head, let it fall to the floor without glancing at it again. I'm dead tired, a horrible middle-of-the-night person. Completely out of sorts and drugged.

I'm standing in an old pair of grungy black sweats, holes just starting at the crotch, and the palest pink T-shirt; no bra. I feel the weight of my breasts stretch against the shirt, know my nipples are erect. I watch the expression on Michael's face change when he looks at me, wonders again if he has the right to be here in the room with me.

I yawn fully, gaping, and kill the light at the bedside table. My day seems so distant behind me, how many hours have passed since my morning run, my reading from Linnea, the margaritas? I'm floating into bed, lay my body down in between the crisp sheets and wait for Michael to do the same, to rest quietly next to me and drift off.

He doesn't. Instead, he stands in his sweats and ratty T-shirt, bare feet, and a smile I can feel through the pitch-dark room. He watches me cozy up to the pillow, prop my hands up under it, and murmur his name.

"Michael? Get in bed. Come lie down. If you don't hurry, I'll be asleep before you get here." I say this to him with the hint of a purr rattling in the back of my throat. I shut my eyes and wait for him, roll the comforter back for him so that he can see both the feather bed and the sheet, but also the bare strip of my stomach just where my shirt has rolled back and exposed my flat belly.

He finally indulges me, runs his hands through his hair for good measure, then folds his body into the bed. When I open my eyes, he's lying next to me. With the slim strip of moonlight that floods the room, I study his body, the space it takes up next to me, the shape it assumes, the rise and fall of his chest with the soft breathing I've come to recognize as his own. His scent.

I reach for his hand and trace his fingers until I lace my own within his.

Michael wakes me at six fifteen. The cloudless blue sky stretches into the room. I'm lying prone, drooling into the pillow, when he kisses me softly on the cheek and I can feel him brush the hair back from my face.

"Are you running?"

"Mmm-hmm. But not till later. What time is it?"

"Six fifteen. It's early. Go back to sleep."

"Mmm-hmm. Okay."

"Can I cook you dinner tonight?" he says.

I open my eyes, expect to find him standing over me, but he's not. He's eye-level, bent at the side of the bed and very close to my face.

"Yes. Of course." I smile at him, a half smile that makes him do the same. "Can I pick something up at the store?"

"No, I'll get it. Anything special you want?"

"Uh-uh." I shake my head, suddenly self-consciously aware of my tousled hair that was wet when I fell asleep and must now be standing every which way.

"Bye, sweets."

I lift a hand from the sheet, just barely, and whisk him away.

25

I had been dreading our first Christmas without Patrick. There was too much tradition in it. Too much familiarity. Christmas Eve dinner at Barbara's was almost too much, and I fought the panic even as I climbed the stairs to her front walk.

"Michael, what are you doing here? Good God, I had no idea."

I kissed him on the cheek and let him close the door behind me, take the packages from my arms. It had started snowing, but it was the wind that was biting through the Christmas Eve night, sending a chill through my bones, even through the long wool coat I wore.

"Miss Christmas Eve? Never."

"But you didn't tell me you'd be here. You never said anything when I saw you last week."

"But of course he's here, Allyson. Michael's family. It wouldn't be Christmas Eve without him. Ever. But especially this year." Barbara's words came at me like daggers. It had taken everything I had to be here, to come to her home our first Christmas without Patrick. I'd planned a trip, booked the tickets for a cruise. I'd wanted to take the girls away; I'd wanted to go somewhere where no one knew us. I'd wanted to forget about Christmas altogether.

Barbara had thrown a small fit when she heard.

"Take my girls away? But, Allyson, this is the first Christmas since Patrick died. You simply can't go on the road. I need you all here. Everyone needs you here."

"I just really think it would be much simpler if we went, Barbara. I think it'd be better for the girls, actually. It's going to be hard enough without their dad around. They don't need any more reminders."

"Nonsense. That's just foolish. The girls need their family around them."

"I am their family, Barbara."

"Well, then, we'll all go with you. I'll book the tickets right now. It'll be fun."

"No, no, really, that's not necessary."

"It's not about what's necessary, Allyson. It's about being together. All of us. The family."

"But, Barbara, I don't know that you are hearing me. We will be together. Our family. The girls and me. It's what I want this Christmas. It's the way I want us to spend it. Just the three of us. Surely you can understand that. . . ."

"No, Allyson, actually, I can't. Not at all."

She pouted then, threw herself into a great piercing silence that lasted a few days and was briefly interrupted by lobbying phone calls she placed to the girls, wedging them in between us like a doorstop.

"Mom, Grandma says we're going on a cruise for Christmas and that you don't want her coming with us."

"Mom, Grandma's feelings are hurt. She says the holidays aren't going to be the same without us this year."

In the end—which was by the end of the week—I'd canceled the cruise. I promised the girls we'd do it another time, but that Barbara was probably right; it was better to be with family this first year after their father had died.

Inside I was fuming. It had taken everything I had, including two scotches before we'd left the house, before I was ready to deal with Christmas Eve. Lady Barbara was like a purring cat; gone were the bouts of silence, the morose pouting and grievous frowns. She'd gotten her way. She kissed me briefly on the cheek, an air kiss of sorts, as she unburdened me of the spice cake I'd made. Michael unwrapped my scarf, helped me with my coat.

"Merry Christmas, Ally," he whispered in my ear.

I searched his eyes for strength. It was there; it was always there. He smiled, barely an upturn of his lips, but enough so that I knew he'd come for me, no one else. Let Barbara believe he was there for her, because this was his family. I had no doubt about what had brought him here tonight.

26

After Michael leaves I can't sleep. I try. I get up, pee, go back to bed, and pull the comforter up to my shoulder blades, decide I'm too warm, strip my bulky sweat bottoms off so I'm lying in just my panties, throw a leg outside the covers, toss from one side to the other. But nothing works and by seven I finally give up and reach for the remote control to turn on *The Today Show*. I can't think of the last time I had a morning like this: slow, quiet, alone.

I smooth the covers and prop myself up against the pillows, listen to the morning song of a bird settled on a branch outside my window. I'm lost within myself. Who am I? A woman with no husband, no children, in a house where I've been labeled with both. A woman who brought a man into her bed last night, not just any man, but a man she's known forever. A woman who was overtaken by everything manly about him but who doesn't know what he is in her own life or what to do with him. I shudder at the thought and pull the pillow Michael had slept on close to my chest; it is filled with his scent and I breathe it in deeply. I shudder, even in the warm morning, the sun flooding the windows and blanketing the room.

Everything about Michael scares me solid; much further than frightened, we're talking downright fear. I let my mind go to him, the new parts of him I have studied and learned so quickly. His swagger, his touch, I let myself go there. And just as quickly, come running right back over the line, deathly afraid of what I might find on the other side. I force myself to think of Michael as I have known him for so long: Patrick's best friend, the father of Becca's best friend, soccer coach, and even downright jerk of a playboy, always a little Betty on his arm, careless, thoughtless, self-centered at times. I force my mind to times when I haven't liked him very much, let it run the course until a sort of resentment fills me and I don't long for him so, balance regaining my senses.

It does not last long. I am a fool, I think, lying there in the morning light, stretching like a contented cat, a sedated smirk running across my lips. I let my mind run to a life with him, a place where he and I are together, where he and I are happy in a different place where things that have come before don't exist. In this fairy tale, my children do not exist; my husband never was, my life is someone else's. *Fool, fool.* I shake the cobwebs from my head, clear the fog.

I don't realize it until much later that afternoon, but I spent the day prepping. Like a girl on prom day, I'd done everything I could all day long to make myself feel more beautiful. A shower that had gone on for well past my usual ten minutes. A quick call to the club for a facial and a pedicure. A trip to the market where I bought wine, cheese, some fruit, nuts, a couple of candles. An hour where I sat reading, nothing in particular, and as I think back over it now, nothing I can remember. I'd lost myself all day, just gone. Like a song I couldn't shake, Michael had played in my mind.

When he opens the front door, arms laden with grocery bags, I am ready for him. I feel beautiful standing in nothing more than capri jeans and a red halter top, barefoot but with sculptured, perfectly polished cherry-colored toes, my hair pulled back off my face, just a light touch of makeup on my sun-kissed cheeks.

"Are you going to sit here while I cook? Just right there, up on the counter so I can watch you?" he asks me when he lays the bags of groceries on the table and drops the set of keys he's car-

rying in his mouth like a dog that has retrieved something important.

"Sure." I pull myself up on the counter, cross my legs, and let
them dangle off the side, and I feel exceptional. He comes to me,
wraps his arms at my waist, and pulls me to the very edge of the
countertop. "My God, you smell good, Ally."

"You like, huh?"

"Yep. Very much."

"What can I do? Let me chop or something." I reach into one
of the tall double-bagged grocery bags and start pulling out
onions, leeks, carrots, three avocados, a white butcher's-wrapped
package.

"Uh-uh. I just want you to sit there. Let me watch you while I
do this. Just sit there and talk to me, yes?" He takes a lemon from
me and grabs a small bottle of coriander out of one of my hands.

"Okay, fine. Sure, whatever you want. Can I fix you a beer at
least? Something?"

"Yep. That you can do." I let myself down from the countertop, open the oversized refrigerator door, and find two cold beers
in the shelf in the door. I twist the bottle caps off both of them
and hand Michael one. He takes his first swallow, long and thick,
and sets the bottle down near the faucet at the sink. I lean into
the countertop with my back, support myself, and run my hands
back and up through my hair. With a clip I've got in the pocket of
my jeans, I secure a mass of hair up into a wild-looking twist, un-
kempt and straggly but back off my face.

"How was your day? Did you do anything special?" Michael
asks me while he slices the leeks paper-thin at the cutting board,
his hands expertly moving up the stalk.

"Mmm, it was good. It was all about me. Weird in a wonderful
sort of way. I did nothing, really. Not much of anything at all."

"Not a bad vacation for being at home."

"My life's a vacation, Michael. What do I do, really?"

"Relax. Enjoy it. It's probably the first day you've had since
Lydia was born, the first real day, all to yourself. Am I right?"

I laugh. Michael is right. I can't remember a time like this when they'd all disappeared, Patrick, the girls, and left me alone to be by myself. No, surely Michael is right. I've been wife or mother, or wife and mother, for the greater part of forever, it seems. "You're right, Michael." I take another long swallow of the beer, cross my arms across my chest.

"It's not a bad thing, Al. It's okay. Really."

"Okay, okay. I'm not complaining." I shift my weight so that I'm up against Michael's back, my legs curved into the back of his knees, and begin to run my fingernails up and down the knit black golf shirt he's wearing. He continues to chop the carrots, small bite-size chunks, but he looks over his shoulder and smiles at me.

I reach into the refrigerator for the Brie, a small bowl of grapes, and a plastic container of olives I've bought earlier in the day at the market. I lay these out on a cornflower-blue serving platter and he fingers off a few of the grapes.

"Michael?" I start in on him, the sound of teasing creeping into my voice.

"Yes, my dove?"

I smile at this, an ironic half smile that sets my eyes to dancing. "How were you about being in my bed last night?"

This stops him chopping, and he reaches for a dish towel to wipe his hands. "I felt wonderful about it. Very at peace with it. Content." He diverts his attention to his chopping again, then adds the carrots to the tinfoil pouch of leeks, potatoes, and two-inch asparagus spears I know he's going to douse with olive oil and sauté on the grill. "Why? How did you feel about it?"

"I've been trying to figure that out all day. Good, I think. Really good. 'Content' might fit just perfectly. And I'm wondering about that, too. What's right about that, and what's not so right about that. I mean I think I've got a good feeling about it and I'm hoping it's right, but I don't know that it should be. Or that I should allow it to be? Do you understand what I'm saying? 'Cause I don't know that I'm doing a very good job explaining myself."

He rinses off the chef's knife he's been using. "Ally, what is it, exactly, you are trying to say to me?"

I get serious with him for a minute, sidle up next to him, and let his height shadow me while I try further to explain. "Look, Michael, I haven't had this for a long time. Not this . . ." I wave my hands around me to indicate the house, the kids, my life as it is here. "Not this stuff, but this." I wave my hands between the both of us. "I haven't had this kind of a thing in a long, long while. Something to make my heart take flight and send the butterflies, well, quite frankly, flying. Someone who just lights me up inside." I retreat to take a seat at one of the bar stools at the island, putting a little physical distance between us. "It hasn't been like this for me, not like it has for you. You've been doing this for a while, making girls swoon."

He shuts off the faucet and reaches for the striped blue and white dish towel again. "Ally, wait. You need to understand something." He walks around the island and comes very close to me, stands right next to the bar stool so that our legs are touching. "I need to make sure you realize this is not like one of my dates, not like the barflies you see follow me to the soccer games. You get that, don't you?"

I can see in his face that he's serious. Instinctively I move away from him, busy myself reaching for an olive. "Yeah, okay, Michael. I get it," I say to him, trying to brush him off.

"Allyson, I need you to understand this. Look at me."

I interrupt him. "I need you to understand something, too, Michael. I can't afford to lose you. Plain and simple, I can't afford for something to interrupt what we have. 'Cause what we have is pretty damn good, maybe the best thing I've got. And no matter how good it could be, no matter how good you think it feels and how badly you want to feel what that's going to be like, it's not worth it if someday it means we can't be together, we can't have lunch at Duke's, I can't look you in the eye at a soccer game. That scares the hell out of me, Michael, you need to know that. I won't do it, you know. I won't do this, whatever this is, this next thing between us, if it means we give up what we have, that someday all this goes away."

"It scares me too, Al. God, it scares me straight. But you know what scares me worse?"

"What?"

"What scares me worse isn't what we might lose if we try this. It's what we might never have known if we don't."

Michael cooks the salmon in butter and olive oil on the grill. I've had this meal of his before, the perfectly prepared couscous, the softly grilled vegetables that have been bathed in a broth of seasonings, and a fish so tender it melts when you bite into it. We eat outside, just the two of us, at the teak table sharing a pitcher of sun tea I'd set out early that morning. I watch him eat, the softness around his eyes, the way his hands move to tell me stories from his day. He refills my water glass before I ever ask him to. Music from the in-ground speakers spills out around us. Citronella candles burn from the corners of the patio.

I know I will make love with Michael this night. There's nothing left in me to doubt any reason not to. The dishes are done, dried, and stacked away in the cabinets. We've settled into our lounge chairs outside and he's covered me with a Mexican blanket I keep in the storage chest by the pool equipment. We've talked for over an hour, until I'm yawning well into the night sky. I'm not at all startled when he takes me gently by the hand and leads me in through the beveled doors. I know he's not leaving. I know he's very much staying with me this night.

We walk, wordless, to my room. I still own this room. He is still very much a guest here. I dial the lights down to dim, start the ceiling fan so that it's turning ever so gently, and he does not complain. I watch him pull the golf shirt over his head, expose his chest, and let him walk to me in his jeans and bare feet, the belt unnotched and hanging loosely at his waist.

I've chosen carefully today, the first time in a long time I've paid any attention to what's on under my capri jeans and top. And what's under them, as Michael discovers when he peels my clothes away from me, is a black bra and black satin thong panties. I've no issues with his seeing me this way; he's seen me in less than this, even when Patrick was alive, on nights when we'd ended up in the pool, skinny-dipping because it was easier than changing or because one of us had ended up being pushed in fully clothed at a party and the only way to keep swimming was to strip away whatever we'd had on, piece by piece, and fling them up on the side, sopping wet.

But I've not felt his hands on me this way. Ever. Felt them as they run smooth over my belly, as he reaches behind me to un-hook my bra and let it fall away from my breasts. Though I've held his hands, I had no knowledge they'd be quite so soft as he reaches between my thighs, guides me carefully, lovingly, onto the bed.

Neither of us stops. There is no conversation between us, for fear we might talk ourselves out of this, come to our senses. We feel everything our bodies will allow us to and I take mental notes. The change in the room, the way the light looks, the changes in my body as if I'm a piano being played for the first time in a long time, by a new artist.

It's hard to know at what point we finish the lovemaking. My sensation is that it goes well beyond the point when we finish making love. And I find myself still drinking in the sensation into the pale morning when I wake with him next to me, curled at my side. When I open my eyes, he is watching me. I'm sure that he has been for quite some time. And I've never seen such a look of contentment on his face, but it is one that I'll remember and hold with me for a long, long time. Of that I am sure.

27

I'm at the gate when the plane pulls in on Sunday, standing with my hands against the glass panes and staring down at the runway guide, large gray earmuffs dulling the roar of the engines in his ears. It has rained all morning; I imagine it has been a rough flight.

Becca's first off the plane, prancing up the runway in her green soccer shorts and a sweatshirt, carrying her stuffed bunny, the headphones to her CD player dangling around her neck, the cord buried somewhere inside her shirt. The cast is an afterthought now; it moves with her body like a piece of her she doesn't even notice, the sweatshirt frayed at the edges where she's cut it in order to get it on over the cast. Becca is playful, eager to be home, lit up like a Christmas tree.

Barbara shuffles up behind her, her walking stick in hand, which she uses to guide Becca in my direction, inching at her all the while.

"Gram, stop poking me with that thing," I hear Becca say to her before she spots me and takes off running in my direction. "Hey, Mom, will you get her to leave me alone? God, it's so ridiculous." She leaps into my arms, stands on her tiptoes, and nearly sends me staggering backward with a bear hug I realize, when she gives it to me, I've been desperately in need of.

I stifle a laugh as Becca's eyes go wide, her frustration mounting, before I hug her back, squeeze the daylights out of her, and whisper, "Welcome home, sweetie" in her ear.

"Hi, Barbara," I say. "Good to have you guys back."

"Yes, I'd say it was just about that time," she says to me, sizing me up.

I can sense the girls have done her in and she'll need a long rest from this communal vacation. I expect I won't hear from her for a few days after I drop her at the house.

Lydia hangs back in the crowd, stuck behind an elderly woman and her overweight son who are lumbering up the ramp. I spot her at a distance and notice that everything about her has changed. She sees me from afar and perceives the same thing. We study each other as she makes her way toward me.

"Hi, baby," I say to her and take her into my arms. She doesn't reach to encircle me, just lets her body go limp against mine, all the while keeping her hands shoved in the deep middle pocket of the sweatshirt.

"Hey, Mom. How are you? You look, sorta, well, different, I guess." She says this matter-of-factly, not accusingly, but I feel the heat rush to my cheeks anyway.

"I was just thinking the same thing about you." I eye her up and down, and she shrinks back from me and moves her feet around a bit, keeps one eye down on the floor. She's got the hood to the sweatshirt pulled up over her head and her sunglasses tucked and hanging from the collar. But I can tell her hair is braided back; one long thick mane of crisscrosses back and forth down her back.

We start up the terminal; make our way to baggage claim and then toward home. Barbara's exhausted, so much so that I catch her dozing off, heavy against the leather in the seat next to me. We drop her off at the house, drag her heavy bag inside the front door, and watch our step as she ushers us back out again, quick to keep us moving. The girls make a break and bolt back for the car just as the largest raindrops start falling from the sky.

The SUV erupts in discussion, a whir of laughter fused with whining, when I start the engine and turn on the defroster to clear the windows of the damp fog that has spread its spiderweb across my front windshield.

"Mom, you have no idea. Don't ever do that to us again," Lydia says, disdain lacing her voice. Becca nods her head vehemently in agreement.

"Really, Mom, it was *bad*. A real car wreck of a week. Grandma was all over us. All the time. Never a minute on our own. It was always, 'Girls, how about we do this today? Girls, don't you think we oughta . . . Girls, what do you think we should have for dinner? Girls, would you like to go see so and so . . . blah, blah, blah. And of course we didn't, you know. I didn't want to see any of her stupid old friends in their stupid old houses. But she made us go anyway. Then it was, 'Girls, don't you think you could put on something nicer? Becca, couldn't you leave that book home this one time? Lydia, don't you think you could smile? Blah, blah, *blah*." Becca's doing her best impression of Barbara, and I have to admit it's good.

I laugh heartily and switch the radio to a station I know they like and I think won't give me too much of a headache. Their voices are music to me, my own special serenade I've missed more than I realized. More than I thought about, I'm embarrassed to admit, even to myself.

"So, what'd *you* do?" I hear Lydia ask me from the backseat, and when I glance over my shoulder at her, I see her staring at me, rocking one of her sandaled feet back and forth in rhythm to the song on the radio.

"Well, let's see. You know, the week went by so fast, even without you guys to cart around. I slept. Ate. Ran every day. Saw a movie with Anna, some old lady flick you wouldn't have liked. Cleaned out the cabinets in the garage, got an oil change, picked up the dry cleaning." In the stop-and-go traffic at a signal that's gone out, I turn my head to look at Lydia, see if she's taking all this in.

She's only half listening to me, so I stop my list litany.

"Hmmm," she chimes in, listening after all. "Well, it sounds like you were kinda busy. We were fine, you know, Mom, just fine. I mean, don't get me wrong, it sucked and all, but we were fine."

"I know you were, sweetie. I know you were."

"How's Michael?" I hear Becca ask, barely looking up. "Have you seen him at all?"

"Um, he's fine, I think. Good. We had dinner together a couple of nights. Sarah's back from camp, got home on Friday."

The moment of silence passes and I hold my breath, both of my hands locked on the steering wheel in a death grip, my jaw locked and tense.

Not a complete untruth. Michael and I had had dinner together a couple of nights. Five of them. In a row. Out, in, him cooking, me cooking, a couple of grilled ham and cheese sandwiches late enough on Friday afternoon to constitute dinner, just after our last afternoon together in bed, and just before he left to pick up Sarah. I'd not seen him since, but he'd left me a bunch of wildflowers on the doorstep this morning. I'd stumbled over them on my way to the grocery store to restock the refrigerator with foods the girls would eat. No more small containers of kalamata olives, cellophane-wrapped wedges of goat cheese.

Lydia calls me out of my daydream, her insistent whine growing louder when I don't immediately acknowledge her from the backseat.

"Mom? Did you hear me? I said, Did you see Eric at all, even once this week?"

"Um, no, honey, I didn't." I watch for her reaction, but all I see is her profile. She cracks the window just enough to let in a hint of the summer storm that's still threatening the skies. It's humid, but I don't complain. The small bit of wind picks the ends of her hair loose, sends them flying around her face in all sorts of directions. "Why don't you call him when you get home? See if he'll come for dinner or something."

"Yeah. Maybe."

"Lydia, it's going to be okay." We're at a stoplight and I take the opportunity to reach out to her in the backseat, just barely reach to pat her crossed legs. "That much I can promise you. Everything's going to be fine."

Becca looks up from her book, looks back and forth between Lydia and me. "What? What's going to be okay? What's going on?"

"Nothing, Bec. Everything's fine." Becca shrugs her shoulders, rolls her eyes once, and refocuses her attention on the last few pages of the book she's trying to get through before we reach the house. Lydia reaches her hand out to me, holds my own for a minute, and I see a single tear roll down her cheek.

At home the electricity is out. The hall runs damp with the smell of heavy rain, the air thick as a musty knit afghan. Rain pounds on the roof and patios, deep pelting sounds that come in buckets.

Ritual sets in. Lydia retreats to her room; Becca to the phone. I surrender to the bath, take a book of matches with me, and light six round, pillar candles. It's just past four, plenty of daylight left in the day, but the skies have gone black, the feeling of Halloween in July.

I hear Becca yell from down the hall, "Mom, Michael's on the phone. Do you want to call him back?"

"I'm gonna have to, Bec. I'm in the bath and the portable phone's not going to work with the electricity out."

A few minutes later Becca appears in the door, rests her head against the frame. "Can Sarah come for dinner? Michael says they aren't doing anything, that maybe we could get together."

I hesitate, just a second, but am certain Becca doesn't pick up on it. If so, she never gives a hint. "I have no idea what we're going to do for dinner. If the electricity stays out it's going to be either sandwiches or cereal."

"Can't we go out somewhere?"

"Becca, you just got home. It's too nasty to be out driving in this."

"Michael thought you would say that. He volunteered to take us to Duke's. He said it's open."

"Call them back and let them know we'll be there at six o'clock. He doesn't have to pick us up, we can make it to Duke's." Becca gives a little cheer and skips out my door and down the hall. And then I yell after her, "See if Lydia wants to go."

I let the water roll up and over me, let my arms go weightless as the bubbles from the jets swirl back and forth in a light rocking motion. Steam rises, condensation drips from the tiles on the side of the tub. I have decided I will not court Michael. No makeup, no high heels. No stunning outfits, no trailing perfume. He gets me as I am.

I dry off, pull on a pair of faded broken-in jeans and a pink T-shirt. Hair damp in a ponytail. I run a Q-tip under my eyes, remove the smeared makeup that's left over from the morning.

An hour later we're officially late and Becca's impatience is growing. We are sitting in the car, the defroster blowing a tunnel big enough to see through the fog on the windshield. I send two long honks through the neighborhood and we wait for Lydia to shuffle from the house in her sweats. She doesn't. The rain has stopped but the skies still threaten. The electricity has been restored and the light is burning from Lydia's room. I see her silhouetted shadow creep across the wall opposite her closet and I'm certain she's torn her wardrobe apart and is searching for something that might suit her at this very minute. Problem is, nothing will and Becca and I could starve and grow old waiting in the car.

I go to the house and leave the front door open, pausing at the stairs. "Lydia? Let's go, Becca's in the car. We're already late."

She emerges from her room and I spy an endless trail of clothes scattered across the bed and onto the floor. She's got the phone up to one ear and a look of excitement in her eyes, the first I remember seeing in weeks. She holds up a hand to me and mouths something that I don't catch.

"Lydia," I say again, a little more softly and with a hint of respect for the conversation she's having on the phone, even though I've got my hands on my hips, the car keys rattling from one of my hands. Holding her hand over the mouthpiece and in a loud whisper, she mouths to me again that she's getting off the phone.

I wait, eavesdropping on the rest of the conversation as she takes the steps slowly, one at a time.

"Yes, uh-huh. Yeah, tomorrow would be fine. I can start then. No, I don't think she'll mind at all. No, it's no problem. Really, I can't wait. I'm so excited about it. Yes, okay, I'll see you then." And then finally, "Bye, Marina." She pushes the button on the cordless and ends the call.

"Mom, you won't believe this," she says to me, a smile breaking wide across the splash of freckles on her face. "That was Marina. She needs me to teach the rest of the summer with her. Only a couple of hours every afternoon, but it'll be easy money. My money. Oh, Mom, please say I can do it? I mean, I told her you thought it would be fine and all. She needs me to start right away. Tomorrow, in fact. I guess Amy broke her ankle water-skiing and she needs someone to take her place. An eight-and nine-year-old tap class, and a seven-to twelve-year-old hip-hop class."

She's talking so fast I can hardly keep up with her, all the while pulling a large gray hooded sweatshirt of Patrick's over her head. The bulk of the sweatshirt covers her waist and hips and falls nearly to her knees. No one would guess what she was trying to hide; from looking at her, they wouldn't even know she had shorts on. I finger the car keys and study a photo frame on the key chain in which one side is Becca's last soccer picture, the other side Lydia on pointe in a simple pink tank leotard.

"Wait a sec, Lyd," I say to her, ushering her out the front door and closing it behind us. "Wait, wait, wait. What is it Marina wants?" The clouds move quickly across the sky, rumbling almost. We reach the Surburban and Lydia pulls herself up into the front passenger seat. I start the car while she continues.

"Amy's been helping Marina teach two tap classes and a hip-hop class this summer. You know, Marina's got so many of those little kids in the class she needs someone to walk around and help them with the moves they can't follow. Anyway, Amy broke her ankle water-skiing and she's on crutches so Marina needs me to take her place for the rest of the summer. Oh, please say I can do it, Mom? Please, please? I don't know what I'll do if you say no to this, too." She's halfway across the console, tugging on my arm and gripping at me with a fierceness of desire I haven't seen in her in a long, long time.

From the backseat Becca interrupts, "Amy broke her ankle. Bummer." She's playing with a piece of the cast that hits up near her underarm and has been chafing against her skin, giving her a rash.

I turn my attention back to Lydia, who is still hanging on me, waiting for my permission to be as excited as she already is. I can see it in her eyes. It's embedded in her soul, part of her body. Even this body.

"Lyd, I don't know," I say cautiously, slowly, "do you really think you should? I mean, considering everything? Everything that's going on, you have no idea how it's going to go. What's going to come of this summer, how you're going to feel about everything. Or, for that matter, how you're even going to feel." I watch her eyes change, watch her look away from me as I back the car out of the driveway, inch it slowly down the street.

"Mom, please. I really, really want to do this." She gnaws on the end of her thumbnail, pulling at a frayed cuticle. It's a nervous habit she's had since childhood, and lately her nails are a mess.

"Lyd," I say, throwing her a look, and she immediately stops the subconscious biting. "Are you sure? You think you can do this? I mean it's a big responsibility for Marina. It means the rest of your summer's shot. What are the hours, what days?"

"One to five every day but Friday." She's turned back toward me, the seat belt pulled taut over her chest, her eyes pleading with me.

"So I have to take you? Every day? And come back and pick you up, right?"

"Yeah." She hesitates only a minute before she shyly asks me, "But you can do that, right? You always take me to the studio."

I'm driving with both hands on the wheel, cautious. I look over at her and take in her enthusiasm again. I know it'll be temporary. In a week or two I'll be dragging her to the studio, reminding her that she can't go to the movies that afternoon and skip out on Marina. I know that as high as she is at this very moment, as filled with the aspiration to do this, she'll sink to the bottom and tire of it in no time. I know this like I know the freckles on her face. I've studied her long enough to know what my saying yes to this means. What the real commitment entails.

But I do anyway. I say to her, "Okay, Lydia, fine. You can do this. If it's what you really want to do. But remember what you've got on your plate this summer. We haven't even brushed the surface of it yet. You've got a whole bagful of stuff we've got to work through, and this job isn't going to make any of that better or go away or not exist or anything. Understand?"

She pumps her head in agreement enthusiastically and lets off a little high-pitched wail. "Oh, thank you, Mom, thanks so much. I'm so excited to do this with Marina. It's even better than dancing, really. You know, it'll be something I can *do* this summer."

Becca shifts in the backseat, the sound of the leather seat sticking to her legs. "What's going on with Lyd?" she asks as if Lydia were not in the car, had not just finished this conversation with me.

"Marina called. She wants me to teach some dance classes with her for the rest of the summer. And Mom says I can do it." Out of the corner of my eye I catch Lydia beaming as she sits up a little taller in the front seat and reaches to switch the radio station to something more her speed, a sense of ownership present in her demeanor.

"Yeah, I got that. I mean, why's Mom so worried about you? What's going on with you? What's all the 'stuff' you've got to take care of?" Becca addresses her sister. Through the rearview mirror, Becca fiddles with the zipper pull on her jacket, running it up and down the length of the kelly green nylon fabric. "Um, well, I, uh . . ." Lydia scrambles for an answer and when she falls short, she goes silent and looks across the front seat of the car for me to rescue her.

I've been waiting for this conversation and have been rehearsing it over and over again. But not here, not as I'm pulling the oversized car into the tiny lot at Duke's, searching for a spot in which to anchor this boat. Nonetheless, Becca's onto us, and putting her off any longer will only frustrate her first, leave her asking and probing with endless questions until she's finally satisfied. I see a spot and inch the car into it, leaving just enough room to get out on both sides. I kill the engine and release the buckle on my seat belt before I turn halfway around in the seat, turn to face Becca straight on.

"Bec, Lydia's got something she needs to share with you. But you need to understand that this isn't gonna be easy for her to tell you. And she's going to need you to understand and support her even if you don't understand. Is that okay?"

The music from Duke's spills into the night air. Lydia shifts in her seat, moves her eyes back and forth between me and her lap and Becca. I can see Lydia tear up, but I don't back off. My intention is not to be cruel; Lydia can't hide from this, so I hold my own. I can see Michael in the far corner booth sipping on a tall beer, talking it up with another man I recognize but don't know.

Becca's not so patient. "What? What is it, Lydia? What's going on? You guys are scaring me."

Finally, with her eyes downward, Lydia takes a big breath and exhales deeply before she says, "Becca, I'm pregnant. I'm going to have a baby." It's barely a whisper, but it echoes off the sides of the car.

"You're *what*?" Becca says, steady and very much like I imagine Patrick would have, had he ever learned the horrible secret we probably would have hidden from him. I hear his voice coming through her and I shift a little more in my seat just to make sure he's not actually there. And I sense the same sensation runs through Lydia, because she jumps when Becca questions her, the sound of Becca's voice startling her.

They stare at each other. I watch them, my eyes darting back and forth, before Becca, still waiting on confirmation of what

Lydia has told her, looks to me. "Mom? Lydia's pregnant? But how can that be?"

I nod my head in agreement and reach for Lydia's hands that are shaking in her lap. She's gone pale, her lips trembling and tears flooding down her cheeks. Becca's really the first unsuspecting person she's tried this on, and her own sister's reaction has met with more disapproval than she'd imagined. I'm thinking to myself that this is a cruel twist of fate, but not unlike the response Lydia's guaranteed to receive from sheer strangers who will see her walking down the street within the next month or two, the obvious pooch probably impossible to hide by that time. This child, this slip of a girl with her middle bulging, a sign to the world that she's more of a woman than they'd think.

"Yes, Becca, Lydia's pregnant," I say calmly and slowly, all the while my eyes on Lydia as if they were my own arms wrapped around her to protect her. "Remember what I said, 'Lydia's going to need your support on this. Even if you don't completely understand it.'"

Becca slumps against the backseat and stares openly at the both of us, her blond hair pouring out around her shoulders and framing her face. "But how? I mean, I don't get it. How can Lydia be having a baby? She's not even married." Her eyelashes flutter open and closed over her round childlike eyes, disbelief settling in. In the seat next to me, Lydia snivels, and I reach for a tissue from the pack I keep in the console. The windows are fogging around us, the front window of Duke's blurring against the condensation on the windshield. I long to be held by Michael, by anyone at this point, who can reassure me that this isn't completely my fault, that I haven't caused us to end up here, this very place where we sit, our little family, trying just to make sense of it all.

Inside, we split. Becca slams the puck on the air hockey table with her friends. Lydia moves to a table where Amy has her foot propped up on the wooden bench, crutches leaning nearby. Lydia spotted her straight off and asked me one more time if taking the teaching job was really going to be okay. When I relented finally, she skipped off to get an update, to hear about Amy's accident and console her, all the while pumping her for information on the classes she'd be taking over.

Michael has a beer waiting for me. And a glass of water. I take four ibuprofens from the small pillbox I carry in my handbag and swallow them together with a large gulp of water. Then I drain half the beer before Michael says, "Hey, slow down, slugger."

"Sorry." I look across the table at him, my eyes heavy with the afternoon and straining under the light at Duke's.

Same Michael, I think, as I study him carefully, the bones that run the rim of his jaw, the late afternoon shadow that's settled in across his cheeks. Same Michael, I say over and over again to myself. Same Michael I've known forever, I process in my brain.

I tell Michael about Becca's reaction, about her sweet question, and he laughs heartily. It makes me smile myself, laugh under my breath. "Write that down," he says to me, reaching to softly trace the knuckles on my left hand. I scan the pub for someone, anyone, watching us. It's not unusual for Michael to touch me, I think to myself, even if Patrick had been sitting right here. Still, everything in me feels different now and I'm sure I'm giving this off, sounding the alarms.

Becca shows up at the table looking for more quarters for the air hockey table. She slumps against me in the booth and drapes her arm around my shoulder. I reach to dig quarters out of my wallet and Michael hands her a couple of dollars to make change with. "Hey, squirt, how was the trip?" he says to her.

"Fine. No, boring. Really boring if you must know. Glad to be home." She's off again, halfway across the restaurant before she says, "Hey, Michael, three weeks and this thing comes off." She knocks at the cast and then waves the dollar bills at him. "Thanks," she mouths and is off to the table, handing two of the bills to Sarah and running one of them through the change machine.

"See, Ally, stop worrying. They have no idea." It's as if Michael can read my mind. He's magnificent in his worn jeans and a mustard-colored sweater and I'm tempted to reach out to him and run my fingernails up and down his forearms, something I know he loves and will send shivers running down his spine.

"Yet. They have no idea yet, Michael." I blush and take another long swallow of my beer.

He studies me back, his eyes boring into mine. "Trust me, they're smarter than you know. They sense everything."

We sit like this waiting on our pizza and calzones, watching our children and falling into a familiar rhythm. Michael entertains me with baseball stories; I'm half listening, more often studying his face, lost in the fullness of his anecdotes, the way he includes me in the most minute of details.

On the way home, Lydia is quieter than I would have expected her to be, her mood suddenly taking a turn. She hasn't touched the radio station; she never moves to increase the volume to a level I can barely tolerate. When I finally ask her if she is okay, she shrugs at me, sinks lower into the cushion, and props her feet up on the dashboard, something Patrick would have had none of, but I'm more forgiving about.

Finally she says to me, "Mom? Does Michael know? About me, I mean? Does he know about the baby? 'Cause I thought we agreed we weren't going to tell anyone, but I could have sworn he knew. It was something about the way he looked at me."

I clear my throat and hesitate only a second, but it's all she needs to know that I've broken her trust. Before I even answer she shifts in her seat, holds strong in her stance. "Oh, great, Mom. You tell me not to tell anyone and then you tell Michael. Just great. I can imagine what he must think of me. Why did you have to tell him? Why? Can't I trust you with anything?"

Becca is in the backseat taking this in, rolling it around in her head. You can see she's trying to decide which side she's going to take. I take a right turn leading into our neighborhood. We're just a few streets from the house and the rain is starting in earnest again, large drops coming one at a time, but quickly, on the windshield.

In a voice meant to calm her, I say, "Yes, Lydia, Michael knows.

I know we promised each other that we wouldn't talk to anyone about it. And I'm sorry I've broken your trust." I watch her sideways as she turns her body away, shrinks against the door's wood paneling.

"Does anyone else know? Did you see anyone else that you told about it, Mom? You might as well tell me now 'cause you know I'll figure it out."

I don't appreciate the tone she's using to make me feel guilty about this as if I've let her down in an irreparable way and can be trusted no more.

"Look, Lydia," I say to her, expertly guiding the SUV into the garage and throwing it into park. Becca's out of the backseat in a flash, looking for refuge in the house, but Lydia waits to hear me out, a look of disdain painted across her face. "Look," I say more softly, "you're not going to be able to hide from this. You have this baby and people are going to know. It was wrong of me to talk with Michael about it, especially after we made a deal that neither of us would discuss it. But it was also important for me to talk with Michael about it, to have his perspective, to have him hear me out on this, to have him help me with it. To have him help us with it." I reach to smooth her hair with my hand, tuck the long almond-colored tresses back behind one ear. "It was like talking to your dad, if you must know, having someone to share all of this with, someone who is my age, like me, looking at it from this side of the fence. That's all. Michael's not here to judge you or me. He was just there to listen, that's all. Do you understand?"

"But he must think horrible things about me. Horrible, horrible things."

"No, Lyd, he doesn't. But people will. You have to know that going in. People will have horrible things to say. People will form opinions about you that aren't true and that will hurt you. The number of people who will accept you for this is small, the number who will look beyond it even smaller. But that's no reason not to do what you think is the best for you and for the baby. You make the choice, you make the decision. And by God, hold your head up about it, okay? Whatever you do, hold your head up about it."

She nods her head wearily and wipes the dampness and smeared mascara from her cheeks where her tears have streaked across her face. Sighing, she opens the car door, hops down from the SUV, and slams the door tightly behind her.

28

The studio is packed with petite ballerinas in black leotards and pink dance tights. My favorite age, eight-and-nine-year-olds, who carry their own dance bags, walk tall with their shoulders perched back like the beginnings of a dancer, and wear their hair swept off their faces and pulled tight into ballerina buns. They giggle, they walk arm in arm, they cajole each other as they pull open the double glass doors into the studio. I pull into the first stall and park the SUV while Lydia begins to protest, an insistent whine starting at the beginning of her sentence. "Mom, what are you doing? You don't have to come *in* with me."

"I'd like to come in. I haven't seen Marina since recital and I just, well, Lyd, if you must know, I'd just like to know that you're going to be okay here." I reach out to tuck her long hair back behind her ear and she pulls back from me, sweeping the mounds of hair up behind her and wrapping it tight with a hair band she's got wrapped around her wrist.

"I've been coming here for like twelve years or something. Jeez, since before I was them." She nods her head in the general direction of two young girls, both carrying square hard-sided cases over their shoulders. "This is my second home if you think about it. I think I've spent more time here than just about anywhere else."

She is right, of course. But this is different. She is different. I want to believe she is eight again, lacing up her tap shoes before anyone else, first to the mirror, stretching her lithe body at the barre. But this isn't my little girl. She sits in dance pants, stretched across a body I don't recognize anymore as her own, am not sure she does either. She's taken to wearing Patrick's oldest sweatshirts, the ones he had reserved for lawn work or a coffee run first thing on a weekend morning, holey across the corners of the embroidered university letters. Her dance bag is packed thick with everything she'll need for the day here, snacks, shoes, extra clothes, her CD player; it is all there, the zipper stretching across the material to close it shut.

We open and shut the heavy car doors in unison. I hold my key chain and dangle it noisily as we cross the parking lot and enter the studio. Marina spots me from behind the office wall and holds up a finger to me to wait while she finishes the phone conversation she is having. Lydia makes her way down the hall to her locker, begins to unfold the contents of her bag and stuff things away. She waves at me and enters an obsolete studio, one used for storage, and begins her stretching. Even now, she's more limber than she has a right to be.

Marina's embraces are world-renowned. They start at your midsection as she takes you full into her arms and warm you all over as she is sure to run her hands, her long, long fingers up and down the length of your back. I am desperate for one of these embraces, and am not disappointed when she flings open the door to her office and takes me in her arms.

At twenty-two Marina is the best the studio has ever had. She'd trained with the San Francisco Ballet since the age of nine, when she was accepted into their program. She'd danced two days a week, then four, then six days, nearly four hours a day. Her body alignment is considered flawless, the turnout of her hips perfect. It is by accident that she's ended up at our studio, home again, not far from the little town she started in. She's never spoken much about what brought her to our studio, what ended her career in San Francisco and started her story here. She has only said it was meant to be, that she is more of a teacher than a dancer. Having seen her do both, I hold the opinion that, in her case, it is impossible to choose one over the other.

"I am so happy to see you, Allyson. It has been *too long.* You've stayed away too long. And thank you, thank you so much for lending me Lydia for the rest of the summer. I didn't know what I was going to do." Marina's a flutter of moving parts, her hands at the cascades of blond hair that she's pulling up as she speaks. She's dressed in a black leotard, a white T-shirt with DANCE sprawled across it, and a lavender-colored gauze of a skirt that shimmers when she moves gracefully even across the floor of the office.

"You've made her summer, Marina. Really, I haven't seen her so happy in a long time. She's pretty excited about this."

"Excellent. I'll put her right to work. She'll be crying for a day off in no time." She smiles a wicked smile at me, but I know she's only kidding.

"We could only hope, huh? Um, Marina," I start cautiously, "is there a time you and I could have coffee one morning this week? I suppose lunch is out with your schedule, but coffee maybe."

She eyes me over a clipboard on which nearly a dozen papers are all clipped together, each one bending out at its own angle. "Is everything okay? What's up?"

"Yeah, yeah. Everything's fine, really. I'd just like to touch base with you on a couple of things, you know, just check in on some things about Lydia. It's fine, really," I say to her concerned face, as she takes a few steps toward me, pulls in close next to me.

"I can meet you for coffee tomorrow. Is seven too early? But, Allyson, you've got me worried. Lydia's okay, right? I mean, it's okay that she's doing this with me, you're not concerned about it at all, are you?"

"No. No, Marina, I'm fine with it. Actually, I think being here is the best thing that could happen to her this summer. I was afraid we wouldn't get her back here for a while, you know, after recital and such a dismal spring. She's fine, really. She will be anyway. And this will be good medicine for her. I'll explain it all to you tomorrow. Seven o'clock, it's perfect for me." I start to back out of her office, pull the heavy door closed behind me. There are only a few minutes before Marina's next class will begin. The studio is full now; bags litter the floor, girls stretched from one end of the long lobby to the other. I step over an errant ballet slipper and around a Diet Coke can that's been left against the wall and make my way back to Lydia's private corner, knock on the two-way mirror, and wave good-bye to her. Before I slip out the studio's front door, I pop my head back in Marina's office. She's engrossed in something on the computer, a spreadsheet, and I'm certain it must be billing she's trying to finish in between her classes. She looks up at me with a start and I whisper across the room to her, "Marina, please, not a word about any of this to Lydia. This is between you and me."

"Of course," she says and I know she understands how important this is to me.

I've seen Marina in street clothes only twice; once when we invited her for dinner at our home and she arrived in a long black skirt and stretch halter top; the second time when Patrick and I bumped into her completely by accident at a bar in the city, Marina dressed casually in slim black jeans and a tight sweater, an admiring and adorable man at her side.

She rolls into the café in black tights, a lilac leotard, black sweatshirt, and tight-fitting leg warmers and folds herself into the comfortable deep purple velvet chair opposite mine, tucking her feet up under her and reaching across the table for my hands, which I place in hers for a moment. Marina exudes warmth; you can't help but be drawn into her. She orders steamed milk and waits for me to start the conversation.

"Thanks for coming, Marina. I needed to talk to you. About

Lydia, of course. I'm thrilled you're taking her on this summer, really I am."

"Ally, please, she's the one helping me out, but may I say, I mean, can I just be honest with you? You don't sound so excited about it. You seem, well, hesitant, I guess, reluctant maybe about her doing this. What is it that's weighing so heavily on you?"

I struggle to find the first words. "Marina, you need to know that this is going to be a really rough summer for Lydia, a rough year ahead, actually. It's just that, well, there's just no easy way to say it." I pause, watching her eyes, before I spit it out. "She's pregnant, Marina. About four months along, due in December, actually." I wait a moment, trying to read her emotions, but they're difficult to sort through.

I'm about ready to start again when she holds a hand up to me, asks me to stop for a second while she absorbs this. She pulls a crumpled tissue from an inside compartment of the large black suede bag that sits at the foot of her chair on the stone floor and runs it along the bottom of her eyes.

"I'm sorry, Ally, I don't mean to lose it on you like this. I just had no idea, no idea at all. It all makes so much sense now. I just can't believe I missed the signs. How could I have missed the signs?"

"Hey, don't sweat it. I've been beating myself up over that for the last few weeks. You can understand why I need to tell you this, can't you? I mean, Lydia, she's being very brave, and very mature about the whole thing, all of it. But she has no idea, none whatsoever, about how her life is going to explode."

"No," she muffles. "No, Ally, she really doesn't. Can I show you something?" she says to me, digging in the corners of her wallet, a compartment under the checkbook where she's got a few things hidden—a receipt of some sort, her Social Security card, a savings book—until she pulls out a wallet-sized photo. She hands this to me, a picture of a baby girl, a newborn identifiable only by the pink ribbon stretched tight around her minute head. Her eyes closed, she's sleeping and oblivious of the photographer. It's a first photo, one from the hospital; I have one each of Lydia and Becca locked away somewhere in their leather baby albums.

Marina takes a long, deep breath and audibly sighs when she releases it. "My baby," she says, "the real reason I left the company. The child I had. That's the reason I couldn't stay anymore after that."

I am visibly shocked, so much so that the hand that is holding the photo begins to shake, just enough to be noticeable. I set the photo down on the table in front of me and lean in to take all of the child into my memory. Her hands curl together up under her chin, her fingers are longer than any I can remember. Dressed simply in a thin cotton sleeper, the kind my own girls wore their first few hours in the hospital, and set against a pink background, confirming, in fact, she was very much a little ballerina herself.

"My God, Marina, when?"

She sighs again, picks up the picture herself, and studies it as if for the first time in a long while. "Nearly three years ago now. I was level eight at the company, my first year as such. You know, at the point where it was not fun anymore, it was just my job, what I did every day, day in and day out. I was exhausted all the time, homesick, longing for a break from all of it, just over-cooked. My body had given out on me, or so I thought. I hadn't had a period in over a year. I weighed twenty-five pounds less than I do now."

I try to imagine what she must have looked like. It's difficult; Marina's skeletal even at her current weight.

"Anyway, in that state, who'd have thought I'd get pregnant? Not me, certainly. And when it happened? I had no idea, no place to go, no one to talk to. Everything I knew was gone and over in a flash, just disappeared, floated right away."

"But you had the baby? Duh, Marina, sorry. I mean, you *had* the baby. Why? You could have changed that, right?"

"Not by the time I'd figured it out. I was two months, then three, and then the rumors flew, the questions started, my boyfriend long gone. It was a disaster. Shipped home. Had the baby, put her up for adoption. Thought I'd go back and start over again. They'd never have me then, not with that tarnished record. There's no going back. Besides, I was done dancing. Done being the person I was then. That's when I came to the academy, started teaching dance the way I wanted to dance, the way I remembered it when I was really little, the time I really loved it. That's what I want for the girls."

"I had no idea. I'm so sorry. I never would have burdened you with all this if I had known. No idea whatsoever, Marina." I stand and reach across the small round teak table to hug her, her cheek dropping in next to my shoulder and resting there.

"Of course not, Ally, how would you have known? No one here knows. No one but Julia, and even we haven't talked about it since she hired me. I've let it go. It wasn't one of my more proud moments. But it was what was meant to happen to me. It took me a long, long time to realize that, but I have no doubt about that now. I finally, finally understand that." She tucks the photo of the baby girl back in her wallet and drops it to the floor so that it rests on top of her bag. "What's Lydia going to do? Four months, she's pretty far along."

"Yeah, yeah, she is. You might not believe it, but she wants to put her baby up for adoption, too. I don't know how she's doing it, what strength she's drawing from, but it's not mine. I'm embarrassed to say I haven't quite got my arms around the whole thing. I'm really struggling with it, actually."

"Why?" She asks this innocently enough, but I'm not sure what to tell her, how to approach it.

"Um, well, I guess I'm just having a hard time understanding how she could do it. How she could possibly, well, how she could possibly—"

She interrupts me, and with love and graciousness gives me permission to be honest with her. She says, "Ally, you can say what you think, ask me any questions you might want to know about. It won't hurt my feelings. It won't change what I've done.

I've done what I've done. It was the best decision, the only decision for me."

"I guess I'm just having a hard time understanding how you could give your child away to someone to raise, to a complete stranger, and have no idea how or where or what happens to this child for the rest of his or her life. It's your baby, someone you've carried within your own body, for nine months." All of it, all the indecision, the superstition, comes bubbling to the top, boils over. I'm mortified at my revelation.

Marina never flinches, just lets her brown eyes rest on my face and leans in to listen to me. She balances her elbows on her knees, her legs crisscrossed under her, and she looks very much like my fifteen-year-old daughter, young and free, but confident and composed. "It wasn't easy, Ally, but consider this. This child was brought through me, but she wasn't mine. She was never mine to raise or rear or even to love every day of her life. I piled all that love up in the beginning, the only time I got to make a decision for her, and made the decision to place her with people who could do for her what I couldn't do every single day. Do I regret my decision? I think about it every day, every single day I wake wondering about her, and wondering when that wondering stops. When's the day that I wake up and not think about her? Maybe it'll be gone when I have my own child, the one I'm destined to raise and have with me every day. But like I said, she wasn't mine. I brought her into this world, but she was meant for someone else."

She reaches into her bag again, this time for a small notepad and a pen. In slanted handwriting, she scrawls something sideways on the lines, then rips the page from the spiral wires and hands it to me.

"Call this woman. I wouldn't tell you to do it if I didn't think it was best for Lydia, or if it wasn't what Lydia wanted. But Elizabeth walked me through all of it. She's better than good. She found her calling a long time ago. Adoption is what she's meant to do. She'll be your rock. For Lydia's sake, and for your own for that matter, you owe it to the both of you to talk to her. She won't push you. But she will be honest with you. She'll answer anything you need her to."

I take the paper from her and fold it in half, then in half again, and tuck it into the inside zippered part of my handbag. Then I reach across the little table that separates us and I take Marina into my arms, hold her tight as can be for a few minutes until she finally whispers into my ear, "Ally, there's a reason for all of this, you know. All of it. I've no doubt why I'm here, why I asked Lydia to teach with me this summer, how God drew us together. It'll make sense one day, just wait. Life has a way of fitting together in pieces we just don't understand, sometimes until much, much later." She stretches her legs and begins to pack up her things. We walk outside and are blasted by the muggy July day, the early traces of humidity already rising from the blacktop. She takes my arm, locks her own around it.

"Ally, one more thing. You should know this. They say the most important person for a woman who is considering placing a child for adoption, the person she will most count on during the entire process, the person who will most likely influence her decision to keep the baby or place the baby for adoption, is the woman's mother. That's you. I didn't have that. My parents abandoned me for my mistake, as they liked to call it, admonished me when I wouldn't have an abortion. They thought we'd be able to sweep the whole thing under the carpet, just be done with it, and two days later I'd be back dancing again, as if I'd had a bad case of the flu, food poisoning, maybe. It took everything I had to stand up to them, make my own choice, do the thing that felt the most right and just and honorable to me." She pauses then, and removes her black hooded sweatshirt, ties it around her waist. "Don't make Lydia do that. Don't make her fight you on this. No matter what you think about it, no matter what would be right for you. You're the linchpin in this. It's critical that you understand that and that you can be there for her. I know you'll do that, Ally.

I can't imagine you being any other kind of mother. Any other kind of person, for that matter."

She kisses me lightly on the cheek, throws her bag over her shoulder, moving with grace down the street. Grace I hadn't noticed before.

29

My plan for the day includes breaking the news to Barbara. It's the thing I dread most.

Lydia's fought me on the idea of abortion, her final parting words "No, absolutely not" before she slammed her bedroom door in my face. So I've told her that it's inevitable that Barbara will know and asked her if she wanted to go with me to tell her. When she went pale and asked me if she had to, I'd finally sighed and told her no, that I would do this for her. I didn't blame her for not wanting to go. I figured, for Lydia, it was somewhat of an extension of having to tell her father, something she'd never have been able to choke out.

Besides, I'd felt an overwhelming sense of maternal protection. With Barbara, you could be sure the reaction wouldn't be good. I knew only one thing. I'd protect Lydia at all costs.

Barbara is dressed in linen pants and a jacket. Bridge attire, as she'd told me on the phone the night before. She had time for tea, but had to be off by ten. I am glad for the prior commitment, and take the long route to her house, leaving myself exactly forty minutes to spend in her company before she cuts me off.

She offers me tea; I decline. She offers me fresh fruit; I politely refuse. Finally, we make our way to the little English garden she meticulously keeps off the side of her kitchen. My sandals scuff at the redbrick patio, and the white wrought-iron chair scrapes as I drag it a comfortable distance from her.

All at once I feel claustrophobic, sick in her presence. "Those girls, Ally. Those girls are a lot of work, you know, just a constant bombardment of bickering and energy and racket and hoopla, all day nonstop." She sips at her tea and places the cup in its dainty saucer with overexaggeration.

"Yes, I know. But it was good of you to take them. I can't thank you enough for the break." I pull and tug at my jeans, inadequate in her presence.

"Well, I can see why you needed the break. And I suppose it was time you had some time by yourself."

I debate for a minute whether or not she's testing me. The moment passes and I know I'm safe. I start the conversation, having rehearsed it over and over again on the drive over.

"I wanted to talk to you about Lydia, actually."

"Hmmmm. Yes?"

"Um, well, did you notice, I mean have you noticed any changes in her? Maybe while you were at the beach together?"

Barbara doesn't flinch, goes on about sipping her tea, holding the English Wedgwood flowered cup and saucer in her lap, her ankles crossed primly. But her eyes bore into me and she clicks her manicured nails against the china the way I've known her to do when she begins to get edgy.

"What, exactly, do you mean, Allyson?" Her glasses hang from the pewter chain around her neck, rocking back and forth slightly with the heavy sighs she emits as she breathes deeply.

I watch her carefully.

"Barbara," I say, rising from the chair and taking a quick lap around the box of a garden. "Barbara, God, I can't believe that I'm having this conversation with you. Oh Lord, this is hard. There's just no easy way. Okay, well, you see, Lydia's pregnant."

"What did you say?" she asks me plainly, matter-of-factly, enunciating each word carefully.

I know I needn't repeat myself; she's heard me plainly, clearly. I stop pacing for just a minute, my hands hanging numbly at my side, the insides of my stomach flip-flopping around. Then I continue, moving, pacing, talking, explaining, rationalizing. Anything to cover the dead space that rests between us. "Four months give or take. She's due in December. I expect it'll be a rough summer, rough fall for us too. We'll get through it. Somehow we'll get through it, we always do." Finally, I say to her, slightly softer, "I'd hope for your support on this, Barbara. There's really nothing more that we need than that."

She sits silent in her chair before she places the cup and saucer on the small glass table next to her and says to me, "Yes, I was certain of it. I could just sense it all along."

"You knew? But how? When?"

"I know my granddaughter, Allyson. I could tell something was different about her, something was bothering her." She was bullshitting me; I could sense it in everything about her, the way she nervously stirred her tea, the ping of the teaspoon against the cup. Barbara doesn't like to be left out. What's more, she hates surprises.

"But, but how could you have known . . . ?"

"I really don't see how that matters now, Allyson." She squares off with me, tempting me to cross her. Inside I know she is seething, plotting. I wait for the explosion to hit and I'm not disappointed when she says to me, "I don't suppose you can explain how you let this happen?"

"I'm sorry?" I say to her, a question, not a statement, because I want to make sure that I've heard her clearly.

"You should be."

I feel my face flush crimson, embarrassment rushing over me in a giant wave.

"I should be sorry? Um, what, exactly, do you mean by that?"

"She's your child, Allyson. *She* is the child, *you* are the adult. She is your responsibility. Her actions are a direct reflection on you. Or have you forgotten that?"

I stand in front of her for a minute absorbing her words, letting them melt, burn their way into my skin. I realize I am not shocked by her response; I simply didn't realize how quickly and with how much force it would come, how full of contempt it would be. I cross my arms over my chest and wait for her to abuse me further. I'm not sure why, but I suppose I figure that once she's done, maybe she'll be done for good.

What's more, as much as I hate to admit it, I'm not entirely sure she's wrong. I've felt this way from the very beginning, very much like I'd let Lydia down.

"Why weren't you there for her? Tell me that. Why?" I watch as she staggers for a minute, attempts to get to her feet. "Why weren't you there for her? What kind of mother lets her fifteen-year-old daughter get pregnant?"

As prepared as I think I am for her, her accusations take me off guard. "I, I have been, Barbara. I don't know what led her to this, I really don't. I've asked myself that question over and over again, but I just don't know how I missed it, what it was that she needed from me that I couldn't give her."

"Well, it's obvious, Allyson. This was simply something you were incapable of handling. Clearly you can't control her. I suppose there was nothing you could have done either way. This is just something you weren't able to handle. This is something Patrick would have handled, it's that simple. This is another one of those things he would have had to take care of." She clears her throat then, tsk-tsks at me, and shakes her head back and forth in disgust. "You'll need to tell me how I should handle this with Lydia. I expect she did not come with you this morning because she's a bit leery of how I might have reacted." She gathers her cup and saucer and starts back up the four brick stairs that lead into her kitchen.

I stand stunned, until she says to me again, "I said, 'you'll need to tell me how I should handle this with Lydia.' After all, I don't suppose she plans to avoid me for the next five months." She turns on a heel and disappears into the kitchen, the sunlight so bright outside that I have to shade my eyes in order to catch even a shadow of her body moving in the kitchen.

I'd like very much to slip out the back gate, into the SUV, and out of the driveway. Her words have stung me, knocked me backward momentarily. I start to object, to right my point of view, before I realize what a wasted effort that would be.

"I'm not sure when Lydia will be over to see you, Barbara. You'll have to take that up with her, I suppose. If you stop to think about it long enough, I'm sure you can understand why she sent me to tell you about all this, about the baby." I steady myself and study her face. She's stern; one might say even tough, hard to crack. But her eyes look older than they had only moments before, soft and sagging in stretches under the lids.

I pick up my bag and start to leave, deflated of my desire to discuss this any further with her. I've done what I promised Lydia I would do; I'd like to take cover before she takes aim at the messenger.

"Allyson?" she says after me, her voice following me down the hall in loud whispers.

I turn on my heel and face her, my hands on my hips. "Yeah?" I'm not expecting an apology, but there is something that's changed in her face that makes me think I might actually get one.

"Well? What's she going to do?"

"She's placing the child for adoption, Barbara. It's what she wants."

She sucks in all the available air in the kitchen. Her lips go tight into a thin line and her face pales. She shakes her head vehemently in disgust. "No, no, simply not. That just can't be. That's her child, her little baby. How could she possibly? How, Allyson? You can't allow it. *I* won't allow it."

I lick my lips slowly and watch her. "You won't allow it?" I can't help but laugh, just a little.

"No. I simply won't tolerate it. That's just not an acceptable alternative to this little problem we've got on our hands. This is Lydia's child, a baby that's born into this family."

I shake my head in disbelief. "Amazing."

"What?"

"Amazing." I laugh again, shaking my head harder this time. "You know something, Barbara, that's what I thought. I just couldn't understand how Lydia could do it, how she could possibly want to give a baby to someone else."

"Well, thank God. At least you haven't completely lost all sense of reason. You will speak with her then. You'll tell her what she needs to do. It won't be easy, but between all of us we can raise this baby. That's it, that's the decision."

"Well, actually, Barbara, I think you were right about something you said just a little while ago."

"What's that?"

"You know, that I let Lydia down, that I wasn't there for her when she needed me."

"Yes, well, that might be true. But, Allyson, you'll make the decisions now. You'll step in for her and take over. She's a child. She simply doesn't understand, there's no way she possibly could. It's your turn to take control over this situation."

"Actually, Barbara, I think she's got a pretty good grip on what's going on. And as for being there for her? I think this time that's exactly what I'll be. Right there for her, no matter what she chooses."

30

I tell Lydia that it would be a good idea for her to go see her grandmother, not because I want to send my child into the lion's den, but because I want a clean slate; I want to play with a full deck. I've given Lydia the PG version of the blow-by-blow her grandmother had delivered. And I've come clean with her about my decision to support her choice for adoption.

"Really, Mom?"

"Yes. I know it's the right thing for you. For everyone."

"All right, I'll go. I might as well get it over with. Can you take me by there later? Maybe after dance?"

"I can take you tomorrow. I'm having dinner at Michael's tonight. You and Becca can come along if you'd like. Or I'll order you pizza if you don't want to go. Michael's barbecuing, so it's your choice." I say this casually, testing the water.

"At Michael's?" she asks. "Really? We never go over there. What's the occasion?" She pauses for a minute before she says, "Okay, I'll go. What time?"

"Six thirty. And he's making ribs, so no turning your nose up at that. If you come with me, you eat what he cooks, got it?"

"Yeah, fine. Okay, Mom, whatever."

I drop Lydia at the studio, double back to pick up Becca, who has an appointment to have her cast checked, stuff a bag of dry cleaning in the back of the Suburban, stack three videos that need to be returned in the seat next to me, and pull back out of the driveway in less than twelve minutes.

"Mom, can I ask you something?" Becca asks me from the backseat.

"Shoot."

"What am I supposed to tell my friends?"

"About what, sweetie?"

"About Lydia. What am I supposed to tell my friends? You know, when she gets all fat and stuff. It's not like we're going to be able to hide it, you know. People are going to know."

I adjust the rearview mirror so we can talk while I drive. Her tone is indignant. From the look on her face I can see her confusion, the bruised ego on her sister's behalf, the weight of the secret she's been asked to keep to without really understanding why.

"Bec," I start, "this baby, it's going to be a really, really hard thing. For all of us, but especially for Lydia. She's going to need our support and she's going to need to feel like we're on her side, even if we're not." As I'm talking I realize it has been a long time since I've checked in with Becca, and in the middle of all this she's slid a bit from my arms. We've not run together, not been out, just the two of us, in weeks. No car rides to soccer practice where we're alone and she can confide in me. No morning carpools to school where I might have caught up on the latest gossip in her class.

"It's just so unfair. You know people are just going to think the worst of Lydia. They're going to think she's a little, well, never mind, Mom, but they're going to think it."

"Becca, what are you worried about? What people will think about Lydia or what people will think about you?"

"It's the same thing, Mom. People are going to think stuff. That's all. I mean, what about when she goes back to school? People don't just get pregnant, you know."

"Yeah, Bec. Actually they do. It happens. And when Lydia goes back to school, she's going to have to deal with all of that. It isn't going to be easy. But I sort of get the feeling that this isn't about her anyway. That this is maybe about you, and what you think about Lydia. So, what do you think?"

"I think it's the worst possible thing that could have happened to us this year. Doesn't Lydia know our family *does not* need this?"

"I don't think it was her intention to get pregnant, Becca."

"It's still not fair, Mom. It's just not. It screws everything up." Becca's hard, stubborn, and obstinate when she wants to be.

"No, Bec, it's not fair. But it's what happens. It's just what has happened. Nothing's been fair about it, but it's what's happened. That's how life goes sometimes."

In the parking lot at the clinic, I say to her, "Michael invited us for dinner, you want to go?"

"To his house? All of us? Why? We never go to Michael's." She sounds remarkably like her sister.

She's right, of course; we never go to Michael's. In earlier days, days when Sarah and Becca were still toddling around in diapers and we didn't have enough cash for a babysitter, yes. We'd sit in the grass-lined backyard and drink gin and tonics long into the summer nights, Michael on his guitar, Leslie and me doing karaoke before it was popular, Patrick cursing our Bohemian ways.

"Mom? I said, 'what's the special occasion?'"

I surface from my daydream, aware that Becca is staring at me.

"Huh? Oh, um, nothing, really. Just in the mood for a barbecue, I guess. He called earlier and wanted to know if we would be, too. Lyd says she'll go, but if you're not up for it, I'll order you pizza. Your choice." I'm still perfecting casual, still rehearsing the words even as they leave my lips.

"Is Sarah gonna be home? I haven't talked to her all day." Becca is loping across the steaming blacktop of the clinic parking lot, her short legs carrying her faster and farther than people a foot taller than she can walk.

"Think so. You can call her when we're done here if you want."

"Okay, yeah, I'll go. What's Michael making?"

"Ribs," I say, and watch the expression change on Becca's face. One of her favorites.

"Yep, uh-huh. I'm in."

Becca's seen a pediatric orthopedist specialist on and off for the last six weeks. His primary concern has been the amount of time the elbow needs to heal with the pins set in place, but he's promised her that if things look good this go-around, he'd schedule the appointment to have the cast taken off within the next few weeks. And he's warned her that it'll be nothing like what she's expecting. Worse. Starting with physical therapy an hour a day, five days a week.

She's ready.

She sits tall on the examining table, rocking her feet back and forth, and practically jumps off the table and across the room when Bruce Cleveland walks through the door. Nearing fifty, Dr. Cleveland is attractive but short, more so than I realized the first time I shook his hand, until I stood at the end of the appointment and came eye-level with his piercing slate-blue eyes.

"Hiya, Dr. Cleveland, it's going great, really, really great," Becca says to him before he's even opened her chart. "When can we get this thing off?" She knocks at the cast to indicate specifically what she's talking about, as if he needed clarification.

Bruce laughs a hearty laugh, pushes back his lab coat, and puts his hands on his hips. He's dressed in a black sweater, gray pants, and loafers, and for a minute, just a minute, I'm left wondering again if I should have taken him up on the offer, *drinks some night out*, which he'd made on the phone the night after Becca's first appointment.

I'd declined, embarrassed and flushed hot, without so much as a moment's hesitation, caught completely off guard by his call. He'd apologized, said he'd hoped he hadn't offended me, which he hadn't, and we'd gone on to have a conversation where we'd both talked nervously over each other until I'd finally begged out.

Since then, at every appointment, he's come to greet me first with a warm handshake and the same piercing eyes. Which is what he does, even before Becca gets his full attention. Then he's all Becca's, prepared now for her constant barrage of never-ending questions, the attempt to pin him down on exact details. He moves her arm this way and that, elevates it up and down and in circular motions that check her range and fluidity, and finally, after recording six or seven lines in the chart, asks her if she's doing anything the following Thursday.

She appears crestfallen. "I dunno. Mom, are we doing anything on Thursday?"

"Um, I'd say you're probably getting that thing off, huh? Bruce, whadda ya think?"

"Um, well, we could wait till Friday, if that works better for you. Allyson?"

Becca interrupts our banter. "Very funny, you guys. No, we're not doing anything on Thursday. What time? Can we do it first thing? Please?"

"One thirty, Rebecca. Don't be late." He hands her an appointment card on which he's scribbled the time of her appointment. "You can save that one for the scrapbook," he says, nodding at the card.

"We won't be late. No way," she says to him and jumps from the table, landing squarely on both her feet before she tackles him in a hug he's barely expecting. "Thank you, Dr. Cleveland. Thank you, thank you."

31

Michael is late to arrive home from work. He's called my cell twice and apologized, promising me that Sarah is home and telling us we should just kick up our heels with her until he gets there. For Becca this is second nature; she's a regular in this house. Lydia, like me, stumbles at first until she finally settles in to watch *Entertainment Tonight* on the television in the family room. She stares at me while I lean awkwardly against the bookcase staring at Michael's books, trying to figure out how to make myself a little less obvious. Michael's house, like mine, is completely different with three teenage girls rumbling around in it.

I'm left wandering from the small kitchen to the den Michael uses as an office and finally to the living room, where I pick a CD and melt into the oversized leather chair and ottoman that smell distinctly like the place Michael goes to read. His earthy aftershave is worked into the leather.

When Michael finally arrives, shirt disheveled and arms laden with brown shopping bags, he's quick again to apologize, even quicker with a kiss full on my lips before I have the chance to pull myself from the depths of the chair, before I have a chance to do a once-over of the room, before I make sure we're in the clear of prying eyes. He leaves me there, soaking in my reverie, lounging in the comfort of his being in the house with me, me in his home.

Michael takes his time with dinner, tends to it while I soak in the last of the late afternoon sun, warm enough to keep me lazily lounging on a teak chair on his deck near the barbecue. His house backs to the woods, and he's built a sunporch that protrudes over the south side of his backyard and leads out to the deck. You could get lost in his sunporch, so filled with books and paintings he's picked up here and there, but the double doors that lead to the back deck will, eventually, draw you outside where the sun sets just over the low side of his home.

We're alone in the backyard when he says to me, "You look beautiful, just sitting there. I could get used to you being there."

I'm not so sure. I'm on edge, wary of the girls and where they might be, half expecting Lydia to come creeping up on the two of us like a cat looking for something wonderful to pounce on. I've got my feet pulled up under me and am sucking on a bottled water, passing on wine, even with the sly look Michael throws me, the way he half tousles my hair and tells me not to worry about things.

"You'll tire of me, Michael, just wait."

He wraps his mouth around the neck of the beer he's drinking, runs his tongue along the inside of the bottle, and shakes his head in disagreement.

No one complains about Michael's cooking; so tender are the ribs that the meat falls from the bone when you try to pick it up with the tongs. His salad is simple but fresh, and the corn sweet without adding even a drop of butter. We'd have been mistaken for a family, should some stranger have wandered into the backyard that night.

Even I lose track of where we are. Until later, when drying dishes in the kitchen, the girls sitting discussing the latest heartthrob at the kitchen table, Michael reaches over and encircles me at my waist, kisses me full on the mouth again. A second flashes, then another, before I open my eyes, and adjust to the surroundings of this different kitchen, this different locale altogether. And then my eyes meet Lydia's.

She says nothing.

I say nothing. Rather, I watch as her face goes white, then a shade of deep scarlet.

Becca and Sarah continue on with their banter, just a faint dull echo in the back of my head somewhere. Michael is very aware of the shift in the room, but he's in unfamiliar territory. He stumbles briefly, then recovers quickly, making his way back to the sink, pulling the dishes one by one from the soapy tepid water and stacking them on the drying rack to the side of the sink. Silent.

"Lydia, I need to talk with you." I don't ask her, yet my voice leaves everyone wondering if it's a request. I wipe my hands on the green-and-white-striped dish towel.

"Not right now." Those eyes, just slits really, but full of hurt and anger and frustration and confusion. She shrugs me off, glued to the seat cushion.

"No, actually I think right now would be a good time." I make a move toward her and square her off in the chair. Something about the tone stops the banter at the table and both Sarah and Becca are left staring at me. Becca asks, "What's wrong, Mom?"

"Nothing, sweetie, nothing at all," I say to her, clearing my throat and running a hand to smooth down the long mane of hair that hangs down to the middle of her back. "Just need to talk to Lydia for a minute. We should probably go in a while, too." I say this more quietly, my voice catching in a whisper that takes most of my breath away.

Michael eyes me from the sink, a raised eyebrow as if to ask what he can do for me. I dismiss him quickly without meaning to. I follow Lydia out of the room and down the narrow hallway toward the back of the house, her hips swinging with purpose, her thonged feet clip-clopping on the hardwood in the hall.

"Lyd, I'm not sure what you want me to say, because I'm not sure what there is to say." I pull a Kleenex from my pocket, twist the ends back and forth. "This thing between Michael and me? It hasn't been going on long, so it's not like I haven't told you about it on purpose. It's new and I'm not even sure what it is, or what I want it to be, so I don't want you to think I've been hiding something from you. I don't want you to think I was lying to you about something."

She's staring hard into the aquarium tank in the corner of the third bedroom that rarely sees guests in Michael's house. On the bed, two rows of throw pillows are lined up precisely against the down comforter, the matching set looking like something that was taken directly off the showroom model. I reach for one of these pillows and hold it close against my chest, waiting for her to say something in retort.

When she doesn't, I try again. "Lydia, I want you to understand that Michael and I know that this might be very, very hard for you and your sister. And for Sarah. That it might be a really, really weird thing. Believe me, it's weird for me, for both of us. I'm not sure about it, any of it at all. It's not something that we planned, that we talked about or thought about. Ever. It's just something that happened, really, just something that we sort of fell into."

She's taken with a deep-orange-striped fish that's made his way to the side of the tank and is hanging there, suspended in the water, making small fish kisses at her against the glass. His black eyes bulge from the side of his head.

Lydia knocks slightly on the glass.

"You're not supposed to do that. It scares them," I say to her.

She scoffs, turning her head to look at me.

I watch as the fish darts in and out of the plastic seaweed and small ceramic caves in the tank.

She crosses her arms and cups her elbows in each of her hands, makes her way across the room to the waist-high bookcase, and leans against it, keeping her eyes on the floor. She slips her flip-flop off and twists her toes through the fringe on the area rug, winding the small threads around her big toe. "Lyd? What can I tell you about this? What do you want to know? No more secrets. Just ask me a question and I'll try my best to answer it for you. I know you're probably still trying to take in what you just saw out there. I'm sorry, Lydia, really, that's not at all how I wanted to tell you about this. Not at all."

"How long?" she says, choking out the words with a hiss.

"I'm sorry, honey, 'how long' what?"

"How long have you and Michael been like that? How long has he been kissing you like that?"

"Not long, Lydia. Vacation. When you and Becca were at the beach with Barbara. Couple of weeks now. That's it. Really, if it had been any longer, I would have told you. You have to know that. I just wasn't sure about the best way to tell you and—"

"Not since before Dad?" she interrupts me, seething, and before she can even comprehend what she's asked me, there are tears streaming in long waves down her cheeks, her eyes red at the rims. Still she holds tight, her body rigid and locked away from me.

I want to shake her; I want to ask her if she's kidding. These are the words that come into my head, form in my mouth. But before I spit them out at her, I roll them around on my tongue, realizing how deeply she's been cut by a moment's indecision.

I go to her, but don't take her in my arms. Rather, I stand next to her, side by side, and touch her arm, rest my hand over hers so that my fingers lie one on top of hers. And very softly I say to her, "No, Lydia, not since before Dad. This was not something that happened before your dad died, not by a long shot. I loved your father very much. He was everything I had always wanted, everything I thought I ever needed. Michael was always a part of our lives, but not a part of my life. Not mine alone. Michael was part of your dad's life, too, you know. He loved your father very much."

She listens to me without looking at me, but I'm confident she's heard what I've said. Finally she says to me, "Okay, Mom." She buries her hands deep in the pockets of her jeans, of my jeans that she's wearing, so that they slink lower at her waist and her belly protrudes slightly over the waistband. "If it's okay with you, I think I'd like to go home now. I really don't want to be here anymore."

"Okay," I say to her and she follows me down the hall. Michael is sitting very still and very straight in the chair at the end of the kitchen table, an empty beer bottle in front of him. With the

index finger of his left hand he spins the bottle on its rim and
catches it before it falls still on the table. His brow is furrowed;
he's busy with his thoughts. The kitchen is spotless.

"Michael, we're gonna go," I say to him as he lurches to his
feet, watching Lydia all the while. "Where's Bec?"

Michael pushes back from the table, and the sound of his chair
scraping the floor reverberates across the room. "They're in Sarah's
room. Let me go for them," he says, clearing his throat and moving to pass me.

"No, it's okay. I'll go." I brush his elbow and feel the bolt of
electricity that runs between us. I know he feels it, too. I eye
them both, Lydia with her head hung low, and leave them alone
in the kitchen. I hear Michael clear his throat again and pick up
the beer bottle from the table to make his way toward the recy-
cling bin he keeps under the sink.

When I return to the kitchen, Becca in tow and protesting,
Lydia's boxed herself into the far corner between the refrigerator
and the pantry. The baggy T-shirt she's wearing hangs like a
minidress over the black jeans. Michael stands close to her, close
enough to reach out and touch her, maybe hold her if she'd let
him, which she definitely will not. Not at this very moment anyway. But I can tell they've been talking, Michael doing most of it.
He stands his ground, backed up against the corner of the island,
his hands shoved low and inside his jeans pockets. They both
look up at me when we walk back into the room and I say,
"Ready, Lyd?"

Lydia takes this opportunity to bolt as fast as she can from
Michael, brushes past him and out the front door. "Al, I'm so, so
sorry. Really, I didn't mean for that to happen, it just came over
me. I don't even know what I was thinking, it was just so damn
natural." Michael starts to apologize, running through the lines I
know he's been rehearsing in the back of his head somewhere.
He sidles up next to me, drapes an arm around my shoulder, and
pulls my head to his chest so that it rests there for a minute. I
suck in every ounce of Michael, let every last drop of him penetrate my sinuses.

I gather my bag, retrieve the black sweater I've left thrown over the leather lounger in the living room, and make toward the front door. I hold up a hand to him to indicate he doesn't need to apologize further. "Michael, it's okay, it was bound to happen. She'll be okay. I may need a few days with her, though. Give me that, okay?"

"You call me, Al. You'll know when." And with that he kisses me square on the cheek, not in an unfriendly way.

"Thanks for dinner, Michael. Thank you for everything."

32

I expect Lydia to freeze me out. Cold shoulder, silent treatment, a complete shutdown. She doesn't. Rather, I'm subjected to a wrath of very angry, haughty, brazen, ill-tempered, bad-mouthed arguments during which, over the following days, she declares me to be incompetent, inept, uncool, useless, and downright wretched. She berates me constantly, snubs me repeatedly, and condemns me consistently.

This, of course, unless I'm driving her to and fro. Her course of action then *is* the silent treatment coupled with one-word answers and long periods of quiet, save for the thin stream of muffled screaming coming through the headphones of her CD player.

Finally, I've had enough. I break her down the only way I figure I know how. I confront her about Eric.

I say to her, "So, Lydia, no news from Eric, huh? Is he going to spend what's left of the summer ignoring the fact that he's going to be a father or do you think he might stop by one of these days and check to see how you are doing?"

This takes her by surprise. We're stopped at a light two miles or so from the studio, her second to last week of teaching before a short break and then school again. I push her further. "I was thinking, Lydia, this might be the time to call Eric, have him over, sit down, and have a long talk about all of this. Maybe even invite his mom and dad, too. After all, I'm sure they're going to want to have something to say about all of this, this . . . well, quite frankly, this little situation that you and Eric have found yourselves in. It's probably a good time for us all to get on the same page about what you're going to do about this baby. You're moving along pretty quick here, you know. There really doesn't seem to be a reason to wait."

She is so taken aback that she's left searching my face for recognition. It's quite possible it's the first time she's looked at me in two days. Still she says nothing.

"Lyd, did you hear what I said?" I ask her again, knowing I've got the upper hand on this conversation. "Now's the time, you know. Dinner might be the best way to sit down and talk about all of this, get it all out on the table. I mean, here it is the first week of August and you haven't even seen Eric all summer. He's practically disappeared on you, which quite frankly, is a little more than disappointing. He does have some responsibility in this. And some choice, too." Finally, in a very meek voice, I hear her chirp from the backseat, "Okay, Mom, I guess so. I just, I just don't know . . ." She trails off.

"You just don't know what, Lydia?" When she doesn't answer I start again, making a wide right turn into the studio and parking the car in the first stall. "Fine, it's settled," I answer confidently, tucking a loose strand of hair behind my ear. "Do you want to call him or shall I?"

"Um, I guess I should call him first. I don't really know what to say, though." Her voice is a whisper at best, just barely audible, certainly not the same girl who had told me, just hours before over Cheerios, that I have "no idea what the process is for getting your driving permit, that you just don't know anything."

"Well, I guess you could start with, 'I think it's time we talked about some of this stuff.' Does he even know what you think you're going to do about all this? And, Lydia"—I turn so that my body is perpendicular with the steering wheel and face her head-on—"do his parents even know about this baby? Or is my phone call to them going to be the first time they hear about this?"

"No, Mom, please. Let me call him first. I don't know," she

wails, crying openly now. "I don't have any idea, I really don't. I don't think they know. If they did, they'd probably have called you or something. I mean, don't you think so? Don't you think they'd care even just a little bit?" With the back of her sweatshirt sleeve she wipes snot from her cherry-red nose and sniffles loudly.

She's breaking my heart, chipping away at it in little bits. I'm pushing her, purposefully.

"Okay, Lydia, this is what we're going to do. You can have this afternoon to call Eric. I'll give you that. See if you can get him to come over by himself first. See if he's willing to sit down with you and with me and we'll talk some of this through. If not, let him know I'll be calling his mother. They need to know. And they need to be involved."

After Lydia leaves I sit in the car for a few minutes, soaking the sun in through the open window. The engine idles sharply in the afternoon heat. I dig through the bottom of my purse and come up with the crinkled paper on which Marina had scribbled the number for the adoption agency. Marina's strange strong slant screams at me from the paper until I pick up my cell again and finally punch in the numbers, waiting for someone on the other end to pick up. My skin is prickly with nerves I try to shake off.

I hang up twice before letting the number ring through. Each time, just before I hang up, I think about this baby, this child. In my mind, no matter how hard I try, I'm left staring into Lydia's face the first time I set eyes on her. I swallow hard and try to let the image go, let it float away from me.

When I finally connect with the agency, I'm on hold for nearly ten minutes before Elizabeth Peters comes on the phone, apologizing before she even stops to introduce herself.

"A birth mom, actually, in labor. There's nothing you can do about it when they call. You just have to take them. She couldn't think straight, didn't have a car to get to the hospital. I've called for a taxi. She'll be fine. The contractions are early. How can I help you, Mrs. Houlihan?"

"Um, I'm actually calling about my daughter. She's pregnant.

And I'm trying to get some information on your agency on her behalf."

"Oh, I see. Well, is she there? May I speak with her?" she asks me.

"No, actually, she's not here, she's teaching right now. She teaches dance, actually, well, just for the summer really, it just worked out that way anyway. It has kept her busy. She's really needed the distraction and this has been so good for her." I stop, take a breath, and realize I'm rambling, scattered, all over the map. "I'm sorry," I say, "I wasn't actually expecting to make this call today, I'm a bit unprepared, I think. Lost, really . . ." I trail off, hoping she'll take the lead.

"Mrs. Houlihan, how far along is your daughter? What is her due date?"

"She's almost five months, due mid-December, actually."

"And does she know you are speaking with me?"

"No. Well, sort of. She says she wants to put this baby up for adoption, it's been her plan from the beginning, but she doesn't so much know that I was going to call you today. Truth is, I didn't know I was going to call you today. I just sort of, well, I just sort of needed to get some more information on the whole thing. What we do, who we should talk to, where we go next. I got your name from Marina actually, Marina Kensington. She referred you. Actually, she referred to you as a godsend."

There's silence on the other end of the line as if she is waiting for me to go on. Finally she says, "Mrs. Houlihan?"

I interrupt her and ask her to call me Allyson, "or better yet, you can call me Ally. Mrs. Houlihan has always seemed too formal to me. And, well, it reminds me of my mother-in-law."

She laughs and starts over. "Ally, how old is your daughter? There's a chance I should be talking to her directly rather than speaking with you. In case there are issues of confidentiality, you see."

I swallow hard and tell her that Lydia is fifteen, that she has just finished her freshman year, and that she's a baby herself really. She lets me go on in long strings and I sense that she's taking notes, scribbling maybe on a lined white steno notebook.

"She's not my youngest birth mom, Ally, not by a long shot, if that's what you are thinking. I see pregnant girls who are just barely teenagers. And I have women who are probably older than you. It's all over the board."

I swallow hard. "Marina spoke very fondly of you, as if you were the only one who supported her at the time when she needed the most support in her life."

"Tell me something, Allyson, how do you feel about your daughter's decision to place this child for adoption?"

"I'm getting my arms around it," I say to her, and then pause before saying, "It's the best thing for her, the best thing for the baby."

"If I can be honest with you, Ally, you don't sound completely sold on the idea. What is it you are unsure about?"

"Everything, actually. Let's just say it's not something I could do myself."

"Is it something you can stand to watch your daughter do?"

I glance over my shoulder at the studio and catch a glimpse of Lydia crossing the hall from the warm-up studio, scooping girls along the way and shuffling them into the dance studio. "I think so. Actually, I don't see much of a choice around it."

"I see."

"Look, Elizabeth, if it were up to me, none of this would have happened. But I'm past that now. Now I'm just trying to figure out the best thing for us, for Lydia, actually. And I'm coming around on the idea of adoption. It's going to take me a little time. I'm not saying I won't permit her to do it, but it's just not what I'd choose for myself."

"Okay, we can start there. I appreciate your honesty. Tell me what makes Lydia want to place her baby for adoption."

It's something about how she says this to me, "Tell me what makes Lydia want to place *her* baby for adoption," that it clicks for me.

"She wants the baby to have a good home. She thinks there's someone out there that was meant to raise this baby, not her. She knows she can't do it. If we were to keep this baby, there's no doubt I'd be the one to raise it. Lydia can't even drive yet. She's barely started babysitting. She doesn't know the first thing. She doesn't have any grand ideas about doing this herself."

"And you? Would you want this baby? I can understand if you do. I run into plenty of people who think it's their responsibility to do this for their daughter's, or for their grandchild's, sake."

"I've considered it. But it's not fair to Lydia. And in the end, I suppose it's not fair to this baby either. To be that selfish, you know."

I take notes on the back of an empty lime-green envelope, a stray that has been stuck in the bottom of my black bag since my birthday. By the time we finally hang up, she's promised to put a packet of information into an overnight express for me, and I've promised to call her again in the next few days. I have an image of her, a stout woman in her late forties, short brown hair, stylish glasses hiding warm eyes, lots of freckles.

I start driving again, steering the wheel with my left hand while the fingers on my right punch out Michael's office number as if I'm reading Braille.

"Hey, Michael." I breathe a long sigh into the receiver. "Do you have time for coffee?"

"Yes. Absolutely. Now? Just tell me where to meet you, Ally. God, I've missed you. I've been so worried," Michael breathes effortlessly into the phone.

"The baseball field across from the theaters. I need to walk. I'll get the coffees, just meet me there in half an hour or so. Man, Michael, I've missed you too, you have no idea how much."

"I do, Al, I think I do."

It has been four days since I've seen Michael. I arrive at the park first and find an uncomfortable wooden bench just west of the gated dog park where a black terrier is backed into the corner, his tail tucked under his backside.

Michael takes the coffee from me but sets it down on the

cracked cement sidewalk and pulls me by both hands up and into a tremendous warm embrace. I melt into him, letting every part of me touch him head to toe. We're like old lovers who have gone years without seeing each other, only to plan an afternoon together, a simple chance meeting. When he pulls away, he cups my chin with both his hands, closes his eyes, and kisses me.

"Can we walk? I don't think I can sit still here with you."

"Yes, of course."

We stroll. Slow, soft steps that fall in rhythm with each other through the adjacent park lined with snapdragons and rose trees. Heads bent together, leaning in and hanging on each other's stories. I listen to him describe the uncomfortable meeting he's had with Leslie the night before, the discussion again about child support, the run he took this morning just on a whim hoping he might, somehow, have bumped into me, the problem he's having with a client.

I tell him I've called an adoption agency, and that I've told Lydia to invite Eric over for dinner so we can sort through things. I leave out the brutal last four days, the harsh words, the seething rage she's hurled at me like a child spraying food across the kitchen. He stops and we stand facing each other on the sidewalk, forcing a mother pushing a stroller to dodge around us.

"Good for you, Al. That's great. I knew you would come around on it." He smiles down at me, gracing me with his wide grin and brushing the hair back behind my ear. "How is she, Al? Will she ever forgive us? Forgive me?"

"Yes. She will forgive us. Eventually. May not happen now, may not even happen for a while. But she'll soften, you'll see."

"I'm so, so sorry, Ally, I don't know what happened. In the kitchen, I mean. It just overtook me, something I didn't even realize was happening."

We walk on, silent. "I know, Michael. I understand."

"When's Eric coming? And how do you think this thing will go?" He runs his free hand through the masses of hair; he's due for a haircut, one every few weeks or the nest becomes unruly, unfamiliar.

"She's got to call him first. Let's see how that goes. He might come, might not. And if he does, we'll have to see how *that* goes. I haven't seen him since before the beach, Lydia's birthday, maybe, or just after that. Really, I don't know, it's been a while. He's got to be scared shitless, just a kid, both of them, really." I finish the last of my iced coffee and toss the plastic cup into a garbage can.

"How can I help you with this?" His eyes plead with me. "Do you want me to talk to Lydia?"

I laugh, and eye him up and down. "You're crazy, Michael. She'll tear you apart right now. Sorry," I say, when I see the hurt register on his face, "but she's not ready yet." We walk on a little farther before I add, delicately, "And neither am I, really. This is something I've got to do with her. Try to understand that."

33

I find Lydia at the kitchen table, a glass of water dripping condensation so that it puddles up around the papers she's rifling through. The box is addressed to me, but it doesn't take long for her to figure out what it is, and I can tell she's torn into it ferociously, the pull tab ripped ragged from one end of the box to the other.

Profiles from prospective adoptive families are spread from one end of the table to the other. "The world's most intimate job applications," I tell Michael on the phone later. Pictures and letters and pages of information about people who want a baby; not just Lydia's baby, but any baby they can get their hands on. Their stories pour out, each one unique, though no less heartbreaking than the other.

Becca and I are just home, Becca struggling with the immobility of the pale, pasty arm that she holds gingerly, cautiously, as if at any moment it might break again and she'd be forced back into another cast. She'd done beautifully, smiling wide-eyed through the whole procedure until the cast was cut, then cracked, away from her arm.

It ached; she'd said so in the car. More than she realized it would.

And before we'd left Bruce Cleveland's office, "Are you sure I can't convince you to have a drink with me?" he asked once again, while Becca, shock registering on her face at words foreign to her own ears, sulked against the wall. She leered at me waiting for my response, appalled that I wasn't quicker on my feet.

"Um, no. No, Bruce I think I'd better pass, but thank you. Becca and I will miss our appointments with you. We'll have to stop in now and again on you." I felt my own face go hot, seeped in embarrassment.

"Well," he said, fact-checking and editing the notes in Becca's chart, "you won't get away from me that quickly." He turned toward Becca. "Easy does it with that, soccer star. Start slow and don't push it. You've got plenty of time to work on that arm, and lots to make up for. It's going to take a while. You're set at rehab starting Monday. Every day until we've regained at least fifty percent mobility and I see some rotation and more movement coming back, okay?"

Becca barely nodded at him, and she pulled back stiff from the embrace she found herself within. She sulked out of his office, dragging her blue and white Adidas sandals across the floor. I smiled weakly at Bruce and followed Becca out, opened the heavy door to the waiting room, and propped it open with my foot as Bruce devoured me into his own bear hug. Clearly he's missed the cues.

We walked out in silence, Becca gingerly touching her arm. She worked at picking off some of the leftover plaster flakes that were stuck to her pale arm hairs. Finally, disdainfully, she spat, "I didn't know Dr. Cleveland had asked you out. Like on a date, Mom? A *date*? You weren't really considering it, were you?"

"Drinks. It's different than a date, Becca." Having been through this earlier in the week with her sister, I was not in the mood to be accused for something I've not done.

"Drinks *are* a date, Mom. Duh."

"Look, Becca, the fact of the matter is that I didn't go on a date with Dr. Cleveland. I passed. I don't really know why, come to think of it. He's an attractive man, and, well, why shouldn't I go have drinks with him? But I didn't. It wasn't for me. Now, can we just move on?"

But still, even after the long drive home in stop-and-go traffic, she's relentless and announces to her sister the minute we walk into the kitchen that Dr. Cleveland had asked me on a date.

Without realizing what Lydia has unearthed in the box propped open at her feet, I know anger has seeped back into her soul. When she turns from the pile of pages she is studying, she mouths bitterly, "Gee, Mom, I wonder what Michael would think of that."

"Michael? Why in the world would Michael care, Lydia?" Becca smarts back at her.

Lydia ignores her sister's question. I glance sideways at the return address on the box before I take a few cautious steps and sidle up toward Lydia's chair. She flashes me a look that stops me cold, fire in her eyes, underlying the hurt she's masking as anger.

"Where did you get these?" she hisses at me. "Who did you talk to? How could you, without even telling me that you were going to?"

I was almost certain she'd have thought I'd done her a favor. "An agency. Not here, Lydia, the agency is in California. A woman who was quite helpful, actually. I liked her very much. She had some very positive things to say about adoption and she seemed to understand where you were coming from."

"Oh, so now you *like* the idea, Mom? You haven't exactly been pro-adoption, but as soon as you talk to some woman, you think maybe it's not a bad idea after all? When I've been telling you all along that it's what I wanted to do? You mean to tell me that you couldn't have at least told me you were going to talk to someone? Couldn't I have at least talked to her? I told you I wanted to do this. Can't you even let me own a little piece of it?" She pauses, flipping rapidly through the papers, flinging them this way and that. "I mean, after all, Mom, this is *my* baby. *Mine.*"

I steady myself on the chair back, and stare down at the photos spread like an album across the table. "Jesus, Lydia, I'm sorry if this surprised or hurt you. I was only trying to help. I figured maybe, just maybe you were onto something."

"Don't you get it, Mom? It's not your decision. It's mine. God, don't you see? This really doesn't have anything to do with you. It's my choice, Mom, not yours. It's just not yours."

"Now, wait a second, Lyd—" I begin, explosive.

She's quick to fire back, "No, you wait a second, Mom. I don't get you. Two days ago you tell me I've got to call Eric, that I've got to get him over here so he and I can take some responsibility in this. Now you tell me you want to be in charge of it. Which is it? 'Cause if you ask me, it's my doing. And you know what? I don't need you calling some woman in California. I don't need your help with this at all. It's fine, Mom, I'll figure it out. I'm the one sitting here with this baby inside me. Look at me. I look like some sort of sick cartoon character, that's what I am, some sort of wicked messed-up girl." Her eyes pierce with rage, but behind them is the hurt, the emotion of something else that has happened, something that's stayed with her.

I pull the chair out from the table and set myself down in it, leaning full into the pinewood spokes. "Lyd, what happened? Is everything okay? What's going on, baby?" I reach out to smooth her hair, but she bats my hand away, furious with me for interfering.

She stands and begins to shuffle the papers together, pictures stapled to each of the corners of the profiles. "No, Mom, nothing happened, nothing at all. You got your wish. Eric finally called me back. He'll be here at seven o'clock. You can figure out what you think I should say to him then. I'm sure you know what's best. I'm sure you've got this whole goddamned thing worked out, don't you?"

I watch her cradle the papers in her arms and hold them tight to her chest. From below the mess of pictures, papers, and black ink, the bottom of her belly protrudes, stretched across nylon gym shorts that don't fit her properly anymore. She walks away from me then, shoulders back.

"I was only trying to help, Lydia. A little bit, that's all. I was only trying to help you do what you said you wanted to do."

"How would you even know what it is I want to do, Mom? You haven't even begun to listen to me."

No one knocks at the door or rings the bell until 7:35. I've been pacing the hardwood in the entry hall for fifteen minutes wondering if Eric will come. Lydia has been locked away in her room; Becca has retreated to Sarah's without so much as a word but to let me know where she was going after she'd finished her dinner. I'd snuck a cigarette, then a call to Michael, asking him to keep Bec as long as he could and run her home sometime after the prime time shows ended. He'd asked if I was okay and I'd given him the highlights.

When I open the door, Eric is standing with his back to me, staring back into the courtyard, his hands shoved deep in the pockets of worn jeans. His hair is longer than I remember, touching the tips of his collar, the makings of waves starting to curl upward. He turns and takes me in before he says, "Hiya, Mrs. H. Haven't seen you in a long while. Is Lydia here?"

"Come on in, Eric. She's up in her room. Why don't you wait for her in the family room? Get yourself something to drink if you want. I'll go get her." He shuffles across the floor, his pants hanging low. I watch him disappear around the corner before I take the steps two at a time.

I don't bother to knock; I just crack the door a bit and peek inside. She's got her headphones on, the music loud enough for me to make out the words to a new song she's been singing the past few days. She sits upright, yanks the headphones from her ears, and throws them across the bed with one hand while the other moves to pull down her long T-shirt.

"What?" she barks at me.

"Eric's here. He's in the family room." I back out of the room and begin to close the door behind me.

"Mom?" Her voice softens. "Aren't you going with me?"

"I figured you two probably needed some time on your own. It's been a long time, Lydia, a long, long time since you've seen him. Why don't you give each other some time to talk, be okay with each other in the room, just work through some of the awkwardness?"

"Um, okay, I guess." She pulls a pillow close to her chest, hugs it to her body, and rests her chin against the piping running along one side. "It's just, oh God, Mom, I have no idea what to say to him. Where do I even start?"

I don't want to help her, but her voice shakes with trepidation. "Try this, honey. 'Hey, how's your summer been? What have you been doing?'" I'm not much help, but I move to the side of the bed and offer her both of my hands, pulling her to her feet. "Start there," I sigh, "and just see where you go."

"Can you come down in a few minutes? Just make your way through the kitchen or something. I'll feel better if I know you're going to come down." She wraps her arms around my neck then, begging me and holding tight while she presses her body into mine. Even well into her second term, she's tiny. I've been so focused on her midsection I've forgotten about the rest of her. Her arms are long slivers, her legs storklike but toned. I draw her to me; pull all of her as close to me as I can get her.

"Okay, Lyd," I whisper into the cascades of hair that fall at her shoulders. I breathe in wafts of her strawberry shampoo mixed with a vanilla lip-gloss, and promise her I'll be downstairs in a few minutes. Before I go, I say to her, "Lydia, I'm sorry I didn't tell you about the adoption agency. I should have, really I should. I just wanted to help. You don't have to use this one if you don't want to. You don't have to look at any of these pictures or talk to any of these people." I steal a glance over her shoulder and see she's moved the sea of profiles to her bed, stacked them in a few piles that I'm sure must have some sort of order to them; a few stragglers lie sprawling on their own. "I just, you know, I just didn't know what to tell you about the whole thing. So I thought maybe I should find out a little more about it. I mean, you might be onto something, here, Lyd. And I know it's your baby, I do know that. But *you're my baby*, Lydi, you're *my* little girl. And I just wanted to help you. That's all."

"It's okay, Mom. I found the right people."

"You what? Already? But how?"

"Yeah."

"But, Lyd," I say to her, fear washing over me. "How could you possibly know? How?"

I stare at her, stunned, when she reaches for her brush and rakes it through her hair a couple of times. She watches me through the mirror over her dresser and finally says, "I'll show them to you later."

"Oh. Okay." I don't push her further.

"Later. I promise," she says, holding the door open for me, waiting for me to leave the room with her. She doesn't dare leave me to rifle through the stack and offer my own opinion. I trip out, stumble on the hardwood, and falter over my very own feet.

Lydia and Eric sit at opposite ends of matching couches, with their backs against the armrests at each end. With his left hand, Eric expertly maneuvers the remote control and the television channels whirl by. Lydia's staring at him; he's focused intently on the big screen wedged into the entertainment unit at the far end of the room. Baseball, fishing, MTV, a game show, a JAG rerun, some movie I know but can't, for the life of me, remember the name of. They go flying by, a few first moments, and then on to the next channel. I'm amazed he can follow any of it at all.

I clear my throat and watch them from the kitchen, making a list of things I need at the store. Nothing, nada, zip, zilch. I sneak a peek and she's trying her best to keep up with the shows. I hear her ask him a question about the baseball game, something I know she knows the answer to without asking, but she does anyway, with a voice that isn't her own. We both look at her like she's crazy.

"Eric," I call at him, my head still focused on the pad of paper in front of me, the notes where I can barely make out my own scribbles. "Can you help me move some bags of potting soil out of the back of the Suburban? I was going to have Michael do it this weekend, but since you're here, maybe you can lift them. They're just too heavy for me to do on my own . . ." my voice trails off.

He shuffles over to me at the countertop, pulling his baseball cap low and tight across brow. "Sure, you wanna do it now?"

"Um, yeah, let's." I place my pen at the top of the notepad and lead him out of the kitchen. "Lyd, we'll be back in a few minutes."

He's quick with the bags, stacking them three deep in the utility area just behind the fence. His body is lean and underdeveloped, lanky, but he hauls the weight, throws the bags over his shoulder, and steadies them against his collarbone. On his third trip I weigh my words carefully.

"How's your summer been? We've hardly seen you."

"Yeah, it's been busy. Not much of anything really. Just hanging around and stuff." He's stiff with his words and controls his response.

"Well, you know you are always welcome around here, you can stop by any time you want."

He stops then, having placed the last bag on top of the pile, and brushes his hands against the jeans he's wearing. My back is to the setting sun; I can feel the last bits of it warming my shoulders. Still, nightfall is close enough to touch, to feel in the air. He squints at me, dazed.

"You'd really want me to come by, Mrs. H.? With all this, um . . . stuff that's going on? I mean, the . . ." He swallows hard now and I can see he's trying to find the right words. "I mean the baby and all. You'd still want me around here?"

I lean up against the back of the car, set the edge of my butt down on the chrome bumper, and cross my legs at the ankles. "Yeah, Eric, actually I would still like you around here. It'd be nice to know what you're thinking about all of this. What you *and* Lydia are thinking about all of this. Together. I know she's got her ideas. But what're yours?"

"You know something, Mrs. H., no one's asked me that. Not Lydia, anyway. I don't know. It's Lydia's decision, really, you know, it's her choice. I told her that right up front. And that I'd be okay with whatever she did, you know, just whatever decision she came to about all this." He's quiet for a minute, contemplative. "I mean, what am I supposed to say, you know? I just want her to be okay with all of it."

"Have you told her that?"

"Yeah. I told her that. I think she thought I was putting the whole thing on her. But I wasn't, you know. I just didn't know what to tell her. I just couldn't believe it had happened." He goes away for a minute, drifts off into some sort of daydream. His eyes are closed, his head back, and I can imagine he's thinking of a simpler time, when none of this existed. "It was just such a mistake. This baby, such a big mistake."

"I don't know about that," I blurt forth, surprised to hear myself saying it.

"How could you not think it was a mistake, Lydia getting pregnant? It's the worst thing that could have happened, you know, the absolute worst." He shakes his head in disgust, eyes wide and full of repentance.

"There's a difference between something that happened and something that was a mistake, Eric. I'm beginning to think that this was one of those things that just happened, for some reason other than one we can explain. Maybe someday we'll get it, maybe not. But I don't like to think of it as a mistake, you know. A child, no matter how he comes into this world, shouldn't be thought of as a mistake." I shiver in the dusk. At the other end of the street the Baker boys race toward home on their bikes, eager to see who can make it before the last streetlight comes on.

Then I say to him, "And, Eric, it's not the worst thing that could have happened. Trust me on that, okay?"

He clams up at the kitchen table when I offer him lemonade and invite Lydia to join us. She eyes the both of us suspiciously and knows we've spent far too much time together outside to have just been unloading a bunch of dirt. But she doesn't ask. Rather, she takes her place at the long pine bench, settles in against the grain of the wood, and leans her head into her hands, her elbows resting on the table.

"Lyd, you want to talk at all about all the stuff that's going on? You know, maybe let Eric in on some of what you're thinking?"

She shrugs and sighs long. "Not much to talk about, really. I'm putting it up for adoption. I told you that." She raises her eyes from the table to find his, but he's stuck on digging something from underneath one of his fingernails.

"Yeah, you told me. I know. That's fine, if that's what you want to do."

"That's it, really. I'll have the baby and then it'll be done with, you know, you won't have to worry about it."

He nods in agreement and shrugs back at her. Then just a little more softly, "Yeah, okay. Whatever."

I sit in between them, in referee position, at the head of the table. I could easily reach out for either of them, for both, but I keep my hands together, one resting on top of the other, and watch them back and forth like a tennis match with quick, but lobbing, powerless volleys. Tension settles thick in the air. I'm left wondering how these two people, these two children who are barely capable of a conversation together, were capable of going to bed together, of having sex, of making love. Forcibly I push the images from my mind, cover my face with my hands, and rub my eyes vigorously.

"What's wrong, Mom?" Lydia asks me. She rubs her feet together, a habit she's had since childhood. I reach for her hand and hold it tight, offering a weak smile.

"I'm fine," I say, though not convincingly. And then, to Eric, "How're your mom and dad with all this? Do they know?"

"Yeah, they know. My mom asked me where Lyd had been. I told her we were just taking some time apart." He checks this explanation with Lydia at the table and watches for her reaction. When there is none, he goes on more softly now. "She'd heard Lydia might be pregnant—I don't know who told her—but she asked me, you know, just right straight up. I wasn't gonna lie to her, what good would that have done? So I told her. She cried, my dad yelled. They both said it was the biggest mistake of my life. They wanted to come over tonight, but I asked them not to. I thought maybe I should come, at least this first time, to talk things through."

I watch Lydia tense at his words, her back straight and rigid. It's the first time she's heard of herself as the subject of a rumor, though there'd be many more to come. For now she bristles.

"Yes," I say this time, "I suppose some people will think it is just that. One big mistake. Like I said to you outside, Eric, I'm not so sure."

Now it's Lydia who looks at me half crazy. "God, Mom, how can it not be? I'd do anything to take this back and make it all go away," she groans.

"It was meant to happen is all, Lyd. It was just meant to happen." I lace my fingers inside her hand and rub my thumb against her pinkie. "That's pretty much the only way I can think to describe it."

34

The phone bolts me awake at 7:42. I sit straight up in bed and fumble across my nightstand to answer it.

"Mrs. Houlihan?" An unfamiliar voice.

"Yes."

"Mrs. Houlihan, I'm with the school district for your daughter, um, well, I had it here just a minute ago, yes, well, give me a minute, will you?"

There's a sound of shuffling paper at the other end, and I ask, "Is there something I can help you with? I have two daughters. Do you know which one you are calling about?" I yawn and wait a second more.

"The one who will be a sophomore at Jefferson in the fall, Mrs., ah yes, here it is, Lydia. I'm calling regarding your daughter Lydia."

I pull the covers around my chest, the creased sheet still crisp. "Yes, what about Lydia? Is something wrong?"

"Well, we understand that she might be, well, I'm not sure you're quite aware of this, but I'll go ahead and say it anyway." She pauses a minute before she lowers her voice almost to a whisper. "Actually, Mrs. Houlihan, we understand Lydia might be pregnant."

"Yes," I say indignantly into the phone.

"Oh, well, I see. Um, well, if that's the case, Mrs. Houlihan, have you made alternative arrangements for her when school begins at the end of the month?"

"What do you mean, 'alternative arrangements'? You just said yourself she's going to be a sophomore at Jefferson. She just finished registering for her classes last week."

"Yes, well, ma'am, I'm very sorry, but Jefferson cannot admit her if she is pregnant. Not, at least, until she has the baby. We can suggest an optional—"

"What?" I practically scream into the phone. "What the hell are you people talking about?" Now I'm wide-awake. And I'm pissed. "Why can't my daughter start school in three weeks like every other student? What in the world does her being pregnant have to do with her education?"

"I'm sorry, Mrs. Houlihan, but the school district regulations specifically state that any student who is pregnant is not permitted on school grounds. There's an issue with liability, you see." She's perky, and by the amount of page turning I make out in the background, I have no doubt that she's flipping through the district guidelines, ready to read me the specific regulation. She goes on, clipping away, "You can imagine what a problem we'd have if she were to go into labor during the school day. The high school is just not, well, it's really not a suitable place for her to be, given the circumstances."

"I'm sorry, I didn't catch your name," I say, curt, clipped bites into the receiver.

"Lois. Lois Stevens. We've been checking on all the students who have recently registered, making sure they've met all the appropriate requirements for the upcoming school year." She's amazingly cheery.

"I'm sorry, Ms. Stevens, but is it the liability the school is worried about, or the appropriate nature of having a pregnant fifteen-year-old on campus?" I ask her.

"Um, well, actually, I guess it would be both, Mrs. Houlihan. But I do not make the rules, I only am calling to let you know. I'll be happy to pop a list in the mail of alternative scholastic choices that will meet Lydia's needs until she has the baby. Um, may I ask, when is she due?"

"December."

"Well, see then, she'll only miss the first semester. Back in school in no time. Has she decided what she's going to do with the baby?"

"Ms. Stevens? I do not see how that is any of your, or any of the school district's, business. Do you?"

"Well, as I said," she replies, suddenly more abrupt, finally comprehending my tone, "I'll just pop that list in the mail then."

"You do that," I grumble through the receiver before I hear her click off. I sit for a minute in my pink and white shortie nightgown, holding the receiver tightly in my hand until my knuckles go white, before I slam it down into the cradle and scream into my pillow.

Lydia takes the news better than I thought she would.

"Fine, Mom, whatever, it's okay. I don't want to see anyone anyway." She's lying on her left hip with a pillow wedged under her right leg. I can tell she's been up for a while; she was awake when I knocked softly on her door at eight thirty. And when I walked into her room, and inched closer to the edge of the bed, I could see she'd been crying, a smallish wet spot covering the striped pillowcase under her chin.

I'm sitting on the edge of the bed. "I know this is important to you, honey. It's tenth grade. I'll rally for you, honestly I will. We just need to figure out what gives with all this. I want to talk to Anna, see if she knows anything about what's what at the high school, see this 'list of alternative choices' and understand better what our options are before you make any decision at all. Anything. Okay? I just wanted you to know there might be a chance we have to do things a little different right now."

She sniffles against the sheet and clears her throat. I start rubbing her back, the way I know she likes it best, with the tips of my fingernails, just softly so there's barely even a trace of a mark. She snuggles closer under her down comforter, hugs the down pillow to her chest, and lets out an enormous sigh I imagine she's been holding on to for a while.

Finally, very quietly, she says to me, "Mom? Did you want to see the people I picked?"

I'm confused by her question, and then it dawns on me, the profile she mentioned the night before. She reaches across the bed to her desk, where a stack of papers is haphazardly tossed together, and pulls out the bottom profile and hands it to me. I take it with both hands, delicately, as if I'm receiving a gift. Two smiling faces stare at me from the photo stapled to the front of the profile, a sandy-colored cocker spaniel sprawled in between them.

I stare at the photo for a long while, taken on a brilliant day, and wonder if they've dressed specifically for the shot. She's in a lavender and white pin-striped cotton blouse; he's in a pale blue oxford. When I flip the photo over, careful not to bend it at the staple where it's attached to the paperwork, I learn their names are Melinda and Reid, they live in a suburb of Denver, and most surprisingly, they are three years younger than I am. I flip the photo back over and stare at them a long while more.

"Read the profile, Mom, go ahead," Lydia urges.

I stare up at her and am taken by the way her eyes plead with me for approval.

Melinda's handwriting is precise and loopy, as one would imagine a schoolteacher's would be, so I'm not surprised to learn that she's taught fifth grade for thirteen years. An engineer by trade, Reid says his passion has always been to open a restaurant, and I learn that he's quit his day job five years earlier to open his own place in downtown Denver. They like snow skiing, traveling, and they're Episcopalian. I skim through the first page of their profile, a series of questions you might expect to fill out at an initial doctor's visit. Then I flip back to their photo. It's a four-by-six shot. The dog, Misty, is sitting more on Reid than on Melinda.

Melinda is thin, her features tiny, her eyes bright. She has on a pair of black shoes that are very similar to ones that I own. She carries a darling Kate Spade handbag that, in the picture, is placed on the sidewalk near her feet. Reid appears protective, but more staged in the photo, more apprehensive maybe. His smile lacks sincerity, as if he's been asked to sit there for too long. But he's not unhandsome, and there's a semicharming, very boyish characteristic about him: dimples. His hair is auburn, a burnt reddish brown tint and cropped short, but blessed with good genes, he has all of it.

For the life of me I cannot figure what has possessed Lydia to pick these people out of a stack that must include nearly forty profiles Elizabeth has sent me. She's got her arms crossed against her chest and is chewing nervously on the end of a frayed cuticle on her thumb, awaiting my approval; her eyes bore into me, watching me read every word, watching the way I stare endlessly at the photo.

I choose my words carefully, realizing immediately the impact they might have.

"Honey, what is it you liked about them?"

"Did you read the letter?" she says nervously, abruptly.

"What letter?" I flip through the pages quickly until I land on the last two sheets stapled to the back. It's a copy of a letter that's clearly been on the Xerox machine a few times.

"Right there, that's it." She bends the papers back for me and hands it back.

As I finish the last paragraph, I understand why Lydia has chosen them. I understand exactly what has touched her so deeply that she resoundingly has already made up her mind about these people before she's even spoken two words to them.

We're not sure what has led us to this path, why God has chosen this fate for us. Things don't often make much sense. The things we thought were supposed to have happened haven't. The things we never expected, not in a million years, tear blindingly through our lives, all of our lives, and we know there must be a reason for that as well. We've stopped asking why and move forward with the will to come to a place where we can best live with what we have, letting peace and strength guide us.

When I finish the letter, I look up at Lydia. She is staring out-side the open window, the sunlight pouring in on her face.

"Do you understand now?" she asks, without looking directly at me. "Don't you see, Mom? It's as if Daddy sent them."

"Maybe he did, Lyd. Maybe he did," I say to her.

Looking at Lydia standing there in the window, sun-kissed and somewhat free with her decision, I can't argue with her. She looks as if an angel has touched her.

35

I've promised myself I'll make some headway on my closet. Kept neat and orderly by one of those wall-to-wall organizer systems we had installed when we bought the house, my sweaters are stacked in rows, my shirts and slacks hung evenly on heavy wooden hangers, my unmentionables tucked away in rolling drawers. But since Patrick's death, my closet is a place where the walls come crashing in. I try my hardest to dart in and out, avoiding all contact with the last remaining things Patrick left behind: his clothes, his shoes, even his watch, which was recovered and which I set in the same place he would have, on his dresser, months and months before.

It's nearly four in the afternoon before I make peace with the mission, having procrastinated long enough. I'm still struck by the slightest trace of Patrick that lingers either within the fabric of his dark suits or in my imagination, I'm still not sure which. He was all honey and musk, warm and inviting. It hangs in the air the minute I step into the small cave.

Patrick took up much less space than I did, still does, but in all this time I've not crossed over, not stolen a single hanger from his side, not moved a shoe or a tie, not rearranged the sweaters that are still piled high on the shelves. It's not like me to have left them over the summer months, perfect targets for stray moths. But come April, when I'd sent my own wool clothes to be dry-cleaned, bagged, and put away, I just couldn't manage to bring myself to do his. So there they rested, same spot, same stacks. The last of his dry cleaning, that which came back long after the funeral, still in the same bags.

There are a few things I cannot part with. A sweatshirt he'd worn running and on weekends that I couldn't bear to see go to the Goodwill. The sweater I'd given him our last Christmas together, a mesh of colors in soft lamb's wool that would be large and roomy on me but that I knew I'd need later. I wrap it around me, breathe all of it in. Patrick had only worn it a few times; still, it felt of him, the way he'd have touched me had he been inside its folds. A man's jewelry box with his wedding ring, a pin bearing his family crest, a few things Barbara had passed on from his father. I move the entire teak box to the bottom drawer of my dresser and set it there for keeps.

The rest I'm folding and stacking in neat piles, jeans, casual slacks, suits, oh, the endless suits. Dress shirts in blue and white, golf shirts that range as wide as the courses he'd played. I'm standing knee deep in clothes, perspiration beading at my neck, when I hear the doorbell ring downstairs. Michael's been out for a run, his cheeks a deep blotchy red and the curls damp at the nape of his neck. He stands bent at the waist, hands on his hips, dripping sweat when I answer the door. I take all of him in, top to bottom. He's dressed in his soccer shorts and the white tee clings tightly to his chest, soaked with perspiration and creased from where he's used it to wipe his brow.

He takes water when I offer it and drinks the bottle in nearly one long gulp. "Jesus, it's so damn hot tonight. What in the hell was I thinking running today?"

"I've got news for you. Compared to my closet, where I've been sorting for the last three hours, this is tepid. It's about 110 degrees upstairs." I push my matted bangs back and take a long drink from my own bottle.

"Right. So that's what you're doing. I'd forgotten. Cleaning day." He pauses then, stretching before gently prodding, "How's it going?"

"It's going. Wanna see?"

"Um, actually, no. I think this is one of those things you gotta do on your own, Al. I think I'll pass, if that's okay."

"Well, I could use your help with something. Since you're here and all," I say to him, carrying my water with me and heading down the hall toward the stairs. "If, that is, you can stay for a few minutes."

He follows me up to the bathroom that separates my bedroom from the closet I'm cleaning. "There." I point out to him the hook on the bathroom wall that's pulled loose and left a gaping hole next to an identical hook that holds my towel. "It pulled out this morning and it's bugging the crap out of me." He fingers the hole; digs a bit at the white calk that has frayed around the corner. "Can you fix that for me? I'm good, you know, but I still haven't mastered all this manly-man household stuff. I tried screwing it back in this morning, but I'm afraid I've made a bigger mess out of it."

"Yeah, I can fix that, no problem." I head back into the closet then, just as I hear him turn and take the stairs two at a time, heading for the tool bench Patrick had assembled long ago on the side wall in the garage. He returns a minute later with the electric drill, some calk, a new screw, and some sort of molly bolt he thinks might do the trick.

"It's hot, Al, damn, it's hot. Don't you have the air on up here?" I hear him move the pile of clothes I've laid on my bed, before he flops down and lets out a long sigh.

"Yeah, it's on. You'd never know it, though, would you?" I emerge from the back of the closet and move to where Michael lies sprawled on the bed. I catch myself in the mirror above the vanity. My cheeks are flushed and bits of hair have pulled loose from my ponytail and fly limply around my face. I've failed to put on makeup today, but my face feels as if it is melting anyway. Still, I feel beautiful in his presence; he does that to me. There's nothing more I'd like right now than to turn on the fan and lie naked next to him, let the air blow over the both of us. The girls are long out for the night, Becca at a soccer sleepover celebrating the end of the season; Lydia at the movies with a group of girls who still accept her, despite the ever-protruding belly, the secret she can't hide any longer.

He sits up slightly, resting his weight on his elbows, when I come into the room, but relaxes a bit when I walk around the bed and switch on the fan. The whirring stirs the room, sending the pages of the *Mademoiselle* magazine on my nightstand fluttering until I throw the copy in a basket on the floor. The air feels so good it sends shivers over my damp skin.

I lie on my side, my legs curled at the knees around one of the throw pillows from my bed. I'm staring at him long and hard, refusing to look away until he meets my eyes. Still he watches the fan, his head back and his eyes intent on the middle of the ceiling and the constant whirring the blades make.

"Al, maybe we should head downstairs, hang out down there for a while?" he says quietly and softly.

"Why? Michael, am I making you nervous?" My voices teases him.

He rolls toward me but doesn't lean in. He keeps his balance, the line of his body parallel to mine. "Yes," he breathes quietly, "you are."

"Why?"

"Where are the girls, Al? Are they around? When will they be back?"

"They're out, Michael. Bec's at Jessica's, the soccer sleepover, remember? Coach?"

"Very funny. And Lydia? Where's Lyd?" He sits up, anxious all of a sudden. "God knows we don't need a repeat performance of the other night."

"Movies. She won't be back until late, Michael. Relax."

"It's so damn hot," he says, "the hottest summer, really. You can feel it, just that wet, muggy feeling, even in the air-conditioning. You know what I mean?"

"I have an idea. Wanna take a shower?"

He eyes me, arching an eyebrow in my direction, trying to decide if I am serious. I leave him sprawled across the bed, his eyes following me as I peel off my shorts first, then my tank top, dropping my panties and bra just outside the glass door. I reach inside to set the water temperature to lukewarm, cool, almost. I take one final glance in his direction before I step inside the enclosed shower and wait for him to join me.

Neither of us expects Lydia, of course. The door-slamming, foot stomping, Mom-calling, goes unnoticed by the both of us as distant background noise, something we're casually aware of, but neither concerned nor heedful of. It's not until she's in the bedroom, nearing the bath and calling my name somewhat persistently, that I even flinch. When I do, panic comes over the both of us, rises like bile in my throat.

I manage to wrap myself in a towel before she struts into the bathroom and plants herself on the edge of the bathtub as she's sometimes been known to do. I'm covered but suspiciously self-conscious, dripping wet and flustered, when I meet her at the door between the bedroom and the bath, usher her the other way. With the water still running, she's immediately quizzical.

"Mom, what're you doing? You're dripping wet." ·

"You startled me, Lydia, my God, scared me cold is more like it. I didn't know you'd come home. I, I wasn't expecting you back this early. I thought someone was in the house." I pull the towel tight around me and scold her with a furrowed brow. She spots Michael's running clothes, recognizes his familiar sweatshirt strewn on the side of the bed, and purses her lips at me, anger overwhelming her face.

"What's Michael doing in the shower, Mom? God, Mom, are you kidding me? You two are really too much," she hisses, turning on her foot and beelining for the bedroom door. She's got one of Patrick's old sweatshirts, one that she'd rescued before I'd started decomposing his closet, tied around her waist, just under where her shirt is bunched up to hide her stomach.

I let her go, watch her stomp out of the room the same way she used to as a child, stubborn and unwilling. Lydia had often barricaded herself in her room for hours when she thought she was deserving of an apology; little has changed in all these years. I lis-

ten to her make her way down the hall, the door slamming hard
and swift behind her in a force.

I meet Michael coming out of the shower, a towel wrapped at
his waist and his hair damp in tiny rings. His face is contorted
with worry, his eyes sad with mistakes. He tells me that he's worried about the damage he's doing to my relationship with the
girls.

"I shouldn't have come, Ally, it's just not okay with the girls
around. This thing between us, we can't ever expect them to
understand it. You were right about that, I had no idea how dam-
aging it would be."

I want him to stop talking, stop thinking. I want the world to
stop moving, stop revolving and swaying and rocking and making
me so seasick. I long for stillness and freedom from disturbance,
commotion, and agitation. I want things to be simple again.

I watch Michael towel himself off and then slip back into his
running clothes, his back turned to me, the broad shoulders still
so delicious-looking. When he's dressed he bends down to me,
balances on bent knees, eye-level with me and kisses me, tenderly on the lips.

I watch him go, quick and stealthlike, as quiet as he can for
fear he'll draw the bear from her den. I hear the front door open,
the alarm chimes echoing throughout the house, then close quickly
and firmly.

36

"Can I have her, just for the night, dear? It'd be good for you and Patrick to have a night away. You could use it."

I'd smiled weakly at Barbara; she was right. What bothered me most about it was that the cracks were visible. They must have been. She seemed concerned, and it wasn't often that she was genuinely concerned. Involved, yes, but rarely concerned.

"It'd be great, Barbara, truly wonderful. Are you sure you can handle her? She's not easy these days. Or nights." It was true; Lydia was beyond difficult. At four months she ran the risk of colic gripping her from 8:00 a.m. until she cried herself out just before dinnertime. Then up, sometimes all night, sleeping in the smallest, shortest of waves. I was nearly out of my head, just short of delirium. A night out, a night away, was exactly what I needed.

"Of course, Allyson, I've raised four of my own children and it's not as if she's the first grandchild. I'm barely out of practice. I'd love to have her. Saturday night. Plan something nice for the two of you. Go to dinner, see if you can put some makeup on and a dress or something. It has been four months. See if you can make something of yourself."

Her words made me wince, but I couldn't argue. When I gave myself a quick once-over, I was embarrassed to find I thought I was more than appropriately dressed in a pair of Patrick's old, holey sweats and a worn, stained T-shirt. No wonder Patrick hadn't glanced my way. My unwashed hair was pulled into a loose ponytail, and my face was without makeup. I was officially a mess; the woman I swore I'd never become.

"Okay, Barbara, you're right. Thank you. Thank you so much."

"Go out to dinner. Spend some time talking. Have a bottle of wine. Sleep in."

"Oh, heaven. It sounds like heaven."

"I'm not so sure," Patrick said skeptically, later that night when I'd told him about his mother's generous offer. "Do you think she can handle her?" He cradled his daughter in his arms, his tie pulled loose at the neck and his top button open at the collar.

"She raised you," I said to him. "And you survived." I'd had the afternoon to get used to the idea and it had grown on me. I wanted a night out with my husband. I wanted to feel beautiful again. I needed to break the monotony.

Patrick held Lydia at arm's length and stared into her sweet face. "She likes to sing, Lyd," he said to her, "really, really loud. And she's horrible. Just pretend you've nodded off to sleep and she'll leave the room."

I stifled a laugh under my breath but beamed widely. "Does that mean we can go, babe? Really?"

"Sure. Why not? It's a night. If she's willing to babysit, I guess we shouldn't turn her down so quickly."

I wrapped my arms around his neck and kissed him full on the mouth. "Mmm, excellent. Wonderful."

It had been better than wonderful, greater than fabulous. It had been our night. We'd done the things we needed to do, fallen naturally back into a routine that came so easily to us. Talked and ate and held hands and taken a long walk together and slept. Oh, how we had slept.

I should have known; should have sensed it coming. Like a well-planned menu, Barbara had been the perfect hostess.

The house was empty when we arrived Sunday at nearly noon. Quiet, too quiet. Patrick used his key and let us in. The coffee cups were still on the table, the paper stacked together in a heap. Patrick flipped through it absentmindedly.

"Where do you think they are?"

"No idea."

"Think everything is okay?"

"They'd have called us if it wasn't, Ally. They're just out somewhere, that's all. Don't worry."

I wasn't, actually. I really wasn't. Strangely calm and still reveling in the full night's sleep and peace I'd been blessed with for the last eighteen hours, I made my way outside and into Barbara's overgrown, but beautiful, garden to sit for a few minutes more in solitude, let the morning sun warm my shoulders.

Patrick had heard them first, the key in the lock and a commotion at the front door. He went, he told me later, so that he could get his hands on his daughter. He'd had a sudden feeling of missing her, of her being gone from him.

"Oh, Patrick, darling, we didn't expect you quite so soon. Didn't you have a good time?" Barbara asked him accusingly.

"Great time, Mom, great time. But we were missing her, you know. We were missing our little darling girl . . ." And that's when he saw her. She was buckled into her infant seat, snugly and sleeping, draped in a blanket he didn't recognize but could sense the meaning of right away. He pulled it back from her and she lay in a gown. I knew it had to be the gown Michelle had worn, the gown that had been passed down to Kathleen. I'd seen the photos, Barbara some forty pounds thinner, standing proudly, displaying her daughters the day they'd been baptized.

"Mom?"

"Hmmm?" she said, her back to him. She'd turned and was busying herself at the credenza.

"Why is Lydia dressed in this gown?" I heard him say the words more clearly than I'd ever heard him ask anything before. Loud, booming, he'd actually woken the baby. I was frozen, unable to get to her, even as she started to stir, whine, mew. Barbara bent to unbuckle her until Patrick said harshly, "No, Mom, don't.

Ally can get her." Then to me, he turned, sternly, and said, "Ally."

I found the courage. More than the courage, I found the fury. I treaded across the hardwood in my Keds and bent to rescue my daughter. She was all dress, long and flowing and overpowering. I waded through the layers of tulle and chiffon and lace and picked her up.

"Mom?" Patrick said again, but this time moved toward her to corner her. He took her by the arm, forced her to look at him.

"Yes, yes . . . what is it, Patrick?"

"Why is Lydia in that dress?"

"It's a baptism dress, Patrick," she said just as sternly, matter-of-factly, right back at him.

"I'm going to ask you one more time, Mom. Why is Lydia in that dress?"

"Because that's what one wears when one is baptized, of course."

"When one is *what*? You had our daughter *baptized*? You *had our daughter* baptized?"

I held Lydia close to me, purring into her ear, stroking her bald head and bouncing her up and down a little in my arms, until Patrick ordered me to undress her. That's how he said it: "Ally, undress her. Now."

"You had our daughter baptized," he said again, not a question this time, but a statement.

"Yes, Patrick. I didn't realize that would upset you so greatly."

"Mother, how could you not think that would upset Ally and me? How, in God's name, did you think we'd be okay with that? We've told you where we stand on having Lydia baptized. It's not in the cards. We wanted to expose her to a number of different religious backgrounds and let her choose which one feels right to her. How, how, could you not understand that? We have been over this time and time again."

We had. From the minute I'd told them I was pregnant and they'd first assumed we'd have him or her brought up in the church, Patrick had redirected them, counseled them, prepared them. It was his decision, actually, his choice.

"Patrick, what difference does it make to you? If you don't believe in the church, then the fact that we had her baptized in something you don't believe in really shouldn't matter to you. It was important to me. And to your father. End of story."

Patrick openly glared at his mother. It was the first and only time I remember thinking he might actually hate her.

"You had no right."

"Sweetie, honestly, you really shouldn't let this upset you so. Think of it more as a blessing. It's not as if we chose godparents for her, or even had a bunch of people there to witness this. It's just something your father and I wanted to do after church with Lydia. She was such a good baby too, so accepting of the holy water." Barbara cooed at Patrick, willing him to make peace. He wasn't budging.

"Ally," he said to me, his eyes still on his mother's adoring face, "get the baby bag. We're out of here."

I whisked Lydia past Patrick's father, who held his head in a downturn. I wanted out. I wanted to run. I wanted to hold my baby close and tear through the halls and through the front door.

I was lucky; Patrick felt the same way. Safely tucked in our new Volvo station wagon, we backed the car out of the driveway and down the hill. There was no conversation; there was no need for any.

37

Becca begs to run with me Sunday afternoon. It's the first thing she wants to know when she arrives home from the soccer sleepover, her hair long and stringy around her face, needing to be brushed. She's wearing baggy sweats and a T-shirt and drops her canvas duffel and sleeping bag on the floor in the entryway.

"Did you run this morning, Mom?" she says, her tone just slightly off, her tempo just a hair more curt than I'd have expected.

"No, Bec. I was thinking I might take a short one later. This afternoon, 'round three or so, after I get all this stuff over to the Goodwill. Why?"

She is lingering over the stacked boxes at the foot of my bed, slowly sauntering through them like a mother who'd packed up her infant's clothing, the things that no longer fit. She pauses on nearly every item, unfolding each shirt or pair of shorts. Occasionally she stops and tosses something of Patrick's into the pile she's claimed for her own, her stash of things she is unable to part with. A baseball hat Patrick had worn most times he played squash, the brim stained with sweat. A knit vest he'd worn with jeans to the father/daughter Christmas dance they'd been to only a couple of months before he'd been killed. A pair of old jeans, holes in the knees and frayed at the cuffs, that he'd worn most Sunday mornings while cooking pancakes; I'd almost saved those myself but couldn't justify a reason. When she is done, she repacks the things she is willing to let go, folding each of them carefully back into the boxes I've labeled. On her way out the door, she turns to me, the baseball cap perched backward so the adjustable plastic band runs across her forehead, and says, "I want to go with you when you go. On your run. If that's okay." And before I have a chance to answer, she is gone.

Becca waits three minutes into the run before the questions start. I'm focused on her arm, obviously tender and sore, weak and not used to the constant swinging motion, the pounding redundancy of the run. I ask her if she's okay, if she's sure she's ready to start running again, at the same time she pings me with the first of a battery of questions.

"April wanted to know what I thought about you and Michael dating, Mom. She asked me just like that. 'Gosh, Becca, what do you think of your mom *dating* Michael?'" She leaves the sentence hanging. The space between us has never felt quite so empty.

"What did you say to her, Becca?"

"What do you think I said, Mom? I told her that she didn't know what she was talking about, that you and Michael are just friends, that Michael was Daddy's *best* friend. I told her to stop talking about it 'cause it just wasn't true." Becca keeps me moving faster than the pace I'm used to, and I'm straining to keep up with her as the frustration she feels comes pounding through in every footstep. "Why, Mom? What should I have told her? Is there something else that I should have said to her? You tell me." Her tone is sarcastic, accusatory, angry.

"It's true that Michael and I are friends, Becca. First and foremost. You know how long we've known each other? Longer than you've been alive. Forever, almost." I pause and let my breathing catch up with my words, realizing that I'm panting. When I go on, my words are more measured, each one carefully chosen. "I don't think I'd have gotten through the last year without Michael. If you think about it, I don't know if any of us would have." I steal a glance sideways at her then to see if she's watching me, but she's stoic.

"And yes, it's true that Michael and I have feelings for each other. Feelings that go beyond what he or I realized before. And, before you ask me whether or not this happened when your father was alive, it didn't. Okay? You gotta understand that, Bec. 'Cause all this stuff just sort of evolved this summer, much longer after your dad was gone. What Michael and I have now, what we might have or even feel for each other, none of it was present when your dad was around."

She stops cold. "All what stuff, Mom?" she spits sternly and forcibly at me. "What are you trying to tell me about you and Michael?" Angry, she holds her own.

I stand in the middle of the street, heat rising up from the long afternoon sun beating down on the black pavement. When I stop running my face turns beet red, my heart beating against my brain in quick, strong pulses.

"This dating thing, if that's what you want to call it, or if that's what April wants to call it, who knows? I don't know what to call it. I don't even know what it is. All I can tell you is that it's important to me that Michael's around right now, important to me that he's in my life, in our lives. Important enough to me that he and I are willing to risk a whole life of friendship to see if there's something else there. And I can't tell you how hard that is, how much I want to run from that. Run until I can't be caught. But it's too late, sweetie, much, much too late. I need Michael around me. I want Michael around me."

I'm anticipating her anger. Becca stands firmly rooted in place, hands on her hips. She's almost breathless and I can tell her brain is working overtime, pulling pieces of knowledge and logic from places she can't even remember and processing these with warp speed. She locks her hands behind her head and stretches to her left side while saying to me, softer now, "What do you think Daddy would've thought of it?"

"Oh, Bec, I don't know." I start to walk slowly down the street. She follows me a step or two behind. I can hear her dragging the tips of her tennis shoes the way she used to sometimes do when she was very young. The scraping sound used to drive Patrick nuts.

"I don't think he'd be mad, Mom. I really don't." She puts a hand on my shoulder then, and I stop to look at her.

"I'm not so sure, sweetie." I clear my throat and throw my head back a little. "But what makes you say so?" We're in the neighborhood next to ours, just barely a few blocks away from our house, and we know plenty of people here.

"I just think Daddy would have wanted you to be happy, is all. I mean, no matter what happened, I think he'd want you to be happy." It's almost a whisper, but from her I swear it's a proclamation.

"You know what I think, Becca? I think Daddy'd want us all to be happy. That means you and Lydia, too. All of us, no matter what. That's what would have mattered to him most."

"We will be, Mom. We all will be."

Becca beats me home, not by much but enough so that she's already stretched and lying flat on her back on the grass in the front yard staring up at the clouds when I pull in, panting and relieved to be done. She tosses the stack of Saturday's mail at my feet. I leaf through it until I get to a thick envelope from the school district, *L. Stevens* scrawled above the district office's return address. I take a seat on the grass just far enough out of Becca's reach and run my thumb under the seal of the envelope, slitting it open in one long stroke.

To whom it may concern: Blah, blah, blah, your daughter Lydia is ineligible for classes this semester, blah, blah, blah, growing concerns over the perception her current condition might portray at the school, blah, blah, blah, cannot allow her on school grounds, blah, blah, blah, make the following suggestions as alternate education for her at this time:

1. She may attend continuing education at a school for teen mothers.
2. She may be homeschooled by a parent or guardian and will

be reinstated in her current class after the birth of her child, pending examinations.

3. An appropriate district-appointed sponsor may tutor her.

I fold the pages in thirds and stuff the whole thing back into its envelope before I give up on my stretching and scoop the rest of the mail up with one hand and head back into the house.

38

The warm sweet stench of burning trash floods the air and burns my nostrils. Almost overnight the air smells differently, crisp and fresh.

From the kitchen table where she's sat most of the morning, Lydia doodles in the margin of her large history book with an over-sharpened pencil. "I invited Melinda and Reid to come out for the weekend. They wanted to meet me."

"You did what?" I ask, with much too hard an accusatory tone. I'm holding a wooden spoon in my left hand, ready to mix together the guacamole for the steak fajitas I'm cooking for dinner.

"I invited them," she says, her eyes boring right back into me. "They'll be here Friday. They're taking me to dinner." She goes back to her doodling, small flowers down the margin, inside and outside the spiral rings of the notebook. "They said you could come if you wanted to." She concentrates hard on the notebook.

"Lyd, when did you talk to them?" I ask her, suddenly feeling very small, my voice shaking with every word.

"Yesterday afternoon. They called again and said they'd been talking about how they really wanted to come out and meet me. They wanted to know if that would be okay, so I said yeah. I mean, God, Mom, I've only got a couple of months left. Why shouldn't they come out here?"

I watch Lydia through narrowly slit eyes. She flips forward to the end of the chapter, to the study questions I know she should be working on, preparing for the test the tutor is giving her on Thursday. She taps the pencil against one of the questions in the study guide before flipping back a few pages again.

"Lydia?"

She looks up at me from where she sits cross-legged at the table. "Yeah?"

I long to reach out and grasp her by her wrists, hold her tight at arm's length and shake her with a jolt, just enough to bolt a sense of something into her. For the first time I'm certain I know exactly how Patrick must have felt, all those times, shut out from Lydia's world.

"Did you want to meet them? I mean, are you glad they're coming out here?" I ask her.

"I dunno, I hadn't really thought about it until they brought it up. It seems like it might be a good idea."

"Does it matter to you if I meet them? Is it something that you want me to do?"

"God, Mom, I don't know. I just found out they're coming. It's not like it's *that* big of a deal, you know."

"Actually, Lyd, I think it's a huge deal. I mean, these people are going to adopt your baby. They're going to raise this kid, you know. It's a damn big deal." I empty the plastic tub of vegetables I'd cut earlier in the afternoon onto the sizzling skillet and listen to the pan hiss and sputter. An aroma fills the kitchen, warm and generous, and when I turn back to the sink to rinse the containers, I catch Lydia watching me, spying.

I smile at her from across the island, force my eyes on hers, and wait. She turns back to her spiral notebook, jots a few points down in her outline.

I take a deep breath in through my nose, a long, rib-expanding breath that I hold inside me for a few seconds before I can move. I turn the temperature on the meat and vegetables to simmer and walk out of the room into the den, where I pick up the cordless phone and dial Michael's number.

He answers on the first ring, recognizes my number from his caller ID, and greets me with "Hey, gorgeous."

"Michael?" I say, my voice quivering. The hot lump in my throat has grown hard. "What's wrong, Al?" he asks with alarm.

I clear my throat again. "Michael, they're coming. Those people. That couple that Lydia picked. They're coming here to meet her."

"They are? When?"

"This weekend. Lydia just told me. I'm doing the best I can on this, Michael, but my best ain't very good." I nudge the door to the office shut with my foot, giving me just a little more privacy.

"This weekend, huh? Well, that's great. Sounds like it's as good a time as any. Maybe it's time to meet them, Ally."

"I want it all to be over and things to go back to where they were. I just want normal back. I just want my daughter back, Michael. I need Lydia back."

"Are you okay, Al?"

"I will be. Here's the thing, Michael, I've told Lydia that if she wants me to meet them, I will. And I've told her that if she wants to skip out with them and have me never lay eyes on them, well, I've told her that's fine, too. I'm not so sure that was the best decision, you know?"

"I think that was absolutely the best decision, Allyson. She'll figure it out. And my bet? You'll be the one standing right next to her when she opens the door on Friday afternoon."

"Mmmm, God, Michael, I don't know. I really don't know what she needs from me." I hold the receiver up to my ear and throw my head back, blinking at the recessed lights.

"The point is, Al, she does. Need you, that is. She just doesn't know how much yet."

39

Melinda and Reid Ramshorn are punctual. I hear their car idle in the driveway before the front doorbell pierces through the walls of the house. Lydia is in her room, music wafting from behind the door like the smell of pancakes on a lazy autumn morning. At the bottom of the stairs I wait patiently for her to emerge from her room. When she doesn't I start up the stairs. I've taken the first three steps when I hear her shout, "Mom, can you get the front door? I'm not quite ready."

I've fussed over my outfit all day until finally deciding on pressed khaki pants and a black short-sleeved mock turtleneck sweater. I'm wearing black loafers, which feel strangely new, having spent most of the summer barefoot, the feel of the hardwood floor more familiar than the leather upper tucked inside the soles of my shoes. My feet are sweating, I think to myself, taking wide paces toward the front door; my hands are sweaty, I think, rubbing them fiercely down the front of my pants and stopping to smooth out any wrinkles before I open the door.

Reid rests one hand assuredly on the small of his wife's back; extends the other hand to me in a firm but warm handshake. "Allyson? We're Melinda and Reid. It's so good of you to have us to your home. Thank you for including us."

When I turn around, Lydia's standing at the top of the stairs. She hesitates and lingers carefully on the third step from the landing, the midway point between here and there, like a cat deciding if she's going to come and curl herself through your legs or jet wildly and hide under the nearest piece of furniture.

"Lyd," I say, pausing to clear my throat, "come on down and meet Melinda and Reid. They didn't come all this way for you to stand on the stairs looking pretty." Static hangs in the air; the jolt of tension lies thick in the room.

The silence in our home is endless and hollow. Lydia fidgets with an imaginary splinter of wood on the banister, then takes the steps slowly, cautiously.

A few minutes later, just as we're beginning to get comfortable with each other, the doorbell pierces the air again, leaving us all to stare wide-eyed down the entry hall and prompting Reid to ask, "Shall I answer that?"

Lydia looks to me, I look to her; we're not expecting company. Her eyes plead with me, *Mom, who in the world could be stopping by now, of all times, why now?* I can't say I disagree with her; there really couldn't be a more impromptu interruption.

It's Michael.

I blink against the afternoon sun, shielding my eyes. His presence confuses me, so I whisper to him, "Michael, what are you doing here? We've got company right now." I step out onto the front porch and pull the door behind me.

"Allyson, are you going to invite me in?" He says this matter-of-factly, as if it's the most innocent of questions he could ask.

I whisper to him harshly, "Don't you remember who's here right now?" My voice squeaks with anticipation and uncertainty.

"Yes, I remember. I know," he says calmly, his hands clasped together in front of him, relaxed.

I eye him carefully, raising an arched eyebrow, until he says quietly, almost under his breath, "I thought you might need some help through this."

I take both of Michael's hands in mine and bring them to my lips, kissing them tenderly and repeatedly. "Thank you, thank you. I know you wouldn't have come unless you thought I would need you."

"And do you?"

"Of course, Michael. Of course."

We walk into the house together, hand in hand, breaking the ongoing conversation in two. I introduce Michael to Melinda and Reid and watch Reid shake Michael's hand, firmly and with sincerity. Man-to-man, I think; there's really no other description for it. Michael moves around to the back side of the coffee table, takes the seat on the couch next to Lydia, and puts just enough distance between the two of them to provide support, yet ensure her independence.

Lydia cozies to him, draws her feet up on the couch next to her, and rests them just left of Michael's thighs. I breathe a long, deep sigh, relief. "I've interrupted your conversation, Lyd, go on," he says to her, encouragingly.

They stay for dinner, a concoction of cioppino that Michael cooks, the sweet smell of steamed rice hanging in the kitchen before he throws it, last minute, into the soup. Sometime just after eight, Lydia asks if she can meet friends for ice cream. Michael throws me an encouraging look to let her go. I can tell he thinks it would be a good idea for us to spend some time with Melinda and Reid on our own. I don't relish the idea, but I take his lead anyway. I grant her permission and she scuffles from the kitchen, returning a few minutes later and throwing her arms like a small child around Melinda's neck, surprising her. I watch them embrace and grow hot in the face with jealousy. Melinda and Reid begin to excuse themselves, but Michael offers them coffee. When Lydia's gone, the sea change in the room shifts. The lights dim, we settle down to make conversation.

Reid starts. "Lydia didn't say much about the baby's father. Is it the boy she mentioned, Eric?"

"Mmm-hmm," I answer him. "Sixteen. A grade older than Lyd. A nice kid, generally. Pretty quiet. Keeps to himself. They've had a rough summer, all this. They're kids, really. The conversation between them about the whole thing is at a minimum."

He bows his head, but asks cautiously, "Is he supportive of Lydia's decision to place the baby for adoption?" His speech is rehearsed, politically correct, but his emotion is raw. He takes his wife's hand, loops his fingers through hers. Melinda sits straight-backed on the hard chair, perched on the edge of her seat. I can tell this is a tenuous subject for them; a list of endless questions masked behind her eyes.

"He is," I answer and watch them both breathe a sigh, slightly audible, clearly visible. "Not much of a choice, I'd say. They're so young. And Lydia's been so hell-bent on adoption from the beginning that I don't know that she, and consequently he, ever really considered anything else."

Melinda and Reid hang on my every word. They seem eager to know everything but are cautious about what they ask, what they feel they can know.

Michael breaks the impeding silence. "Is there something you want to ask Allyson? About the baby, maybe? Or about Lydia? Anything? Al, you're okay with that, right?"

I want to slug him outright. I'm not in the mood to disclose my family history; I'd like them to go, actually. I've had just about enough togetherness, just about enough extended family. They've come, they've met, they've visited.

But I smile politely and nod my head.

"Um, there's about a million things, actually." Melinda laughs nervously, watching my face. "Maybe even more than that. I'm sorry, I'm not sure what's okay, what's off-limits. What we should, or shouldn't ask you. It's an odd thing, this whole thing." Her hesitation is painfully obvious.

"I guess, you know, I guess I'd like to know a little about you, Allyson. About you and Michael, maybe. How long have you known each other?"

Michael laughs. "Actually," he starts, affection warming his voice, "we've known each other for what seems like forever. Maybe longer. Only not like this."

"No," I say, blushing despite myself. "Not like this. Michael and I have been friends since college. He was very good friends with my husband. With both of us, actually. I lost my husband a little over a year ago," I add quietly.

Reid says in a clear voice, "Lydia told us. I'm very sorry."

I shrug my shoulders and bow my head because I can think of nothing else to do. "Thank you." I wonder about what else Lyd had told them.

"Is there something you want to know? I mean about Lydia? Or about the baby?"

"We asked about the birth father, Allyson," Reid starts, "because we had an adoption fall through before this one. It was the birth father, actually, in the end, who decided to raise the baby. He was older, in his twenties, but still. It's a big red flag for us. I don't know that we can go through that again. It was, well, it was near beyond words to have that baby torn out of our arms. I just don't think we could do it again."

Now it's my turn to tell them how sorry I am, but I can't quite get the words out. I hadn't thought about it before, what this must be like from their side. "I'm so sorry. That must have been very difficult."

"It was," Melinda says in a short final way that indicates that she does not want to revisit the details.

I don't push her further, I simply say to her, "I can't imagine you'd find yourself in that position with Eric. He's sixteen. He's told Lydia this is her decision."

"And you, Allyson?" she asks me, more boldly now. "How do you feel about Lydia's decision to place her baby for adoption?"

I feel my face flush and grow hot beneath her question. Finally, I say to her, "It's Lydia's choice."

She waits a minute and lets a bit of silence fall over the room. I sip my coffee, and shift against the wood chair. "But that's not what I meant. How do *you* feel about her decision? Is it something that you're happy with? Are you at peace with her decision?"

"Actually, Melinda," I say, "I'm not very happy about the whole thing. There's not so much in it to be happy about, from where I sit. It has been a hell of a year. And if you mean, am I pleased with her choice to give up her baby? Well, no. I've had a pretty damn hard time with it, actually. I can barely stand to think about what it's going to be like for Lydia. And I know she doesn't have the foggiest idea. But I meant what I said. It is her choice. She and I have been to hell and back on this, but she's held firm. I've got nothing left in this but to support her decision. It's her choice. I'll get along with it."

She waits awhile, pulled in tight against her husband's arm, and watching them I feel a pang of jealousy that stabs me in the heart. Even with Michael sitting next to me for both companionship and warmth, I can't help but long for what I had, what is very obviously apparent between these two. Finally, she says, "Thank you, Allyson. I appreciate your honesty."

They leave the same time Lydia is coming in. I watch Lydia dive into Melinda's arms again. My stomach clenches as I bear witness to the relationship that has begun between this woman and my daughter, the buds of a bond breaking through the soil.

When they're gone, Lydia starts in with questions.

"What did you think? Did you like them? I really liked them. I think they'll be great. Do you think she's going to be okay as a mom? She really wants a baby. I think she really wants a baby, don't you, Mom?" Lydia's breathless, barely coming up for air.

I'm floating off somewhere, in a time long, long time ago. A time before I was a mother, when I was just a wife, just before I found out I was going to be a mother. I'm drifting in a smaller place, the smell of the condo we lived in, a cool, musty smell that I never particularly liked, poisoning the ends of my nostrils. I'm nauseated and moody, overcome with emotions I haven't yet identified but will later come to recognize as the sheer panic that follows me along the days and weeks of my pregnancy as I balloon out, wondering what it was we'd undertaken, awed by the involuntarily movements that had taken over my belly, woken me in the middle of the night.

"*Mom?*" Lydia's insistence jolts me back. "Hmm, uh, yeah, honey, what was it?" I'm glassy-eyed and glazed and not completely there. Lydia faces me, her hands on her hips and annoyed, but persists anyway.

"I said, 'Do you think she wants to be a *mother*? Do you think she'll be okay?'"

"Lyd, I think there's nothing more she wants in the world. Nothing more she's ever reached for and not been able to have. I think she'll be just fine."

Lydia throws her arms around me in a bear hug and squeezes me tightly. She moves from me to Michael and stands in front of him, stealing a sip off the Diet Coke he's drinking.

"Thanks, Michael," she says, handing him back the can. "I'm glad you were here tonight."

"No problem."

She turns to head out of the kitchen and retreat to her room. Before she escapes, Michael calls for her and she turns to take him in. "You're doing the right thing, Lyd. Really you are." He waves her off then. His words echo in my head, pounding.

She nods her head at him and plods out of the room in stocking feet, her gait a little slower and more full than usual, but no less meaningful.

40

I haven't tucked Lydia into bed, truly pulled the covers up to her chin and smoothed them clean, and planted a kiss on her forehead in a time longer than I can remember. But tonight she allows me to do this. She's got on her headphones when I knock softly on the door, and she's reading, but yawns and tells me she's ready to go to sleep. She asks if I'll shut off the bedside lamp, which I do. Then I pull the covers so tight it's as if I've wrapped her safely in a cocoon. Her auburn hair cascades across the pillow, and the moonlight from outside the window floods her face on the pillow, providing a hauntingly beautiful profile of my child. I stoop to whisper into her ear.

I say to her, "Michael's staying here tonight."

I close her door behind me, and pull it tight until I hear the handle click into place. I can hear the water running. Michael's drawn me a bath, and when I walk into the bathroom, he sits tub-side, barefoot in his jeans and a T-shirt, stirring sea salt into the water and swirling it with his hand. The bathwater goes murky with every swirl, then settles. Seeing him there, perched on the edge of the bath like that, jolts me for a minute. I rub my eyes furiously, pressing my fingertips hard into my eyeballs.

I peel away my clothes, drop the khakis on the floor, and strip the black sweater over my head and let it fall in a pile. I push down my panties and unhook my bra until I'm standing in front of him.

"I wanted to light some candles for you," he says.

"That would be lovely."

"But I couldn't find the matches."

"They should be in the top right drawer, all the way in the back."

"They're not. Empty box." He holds up the evidence and shakes the small box without a sound.

"Downstairs in the hutch. Middle drawer. There should be a whole pack."

"Okay."

I take two steps toward him. He stands, then runs his hand over my ass, full and supple, and then down the back of my thigh before walking past me.

I dive into the bath and beads of sweat pop at my temple. There aren't enough bubbles to cover my breasts, but I slink down under the water and let it ripple over the top of my chest, just at my collarbone. When Michael reappears in the doorway, he's holding a box of stick matches and the two round pillar candles we'd lit earlier in the kitchen. He sets one of the candles on the tile next to the bath, the other on the vanity just to the left of where I'm reclined. When he lights them, the flame flickers and sputters, dancing off the tiles, the walls, and the ceiling.

"Enjoy that," he says to me before blowing out the match. I watch the smoke swirl around his face.

"I will. I am. Mmmm, heaven, really. Do you want to join me?" I say this to his backside as he's slinking from the room.

"Yes, but I'm not going to. You need this. Twenty minutes on your own, that's all you get. Then you're mine."

And with that he disappears from the doorway into my room. I hear him pad across the floor and down the stairs as I drift off in the quiet lapping of the water around me, my head back and the ends of my hair damp with a mixture of sweet-smelling, oily bathwater and salty perspiration.

I must soak for half an hour, barely moving, my eyes closed most of the time. I concentrate on the nothingness of the moments alone, the sheer black and endless slate that hides behind my eyelids. It's difficult at first. Images of Melinda and Reid run back and forth in my mind: the way she brushes back her hair over her left shoulder, the way he constantly clears his throat and ends his sentence on an upbeat, leaving you not sure if he's made a statement or is asking you a question.

I reluctantly pull myself from the bath and sop up the water that has beaded over my body, residue from the bath oil. When I'm dry I put on a short silky robe, and head down the stairs in search of Michael. He's stretched on the couch, a discarded copy of *Investor's Business Daily* next to him and ESPN turned low on the television. He's engrossed in highlights of the Ryder Cup, and tearing him away from the show proves challenging, even as I hold his hand in mine and run it up under the slip of a robe I'm wearing.

I ask him, "May I turn this off?" Apparently that gets his attention. I take the television controller from his hand and he releases it willingly.

We kiss for what seems like an hour, my lips swollen and my cheeks rough against his late-in-the-day shadow. When I finally can't take any more, and am convinced there isn't a part of his mouth I haven't explored, or a point on his neck or forehead that I haven't yet run my tongue over, I pull him from his spot on the couch.

I know the places he likes to be touched; he knows the things that send me over the edge, my back arched in agreement. But it's the holding on to me, much later and long into the night, the patient and calm listening, during which I fall most in love with Michael. His arms wrapped around me, he wipes away the silent tears that fall first, quickly, from my eyes, the ones I fail to wipe away, but just let go, running in long lines down the sides of my face, and draining into my ears. These first tears fall with the largest of lumps in my throat, so big I can hardly get the words out, and he knows that and keeps telling me it's okay, that everything will be fine.

"Michael?" I finally say to him, rolling over on my stomach, my breasts lying on his chest. He reaches under my chin and pulls me toward him, kissing my tear-soaked face in all sorts of spots.

"Yeah?"

"How do you know it's going to be okay? How can you be so sure of it?" I prop myself on my left elbow and trace the line of hair that runs down his chest.

He pushes my hair back behind my ear before he answers me. "How can it get any worse, Al? I mean, this is it, you've hit it. It can't get any worse. We just won't let it. It's time for it to start getting better." He wraps his arms around me tightly, catching me at the rib cage.

I take a single deep breath, a hiccup of sorts. When I lay my head down on his chest, I can feel it rise and fall with his breathing. I place my hand against his heart and feel it beating regularly, comfortably. "It is time for things to start getting better, Michael," I say to him.

"Al? Did you like these people tonight? They seemed okay, don't you think?" He's running his hand down over my head, listing his fingers through the fine bits of my hair.

"They're fine. They want a baby so badly. Everything about them wants one."

"Uh-huh."

"They're going to be fine, Michael," I say, choking back a sob.

"Then what, baby? What is it?" He pulls me up toward him so that we're eye-to-eye, sharing his pillow.

"I don't know, Michael, I just don't know." I take in a deep breath that helps me to control my words, and I wipe away at the tears with the backs of my hands. "It's just a scene I can't play out, you know. That minute in the delivery room when my daughter goes from being a daughter to being a mother, what's that like? Does she have any idea what it's going to be like?

'Cause I don't. I can't picture it. I can't make sense of it. If I only knew what that very minute was going to be like, maybe, just maybe I'd have the strength I need, enough strength for the both of us, 'cause I know I'm gonna need it. I know that minute's going to come and I'm not going to know where to draw from."

He sighs and lays his head back on his pillow, pulling me close to him, cheek to cheek now. "Al, do you remember the minute they handed you Lydia for the very first time?"

"Barely." I laugh, smiling and wiping away the last of my tears. "God, I barely remember the minute at all. I think I was in shock at how beautiful she was, how simply undeniably remarkable everything about her was. It was as if heaven and earth had stopped."

"And from where did you draw the strength to go on?"

I stop, silent for a minute, and think. Surely it wasn't Patrick; the awe had left him just as speechless, just as paralyzed.

"God, Michael, I don't know. I suppose, if I think about it, I drew it from Lydia herself. From everything she needed from me."

He turns his head and looks at me then, waiting for it to register, before he says simply, "Bingo."

41

The last heat wave of summer, the one that comes despite the pumpkins that are already strewn across empty lots, arrives in mid-October. Temperatures rise into the midnineties and the humidity turns the sky into rolling gray clouds that rumble but produce virtually nothing, save an episodic spit that drops in large splotches on the windows.

At the kitchen table, Lydia has been working on an Algebra II problem that is giving her trouble. I know because she's written and erased it in her notebook no less than half a dozen times. She's slumped over the table with her head resting in the palm of her hand, her fingers wrestling with the bangs she's had cut only days before. I can empathize; I hated algebra, and her bangs will be a nightmare to grow out.

I remind her of her doctor's appointment for which we must leave momentarily.

"Can't you cancel it?" she bites, seething at me through hissed teeth.

"No."

"Uh, jeez, Mom, great. Fine. Okay." She slams down the pencil, leaving it wedged in the spine of the book, and makes her way up the stairs. When she doesn't reappear, I start to get anxious. I call to her from the bottom of the stairs. She emerges from her bedroom, no more dressed or together than when she'd left the room, the painted nails of her bare feet protruding over the edge of the floor above me.

"Yeah, okay, Mom, give me a few minutes, will you?"

"We don't have a few minutes, Lyd. Get moving."

I'm still standing in the same spot at the bottom of the stairs when she comes back out of the room, the cordless phone receiver up to one ear, her shoes and purse in the other hand. She's all giggles and gossip as she takes the stairs casually, swinging her hips back and forth.

She reaches the place where I'm standing and flops down on the bottom step, struggling to get her white Keds on her feet and lace up the shoes, all the while balancing the receiver between her ear and chin. I recognize April's high-pitched giggle at the other end of the phone line, nonstop chatter.

"Lydia," I say urgently. I cross my arms over my chest and move in front of her, pointing at my watch, signaling to her that we need to go.

"Lydia, we need to go," I say a little louder, hoping April might catch the tone of my voice and give in. I bend down and pull the shoe on for her, pulling the laces tight across the arch of her foot.

"Ouch, Mom, jeez, that hurts. Just a second, will you? I'm almost done."

"No, Lyd, you *are* done. Tell April you'll call her later. Tell her there are a few things you need to take responsibility for. Right now."

"Hey, April, I gotta call you back. My mom's havin' a cow and I gotta go to a doctor's appointment. I'll call you later. I still can't believe he said that to Maria. She so must have died. She has got to be so over him by now . . ."

April's voice trails off when I grab the receiver. I scratch Lydia with my nails as I reach for it.

"Oh, Jesus, Mom, relax."

"No, Lyd. We're late. That's it. In the car. I'm serious. You have absolutely no consideration for anyone but yourself sometimes. Just absolutely none. Do you have any idea what it's like at the doctor's office? They run a business, you know. You need to be there when it's your time. It's called an appointment."

She moves away from me, her hand up to her cheek where I've drawn the smallest bit of blood, her face an angry red from my berating marks. She slumps next to me in the front seat of the car and stares out the window as I start to back out of the driveway and make my way out of our neighborhood. We're both silent and fuming.

I steal a glance in her direction. She's furious with me; it's evident from the body language. Crossed arms, not dissimilar to mine only a few minutes before, furrowed brow that cuts deep into her forehead, dark eyes. I try to warm her up.

"Hey, Lyd, look, I'm sorry I got so worked up about it. But you've gotta realize that people keep schedules. They can't work around you. You need to be somewhere when you're supposed to be. April can wait."

Silence.

"Do you understand, honey? I'm not angry with you, I'm just trying to make sure you get it."

Silence.

"Lyd?"

"Yeah, fine, Mom, whatever. It's fine."

"It's not fine. I want you to understand why this is important. Life's not just available when you are. You don't just get to play when you want to play. It's a full-time deal."

"Yeah, okay, I get it. Fine."

We pull into the medical center parking lot just as the rain becomes purposeful. I reach behind my seat for an umbrella I keep wedged into the net basket, and start to open my door as she stops me, her hand on my arm.

"Hey, Mom, why don't you just hang here? I think I've got this one."

"What? You don't want me to come in with you?" Shock registers on my face; she can sense that she's stung me badly.

She looks me dead in the eye anyway and shakes her head. "No." She opens the door and hurls herself out onto the pavement, rain spotting her clothes. I'm so stunned that I never offer her the umbrella; I'm still clutching it when she slams the door hard on me.

I know she's done this to get back at me, to punish me for the way I've treated her, but still I'm hurt. For sympathy, I dial Michael's office line.

"It's Michael," he says through the receiver.

"Hi." I say it meekly, almost afraid he won't hear me the first time, so then again, "Hi, Michael."

"Hey, babe. What's up?" I hear him shuffling through a stack of papers, his attention not mine yet.

"Um, just waiting on Lydia, actually."

"Where are you?"

"In the parking lot at Peggy's office. We had a bit of a, well, we had a bit of a disagreement. She didn't want me to go in with her so I'm sitting here listening to the rain, watching the windows fog up." As I replay the story for him I waver between angry and hurt, frustrated and displeased.

He interrupts me. "Wait, let me get this right. You're still sitting in the parking lot, Al?"

"Yeah, I mean what else was I gonna do? She wanted to do this on her own. I think it's her way of controlling it, of reminding me that this whole thing, this whole bloody mess is hers to deal with."

I hear him laugh at the other end of the phone. "And you're still sitting in the parking lot? By yourself?"

"Yeah." I'm beginning to run low on patience with Michael and get the distinct feeling that he's not going to side with me. Suddenly I feel foolish sitting in the front seat, watching the nurses and doctors, patients of all ages walk through the lot to the hospital. The windows have fogged up around me and I use the back of my sleeve to wipe clean the condensation on the front windshield, leaving a trail of streaks and lines behind me as I go.

"What do you suggest I do, Michael?" I'm a bit snippier than I mean to be. After all, I've called him. If he turns on me now, I'll have no one left to confide in.

"I suggest you walk your sweet ass up the stairs to Peggy's office and take Lydia in to her appointment."

"But—" I stammer and start, but to no avail. He cuts me off before I even get the hint of an excuse out.

"But what, Allyson?"

"But, well, she doesn't want me in there. That's that. She made herself pretty damn clear when she slammed the door and walked in there on her own."

"Yeah."

"Yeah, nothing. Yeah, that's it. I don't see how I just walk in on her. I was just lecturing her about taking responsibility for some of the crap in her life, this included. And now you want me to go rescue her?"

"I didn't say that." He's terse with me, scolding as if I were a child who wasn't listening.

"Well, what is it you're saying? 'Cause frankly, I'm not getting it."

"Whose decision is it for you to be involved in this, Al? How old is Lydia?"

"Fifteen, Michael, don't start with the lecturing, we all know she's fifteen."

"Uh, yeah. Okay. Fifteen. Who drove her there? You. Who's paying for Peggy's bill? You. Who gets to decide if you're going to be involved in this? You. And quite frankly, Al, who is the only person in the world who's going to be around to pick her up from all this?" He waits for me then, waits until I finally give in and answer his question.

"Me. Yeah, okay. I get it." I can hear Michael's calm deep breaths through the other end of the phone. I wedge myself out of the driver's seat, collect my purse, and pull the keys out of the ignition.

I check in with the receptionist, someone who's been with Peggy as long as I can remember. Michelle shows me to Lydia's exam room, then knocks before opening the door. Lydia's robe-clad and barefoot, sitting on the edge of the cool gray examining table covered in white paper. Peggy's perched on the other stool and smiles when she turns to see me.

"Ally, hi, we were just getting started. C'mon in." Peggy greets me with a bear hug. I see Lydia roll her eyes before she asks Peggy, "Dr. Nelson, I'd really rather do this on my own today. Does she need to be in here?" Her head is bowed and she's staring at the floor, twisting her feet back and forth against each other.

Peggy pulls me close in tight. She whispers in my ear, "What's going on?"

I shake my head in response, before letting go, and say to her, "It's okay, I'll be in the waiting room."

It's half an hour before Peggy comes to find me, Lydia's thick chart in her right hand. The waiting room is empty; she takes the opportunity to flop in one of the straight-back chairs next to me. "Not a good day, huh, sweetie?"

"A row. Silly, if you really sit out here and think about it for thirty minutes, which is what I've been doing. Ridiculous." She takes my hand in hers and sets it in her lap, holding it closely. "We've been bickering with each other on and off for days. I just can't get her to the place I want her to be."

"What place, exactly, is that?" She peers at me over the top of her glasses, light bouncing off the bronze wire frames.

"Somewhere where she'll take just a little bit of responsibility for what she's gotten herself into. Just a little more consideration for those around her, you know? A little more reality."

"Ally, hello? Reality? Don't you think she's sort of got a good dose of that like sitting right in front of her?" She pushes her arms out in front of her to make the sign of a pregnant woman, a big belly protruding out into space.

"Yeah. But she got herself there. She's *got* to learn to deal with it."

"Excuse me? How can you say she's not dealing with it? She's here. She's in there. She's made a decision that she thinks is best for her, for you, for the baby. I'm sorry, Al, but she's dealing with it in more ways than some women twice her age who come in here planning to start a family."

I start to protest; start to tell Peggy about how I practically had to drag Lydia here to the appointment, and then fall silent. The door to the waiting room creaks open and Lydia comes through it, slumping to one side in her sweats and long T-shirt. She's pulled her hair, ratty from the weather, up into a single ponytail behind her and fastened it with a comb she'd had buried in her purse. Her face pale and without makeup, she looks much younger to me than she had looked standing just outside the car, making her point in the parking lot, before lumbering off.

"I'm ready," she says to me, flatly.

I start to thank Peggy before she throws a hand up and brushes me off. She pulls me into another of her famous long hugs, drawing me in near her and rocking the both of us back and forth on our heels.

When she lets me go, she says to Lydia, "Two weeks. Michelle made your next appointment, right? Easy on the sweets. I don't want to see you up any more than a couple of pounds next time, missy."

Lydia tilts her head up at Peggy to acknowledge she's gotten the message. I pull the heavy, spring-loaded door open and hold it that way for Lydia to pass through. Just before we leave, Peggy turns to me and asks, "Ally? How's Becca, by the way?"

It occurs to me that I have no idea.

42

Dinner is served precisely at six-fifteen. I am determined we will sit down together like a family tonight. I've cleared the table of Lydia's schoolbooks and set it properly with the red embroidered place mats Barbara had given me as a Christmas gift the year before. Beige linen napkins, full place settings, the everyday glasses, but glass, not the plastic tumblers that are usually lying around the house. I've arranged cut flowers in a vase and chilled tea in the water pitcher; it looks like we're having company. But I'm careful to set only three places.

It takes two shrill calls and a trip upstairs before the girls crack open their doors and see what it is I want.

"Lamb stew. It's just about ready, come on down and have dinner," I say to Lydia, who crinkles up her nose in protest and shakes her head, heaving herself back on her bed.

"I'm really not that hungry, Mom," she says, shrugging me off.

I push open the door with the toe of my foot and, arms crossed at my chest in her door frame, say to her, "It wasn't meant to be a question, Lydia. I don't care how much you eat, but be downstairs in five minutes."

Becca meets me just outside her door, her fingers plugging her nose. "Lamb stew, Mom? Baaaaa . . ." She lets out the noise of a baby lamb through clenched nostrils and follows me down the stairs.

"You love lamb, Bec, what's the problem?"

"Lamb's fine. Couldn't you have just stuck it on the grill? Stew? Eeew. All those soggy potatoes and cooked carrots. Ick."

"Pick out the lamb, then, honey," I say with a sigh, dishing a medium-sized bowl, skimping on the carrots and squaring her off with a couple of extra chunks of meat. At least I've managed to get her to join me in the kitchen; Lydia is still nowhere to be found.

A few minutes later Lydia slides into her spot at the table and I pass her a bowl, which she stares at before wrinkling her nose and shuddering an over-exaggerated shiver one more time. I load the table with steamy corn bread, enough tossed salad for ten people, and a covered pot of perfectly steamed white rice, which I watch Becca spoon and stir carefully into her stew.

Lydia leans on one elbow as if it's too much effort to sit up straight in her chair. She pushes the stew back and forth across the bowl with her spoon. I watch her for a minute in silence and think about how long Patrick would have stood for this. He'd have had her by the elbow and back to the foot of the stairs by now. In tears and up to her room. Forget it; she'd never have dared try.

The phone bolts the three of us upright at the table, and in a split second both Lydia and Becca are racing for the extension in the family room. They stop still, Becca sliding across the tile in her socks, when I call to them, a touch of irritation in my voice, to let it go. A minute later we hear Michael's voice on the machine, up and happy, singsongy and melodic. They both slink back to the table and settle in again.

"Bec, what time's the dance Friday? And did you guys decide if you're going?" I ask her, anticipating the last-minute plea for costumes and, no doubt, the frenetic trip to the Halloween store that will require at least a couple of hours of junior high anxiety mixed with adolescent insecurity, a deadly combination.

"I don't know if we're going. Sarah wants to, Jennie doesn't. I don't know what to wear. There isn't anything I want to be. And it's too dumb to get dressed up anyway. I'll feel like a freak. We don't know if anyone's going, so we don't know if we want to go. It might just be a bunch of seventh grade boys. Kinda lame, Mom, you know?"

"Um, hello, you're in seventh grade, lame-o, what do you care?" Lydia pipes up from her chair.

"Um, hello, it's my dance so I can decide if I care about who's going or not, lame-o. And I don't know if any eighth graders are going," Becca fires back.

"Well, like any of them are going to want to dance with you anyway. Yeah, right." Lydia snickers, mock disgust in her voice.

I watch Becca's face fall, red and splotchy at first and then fuming with anger. She winds up and throws Lydia the best curve ball she's got. "Like anyone would want to dance with *you*, looking like *that*. Oh, I forgot, you don't get to go to your dance 'cause you can't even go to school." Flat, perfect delivery.

"Becca, enough," I say in a short and decisive breath that cuts through the air and across the table.

They fall silent with each other, and all that's left in my kitchen is the sound of scraping utensils moving back and forth. Lydia's furious, but more hurt. You can see it if you look into her eyes, you don't even have to go that deeply. She's doing a good job, a valiant effort, really, trying to disguise her anguish, the knife that has cut through her. But I can see the lump in her throat and, no doubt, there's a strange salty taste of tears that's swelling in her mouth. I don't push her to eat the stew. I let her go about the business of recovering from that blow, watch her nibble at a crouton she's picked haphazardly out of the salad bowl with her fingers.

Finally I cut the silence. "Bec, let me know if you need my help for this thing. If not, fine. But not on Friday, okay? Before then so it's not a last minute-crisis, understand?" She nods at me, acknowledging that she's screwed up, sorry instantly.

"Hey, Lydi, sorry about that. That was stupid of me. You look fine." Becca looks up at her older sister and tries to make eye contact, but Lydia's having none of it. Her trust level has diminished.

I glance at Becca struggling to make amends and silently nod my head at her, offering her the encouragement she needs to make good on what she's said. She tries again. "Lydi?" she says again, using the childhood name she'd adopted when she couldn't quite get Lydia's whole name out.

"It's fine, Bec. Fine. I know how I look. I get it. Just go and have fun at your dumb dance. It's fine." Before she gets the whole of the sentence out, she's in tears, small rivers running down her cheeks and her nose instantly cherry red. She dabs at her eyes with the linen napkin, then covers her face and begins to sob.

I look at Becca and she at me; she is unprepared for the show of emotion that she's brought to the surface, like stirring soup. Becca gets up and goes around to Lydia's side, the side with the long pine bench, and sidles up next to her, their thighs and knees touching. She wraps her arms around Lydia, near as she can, and buries her head against her sister's shoulder.

"I'm sorry, Lydi, I'm so sorry. I didn't mean to hurt you. That was really stupid. You're beautiful, really you are. And you'll have your dances, too. You'll see, it's going to be fine. Everything's gonna be back to the way it was real soon. I just know it. You'll see." Over and over again, until it's hard to know, unless you were as familiar as I was with the tones of their cries, the pitch in their snivels, which sounds were coming from which girl.

They melt into one, their arms wrapped tightly around each other. Their faces cheek-to-cheek, I'm reminded of the nights Patrick and I would find them in one or the other's bed. The blond of Becca's mane interweaves with Lydia's auburn tresses, a color you couldn't dream up in a bottle.

"Lyd, can I be there with you? You know, when the baby is born?" Becca asks, then pulls back from Lydia just enough to be able to look into her eyes. "I mean when you are in the hospital. Can I, Lydia? I'd really, really like to be there with you."

I sit stunned in my chair, the words buzzing in my head, and wait for Lydia's answer.

"Of course, squirt. If you want to you can. Yeah."

"I don't want to watch you hurt, but I just want to be there, you know."

"Yeah. Okay."

"Um, Lyd, I'm not so sure how I feel about that," I say, directing my comment directly to Lydia. "You have no idea how it's going to go, you know."

The two of them stare at me, hands tight together, fingers intertwined now in the small space between them. Their red-rimmed eyes stare back at me, daring me to question them on this. I do anyway; I walk right into the fire.

I continue. "It's just that I'm not so sure it's the best thing for Becca, you know. It might be a bit R-rated. And it might be terribly painful to watch, honey," I say to Becca, urging her to back down and think logically.

"No, Mom, it's fine. Becca can be there if she wants to. Melinda's gonna be in the room, so Becca might as well be there too." Lydia lobs this back across the table. My body shivers with anticipation and I wait for Lydia to say the words I'm willing to fall from her mouth next.

And of course you'll be there too, Mom.

Of course you'll be there too, Mom.

OF COURSE YOU'LL BE THERE TOO, MOM!

Say it, Lyd, please say it, I pray silently to myself, motionless in the pine chair, my elbows square on the armrests for support. My back is rigid, my body tense.

Nothing. She clears her dishes, then does the same for her sister.

When they're gone and I hear their giggles drifting up the stairs, I lay my head right down on the table and feel the cool planks of pine, knotty in spots, bore into my skin.

I want to run. I want to go as far and as fast as I can. The evening sun is disappearing, the world fading faster and faster these days. It's the time of year I love most during the day, despise at night, my light gone so early now that I can't, no, won't, take to the streets in long strides. I leave the dishes where they are in the sink, crusting and caked over, and move to the leather couch.

I stare at the phone and hit the Play button on the recorder, listening to the chirpy sounds of Michael's voice light up the room again.

I think about what Lydia is missing and compare it to my own memories. The first times Patrick and I had tried so hard for a baby, waiting on the time when we'd find out, careless and uncommitted at first, lapsing into genuine determination to make a baby together. The first missed period, the sheer tingle down my spine at the thought it might be, could be, would have to be a baby. The way Patrick held my hand as we watched the test turn blue, then again as he watched the doctor listen for the faintest signs of a heartbeat. The same heartbeat that was, in fact, Lydia's. The way we broke the news to his parents, his dad still alive then, and so overwhelmingly proud to be thought of as a grandfather—sitting a little straighter in his chair, his head a little higher, the look on Patrick's face as he crossed from son truly into manhood.

I sink back into the leather and curl my feet up under me, throwing the chenille blanket over my lap for comfort more than for warmth as I think about the time we spent in preparation. Testing strollers, picking out furniture, laughing at the smallest of things. The way Patrick had rubbed and rubbed and rubbed my lower back, so much so that he could almost do it in his sleep, all those nights of discomfort. The last dinner we had together, him somehow knowing this was it, sensing labor coming on—each of us in our own way—silent and preparing for something we had no concept of grasping.

Labor. The hours and the walking the halls, small tears ripping through. Tiny jabs that grew and grew until Patrick couldn't, no, wouldn't, take any more; demanding I take something for the overwhelming pain that stretched over each inch of me. The look of sheer terror on his face as they turned up the overhead lights, bright enough to send a signal to the heavens, he told me later, holding Lydia for the first time in his arms. That's what he had thought, "bright enough to send a signal to the heavens and have the heavens send back our little angel." The dreamy stupid stare I must have had all over my face as he said this to me, convinced this was the end of it all, they could take me now, so perfect was the image emblazoned in my mind.

The minute we walked into the house with her, silent in her infant seat, finally asleep only as we had turned down the street to our small condo. The way we placed her in the middle of the room and, each of us, backed away slowly, made for the couch, and met there like strangers, aware only of this other person that had invaded and infected us with these ridiculous grins. We sat there for as long as she slept, silent and in awe of her endless beauty, taking in each ounce of her, watching each rise and fall of her transparent chest. Completely unaware of the curse she'd cast upon us.

"Mom? Michael is on the phone. Mom, are you down there?" I hear Lydia trip down a few steps.

"Yeah, okay, Lyd, yeah, I'm getting it." I pull myself from the sweet dream, longing to go back.

"Mmm, hey," I say sleepily, choking back a yawn into the receiver.

"Al, you sleeping? It's only ten before eight. Did I wake you? Are you okay?"

"Mmm, I dozed off. I was just sitting here and off I went."

"Oh, I'm sorry. I should let you go, then. You go on, get some rest . . ." Michael's voice drifts, lingering momentarily. I know he doesn't want me to go; I can hear it in his voice.

"Okay," I say to him, knowing this is not the reply he expects.

"Oh, okay, then, well, I guess I'll talk with you sometime tomorrow."

"Okay." There's an uncomfortable silence that falls over the phone, neither of us sure about how to gracefully exit the conversation without seeming as if we're leaving the other feeling left.

"Ally?" he finally says to me. "You all right?"

"Yeah."

"You sure?" Michael feels needy to me and I'm not in a mood to be able to provide.

"Uh-huh, yeah, sure. Fine."

"You don't sound like yourself," he persists.

"Just some ghosts, Michael. The ghosts are chasing me." I'm more than a little annoyed, grumpy from the intrusion, so I say to him, "I'll be fine. I'll talk to you sometime tomorrow." And I hang up the phone.

Instantly I feel worse. I reach for the phone, dial Michael's number back.

"Michael? Did you want to talk tonight? Was there something you needed?"

He laughs, chuckles really, a kind of titter rumbling through his chest. "Oh, I'm so glad you called me back. You sound better even in the instant."

"I'm fine, Michael, really I am," I sigh into the phone.

"Something is bothering you. I can hear it in your voice. But if you're not ready to talk it through, it can wait."

"It's not me, it's all around me. I'm just wallowing in it. I'm allowed."

"You are allowed. You have five minutes. After that, get on with it. It won't do you any good to mope about."

"What's up?"

"I was missing you, is all. Just missing you."

"Still missing me?" I say, purring into the phone.

"Not as much, no. Not now anyway." I listen as he takes a deep cleansing breath, and lets it out in a quick, hot release. "Long day. I had an argument with Sarah, then one with her mother. Then a call from an irate client, then dinner. Alone. Just long. Just wanted to hear your voice. And now? Now the rest of it seems all so far away."

"Hmmm. You know what you need? A back rub."

"Should I leave the front door open and you can let yourself in?"

"Not tonight, Michael. It's a good night, I think . . ." I pause, searching for the right tone. "For each of us to be alone."

"I think so, Al. I think you're right."

"It's not often I'm right, Michael. Just ask my daughters. But tonight? Tonight's a good night for being on your own. Good night, Michael."

"Night, darling."

43

The calls from Melinda come in on a regular basis between seven fifteen and eight o'clock every third night. I'm stunned at the first one, rattled after the second, and annoyed by the third. When it comes to the fourth call, early in the second week of November, I am hurried and short with her on the phone. The conversation goes something like this:

"Hello, Allyson, it's Melinda. May I speak with Lydia?"

"Sorry, she's out again, Melinda."

"Oh, oh, I'm so sorry. I see. Well, um, could you let her know that I've called? We were supposed to speak this evening, I believe. Let me see, have I mixed up the nights? I think it was tonight . . ."

Her voice trails off before I cut her short. "It might have been. But she's out. I'll tell her you called, okay?"

"Well, please tell her to use our calling card number. She has the card so she can reach us any—"

"I'll let her know, Melinda. Thank you."

When I hang up the phone Michael is staring across the kitchen island at me, a damp dish towel in his left hand.

"Mighty short, I'd say," he says to me. His look is hard; I can tell he is disappointed with my attitude.

"I could set the clock by her calls, Michael. Doesn't she know calling Lydia's not going to make the baby come any faster?"

Then, "Damn! God, damn." I shout this as I take the corner too sharply and run my knee into the side of the cabinet. I check for bruising right away.

Michael brings me a small Ziploc bag of ice and sets it on my shin, just below the knee where the mark is still visible, an indent whitening the skin. I limp to the chair at the head of the kitchen table and prop my foot up on the adjoining bench. "I mean," I continue, "doesn't she realize Lydia's a fifteen-year-old girl? It's not like she's sitting around waiting for her calls. And the last time I checked, I don't think Lyd's looking for a new best friend." The sarcasm doesn't just drip from the corners of my mouth, it pours like sweet syrup on pancakes.

"Ally? What's wrong with her calling? Tell me that. What is it that is bothering you so much?"

"Nothing. Nothing's wrong with her calling," I fib to Michael, to myself.

"Ally."

"What?"

"Ally? Look at me."

I do. He's standing with his back to the countertop, but on my side of the island now, leaning against the granite and sipping the last of his chardonnay. "What?" I whimper.

"What is it really? What is it that's got you so amped on this?"

I run the palm of my hand against the base of my neck, massaging the tight spots. Michael moves around the back of me to take this over, a sort of melodic rubbing beginning with his thumbs into the middle of my spine. "I've said it before, Michael. She's missing it. She's missing everything about this."

"Who is?"

"Lydia, Michael. Jesus, don't you see it? She's missing out on the whole thing. She's got this experience of bringing this baby into the world, and nothing about it is right. No baby showers, no nurseries, no registering for playpens and trying out strollers. No whispering long into the night with her husband about what it's going to be like when it's not the two of them anymore. No talking to me about it. None, none whatsoever. No long talks about what it's like to be a mom, to hold your child for the first time." I run my hand up through my matted hair and tug hard on it with a bit of force. Through clenched teeth and an exasperated voice, I say to him again, "She's just missing it. All of it. I'm just so mad about that, I can't stand it."

"Whoa. Time-out, Ally." Michael stops rubbing abruptly and bends down so he's eye-level with me still sitting in the chair. "Hang on for a second."

"What?"

"That isn't what this is about. This isn't her time for any of that. This is something entirely different. And if you take five minutes out of feeling sorry for yourself about how Lydia and Melinda are getting on about all this, you might just realize that. This is not Lydia's time for any of that. None of those things work in this scenario."

"That's my point. It's supposed to go a certain way. Certainly not like this, not at all like this. There's a lot of ways that all this could be. But I can tell you one thing. It's not supposed to be like this. No one's supposed to get *this*."

"Who says?"

"What do you mean *who says*? Anyone says. It's not supposed to be like this."

"Al, it is supposed to be like this. It's supposed to be exactly like this. This is the way it goes for Lydia this time. Maybe next time it will be different. But thinking and hoping and wishing it were something else isn't going to change it. This is what it is. That's all." He takes my hands gently in his and rubs his thumb over my fingers, tracing the edge of each one of them. He nears my wedding band; I still haven't been able to give it up. He traces it, too, with his thumb, a constant reminder.

He starts again. "You see, it's just different. Completely different. It's not about baby showers and registering for new strollers. It's not about planning and going about this as if it's the best, most moving, most earth-shattering thing that's happened in her life, a life she's sharing with someone else. It's not about any of that. It's completely different, is all. It's about Lydia and something that's happened to her, something that's earth-shattering and life-changing, but not at all in the way you experienced it. This is something she'll carry with her all her days. Years from now she'll remember the nuances you and I and everyone else failed to ever even see. I imagine she'll curl up every now and then and think back on it. Maybe there will be parts she'll bury and have to really struggle to recall, but it'll be there for her."

"I just don't know what to do for her, Michael," I choke in harsh whispers, each word catching in my throat.

"What do you mean? You're doing exactly what you are supposed to do, what Lydia needs you to do."

"But it's not what I thought. I'm not who I thought I'd be. I don't even know who I am supposed to be in this."

"Al? Last time I checked, you're her mom. It's a pretty big part," he deadpans.

"But, but . . . Melinda calls, and Lydia comes running. They're in this together. Lydia confides in her, tells her what's happening to her, how she feels about all of this, what the baby is doing, when it kicks, when it's got the goddamn hiccups, when she's got indigestion, blah, blah, blah."

"Ooooooh," he says, long, drawing out the syllable of the word. "Oh, okay, now I get what's got you so bunched up about Melinda." He holds my chin firm in his hand and pulls my face close to his, so close that our noses nearly touch. "Ally, my God. You think Lydia doesn't need you? You think that Melinda's some sort of substitute for what you have with Lydia?"

"But she doesn't need me, Michael. She doesn't need anything from me. She doesn't even want me around."

"You have got to be kidding me."

"I'm not kidding you, Michael. She and Melinda have forged this whole new bond, this whole new thing that I have nothing to do with."

"I'm sorry, Al, but I can't let you get away with that. Uh-uh, no way."

"It's true, Michael, what do you think they talk about when

they're on the phone? The baby this, the baby that, how's it going, what's going to happen. On and on and on. I can barely get two words out of Lydia. Melinda? She gets volumes."

"Wait a second, Al, look." He comes toward me, stands very close, and cups my chin in his hands. "Here's the deal on this. Lydia needs Melinda, that's just part of what's going on here. It's just part of the deal. Think about it. When you were pregnant, you had Patrick. Lydia's got Melinda. You get it?"

I turn and stare at him blankly. I hate to admit he makes sense.

"Go with me on this, suspend your disbelief for just one second." He holds up his index finger at me, right near my face so that it feels as if he's lecturing me directly. "All that planning? All those late-night silly discussions that you had with Patrick when you were lying around eight months pregnant with Lydia? All those promises you made each other about how life wasn't going to change? All that nonsensical stuff and mythical magic that came along with the feeling you had every time you realized you were carrying a little life inside you? Lydia has a little bit of that, too. And Melinda gets to share it with her, not you. It doesn't make sense for you to share it with her. You can't do it." His words cut right through me, sting the surface of my emotions, and make me lash out at him.

"You don't know what you're talking about, Michael. You don't know anything about what Lydia and I have."

"No?"

"No."

"I can tell you this, Al. What you've got with Lydia? What you do for her and what she needs from you? That hasn't even kicked in yet. You think you're missing out on all this, that she's denying you the right to all this? She's not. It's not yours to have, that's what I know. What's yours to have is the part you get back. You get Lydia back. She's *your* daughter. You have no idea what she's going to need from you, what she will require. That's just about to start again."

He turns and walks away from me then, makes his way to the

French doors and stares out into the backyard. "Oh, and by the way, Ally, if you hadn't noticed? People might say that what we have together, well, it wasn't supposed to go this way either. You gonna deny that it wasn't meant to be, that it's something that doesn't have a right to exist because it isn't the way it was supposed to be?" He leaves me there, still standing in the kitchen, before he closes the door and steps out into the chilly fall night.

I stand at the island and watch Michael make his way across the lawn to the swinging love seat. We don't fight, Michael and I, so I'm left wondering what I'm supposed to do. Nothing comes naturally, so I stand there a little longer, waiting for him to come back into the house. He doesn't.

I make my way outside, my head still ringing with his words. He stops the swing long enough for me to get comfortable next to him. We sit very close to each other, a perfect fit. When I shiver at his touch, he rubs the upper part of my arm a little more.

"I'm sorry, that wasn't fair. This isn't about us, you and me. This is about you and Lydia. It wasn't fair of me to turn this into something else."

"Actually, I think it was more than fair," I say. "And it isn't necessarily about Lydia and me, either, Michael. It's about Lydia. You're right."

"You're her mom. It's all going to come back around. You'll see."

"I know. You're right." We swing in silence, Michael's foot giving us a push off the ground every two or three rotations.

"Michael? You're right about us, too. It wasn't supposed to happen this way. And I struggle with the greed in it every day. I don't know if you can understand that, but I do. I battle with that all the time. I think to myself, how do I have a right to be this happy with this man who was so much to my husband and to me? How do I accept that it's okay for me to be like this with him? How do I allow myself to laugh and live and love again when what I had was so beautiful and so right and meant so much to me? How can I possibly replace that? And how can I do it with this person?"

We move to an Adirondack chair, the wood hard against his back. Michael pulls me down between his legs so that I'm sitting with my back on his chest staring up at the endless sky filled with miniscule stars, each of them seemingly blinking back and forth in code across the backdrop.

"I don't want you to be angry with me, Al."

"I'm not," I sigh. "I'm not angry with you, Michael. I'm in love with you. Everything about me is in love with you. I have nothing left but to be in love with you. I've tried rationalizing it, fighting it, letting it roll around inside me and go nowhere, but everything I am is in love with you."

Michael waits for a minute before he finally says something to me, something I won't forget for a long, long time, maybe ever.

"It's okay, Ally," he says.

"What?" I ask him, puzzled.

"You can love us both, you know. Patrick and me. It's okay," he says quietly, almost timidly.

I let the words swirl around in my head and try better to understand what it is he is trying to tell me.

"You can love us both," he says again. "As a matter of fact, I don't want you to stop loving him." He waits a minute more, the silence falling over us, before he says, "I never have."

44

I recognize Melinda's phone number on the caller ID the next afternoon around five. It stops me cold and I think twice about letting the machine pick it up before I finally grab the receiver and hurriedly say, "Hello?"

"Hi, Allyson. It's Melinda Ramshorn."

"Oh, hi, Melinda. Lydia is up in her room. Hang on, let me go get her . . ." I trail off before I hear her voice still clear in the receiver.

"Actually, Allyson, I was hoping I could speak with you, if you have the time. And if that's okay?" She's hesitant, but resounding, practiced.

"Oh, um, sure, okay."

"Reid and I have been talking, actually. About the baby. And, well, there's no easy way to say this to you, Allyson, and no easy way to ask you, so I'm just going to come right out with it, okay?"

"Um, sure. Is everything okay, Melinda?" I say to her, cautious and unnerved.

"No. Actually, it's not."

My heart runs fast, quick deathlike beats that send my heart and blood pumping and my hands shaking.

"You have to understand, Allyson, that this is very difficult for me, for us, actually. Although Reid doesn't know I'm calling you. And I'd appreciate it if you could keep it that way. This is between you and me. I feel as if, well, I feel as if you and I might need to clear the air, actually. I feel as if there is a lot that has been said between us, without so many words. That probably doesn't make much sense to you, I know, but bear with me."

I clear my throat but wait before I say anything to her. The receiver is pressed hard against my ear; I don't want to miss a thing she says.

"Reid and I have been talking, and, well, like I said, there is no easy way, so I'll just come right out and ask you this. We're wondering, you know, we just have to understand all of this as we go forward with this adoption, so we were wondering if you had considered raising this baby yourself.

"I'm sure this is very hard, Allyson, and really, you see, it seems as if maybe, just maybe regardless of what Lydia wants to do, well, it seems that it's really that *you're* not ready to give up this baby. So I'm sure it had to be something that you'd considered. I mean it does happen, it's not that far-fetched."

"No, I suppose it isn't," I say to her, melancholy sinking into my voice.

She waits a long minute then, and the silence that creeps in over the phone wire, in between the both of us, is painful. I have no idea what to do with it until she says, "Well, maybe that's all I really needed to know. Maybe, I just wanted to see if . . ."

Her voice trails off before I say to her, "No, Melinda, wait."

She sighs deeply, a long exhale that fills the empty space. I sink onto the bottom step of the stairs, folding my legs up so that I can rest my chin on them.

"Allyson, please, it's okay. I can't imagine what you must be going through, I really can't. But I don't want this baby if you think it really belongs with you. I couldn't possibly imagine the place you must find yourself in about this. But you have to know that it's not my intention to take this child from you. It just simply isn't. I can't sit here and tell you that it's best for this baby, or best for Lydia. You're her mother. My God, Allyson, you would know that far more than I would."

She waits, patient, until I can finally talk.

314   *Deborah J. Wolf*

"This is not my child, Melinda, not my decision. This is not at all about me," I whisper into the receiver and hear her choke at the other end of the phone, break free into a sob. At the same time, I look backward once again toward Lydia's room and I find her, standing on the landing above me, and with everything in her, looking right into me.

45

The first flakes of winter drift quietly out of a gray bleary sky on the first weekend in December. Earlier in the day I cleaned the fireplace, swept it until there was nothing left of the late autumn fires we'd already burned, more wood than I'd remembered in past years. Patrick had disliked fires, couldn't stand the mess they made or the smell they left lingering in the house. Michael shares my desire for a fire burning every night, regardless of the cleanup. We've already burned through our standard annual delivery, and just this morning Michael called for more. I listened to him on the phone in the other room where he sat stretched watching a football game as he recited the numbers to his credit card, then my address, both burned in his memory.

Melinda's calls have been more frequent now, the last this morning just after nine o'clock. The house quiet, she'd caught me alone in bed nestled against two thick down pillows, flipping channels and working on my Christmas list. She begged my opinion about car seats.

"Better decide soon," I said to her. "This baby could come any day."

I sensed the arrival of Lydia's baby before she ever went into labor. Felt it and knew it in my own loins maybe, quite possibly, before she felt the effects of the first cramp, before the first contraction rocked her. Those came Saturday night, long after Michael and I had cuddled on the couch like two teenagers, making out in the night, the darkened room lit only by lingering embers of a fire we'd built hours earlier. I heard Lydia's door open, not nearly soft enough for her to be treading downstairs for water, but with much more purpose, her feet tripping as she padded across the wood floor. "Mom!" I heard Lydia cry out, and reached her just as she doubled over, turning to face me in the hall. Her sweats were damp, not nearly qualifying as wet, but soggy enough so that I knew what had happened. The proof evident in her bed, on her sheets, her water had broken. She was two weeks early, and convinced she'd be late, none of us was prepared.

I'd dressed Lydia, ordering her to take off her sweat bottoms and underpants, directing her to step into a clean pair of maternity pants that I'd located somewhere in her bottom drawer. She sat on the side of her bed, her hands wide and gripping at the underside of her belly. I kept one eye on her, as I threw things into a duffel bag—a pair of pajamas with a wide elastic waist, a favorite sweatshirt that had been Patrick's, her slippers, a pair of tennis shoes, two pairs of underpants, her hairbrush, and then, last minute, her portable CD player and the few random CDs that lay scattered on her dresser. She was far quieter than I thought she was capable of being.

"My journal, Mom. Can you grab my journal?"

I watched as she pointed across the room to her far table where a fabric-covered book lay prone on the table, a ballpoint pen resting in the spine. I reached for both and dropped them in the bag.

"Mom?" she whispered again. I wasn't sure if it was a conscientious effort on behalf of Becca still sleeping in the next room, or if the whisper was all she could manage.

"Yeah, honey?"

"How bad is it going to hurt?"

"It'll be worse than this, Lyd. A lot worse." She looked back at me with steel in her eyes as I finished my thought. "And then it'll be better. I promise."

I'd wondered how Lydia would be in labor, whether she'd be overcome with pain so severe she'd beg me for anything in my

power to make it stop. I stepped out in the hall to place the call to
Melinda and Reid. In the labor room primped by a French coun-
try armoire and Laura Ashley curtains, she said to me, "I'm fine,
Mom. It's going to be fine. Just see if you can get Melinda here in
time."

"She's in labor. You need to get on a plane," I said to Melinda,
and waited until I was sure she was awake and comprehending
what I meant. "Now, Melinda. You've got to come now."

Michael had brought Becca to the hospital. In the waiting
room, as I warmed in his embrace and he rubbed my back, he re-
ported that it was the first time he'd heard Becca swear, when he
woke her softly and told her that we'd gone hours before.

"Shit, Michael! *When?*" she said loudly, kicking back the covers and jumping out of her bed.

That was all she'd said to him, eyes blazing and hard, tearing
right through him. He couldn't get his own things together fast
enough, grabbing for his wallet and sunglasses as she pushed him
out the door and into the refrigerator-like air in the garage. She
refused to speak to him again after he'd suggested they make
their way through the drive-through, assuring her that I'd have
called him if things had gotten close enough.

"Jesus, Ally, I must have told her fifteen times that it could
take all night and all day today. She just wouldn't believe me."

"I can only imagine, Michael. She was determined to be here,
no doubt about it. She's in for a long haul, I think. We all are.
This is going to take a while. Only person in charge in there is
Lydia."

"Don't you mean the baby?"

"No. I mean Lydia. You should see her. She's got the strongest
resolve I've ever witnessed. I think she had a discussion with
that baby, told it not to even dare think of making its way out
here until she was good and ready. And that ain't happening until
Melinda makes it. Strangest damn thing I've ever seen."

I watch as he slumps into an easy chair in the corner, and
slurps at the large coffee. His glasses on and his hair disheveled,
with more than a day-old beard, he looks stunningly gorgeous to

me. When I kiss him on the forehead, he draws me in, wraps his arms around my waist, hooking his thumbs through my belt loops, and kisses me square on the belly.

"You're beautiful, truly lovely."

I rake my hands through my hair and rub the sleep and left-over mascara out of the corners of my eyes. I'd felt neither beautiful nor lovely, until Michael bestowed the words upon me.

By noon, the contractions have stopped altogether.

"They won't send us home, will they, Mom?" Becca moans from the corner chair where she is reclined taking in an episode of *The Amanda Show*.

"Uh-uh. Not since her water broke. There's no going back now." Leaning over the metal bed rail, I stare down at Lydia. She is tired, and aches. She rolls onto her right side, away from me, and studies the door. I am convinced Lydia has stopped her own contractions, hell-bent on Melinda being here before she lets things run their course. I am still struggling with my role until she rolls back toward me, onto her left side, and looks up at me, whispering, "Mom, you're not going anywhere, are you? No matter how long it takes?"

"No, baby, no. I'll be right here, long as you want me."

Peggy orders Pitocin just after one o'clock. Lydia begs her for more time, but Peggy is practical.

"It'll take a while for it to kick in, sweetie. And I've started you out slow, okay?" she says to Lydia, brushing the hair back from her face. "But we've got to keep you moving, understand? You can't linger here all day doing nothing. It isn't good for anyone, especially for the baby."

Lydia swallows a hard lump and blinks back the tears in her eyes. I start praying, willing Melinda and Reid to arrive.

Sometime after three, when Lydia's contractions are heavy enough to demand an epidural, I usher Becca out of the room. I bring Lydia her third bucket of ice chips and work on her lower back until the anesthesiologist, a small humorless Chinese man, makes his way into our room. He slowly tapes off the area on her back, dousing it with antiseptic, before he threads the needle into her spine. Hypnotized, Lydia hunches motionless over the side of the bed. Her pink-painted fingernails drive into my hands until they go prickly, then numb.

Melinda Ramshorn walks into the hospital room a little less than an hour later. Lydia is propped on her right side, and doesn't see her come into the room. My eyes meet Melinda's first, her tiny frame filling my line of vision. It's hard to know whether it is a look of sheer relief or sheer fear that washes over my face, but either way Lydia glances over her shoulder, gathers up the backside of her hospital gown, and manages to roll over.

"You made it," I whisper. "I didn't know if we could wait much longer."

Melinda is timid and stiff at first, unsure of her surroundings, unclear about what awaits her. She brushes the hair back from her face, tucks it neatly behind her ear, and stands in the middle of the room, both hands clutching the handle of her pocketbook and frozen.

"Lydia's been waiting," I encourage her, patting the side of the bed, a signal that it is okay for her to approach. She does so, but cautiously. I stand by the window and as she strokes Lydia's arm, brushes back the matted hair from her forehead.

"I swear she held off her own contractions."

Melinda takes in the room for the first time, the monitor beeping to the side of the bed, spitting out a constant running tape of Lydia's vitals. I pick up the remote and switch the television off.

"I'm so glad you made it," Lydia says sleepily to Melinda. "I didn't want to do this without you." Melinda stares from Lydia to me, and then back to Lydia before her eyes rest once again on me.

"They gave her the epidural about an hour ago. It's taking effect. She's feeling much better now. She was very worried you wouldn't make it, and she didn't want to start without you." I motion with my head to the monitor and watch as the numbers go up, 106, 109, 112, 122. "Contractions," I say, just as Lydia winces and shifts in the bed, curling one leg up under her. "They're getting stronger now. She's feeling a lot of pressure."

"How long? How much longer do you think it'll be?" Melinda takes a quick breath in, a hiccup of sorts.

"Not long. Peggy should be in any time. Our doctor. You'll like her, she's a longtime friend of mine. It's going to be fine, really."

Becca returns from her walk with Michael, licking the last of an ice cream cone and wiping her mouth with a napkin. I introduce Melinda to Becca for the first time and watch as Becca sizes her up. She starts in with the questions right away. "Do you have the baby's room done? Do you care if it's a boy or a girl? Are you going to tell him or her that they're adopted? Will you love the baby just like it's your own?"

"It will be hers," Lydia pipes up from the bed, rolling on her side toward Melinda. Her back to me, I start rubbing just at the base of her spine. "More on my hip, if you can, Mom. *Please.* Just a little bit lower." I readjust and center the pressure from my thumb just below Lydia's left hip, moving it in a constant circular movement. "Thanks, that's so much better," she says to me.

"I didn't mean it wouldn't be her baby, Lyd. I just mean, well, you know, her own baby, like from her."

"It's the same thing. Ugh," she moans, sucking in air with the contraction that's overcome her and holding it in deep in her lungs as if she were smoking a cigarette. "Oh, Mom, oh, oh, that hurts so much, oh, Mama."

"Let it out, Lydi, nice and slow," I say to her. "Just let it go."

"Yeah, okay, I get what you mean." Becca's relentless, having climbed up the end of the bed and planting herself just below where Lydia might want to stretch her legs. "Bec, can you move all that stuff in a pile over by the window?" I motion to her backpack and coat, a few random things of my own scattered on the table.

Becca jumps down from the bed, starts piling things in the corner. I hear Becca ask Melinda the last question again. "So, will you love the baby just like it's your own?" She's pointed and doesn't back down, still searching for the answer to her question.

"She's a tough one, huh?" Melinda motions to me.

Nodding my head in agreement, I tell Melinda, "You have no idea."

"Yeah, Becca, I will. We both will," she says, making mention, for the first time, of Reid, who I imagine has joined Michael in the waiting room, his loafered feet never making it past the striped curtain pulled across Lydia's door. "Remember, this is it for us. We don't know anything else. In our family, this is how we make a baby, how we have a family."

That seems to satisfy Becca, who fumbles for the remote and switches another show back on. The electricity from the set settles over the room before the sound and picture come on.

"Hey, Bec?" I say to her.

"Yeah?"

"Shut that thing off when things get rocking, okay?"

"Yeah, fine."

"She wanted to be here," I say to Melinda, but it's Lydia's face I'm watching. She's gone ashen. Through clenched teeth and dry, chapped lips she says to me, "Mom, can you go find Peggy?" before she draws her knees up as close to her chest as she can get them.

Melinda goes pale, near white. It occurs to me that for Lydia and me, this is the end of something, while for Melinda it's only just the beginning.

Up the night, the day, and probably more, Peggy looks undaunted and courageous, almost peppy. She hugs Melinda with a tight and full embrace, before she dons gloves and lifts the sheets and blanket from Lydia. This piques Becca's interest and she gives up on the show.

"You ready to do this, Lydia?" Lydia nods her head and glues her eyes on Peggy. The sound in the room changes, tiny metal clinks and scrapes becoming prominent. The light in the room changes, the pale sky outside the window fading to the sharp overhead lights. The air in the room changes; it moves with an ebb and flow that Peggy and Lydia command.

Just as Lydia is getting ready to push, I do not know where to stand and I find myself lost in the middle of the room without a job. Becca and Melinda flank either side of Lydia, using one arm to prop her head up on a pillow, the other to help pull back her knees. Light-headed, I'm caught floating somewhere in the room, until finally, from a distance, Peggy barks an order at me.

"You're not going to see anything from over there, Ally. Move around! Come down here with me!" I lift my head from the fog and strain to make out the words, thick and slow, flowing from my friend's mouth. I barely recognize her under the rank-and-file plastic mask; only the familiarity of her eyes draws me in and pulls me to her side, close enough to see everything I'd missed in the birth of my own daughters. I find myself in the same place Patrick had been, looking back up at the miracle created. With a hand covering my mouth, tears streaming down my face, and the echoes of my daughter's voice, "Mama, Mama?" vaguely surreal somewhere within the room, I watch as Maya Elizabeth Ramshorn makes her way into the room, strewn with mucus, transparent and veiny, loud and pissed.

"Who wants her?" Peggy says, cutting the cord, and holding the shrieking child with two hands as we all stare shocked into the face of this beautiful creature.

"Hand her to her mother," I hear Lydia say in a gasping whisper. She's breathless and turns her face away, tears streaming onto the pillowcase. A nurse suctions the baby, and begins to wipe down the mucus from her face and body. I look again, not at the baby this time, but at the look on Melinda's face, so overcome and joyful she's speechless.

"My God, a girl," I hear her whisper. "My God, she's so beautiful. Oh God, thank you, Lydia, thank you. She is so beautiful."

I move to Lydia's side, and bend to soothe her face, wipe away the tears, and rake back the hair that's plastered against her cheek. I'm close enough to feel her hot breath on my cheeks, and whisper to her face, "Open your eyes, Lydia, I want to see your beautiful eyes. I love you so much, sweetie. You did a great job. I love you so much. I'm so proud of you. You did it, you got through this. I knew you would, baby. I just knew it." She reaches her right hand out for mine and I take it, grasping it in my own, and hold it there as Peggy comes to the side of the bed.

"Couple of things I need you to do, sweetie, and then we're

done. There's some small tearing that I want to stitch and we'll be out of here, okay?"

Lydia's eyes wander off, dazed, as she listens to Peggy and follows each of her instructions. She allows the nurses to come in and massage her abdomen, never flinching when they place ice packs on her stomach. It's only then that I am aware Melinda is no longer in the room, she and the baby, the plastic nursery on wheels rolled off somewhere else.

46

Lydia agrees to a mild sedative shortly after everyone clears the room. Her eyes get heavy and she falls off, not dissimilar to the way she'd go out as a child, just as she could anticipate the end of the story I'd be reading to her. Peggy hooks her arm through mine and pulls me from the stiff wooden chair I'm sitting in next to the bed.

"C'mon," she says to me. "She'll be out for a while."

I let Peggy lead me outside into the hall before I go limp from exhaustion. "She did great, Allyson, just beautifully. She should be able to go home tomorrow," she says softly into my ear. "She's going to be fine."

"Mmmm," I mumble back and let my chin rest on her shoulder. "God, I'm so glad it's over." Dizzy and lacking both sleep and food, I'm feeling more than a bit light-headed. Peggy guides me down the hall; I stagger even with her arm around my waist into the waiting room, where Becca is giving a blow-by-blow description to Michael and Eric. I'm bewildered by Eric's presence and ask him, not in an unfriendly way, what he's doing here.

Confused, he says to me, "I thought maybe Lydia would want me to be here."

It takes me a minute—as I stare at him blankly—before I answer, "Oh, right, yes, of course. Sorry."

Michael guides me carefully down onto the ottoman. I sit,

feeling very awkward, with my hands shoved between my knees, as if I don't know what to do with them, my feet turned inward.

"Her name is Maya," I say, because I can think of nothing else.

"Maya Elizabeth, Mom," I hear Becca say in a know-it-all voice, as if I've stolen her thunder. "I already told them. It's a great name, don't you think?" She tut-tuts her way across the room to the soda machine, and I watch as she drops five quarters into the coin slot and pushes the button for Minute Maid lemonade. The plastic bottle drops, echoing throughout the room.

"Do you want to see the baby, Eric?" I hear Michael ask.

"Um, I'm not really sure. Do you think I should?"

"I think it's up to you," I answer him.

He nods, keeping his head low and bowed. Becca takes the bait, jumps in. "I know where the nursery is. I can show you."

When they are gone, Michael sits forward in the chair, his knees on either side of the ottoman, and pulls me back against him. It's only a few minutes before I'm drifting off against his chest, lulled by the melodic beating of his heart, the shallow rise and fall of his breathing.

I wake an hour later curled into the chair, my body stiff and uncomfortable. Michael's gone and I'm in the room alone, the picture from the television on but without sound. I pull off the thin blanket that someone has draped over me and crumple it up in a heap in the chair. I pad off to Lydia's room to see how she's doing, the soft tread of my tennis shoes squeaking on the freshly mopped tile floor.

Lydia is awake, propped by two large pillows, staring out the large-paned windows in her room. She turns her head ever so slightly toward me when I enter her room and let the door swing closed behind me. Tears are streaming down her face, her red cheeks, and she blows her nose noisily with a crumpled tissue she holds in her hand.

"Hi, baby, how're you feeling?" I take in the contents strewn on her side table: a pink plastic water pitcher, a half-filled plastic cup with a bent straw limply folded over the top, her CD player and headphones, a box of Kleenex, six or seven crumpled and frayed tissues tossed in a small heap, a small vase with three yellow tulips. "Your flowers are beautiful," I say to her because I can think of nothing else to start with.

She blows her red, raw nose into the tissue in her hand and leans her head far back into the pillow. Her eyes are swollen, red-rimmed, and tired, and she's got her glasses on, making her look even younger than her fifteen years. The freckles on her face are joined together in blotches. She's a virtual mess and yet I can think of nothing but how beautiful she looks to me.

"Michael," she says, motioning toward the tulips, and sucking in snot. I think to myself that I should have known that.

"He let me doze off—Michael, that is. I was out cold in a chair in the lobby. I'm sorry I wasn't here when you woke up."

"I didn't sleep much," she manages, her nose clogged and nasally, leaving her sounding like she has a nasty cold. "Michael took Becca over to hang out with Sarah. She couldn't wait to tell Sarah all about the . . ." Her voice trails off before she gets to the word *baby*. "He said to tell you he'd be back later."

"Okay." I take my place in the hard wooden chair next to the bed, pushing the swinging table out of my way. "Are you okay, sweetie?"

From the bathroom I hear the sound of the toilet flushing and look quizzically at Lydia, raising my eyebrows as if to question her.

"Grandma. She got here about half an hour ago. I guess Michael must have called her."

Shit.

Lady Barbara is the last person I am prepared to see. Still, I should have expected her. I look around and spot her purse, her raincoat thrown over the back of the chair in the corner. I should have known Michael would call her. Damn him.

I manage a weak smile at Lydia and wait for Barbara to make her way into the room. Lydia closes her eyes and leans her head back on the pillow so that the tears that fall from the corners of her eyes roll vertically down her face and into her ear canals. Her lower lip trembles as if she might burst at any minute.

"Hello, Allyson," Barbara greets me loudly, filling the room with her presence. She emerges from the small bathroom wiping her hands on a piece of paper towel and disposes of it quickly. "When did you get here?"

"Hi, Barbara." I rise from the chair to greet her, make a place for her in the spot I've unsuspectingly taken from her. She motions at me to sit, but I don't. I'm more confident on my feet; feel as if I can move more quickly. "I've been here, actually. Just catching up on some sleep and trying to let Lyd do the same. We've had quite a night, quite a long day."

"So I heard. I haven't had a chance to see my great grand-daughter yet, but Lydia tells me that everything went as well as could be expected."

I swallow hard at her reference to the baby and move my eyes cautiously to Lydia, watching her wince at Barbara's words. Barbara's calculated, deliberate. I surmise she's been working on Lydia since the minute she walked in the room.

"Lydia did a great job. I think we're all grateful to have it behind us, don't you, Lyd?"

I watch my daughter bury her hands beneath the sheets, squirming. She turns her face from me and lays it down on the pillow. I swear I see her swallow down a lump in her throat. Her chin quivers; she's frightened.

"Behind us? Nonsense. The fun's just beginning now, isn't it, Lydia? So much to do now that the baby is here. Good grief, we'll be busy." Barbara barely blinks, never takes her eyes off me. I feel her hard stare, her cold look.

"Barbara, you know where we stand on this, what Lydia has decided to do about the baby," I stammer, angry with myself for the break in my stride, my confidence shaken. I walk toward the bed to stand by Lydia's side, folding down the metal side rail that separates us. The sheets feel rough and starchy, like something that has been bleached too often. I notice Lydia's changed into her sweat bottoms; they stick out from underneath the clean hospital gown she's got on.

"Well, I know that Lydia *was* considering the idea of putting this baby up for adoption. But really, Allyson," she says, her voice threatening condensation, "we've just been sitting here having the nicest talk, Lydia and me. We've been chatting about the wonderful aspects of motherhood, the sweet simplicity of it all. When it comes right down to it, there's really nothing better than being a mom. And now that Lydia's a mom, well, I just know she'll be so terrific at it. And after all, she'll have you and me to rely on, our help with all of this. You'll see, everything is going to be just fine."

Bile rises in my throat.

"Barbara, you know where we stand on this," I say again. "You and I have been over this no less than a dozen times. I know this seems really hard. Trust me, I understand that. But this is the best decision for Lydia, for the baby." I square her off so that my body blocks Lydia's. I feel like a lioness that is left pacing in front of her cave, protecting her young. From behind me I hear Lydia wail before she breaks fully into uneven heavy sobs that send the bed frame shaking. With my hand I reach behind me and find her shoulder and grip it tightly, refusing to let go.

Barbara frowns.

"Perhaps you should ask her again, is all I'm saying, Allyson. It certainly wouldn't hurt to ask Lydia what she's thinking about all this now that the baby is here. After all, people do change their minds. Isn't that right, Lydia?"

I turn to face my daughter. She has bent her legs and pulled them up so that her heels are close to touching her butt. With a tissue that is barely in shreds, she is blotting her eyes, but the tears come faster than she can wipe them away. She looks so young; I can't think of a time when she has looked so young to me.

I brush back matted wisps of her hair, pushing them back from her face, and spreading them out across the pillow in the shape of a large fan. "You've got a lot to grieve on this, Lyd, don't be afraid to let it all out, just let it go." I watch as she balls up her fists and presses them under the frames of her glasses, deep into her eye sockets, rubbing them furiously as if she could rid the images that are already haunting her.

"Oh, Mom, God, Mom, I never imagined it would be like this."

I bend down and whisper into her ear, "Just let it go, Lyd, you don't need anyone's permission. Just let it all out."

I gently stroke her hair away from her forehead and kiss her softly. Behind us, Barbara is pacing. I can hear it in her even, heavy steps, back and forth, back and forth.

"I was telling Lydia that I was certain Patrick was here with her today. He simply must have been. Like an angel watching over her."

I never stop stroking Lydia's forehead, back and forth, back and forth, but inside an alarm sounds. I know from the tone of Barbara's voice that she has worked Lydia into a frenzy of guilt.

Lydia turns to me. "Do *you* think Daddy was with us today, Mom? Do you?" Before I can answer her, she interrupts me again. "'Cause I think Grandma might be right. I swear he was. I could just feel him."

"Then I'd say he probably was, Lyd. That happens to me all the time."

"Really? Like when?"

"Oh God, Lyd, all the time. In the morning when it's very quiet in bed and I'm alone by myself, wondering how I managed to sleep through another night without having awoken even once to check for him next to me in bed. When I'm doing the most mundane of tasks—the dishes, let's say. Your dad was a good dishwasher and he and I used to spend a lot of time talking together when we would stand in the kitchen washing, you remember? Gosh, sometimes it's just when I walk across the room . . . he used to sit and watch me, just the most ridiculous grin on his face from his spot on the couch. In the coldest of nights, in the warmest of days, I feel him all the time."

Barbara interrupts the solitude Lydia and I share. I'd almost forgotten she was still in the room until she says, "I was telling Lydia that I just knew how important it would be to Patrick for her to keep and raise this baby. I mean, he just never would have allowed her to give this child up. He just simply wouldn't have heard about an idea like adoption. Now, I'm not saying that he'd have been happy about the idea of Lydia getting pregnant and all, but there is just no way he'd ever let someone else raise his own flesh and—"

"Barbara! Please!"

"What, Allyson? All I am saying is that Patrick would have had a solution for this. He certainly wouldn't have heard of adoption. It would have been extremely disappointing to him that Lydia would even be considering such an idea. Honestly, Ally, sometimes I wonder if you knew my son at all."

Lydia is crying again, the tears coming more quietly now. They run down her face in long streaks that I swear could turn to small rivers. I smile at her daintily before wiping them away with the back of my hand and then turning to face Barbara.

"Did you mean 'your son' or 'my husband'? Because honestly, Barbara, sometimes what *I* wonder was whether or not you knew *my* husband?"

She fumes at my insinuation, fumbles for something to say to me. Finally, she walks past me to Lydia's bedside. "Honey, I know you've had a long day and there is so much to think about." She reaches out for Lydia's arm and clamps her wide hand down around her elbow. "Remember what we talked about earlier. Remember all the things I've told you." She bends to kiss Lydia on the forehead then, the place where I have so carefully been stroking her head, before whispering just loud enough for me to hear, "I think it's time I go see that great-granddaughter of mine now, don't you? I'll come back later, Lydia. Get some rest."

And with that, she's gone.

47

There's not much room in the adjustable hospital bed, but I force my way in anyhow. I want to be close to Lydia, close enough to hold her. She obliges me by scooting as far as she can toward the rail on the other side of the bed.

Every fiber in my being wanted to run after Barbara, escort her down the stairs and out the front door of the hospital. Everything in me wanted to call Peggy and ask her to have Lydia's baby moved away from the viewing window in the nursery. I longed to push Melinda and Reid in front of the woman; let them duke it out with her. But I stayed. I stayed, long and still, next to Lydia in the small bed, our breathing finally relaxing and falling into rhythm together.

I waited a long time, until finally I couldn't stand it any longer.

"Lyd, what'd Grandma say to you?"

"Oh, Mom, everything. She's so certain that adoption isn't a good bet, that I'll regret it. She thinks I'm ready to be a mom, I guess, though I have to sort of laugh at that. I don't know the first thing about being a mom. I wouldn't have a clue."

I breathe deeply. With Barbara out of the room, Lydia sounds more relaxed, more sure of herself. And then she tells me, "She thinks Daddy would be so disappointed with me if I gave the baby away. She just kept saying to me, 'Your father wouldn't stand for this, Lydia, he just wouldn't. Family is family. You don't just give away a baby.' God, Mom, I don't know. What do you think? Do you think Daddy would have wanted me to keep her?"

I think hard for a minute before I answer her. I want to do so truthfully, honestly. In some regards, I wonder if I know what Patrick would have thought. Would he have been supportive or would Lydia have had to drag him along to accepting this as the best choice, like she had done with me? Would he even consider the option or would he have laid down the law? I really don't know.

"I think Daddy would have wanted you to do what was right for you. He loved you very much, Lydia. Very, very much."

Sometime later we both doze off, my right arm propped under her neck and long numb. Michael wakes me when he stops by to check on us. I squint at him through the bright light that bleeds into Lydia's hospital room before I get up and pad across the tile floor. I close the door gently behind us and walk down the hall with him.

"How's she doing?" Michael asks me, wrapping his arm around my waist and pulling me toward him.

I stiffen, cross my arms over my chest, and shrug my shoulders. "She's okay."

"Just okay?"

"Barbara was here, Michael."

"Oh. And? Is everything okay?"

"Let's just say she's made her opinion known about what she thinks Lydia should do. And adoption is nowhere on her radar."

"I see. She hasn't changed her mind, huh?"

"Nope. Did you expect she would?"

"I was hoping she would keep her opinion to herself, actually. It would be the best thing for everyone."

"When was the last time Barbara thought about everyone? Or anyone for that matter?"

"It's not that she means to . . ." Michael starts to cover for her and then stops cold, his hands shoved well into the pockets of his jeans. It's late and the corridor is deserted. The hospital feels cold, sterile. I wrap my arms tightly around myself and rub my shoulders for warmth. I look back at him, then at the floor, then back at him, waiting. Finally he says to me, "Okay, never mind." He takes a deep breath and then asks me, "Do you want me to talk to her?"

"No. No, thanks, Michael, but no. I need to deal with this one. Lydia and I. We'll be fine."

He smiles wryly and winks at me. "I know you will. I know that." He pulls me tight and wraps both of his arms around me. I bury my face into his chest, just lay it right down there and sigh. Then he whispers into my hair, "You tell me if you need me." I ask him to keep Becca for me for the night. He agrees, nodding his head with a long yawn.

In the dimly lit room, Lydia stirs when I settle into the side chair that reclines. I'm pulling a thin blue hospital blanket over me when she rolls over and says to me, "Mom, can we go see the baby?"

"Oh, Lyd, are you sure? It's so late, after midnight already."

"Yeah. I really think I want to, Mom." She throws back the covers and begins to swing her legs over the side of the bed, her stocking feet hitting the cold tile floor. I get up to meet her by the bed and steady her some; she's still unsure of her footing.

"Um, okay, Lyd. She's in the nursery. Do you want me to get you a wheelchair or do you want to walk?"

"No. No wheelchair. I can walk, I'm fine, Mom."

"Okay. Lean on me, okay? Let me take your arm."

We make our way down the hall to the nursery, which is lit and alive with action. Small incubator-like beds line the room. In the center of the room are three wooden rocking chairs; a nurse in blue scrubs sits in one of them feeding the tiniest newborn.

"Hi," she says to us, propping the baby under one arm, the

bottle wedged against her armpit. The child continues to drink. "I need to see your ID bracelet."

Lydia holds up her left arm, two identical bracelets swimming around her bony wrist. The nurse checks them and looks at Lyd. "She's over there. Last one on the left. I imagine she'll be awake any minute if you want to feed her. She's got a great set of lungs on her, that one."

Lydia grips at my arm tightly, her nails digging into the soft part of my forearm. I steady her and whisper, "Are you sure, Lyd? You don't have to go if you don't want to."

"No. I want to see her," she whispers, her lips barely moving.

We make our way over to the small rolling infant bed. Maya is rolled burrito-like in a striped hospital blanket and turned on her side, a pink cap covering her tiny head. Her puffy eyes are closed, her skin blotchy red but a good color. She has Becca's eyebrows, thin and pencillike.

We lean into the plastic bassinet, our heads pressed together, and in awe of the tiny, beautiful creature that lies before us. Her long, thin fingers begin to uncurl just slightly before she yawns, then sighs deeply. The nurse was right, she doesn't last long with us staring her awake, and before we know it she begins to emit small puffing chirps that gradually grow louder into wailing cries.

I pluck her from the bed and cradle her to me, hushing her and turning her in toward my chest. "Shhh," I say to her, "you're all right, baby girl." I bounce slowly, my body settled into that rocking motion that just overcomes a woman.

The nurse smiles at us feebly and I nod my head at her. "You were right," I say, "she's starving."

"Her bottles are in the top drawer," she says to us. "Just pull the wrapper back and you can feed her."

Lydia pulls open the top drawer that reveals a stack of tiny diapers and ten or twelve bottles already filled with formula. "This?" She looks at me strangely, holding one of them up to me.

"Uh-huh," I say, moving Maya up on my shoulder and patting

her back gently. "Bring it over here, Lyd, and we'll feed her." We make our way to one of the rockers, Lydia's long sweat bottoms dragging on the floor.

"Do you want to feed her or do you want me to do it?" I ask her.

"Um, maybe you should do it, Mom," she answers me, and I take the chair, settling back and reaching for the bottle she's pulled from its wrapper. I suck in the sweet smell of baby—Maya's had her first bath—and nestle the tiny nipple into her mouth. She fights it at first, then relaxes and settles against the crook of my arm, lapping at the nipple and sucking at the formula. It dribbles some down her cheek and into the crease in her neck and I ask Lydia to get me a burp cloth.

"This?" she says, holding up a cloth diaper.

"Mmm-hmm."

Lydia watches her daughter drink from the bottle, taking her in and gathering enough strength to ask me to step aside. Finally, she says to me, "I think I want to try to feed her, Mom. Okay?"

"Of course, honey." I rise from the chair and wait until Lydia is settled into the rocker, a pillow between the wood spokes and the small of her back, before I hand the baby to her. She's timid at first; afraid she'll break her, or worse yet, drop her.

I don't quite know what to say, watching her, so I say nothing. I lean against the melamine cabinets and cross my arms in front of my chest and just watch.

Lydia stares into the baby's face, really studying her, as if taking in everything about her. She's stiff and barely moves, but just stares into her face, bending finally to kiss the child on her forehead.

"Do I have to burp her?" she asks me. "I don't know how to do that." She looks panicked, fear running across her furrowed brow.

"I can do it for you if you want."

"Can you show me?"

"Sure." I take Maya from her arms and hold her upright against my chest, gently patting and intermittently rubbing her back. She produces a small burp, enough to make the both of us smile, then giggle, before we proclaim her brilliant.

"Do you like her name, Mom?"

"I do. It's unusual, but I like it. Seems to suit her, don't you think?"

"I'm not so sure, actually. I guess so. I guess she'll grow into it." Lydia pauses for a minute, coming to my side and running the tips of her fingertips over Maya's bald head.

"Careful," I say to her. "She's got a soft spot right here." I take Lydia's index and middle fingers and run them over the top center portion of the baby's head. "Feel that?"

"Eeew. What's wrong with her?"

"Nothing, Lyd. All babies have it. There's not a thing to be worried about. It's completely normal." I switch Maya's position so that she's cradled in my left arm and warm against my rib cage. "Trust me on that one. There isn't a thing wrong with her, she's just beautiful. Perfect."

"I'm thinking of changing her name," Lydia says to me flatly.

"Huh?"

"I like Samantha. The agency said I could name her if I wanted to." She looks down at her feet then, testing her own confidence. "I just think I should at least give her a name, you know."

I don't say anything to her at first. After a long pause during which we are both staring into Maya's face, I finally respond. "If it makes you feel better, Lyd, you can name her, sure. I don't see why it wouldn't be okay."

Lydia smiles then and repeats the child's new name, softly and in her ear like whispering a secret. "Samantha. Oh, my baby Samantha, you really are just perfect." Then she turns from me and addresses the nurse. "Can I take her to my room? I want her to sleep in there with me tonight."

"Lyd," I interrupt her, "I don't know if that's such a—"

"It's fine, Mom. Really. I've been thinking about it. I'd like her in there. Just for tonight. Melinda and Reid aren't here anyway. I don't want her to spend the whole night in here. She can sleep in with me."

"We can arrange to have her brought down, sure." The nurse smiles politely at Lydia, but her eyes run to mine, looking to me for help. She's been briefed on the adoption; she knows Lydia's plan. Still, there's not much she can do to say no.

"Thanks."

Lydia runs her index finger under Maya's hand and allows her to grip it loosely. "Just for tonight, Samantha," she says to the child. "Just for tonight."

I don't sleep much, hardly at all. The reclining chair isn't much of a makeshift bed; I can't imagine having to spend more than one night in it. But what really keeps me awake the night through is the presence of this tiny baby in the room. Lydia's pulled the plastic rolling cradle right next to the bed so that as she is dozing off, she can watch her daughter sleep, a goofy lopsided grin on her face. The baby is truly an angel; she sleeps noiselessly, content to be wrapped tightly in her cocoon and propped by a second blanket so that she lies on her side. From across the room she looks like an expensive porcelain doll.

I study the two of them turned in toward each other. Like most newborns', Maya's features are yet to become pronounced. But I memorize every inch of her anyway.

Lydia stirs and then rolls over, her back toward the baby now. I stand as still as I can and take as much of her in as I can, then compare her to her mother. When Maya begins to murmur in her sleep, I pick her up and cradle her against me again. She nestles down into the crook of my arm, and yawns with perfectly pursed lips.

I settle against my chair back and sigh, just loud enough that it wakes Lydia. She opens one, then the other eye, and adjusts to the little bit of light in the room, blinking and squinting her eyes at me.

"Is she okay, Mom?"

"She's fine, Lyd. Try and get some sleep. I'll stay awake with her."

Lydia sits a little higher in the bed and watches me. When Maya emits the slightest peep, she jumps. I let the baby suckle at my pinkie finger, which she does hungrily. "She might be hungry again," I say to Lyd and ask her to hand me another premade bottle from the top drawer, which she does.

"She can eat!" Lydia exclaims, pride settling in.

"She can at that."

Hushed voices float by our room, then down the hall. Otherwise, everything is quiet, so very still.

"What do you think of her, Mom?" Lydia asks me finally, in a hushed whisper.

"Oh, Lydia, I think she's just precious. She looks like you, you know. Just exactly the same as you when you were born." Maya stops drinking from the bottle, sniffs once, and lets a small perfect sneeze go. Lydia and I look at each other and giggle. "She sneezes like you, too." I regret what I've said before I get the whole sentence out.

Lydia looks to me, hopeful. "She does? Really?"

"Yes." I say this more quietly this time.

"How so?" she pushes me.

"Oh, Lyd, I don't know." It comes pouring out of me. "Just something about her. Everything about her, actually. She has your eyes. Same eyes as Daddy, you know. She's got your fingers—long and thin. Maybe she'll be the piano player I've been hoping for." I know I should stop; I can read the look on Lydia's face, the sheer desire to learn as much as she can, to suck as much goodness out of me as is possible in the time she has.

"Really? Oh, Mom, wow."

"Yes, honey."

Silence creeps in again, save for the tiny mewing coming from the baby as she slurps at her bottle. She's fallen asleep while drinking, her mouth wide open. I take the bottle, half finished, and set it on the side table next to my chair, turning her in toward my stomach and rubbing her back until she produces a smallish burp that sends her sleeping body shuddering.

Lydia says to me, as quiet as she can, "I don't know if I can do this, Mom."

"Do what, Lyd?" I say to her, oblivious and in desperate need of sleep.

"This. This whole thing. What I've been planning to do all along. I don't know if I can do it." She holds out her arms then, outstretched to me, begging me to bring the child to her. I do, and she snuggles her down into the covers next to her.

"What are you saying, Lyd?" I ask her. "Are you saying you want to keep her?"

"I don't know, Mom. I just never thought it would be like this. I had no idea how beautiful she would be, how much she would make me want her."

"God does make them that way, Lydia." I brush the hair back from Lydia's eyes and run my hand over her cheek. I know I'm not helping; I know I'm probably confusing her even more. I know the words I should say to her, the encouragement she requires to stay steadfast with her decision. I've been counseled on it. Marina's words come floating back in my head.

They say a woman's mother is the most influential person in her decision.

Finally she says to me, "Maybe Grandma's right, Mom. Maybe she belongs with us. We're her family."

They fall asleep together like this, right next to each other. When I sense Lydia's out again, I move the baby, unsure of what to call her, who she is, whom she belongs to. I stare for a long while at her, the long eyelashes, the small flat nose, the tiny pointed ears. I can pick each of her features and assign them to someone I know. I unwrap her and she starts to stir, whimper, then belt into a lung-curdling scream that leaves me shhh-ing her while I change her small diaper. Only when I have her wrapped again, her arms tucked back inside the blanket and her cap covering her nearly bald head, does she settle back down. She opens her eyes, blinking at the dim overhead light and craning her neck as if to look around. Her lips are small and pursed and perfect in every way and she pushes them out at me as if blowing me small kisses.

All this time Lydia sleeps, a deep slumber that never wakes her, never causes her to stir. Her hands are cupped together under her chin.

48

Lydia's breakfast is delivered on a tray just before seven. She rolls over when she hears the aide set it on the swinging side table, but it's the first time she's moved all morning. I am up, cramped and fighting a crick in my neck from the hard chair, and feeding Maya, who has already sucked down two ounces of formula.

"How's she doing, Mom?" Lydia asks me from the bed, rubbing sleep from her eyes and trying to adjust to her surroundings.

"Fine. She was hungry. Screamed her head off."

"I didn't hear her. Why didn't you wake me? I'd have gotten up."

"It's okay, sweetie."

"Hi, Samantha," Lydia says to the baby, carefully making her way over to the two of us in the chair. "Hi, baby." Lydia kneels down beside us and kisses her on her forehead.

"Do you want to feed her, honey?"

"Um, sure, I guess so. I need to go to the bathroom first, though, okay?"

"Sure."

I watch as she eases her way over toward the door to the bathroom, heavy and plodding. She disappears behind the door for a few minutes and then reemerges, looking somewhat more put together. She has on her glasses and her hair is combed down, and when she comes toward me, I can tell that she has brushed her teeth. I stand and hand her the baby. She is still cautious, and she clings to the small child as if she'll wriggle free from her at any moment.

"She may be just about done," I say to Lydia as she tries to get her to suck from the bottle. "She needs to be burped, though."

Lydia looks at me, hesitantly. "I'm not exactly sure I should . . ."

"Go ahead, Lyd. Try it."

I watch as she gingerly pats her on her back, barely enough to warrant any sort of encouragement. "You gotta hold her head, Lyd, don't let it flop over like that," I say to her. She's all hands and can't quite get a rhythm, stiff and fumbling.

"Here," I say, "support her more with your shoulder. Grab her like you're holding a football close in at the breast. Then really give her a good pat, don't worry, she's not going to break. Rub her back a little too, sometimes that can help."

Lydia works at it, but it doesn't come naturally and before long Maya is screaming, her cheeks turning scarlet purple from the wailing. "Mom, help . . . what do I do now?"

"She's just letting you know she's not so happy, Lyd. Keep at her."

I watch another few minutes, the two of them not finding any sort of synch to the madness, before I finally take Maya from Lydia. Lydia looks relieved, sits back in the chair, and takes a long deep breath, just as Maya burps, then spews a small stream of yellowish mucuslike formula from her mouth. "Oh, better," I say to the baby, wiping her with the burp cloth and getting ready to change her again.

"What should I do?" Lydia asks me, unsure.

"You can get me a diaper, Lyd. She needs to be changed again. And another onesie, right there in the top drawer."

Ninety minutes, two diaper changes, and one bottle later, Lydia looks at me and begs to take a shower. "Please, Mom, please can I get in the shower now? I stink so bad. God, that formula just reeks."

"Okay, Lyd, sure. You go ahead and when you're done, I'll head home for an hour or so to do the same." I'm holding Maya, finally asleep and content, and pacing the floor of the tiny room, when Melinda Ramshorn knocks on the door.

"Hi," she says, timid and visibly uncomfortable, her eyes going immediately to the plastic bassinet next to Lydia's bed. "Can I come in?"

"Um, sure. Yeah, I guess so. Come on in," Lydia says.

"How, how is she?" Melinda asks, timid and unsure.

"Good, she's fine," Lydia says to Melinda, looking over at me for support.

"Did, did she . . . um, did she sleep in here with you last night, Lydia?" Melinda asks, shuffling toward me and stopping short when she sees I don't move an inch.

"Yeah. I, um, well, I didn't really feel very comfortable with her sleeping in the nursery. It was so loud and, well, it was just better in here . . ." Her voice trails off then. "I think she slept better in here, don't you, Mom?"

I nod my head, staring down at the baby, fussing with her blanket as if it needed to be rearranged again.

"Oh," Melinda says.

"Actually, I was just getting into a shower. My mom will watch Samantha, she's going to stay until I'm done," Lydia says, dismissing her.

"Saman . . . ?" Melinda stares wide-eyed at Lydia.

Lyd's quick to interrupt her. "Oh, I named her. You know, the agency said it would be all right. I just, well, I just always really liked that name, is all." She busies herself in the drawer at the pine armoire where I had stacked a pair of clean maternity pants, underwear, and a T-shirt the day before.

"Oh," Melinda says again.

"Melinda, where's Reid?" I finally manage from the chair.

"He went for coffee," she says flatly, her eyes burning through me for help. I watch her gulp back a lump in her throat. "In the cafeteria. We went to see the baby in the nursery, but they said she was in here. We weren't sure, um, really, what your plans were, so he decided he better . . ." Her voice trails off then, and she begins to tear up, expecting, or maybe feeling, I suppose, what hasn't been said.

Lydia starts again, determined to dismiss her. "Well, like I said, my mom is going to watch her while I take a shower. I can come get you later on. Will you be in the cafeteria?"

"Um, I guess so. Yes." She takes a deep breath and composes herself, wiping away an errant tear that she wasn't quick enough to blink off. "I suppose that would be best. Why don't you come on down—or send your mom for us—when you are ready?" Her voice trembles. She's hesitant and unsure of her every move. "Is that okay?"

"Yeah, sure," Lydia says, coming to stand by my side. She doesn't take the baby from me, but she's careful to sit very close to me and run her finger under the baby's cupped hand again until Maya takes it and wraps her hand around it. We watch as Melinda turns and tiptoes from the room, almost as if she wanted to erase the time she's just spent with us.

Lydia and I don't say anything to each other when Melinda leaves. Finally, Lydia closes herself into the bathroom, and a few minutes later I hear the water running in the shower. I rock and rock, refusing to see clear into all this, dazed as if in some sort of trance that the baby has placed over me. I'm only slightly aware of the goofy, lopsided grin that crosses my lips when the baby opens her eyes and looks, I swear, as if she recognizes me.

"I've seen that look on you before, Al." Michael's voice interrupts me, and when I gaze up at him from the chair, he is standing very near me. I'm surprised I've not heard his footsteps, never anticipated his arrival. I've been humming, the sweet sound of "Mockingbird" running through my head.

"Hi."

"Hey." He bends to kiss me on the forehead, running his strong hand over my left shoulder. "How was the night?"

"You're looking at it."

WITH YOU AND WITHOUT YOU   345

"Have you? Have you been up all night? Right there in that chair?" He places a paper cup of coffee on the table next to me.

"Pretty much. Oh, Michael, she's just a piece of heaven, isn't she?"

"She's someone's heaven, no doubt. What's going on, Al? I saw Melinda and Reid in the cafeteria. Melinda was near hysterical and Reid can barely manage a conversation. Where's Lydia?"

"Shower," I say. "God, Michael, I knew this would be hard. I just had no idea how hard it would be."

"How's Lydia?"

"Fighting it." I pause, coming to a stop in the rocking chair.

"You have to trust me on this, Al. We've been over this so, so many times. You know you have to trust me on this, babe."

"Trust you on what?" Lydia says, emerging from the bathroom, thick steam following her. She's dressed in clean sweats and has her hair rolled into a towel. Without makeup she looks younger than her fifteen years, the freckles spread wide across her cheeks and the bridge of her nose, her eyes wide with enthusiasm. "Hi, Michael."

"I was just telling your mom that I wanted to hear what you were thinking, that it seems as if maybe you've changed your mind about some things."

"Michael saw Melinda and Reid in the cafeteria," I say to Lydia.

"They sort of think that maybe you're changing your mind about things, Lydia." He glances around the room then, the makeshift nursery of sorts where Maya had moved in for the night. "They really didn't expect to find you with the baby this morning."

Lydia shrugs her shoulders, brushing past Michael and flipping her head over to unwind the towel. Waves of wet auburn hair fall loose and she begins to brush them with fury. "I can't help it, Michael. I just didn't expect it to be like this."

Michael makes his way to the side of the bed, opposite where Lydia is standing. Even with the bed positioned in between them, he's close enough to make his point. "You didn't expect it to be like what, Lydia?"

"Like this, Michael. Like this. I just didn't know how beautiful she would be, how much I would want to keep her. I can't help it really."

Michael leans on the edge of the bed and I think for a minute that he is going to explode. A small visible vein runs across his temple, blue and curvy like a river. He takes a deep breath and watches Lydia until she is forced to meet his eyes. Her hair, still wet, has made a long spot on her T-shirt down to the middle of her back and still she continues to brush it back and away from her face in long, full strokes.

"I understand your grandmother was here yesterday, Lydia."

Lydia shrinks back from his words. Quietly, softly, she answers him, nearly a whisper I can barely hear. "Yeah. She came by."

"What'd she say to you, Lydia?"

Tears roll down her face before she can choke out the words. "She, she said that I shouldn't give her away, that I didn't understand what kind of decision I was making."

"Do you?"

Softly Lydia answers him. "I thought so. I really did. But what if she grows up to hate me? What if Samantha, I mean Maya, can never forgive me for, for giving her away to people? What if Grandma can't ever forgive me, Michael? She'll think I'm horrible, that I've made a terrible decision."

She stares at Michael then, not sure of what else to say. He watches her carefully, his head cocked to the side, and waiting. He's patient, taking the time to see if she has finished. When he doesn't say anything, she finally comes to my side and takes the baby from me. I get up and stretch. My body is beyond tired, sore and tense and aching. I pace the floor between the chair, the bed, and the large-paned window, back and forth, back and forth. Still Michael is silent with his thoughts.

The large clock over the bathroom door clicks through the minutes. My head throbs in rhythm, a dull sort of storm that is building at the base of my spine and working its way up to my temples and back down again.

Michael asks Lydia if he can hold the baby. She squares her shoulders back and with great pride walks her daughter over to him. He takes her like a pro, just like I remember him to be when I'd seen him hold Sarah a million times before. For all his faults, Michael has always been a wonderful father, doting and dedicated.

"Hi, beauty," he says to the child.

Lydia watches him, her hands shoved deep in the pockets of her sweatshirt. I imagine she's thinking what it might have been like if Patrick had been holding his grandchild for the first time, the look of awe that would gradually have grown over his face. Maya takes to Michael and coos at him peacefully, squirming contentedly in his arms and nestling against his hand.

"Lydia, you don't have to do this," Michael says finally, quietly. "But I know you want to. I know that deep in your heart and soul it's exactly what you know you want to do. I know that you know where Maya belongs, that your purpose in this was to deliver her to her parents, the people who are supposed to have her. I know you know that. I know that's what you want for her."

Lydia stares at him, her mouth a tight, thin line. She grasps the bed rail for support, but Michael catches her arm instead and pulls her close to him, in at the side. He whispers something in her ear. I can't hear them no matter how hard I strain, but I watch him do this with her. I watch as he expertly places Maya on the bed before he pulls Lydia into a full embrace, lets her lay her head on his chest, and allows her tears to come flowing, full-force, from her. He is wordless when she chokes back the sobs, when she belts out the cries I knew then she'd been holding back from me. I am awed by his support, the way he runs his hand down her back and into her hair as if he were melting away every bit of pain, every ounce of distress. I've been witness to Michael's support. I know with all my heart that he's giving her everything she needs to do what she needs to do. And I know, watching the two of them, his arms around her there, that what she needs is to let this baby go.

Sometime later, on a night when Michael is holding me close, a night when the ghosts have come haunting me and I have awoken to bad dreams all around me, I ask him what it was that he'd said to Lydia, what he had whispered into her ear as he held her there.

"I told her she was forgiven," he whispers, stroking my hair. "You've long been forgiven, too, Al. The both of you, you know. There is nothing to feel guilty about now, nothing to harbor anymore. You know?"

"Yes, Michael," I say, nodding my head at him. "Yes, I know."

49

Melinda dressed Maya in pink, of course. It suits her, actually. We watch her together, the painstakingly slow process a new mother takes. I hold Lydia, her back pressed against my chest, our right hands intertwined. Lydia's eyes are bloodshot and weepy, her nose streaming.

Barbara has stayed for a while, heaving her disapproval across the room in great giant servings. She weeps openly, covering her face and shaking her head back and forth.

"Are you sure, Lydia? Are you sure?" she says over and over again until I can't stand it any longer. Finally I am done; enough really is enough. I ask her to leave.

"Barbara," I say, plain as day, "I think it's time for you to go."

"But, but I'm just not ready to let her go."

"Barbara."

"Fine, Allyson," she says and turns on a heel. "Fine."

Lydia had signed the stack of relinquishment papers without regret. That's what she said to me. "I'm doing this without regret, Mom. It's the right thing to do. It's what I wanted to do. It's what I was supposed to do."

"I have no doubt about that, Lyd," I concurred.

"I just need to be able to say good-bye to her. Do you think they'll let me say good-bye one more time?" she said when the last paper was signed.

"Of course, Lydia. You can have as long as you need."

Melinda places Maya in Lydia's arms for the last time and leaves the room a few minutes later. I watch for a while, for as long as I can stand to, while Lydia rocks her, back and forth, back and forth. She takes nearly an hour, maybe more, I lose track along the way. Finally I can't take it any longer either and retreat to the hallway.

"Mom!" I hear her piercing wail call to me from the room, from behind the curtain of the four walls that have been closing in on us. I've been sitting with my back to the wall. Waiting.

"Yeah, honey, what is it?" I rush in. "Are you okay, Lyd. What do you need?"

"Here. You do it, Mom. Please. I just can't. I just . . ." She hands me Maya then, rolling her small wrapped body into my arms as if she were handing me a log for the fireplace.

"It's okay. It's fine, Lyd."

She walks away and out the door. I plant tiny kisses on Maya's forehead, on her eyelashes, on her cheeks. I run my fingers over each of her features again, the heart-shaped chin, the perfect eyebrows.

"Melinda?" I call, barely above a whisper, but she hears me anyway and appears in the doorway, ready at the quick. "She's ready."

50

Michael is often home before me, his midnight-blue Jaguar parked far to the right in the driveway, just in front of the third garage that is filled mostly with boxes, things he still hasn't unpacked, things he says he really doesn't need to unpack.

It's virtually impossible to let the first of December slide by. I think of small children peeling back the first day of their Advent calendars, tiny chocolate treasures hidden behind the cardboard backing. The wind blows me through the door, the cuffs on my coat flapping wildly.

"Damn, it's cold," I say to Michael. "That wind is a joke." He is coming down the stairs toward me, his hair brushed straight back off his temples and curling in wet rings at the base of his neck. He has just showered, and I'm jealous that he's comfortable and warm in gray Polartec sweats. The sweet smell of sausage cooking in a heavy broth hangs in the air and warms my nostrils.

"Good day?"

"Fine, really. Just too much to do."

He senses my mood, my response short and clipped. We've waited for this day to pass us by, the memory fading little by little. He takes my hands and turns them over so they're palms up, then starts to rub them generously so they warm. He stares long and hard into my eyes, still melts me inside when he does that.

"There's something for you. In today's mail."

"What?" I say, peeling off my damp coat and letting it fall behind me on the stairs.

From the pocket of his sweatpants, he pulls a plain white envelope, Melinda's loopy handwriting in red ballpoint across the front. Even without a return address, I know whom it's from.

I take it from Michael, cautiously, carefully, and hold it in my hands as gently as you'd hold a newborn chick, cupping it in a way that it can't leap free or escape. The letter is addressed to me; Lydia had insisted there be no contact ever since she walked out of the hospital room and down the hall away from Melinda and Reid.

I slit the back of the envelope in one quick, long motion and allow the letter, two ruled pages, to unfold. From their midst, a photo drops free, slides itself face down across the hardwood floor so that all you can make out is the watermark on the back of the picture. In one swift motion, I reach for it, pick it up, and settle myself back onto the stair. I turn the photo over and stare into the eyes of the child that mirrors my daughter, the same glow and laughing smile, the beauty etched over her skin, her story just begun.

A CHAT WITH DEBORAH J. WOLF

Dear Reader,

This is my first novel. It took about a year to write and a good deal of time to edit it thereafter. I'd been writing long before that. My mother said I could write the best letter or thank-you note she'd ever known a five-year-old to send: full of detail and description. And I'd always loved a good book report—something I could really sink my teeth into and tell my own story about. Part of that, I'm sure, was due to the fact that I had such an insatiable appetite for reading.

In high school and at the university, I found any opportunity I could to take a writing class. I'd carry a notebook (and I don't mean laptop) with me and write whenever and wherever I could: lunch, in between classes, in the library, on the steps in the university union. I thrived on short stories and authored fifteen or so before I graduated. After graduation, when I was miserably navigating my way through advertising agency life, I bought a *Writer's Market*, which is *the* Bible for anyone who thinks they stand a chance at breaking into writing. I sent a collection of my stories off to various women's magazines based on the description in the book. I had no idea what I was up against, but I could share with you the stack of rejection letters I've saved all these years.

Writing is like oxygen to me. The computer calls to me and I have to stop, go to it, and start writing. I write most nights when the house is quiet and everything from the day is behind me. People ask me how I have the energy to start writing at nine or ten o'clock at night, but for me it's more like the place I have to go, the thing I have to do.

When I finished this manuscript, someone asked me which authors I had tried to most emulate in my writing style. The truth was I hadn't set out with any particular style in mind and the novel just flowed out of me in a way I hadn't expected. But I do imagine that the voice, the style, was influenced by the countless women authors I've read. I'm a huge fan of Jodi Piccoult, Alice Sebold, Sue Monk Kidd, Candace Bushnell, Terry McMillan, and others.

I'll read nearly anything recommended to me by a short list of friends with varying tastes. I think this is a great way to find things you wouldn't choose yourself. It's also one way to guarantee I end up reading at least one autobiography, a few business books, and some sort of historical piece a year.

The other thing I love to do is pick a first-time author and read his or her work. I sort of liken this to a first date. Everything goes into a first novel: all the passion, the work, everything. Khaled Hosseini's *Kite Runner*, for example. Bam, home run.

I had a college professor who told me that the key to writing well was to write about the simplest things in an interesting way. He scolded me once for adding a ridiculous, completely inappropriate car accident scene into a story where it had no business being just because I thought the story needed some sort of dramatic denouement. For this reason, I lean toward authors who write beautifully about the simplicity of life and living. Dai Sijie's *Balzac and the Little Chinese Seamstress* and Leif Enger's *Peace Like a River* are prime examples.

And, of course, forced upon us with dread in high school are some of the well-worn, dog-eared books that sit on my shelf now.

Tolstoy's *Anna Karenina* and Steinbeck's *Of Mice and Men* were my two favorites. All hail Oprah for bringing them back!

People often ask me where I got the idea for *With You and Without You*. I had little idea about where the novel was going when I started the manuscript. I don't tend to draft an outline or a synopsis for my stories, and I didn't for this one. I expected the story would focus much more on Ally and her relationship with Michael than it would on the relationship between Lydia and Ally. But as I said, the story sprang from me with force and it took everything I had to contain some sort of rhythm to the pace.

At some point, I stopped writing and let the story tell itself. I suspect this happens when the characters start to talk to you; informing you about what they're going to do next, what is going to happen. It's a blessing, that moment, a writer's high, if you will.

I have two adopted children and was fortunate enough to meet both of their birth mothers, but *With You and Without You* has nothing to do with either of their adoption stories. Still, I expect some of the story—from the other side—resided deep within my soul and needed to come out.

I wanted to write a story that spoke to women of all ages, something that my mother would read, but also something that women of my generation (and those younger than me) would enjoy. I didn't expect men would enjoy it at all, or that it would be something a man would pick up on the shelf in an airport bookstore. But I've had surprisingly good reviews from men, including one writer friend of mine who encouraged me the whole way through with just a few telling words. "It's good. Keep going."

As soon as I finished *With You and Without You*, I started my second novel without a moment's hesitation or a minute of trepidation. This new novel chronicles the lives of four women in a year when everything in their lives appears to be falling apart. The issues they each face will test their friendship, and they'll come to realize that what they really know of each other isn't necessarily so. The story digs into the deep ties that bind and root women together despite their differences, despite the people they have become. It explores the idea that no one really knows who we are, that there are parts of ourselves we hide even from those closest to us.

Thank you for your interest in *With You and Without You*. I hope you enjoyed reading it as much as I enjoyed writing it.